LLANTARNAM

A Novel

by

Muriel Maddox

First Edition
Printed in the United States of America

Library of Congress Cataloging in Publication Data:
Maddox, Muriel.
      Llantarnam : a novel / by Muriel Maddox. — 1st ed.
         p.   cm.
      ISBN 0-86534-173-7 : $16.95
      I. Title.
PS3563 . A339455L58   1992   91-38366
813' .54—dc20   CIP

Published by Sunstone Press
            Post Office Box 2321
             Santa Fe, NM 87504-2321 / USA

For Pamela, Brian and Alan

The author is grateful for permission to include the following previously copyrighted material:

REMEMBER, by Irving Berlin
© Copyright 1925 by Irving Berlin
© Copyright Renewed
International Copyright Secured
All Rights Reserved. Lyric reprinted by permission of Irving Berlin Music Co.

Excerpt from VOICES by Antonio Porchia as translated by W. S. Merwin. © 1969 by William S. Merwin.

Reprinted with permission of Macmillan Publishing Company from FIREFLIES by Rabindranath Tagore.
Copyright 1928 by Macmillan Publishing Company, renewed 1955 by Rabindranath Tagore.

"The chains that bind us most closely are the ones we have broken."

—*Antonio Porchia*

PROLOGUE

"Everything we have or will ever have, we owe to him," her cousin Cordelia said at his funeral. "Always remember that."

And she had cried then. But not for her grandfather, Thomas Joseph Wyman.

What do we owe him? she wondered now, all these years later. He had built a fortune, yet he had destroyed lives, those of his family, and others. She alone had survived the curse of the Wymans.

Or had she?

BOOK ONE

1863

CHAPTER ONE

Thomas looked up at the pretty painted lady in the red dress with the feather boa and hesitated.

"What's the matter, little boy, don't you like candy?"

"Yes, but—"

"Your parents have told you never to take candy from a stranger?"

How could this lady know exactly what his mother had said? Thomas nodded, staring longingly at the piece of chocolate in her hand. He loved chocolate, but his mother also said that it was bad for his teeth.

"Here, take it." She handed him the candy. "You're going to be a heartbreaker when you grow up." There was something sad in her voice as she said it.

Just then he heard his mother calling him. She sounded angry.

"Thomas, where did you go? I turned my back for an instant and—what is that in your hand? Give it to me!" She ran over and took the sticky chocolate from him, glaring at the lady with the feather boa who had joined two men and was walking down the street. His mother's lips pinched into a narrow line. Then she threw the candy in the mud.

"There! That's where it belongs. Like her."

"But why?" Thomas started to cry.

"Why? Because that kind of woman . . ." His mother stopped, searching for the right word to use. "She's not nice, that's all."

The tears were rolling down his cheeks. "The lady meant to be nice."

"She's not a lady. And stop crying. A big boy of four!" His mother took a lace-edged handkerchief from her purse and wiped his face. "We have to meet your father at the hardware store. You don't want your father to see you crying, do you?"

Thomas shook his head. He was afraid of his father. He was sure his mother was too. Was that why she didn't wear gay-colored dresses but always gray or brown? His mother had a pretty face but sad blue eyes. Sometimes she smiled, but not often.

"Now, let's go." She took his hand.

He could hear the oil derricks pumping away and everywhere there was the smell of oil.

Franklin, Pennsylvania, was one of the leading boom oil towns and the town itself and the area surrounding it was filled with oil derricks. Hotels and boarding houses were packed with gamblers, promoters, farmers, supply people, and real estate dealers. The streets were lanes of deep mud, flanked by busy stores built with false fronts.

Thomas was fascinated by the oil men who thronged the town, their clothing splashed with sand pumpings and spotted with grease and oil.

Oil!

The name had a magic sound.

He did not know what a part it would play in his life.

Thomas Joseph Wyman was born in Franklin six weeks before an event that would change his whole life and the future of his descendants. For on August 27, 1859, in nearby Titusville, a man named Edwin Drake drilled the first oil well in the United States and turned the quiet Pennsylvania countryside into booming oil towns.

But on that July morning in the modest little frame house in Franklin, there was nothing to indicate that Thomas Joseph Wyman would not grow up to be a clerk in the local hardware store like his father.

Thomas was the youngest and hardiest of five children. As a baby he survived the diphtheria that took his two older brothers. His father was wounded early in the Civil War and returned home with a permanent limp caused by a Confederate bullet at the bloody battle of Antietam Creek.

"It was shortly after noon on September 17, 1862," his father said. "We crossed the bridge at Antietam Creek under General Burnside in the face of fierce artillery fire. . ."

Matthias Wyman got up from the table and limped over to the sideboard. He took a bottle of Allegheny rye and poured himself a large glass.

"For the pain," he explained to his son and two daughters. "The cold weather makes my leg throb."

Thomas noticed that his father was drinking more and more and sometimes his speech was slurred. Other times he got angry and shouted at his mother for no reason and made her cry. It was then that he felt like hitting his father, but he didn't dare.

He would make it up to his mother one day when he was bigger, he would buy her a pretty dress and make her proud of him.

And as for his father. . .

All he could do now was lie in bed at night and clench his fists.

He did not know his father was unhappy, trapped in a life he could do nothing about. That knowledge would come later, and when understanding came, his father would be gone.

Thomas roamed the banks of the Allegheny, listening to the frogs croaking and the steady roar of the rapids, watching the steamer packets pass by on their way from Pittsburgh to Oil City. In early spring, when the trilliums and dogwood were out and the lilac bushes bursting with bloom, he picked violets and brought them home to his mother.

Sometimes, then, she smiled, and that made him happy. He loved the woods with the buckwheat and goldenrod, the wild asters and Queen Anne's lace. In autumn the hills were veiled in a pale blue mist and the maples were crimson and gold against the dark green hemlocks. He felt the brown, dry oak leaves rustle under his feet. The air was crisp and invigorating, redolent with mingled scents of apples and spices. His mother would have apple butter simmering in the copper kettle hanging over the wood fire. There would be fried country ham and dandelion greens for supper and buckwheat cakes with honey.

From his bedroom window at night Thomas could see the hills with giant pines along the ridge, the derricks silhouetted against the sky, their flickering lamps yellow sparks of light in the darkness.

By the time he was five he had climbed to the extreme tip-top of an oil derrick.

He went to school, he studied hard, he dreamed dreams.

He watched the people who flocked in from all over the world, hungry to make fortunes.

Someday, he would be part of all this excitement, Thomas told himself. He would be a success and build himself a fine house like the ones in Titusville and Bradford.

And he would use his money to help others.

For what other purpose was money?

CHAPTER TWO

"Me and Ben and some of the boys, we're going to French Kate's after work," Archie said with a wink. "Want to come along?"

"No thanks," Thomas said. "I have things to do."

"Like what?" He nudged Ben. "I bet you've never even been with a woman."

Thomas flushed and did not reply.

Ben laughed.

"What do you do every evening, anyway?" Archie asked.

"Leave him alone," Ben said. "See you tomorrow, T.J."

It was Pittsburgh in the year 1877, a dirty city, where coal dust seeped in even through closed windows, turning the curtains black. Thomas was eighteen, tall and gangling, with blue eyes and dark brown hair. The year before, his father had died suddenly, and with that his dreams of college. There was barely enough money to take care of his mother and his two sisters. He walked all the way to Pittsburgh, a journey of several weeks, looking for any work he could find.

He got a job as a clerk in the offices of the Empire Line. The Empire Line was organized in 1865 by Joseph Potts, a young colonel fresh from the Army. Its fifteen hundred tank cars transported crude oil from the wells to the depots and were painted a bright green, so it was known as the "Green Line."

Thomas lived frugally in a cheap rooming house near the railroad station and sent part of his weekly salary home to his mother in Franklin. He still had dreams, but they seemed more difficult to obtain now.

Still, with hard work. . .

He borrowed books from the public library and spent his evenings trying to make up for the education he had missed. He read Dickens and was now making his way through Thackeray. The librarian had suggested Tolstoy's *War and Peace* and also *Crime and Punishment* by Dostoevsky, but the Russian writers looked difficult. Perhaps later on. He loved the beauty of the language in the books he read and he observed that most of the men he worked with in the railroad office used incorrect grammar.

He wanted to get ahead and he intended to.

And he did not want his first sexual experience with a woman to be in a bordello where he would be likely to catch a disease.

"Hi there, handsome. Want to have a good time?"

The woman was standing on the corner when he came out of the Empire Line offices. She had flaming red hair, a purple satin dress hiked up to show black laced boots, and long dangling earrings. Suddenly he was reminded of the woman in his childhood who had given him the candy, the one his mother said was "not nice."

"My place is right near here, honey," the woman called, as he walked quickly by.

Poor thing, he thought, to have to sell herself like that, and he wondered if she had a family. They must all have families. Life was hard for a woman and he was glad he was a man. He thought of his mother's worn, lined face, how hard she worked from morning till night. There seemed to have been so little joy in her life. If only he could give her a better life before she died, a few comforts, and above all make her proud of him.

It's up to me, Thomas thought.

The October evening was chilly and he didn't have an overcoat. He turned up the collar of his jacket and blew on his hands. He could see his breath in the air. He would stop in a cheap cafeteria for supper, then pick up a new book at the library.

Two years later the Empire Line transferred him up the Allegheny to Oil City, where he worked in their general offices. It wasn't too far from Franklin, so he was able to visit his mother now and then. He was learning more all the time, getting more business experience.

Someday he intended to have his own company.

The year Thomas was born Oil City did not exist, only a collection of shambly houses and a store or two. It was called Cornplanter after a Seneca Indian chief. Now, since the oil boom, it spread out on both sides of the Allegheny River and was growing every day. There were schools, churches, and two daily newspapers. The new oil millionaires were building handsome houses up on the hill and importing fine furniture from Europe.

Thomas lived in a rooming house run by a Mrs. Sadie Plummer, who had lost her husband in the Civil War. She kept his picture on a table in the front parlor and sometimes, when Thomas returned unexpectedly, he would find Mrs. Plummer talking to the serious-looking figure in uniform.

From December to March the Allegheny was frozen solid, with ice piled in great packs and jams. Then in spring came the floods, the angry river overflowing on the low-lying boiler works and the soot-stained houses.

The Empire Line made him their agent in Oil City. It meant a promotion, but he continued to live at Mrs. Plummer's boarding house, where simple home-cooked meals were served. He now had a nice savings' account at the Oil City Bank, and he was only twenty-three.

Someone was playing a Chopin nocturne on the piano in the parlor and he went in to see who it was. It was a new boarder, a young woman who had recently arrived. He'd heard that she was a school teacher.

He sat down and listened. She continued to play, paying no attention to him. When the nocturne finished he applauded. "Beautiful," he said.

She turned and he noticed her large blue-gray eyes. You are too, he thought, but to say so would have been too forward.

She smiled. "Thank you. Do you like music?"

"Yes, very much."

"I'm glad. I teach music."

"Where do you teach?"

"At the new high school on Central Avenue."

You couldn't be much older than the students, he thought, but instead he said, "Is that the brick and stone building with the large clock in front?"

"Yes, that's it."

"You look much too young to be a teacher."

"I'm twenty-four."

He stood up and walked over to the piano. "Excuse me, I don't think we've been properly introduced. My name is Thomas Wyman."

She held out her hand. "How do you do? I'm Ardith Jones."

"Ardith — what an unusual name. I don't believe I've ever heard it before. It's very pretty," he added quickly. "I like it."

"It's Welsh. My parents were born in Wales."

"My family came from Ireland. My grandparents, that is."

"Then you're Catholic?"

"No, Protestant. They were from Northern Ireland, a place called Londonderry."

She nodded. "I've heard of it."

"Since you're staying at Mrs. Plummer's, I guess your family doesn't live in Oil City?"

"No, Rouseville. But I wanted to teach music and the opportunity came up here with the new school."

"I wouldn't mind having you for a teacher."

She blushed and got up from the piano. "I have things I must do now," she said.

"I'll see you again."

And that was how it began. Ardith Jones. He said the name over and over to himself before he went to sleep. This was the woman he wanted for his wife, the woman he had waited for. She was so pretty with her soft brown hair and lovely smile and tiny waist, and her laugh was like a musical chime. Once, when she bent over, he caught a glimpse of a delicate ankle. Would she be strong enough to bear the children he wanted?

He must work harder than ever to be in a position to offer her something. Right now was out of the question, but in a few years . . .

He wanted to protect her, give her the world. Was this what being in love meant?

They did not have the opportunity to be alone together to talk for some time after that. Mrs. Plummer was a strict chaperone and she permitted no hanky-panky. They saw each other at dinner with the rest of the boarders and sometimes in the parlor on Sunday nights, when they gathered for singing.

She had a beautiful soprano voice and he found out that she once had dreams of becoming an opera singer, but of course that was out of the question for a respectable woman. Sometimes he thought it unfair that a woman couldn't do what she wanted in life while a man could, but that was the way it was. A woman was meant to be a wife and mother, to keep house and encourage her husband and raise her children. It was an important role.

That winter his mother died, worn out from a life of toil. She was fifty-six, but looked much older.

He buried his mother on a cold December morning, the ground covered with freshly-fallen snow, the derricks looming like black skeletons beyond the graveyard.

He bit his lip till it bled trying to hold back the tears as the minister read the simple service.

Why did she have to die? he asked himself. She was such a good woman, she asked for so little in life.

One day, he vowed, when he had made his fortune, he would build a hospital wing and name it after his mother.

CHAPTER THREE

Oil City was becoming the hub of the oil industry, and in spite of floods and fires the town continued to grow and prosper. Men came there to make money and make money they did. Soon I'll have my own oil company, Thomas thought, be my own boss instead of working for others. He couldn't do it on his own quite yet, he needed a partner, and he was looking for the right person. It would not be long before he had something to offer Ardith and then he could ask her to be his wife.

Men succeed by fitting their strength to the circumstances of the times and not having too much bad luck, he observed, and thus far he had been lucky. He had always believed that with grit and determination a man could get anything he wanted in life. But was it the same way in winning the heart of a woman? He had little experience along that line. A woman's feelings were fragile, delicate, easily bruised. He had seen that in his mother, how his father hurt her, made her weep. Had she loved him once when they first met, had her heart quickened at the sound of his step, before time and sorrow took its toll? He would never know. He looked at the black armband on his sleeve. His year of mourning was almost up. Then he would declare himself, ask Ardith Jones to marry him and share his future.

It was then something happened that opened his eyes. Ardith had another serious suitor, a young banker with ginger hair and a handlebar mustache. He was coming more and more often to the boarding house to pick her up and take her buggy riding and the other boarders were starting to whisper about them. Thomas suddenly realized that there was no time to lose. He would have to throw his hat in the ring and declare his intentions or else risk losing her.

And lose her he did not intend to do.

Her birthday was in two weeks and he decided to get tickets for the opera and then take her to supper at the best hotel in town.

"Oh, Thomas, the opera! How thrilling!" Her eyes glowed. "And *La Bohème* is one of my very favorites."

"Then you can go?" He felt like an awkward schoolboy once more with his first date.

"Oh yes. How thoughtful. I never realized you liked opera."

I don't, he thought, but I know that you do. He looked bashfully at his shoes and then at her. "And we'll have supper afterward at the Arlington Hotel if you'd like."

"Like? I'd love it! Oh, Thomas, what a grand evening that will be!"

So much for that banker with the ginger hair, Thomas thought smugly, and then wondered how much money he would have to take out of his savings account to pay for the evening. Never mind, it would be worth it.

"Your tiny hand is frozen," sang the fat Italian tenor, holding the chubby hand of the soprano and gazing into her eyes. Thomas started to smile. To him the whole performance seemed ridiculous, but Ardith was enthralled, leaning forward in her seat, her lips slightly parted, tightly clasping the program as a tear glistened on her eyelashes and then ran down her cheek.

When it was over she seemed in a trance, completely carried away by the music.

"Oh, Thomas, that was wonderful!" she said, wiping away her tears.

"You are crying."

"Only because the story is so sad. But the music is so beautiful. How I would love to see Paris! Wouldn't you?"

"Someday." And I'd like to take you with me, he thought. But we wouldn't live in a garret like the lovers in *La Bohème,* we'd stay in a grand hotel. That is, after I make my fortune.

At the Arlington the maître d'hôtel showed them to a table in the back of the room

"Don't you have anything better?" Thomas asked.

"No, sir." He looked them over haughtily, his eyes sweeping the room filled with elegantly dressed men and women. "Everything else is reserved."

Thomas flushed. You bastard! he thought. Someday I'll buy this hotel and then you'll be glad to give me the best table in the room. He was wearing his best suit and he thought that Ardith, in her simple, high-necked gray silk with a delicate gold and amethyst pin at her throat, looked more beautiful than all the over-dressed women in the room with their bare shoulders and sparkling jewels.

They ordered dinner and then he decided to broach the subject. He leaned forward and cleared his throat. "Ardith," he started, "there's something I want to ask you."

"Yes?"

"As I'm sure you must know, I'm very fond of you."

"And I like you very much too, Thomas."

"I just got another promotion and I'm making a good salary now."

"I'm sure you'll go far, Thomas."

"Do you really believe that, Ardith?"

"Indeed I do. You'll have your own company one day."

"That's what I want. The opportunities are here and I mean to make the most of them." He paused. Suppose she turned him down? He did not think his pride would let him accept that possibility. He plunged on. "And I want you to share everything with me, to be my wife."

She looked startled.

Was it possible that she cared for the banker more than he realized, or had his proposal taken her completely by surprise? He waited.

"Well?"

"I don't know what to say."

"Is there someone else?"

"No. It's just that I didn't know that you . . . well, you never said anything to indicate that you—"

"That I loved you?"

"Yes.

"How could I? I wasn't in a position to offer you anything. And then, with my mother's death—"

She touched his arm. "Thomas, I'm sorry."

Was she turning him down gently? "Do you want more time to think about it?"

She smiled. "I don't need more time. I was wondering when you were going to ask me."

"Then you knew?"

"Women have an intuition about these things. I often wondered why you never expressed your feelings."

"It's not easy for me. That is, I guess I'm not what you would call a ladies' man."

"That's what I like about you. You're sincere."

"Then your answer is yes?"

She nodded.

"I intend to do things properly, ask your father for your hand," Thomas said. "Do you think your family will approve of me?"

Ardith smiled. "I'm sure they will."

It was all working according to plan, Thomas thought. Too easily, almost, and he felt a strange premonition. Everyone has to pay the piper, but right now he was young, with his future ahead of him and the woman he loved by his side. He did not know that life often changes our plans.

When they came out of the Arlington Hotel it was snowing. He called a hansom cab to take them back to the boarding house and held her hand under the fur robe. Did he dare try to kiss her? The driver was watching them. Not now, he thought, there would be plenty of time for that.

CHAPTER FOUR

He lay beside Ardith in the large brass bed watching her sleep. Her long, soft brown hair was spread across the lace-edged pillow. He loved to watch her in the evening when she took the pins out and shook her head till her hair fell in waves below her waist, then brushed it till it crackled. She sighed and moved slightly, her delicate hand with the antique gold wedding ring resting on her cheek. The ring had been his mother's.

Should he wake her or let her sleep? He had to get up now and be off to work.

She stirred and slowly opened her eyes.

"Good morning," he said and kissed her.

"Have I overslept? What time is it?"

"Five-thirty." He stroked her face gently. He was still not used to the miracle of waking and finding her beside him. If she was not yet ready for her marriage duties, that would come in time. They had only been married a month. He must be patient.

The year was 1884. They had rented a small house and Thomas was holding down two jobs. He was still working for the Empire Line but he was also engaged in refining oil two miles down the river at Reno. The twelve hundred acres of land overlooking the Allegheny had been named for the Venango Civil War hero, General Jesse Reno.

Thomas had formed a business partnership with Ernst Ludwig, a hard-working German immigrant from the Rhineland. There were many Germans in Oil City and they had their own church, the Good Hope Evangelical Lutheran, where Pastor Vogelsang conducted the services and parochial school in German. As the oil boom grew, each group built its own church. There were Methodists, Catholics, Episcopalians, and Baptists. Thomas and Ardith attended the First Presbyterian Church at the corner of Harriott Avenue and Spring Street.

Thomas got dressed quickly while Ardith prepared his breakfast. He knew that she missed her pupils, but it was not proper for a woman to continue teaching after marriage. What would people think? That he couldn't support his wife, so that she had to work to make ends meet?

He knew that she didn't have enough to do in the small house, and he was gone from early morning to late in the evening. But he had a surprise for her, one that he was saving for her birthday. He had put a down payment on a large corner lot on Third Street where he intended to build a fine house with a music room where she could invite their friends and have musical evenings. Ernst had told him of such rooms in homes in Germany, where his wife Anneliese had worked as a maid before their marriage. Ernst had worked on a farm, but times were bad in Germany and America beckoned with opportunities not offered them at home.

America was the dream, where with hard work anyone could rise to the top.

Thomas finished his breakfast and kissed his wife goodbye.

After he left for work Ardith went back to bed. The days seemed long all alone in the little house. It didn't take her that much time to clean and dust everything. She had planted a small vegetable garden in the back but the early frost had killed everything. She decided to bake some bread. There was nothing nicer for a man to come home to than a house smelling of freshly-baked bread.

She wanted to be a good wife and she wanted to make Thomas happy. She was lucky to have such a good man for a husband and she knew that he loved her. It was just that . . . she pulled the covers up around her and snuggled down in the bed . . . some details of married life . . .

She had been horrified on their wedding night when Thomas told her what they were supposed to do. All her mother had said was, "You must do what your husband wants," and then she had blushed a fiery red.

What other choice was there for a woman? Become one of the pitiful old maids, the spinster aunts that every family had?

She thought back briefly to her early dreams of being an opera singer, of thrilling people with her voice. Sometimes it seemed that only music made her feel truly alive.

Well, that was over now.

Tonight she would do that thing that Thomas wanted her to do.

*   *   *

Their first child was born nine months later in the brass bed. She had
never imagined such pain. She hung on to the knotted sheet, sweat pouring
down her face, as the contractions came one after another. She thought her
insides would be torn apart. The labor went on and on. . .

Finally she lay, weak and exhausted, barely conscious. Thomas was
holding her hand, looking down at her with an expression that filled her
suddenly with fear.

"Is the baby all right?" she asked.

"Of course." He stroked her forehead.

"May I see him?"

The midwife came over to the bed holding a bundle. "A beautiful
little girl," she said, putting the baby in Ardith's arms.

So that was why Thomas looked the way he did. He had been so sure
of a son.

"I'm sorry it's a girl," she said weakly.

"That's all right. The next one will be a boy."

The next one! How could she go through this again? Her insides felt
raw, bleeding. How did women have seven and eight children? She didn't
feel as if she could ever go through this experience again.

They named the baby Elizabeth. Later on she would be called "the
gimme girl." It was as if she knew that she had been a disappointment and
was determined to make up for it in other ways, always living beyond her
means with yearly trips to Europe and designer clothes, for which she sent
her father the bills.

While she was still nursing Elizabeth, Ardith discovered that she was
pregnant again. She had thought that you couldn't get pregnant when you
were nursing. Obviously an old wives' tale.

Thomas was elated. He would have a son.

Money was coming in now from the oil fields at Reno and Thomas
had drawn up the plans with an architect for the house on Third Street. The
foundation would be laid in the spring as soon as the snow thawed.

Ernst knew of a young German girl newly arrived who would live in
the spare room and do the housework and help with the baby. Her name
was Marthe, and she knew no English but quickly learned. Ardith liked
having company during the long hours when Thomas was away, and
Marthe taught her German.

She was carrying this baby differently and even Marthe assured her that it was a boy. She knew all about such things, being one of nine children.

"I hope you're right," Ardith told her. "My husband wants a son so badly."

Her second labor was even longer than her first. She had heard that it was usually easier. But the expression on her husband's face when it was over made it all worth while.

"My son," Thomas said, looking at the baby proudly. "The son I always wanted."

It was the sixth of April, 1887. They named the baby Thomas Joseph Wyman, Junior. He was called Joe, the fairhaired one, and invested with dreams that no one could ever live up to.

CHAPTER FIVE

In the year 1887, Grover Cleveland was president, Pearl Harbor was leased from Hawaii as a naval station, and a poet-journalist named Eugene Field endeared himself to Americans with his moving "Little Boy Blue," which was to become Joe's favorite poem.

It was also the year the Wyman family moved to the new house on Third Street. It was finished just in time for Christmas. Ardith decorated the house with holly and pine boughs, and she and Marthe baked mince pies and made plum puddings and stuffed a huge turkey with breadcrumbs and chestnuts. Another young German girl came to work for them. Her name was Elsa, and she and Marthe slept in the maids' rooms up on the third floor.

The paneled entrance hall had a stained glass window from an old English church and the floor was Italian marble, as well as the steps on the winding staircase. From the high ceiling hung a crystal chandelier that sparkled with colored prisms as the sunlight hit it. The living room was tastefully furnished with antiques and brocades and fine paintings and there were enough bedrooms for a large family.

But the room Thomas was proudest of was the music room. It was all done in blue and white. There was a white marble mantle and loveseats and draperies of deep blue velvet. The ceiling was painted to resemble a delicate blue cloud with a faint suggestion of cherubs and garlands of roses. A Persian carpet of blue and rose covered the floor and the Steinway piano had been finished in antique white. In one corner was a victrola where Ardith could play all her opera records and on a small table was a music box from Germany, a gift from Ernst and Anneliese.

Sometimes Thomas could hardly believe his good fortune. He was only twenty-eight and already he had become rich in the oil business. To think that ten years ago he had walked from Franklin to Pittsburgh with only a few cents in his pockets!

He looked around at his family as they gathered under the Christmas tree. He had a lovely wife, a two-year-old daughter, and a baby son.

What more could a man ask for?

Yes, there was something. If only his mother could have lived long enough to see his success, how proud she would have been!

Two years later their second daughter was born. They named her Sarah after his mother. From the first moment he saw her with her red-gold ringlets and chubby dimpled fists, Thomas felt a love for her that he had never had for Elizabeth, his first-born. He knew it was wrong, but he couldn't help it. There was something cold and calculating about Elizabeth, small as she was. When he tried to touch her, she drew away.

But little Joe was a delight. He had started to walk and they had to put gates at the top of the main staircase and also at the back stairs so that he wouldn't fall. Too many evenings Thomas came home after the children were in bed, but there was nothing he could do about it. To keep ahead he had to work harder and harder.

Ardith's occasional moods of melancholy had increased. He mentioned it to his partner Ernst.

"We have a saying in Germany," Ernst said. "*Kinder, Kirche, Küche.* Children, church, kitchen." He winked and slapped Thomas on the back. "Keep her busy with babies. She won't have time to be moody. Look at my Anneliese."

He had. Anneliese had five children, a round peasant face with heavy blonde braids and a round figure to match. She was a nice woman but Thomas felt that his own wife had more quality.

"I guess you're right," he told Ernst.

Ardith wouldn't hear of having any more children. "We have three already," she said. "A boy and two girls. That's a nice family."

He decided not to bring up the subject again. At least not for a while.

"And since you're home earlier than usual this evening," she said, "you can read to the children. I'm just putting Joe to bed."

Joe was tucked in his bed with the blankets pulled up under his chin. He grinned when he saw his father and stretched out his arms to him.

"Give me a piggy-back ride," he begged.

"That's too much excitement at bedtime," his mother said. "But would you like your father to read to you?"

"Oh yes!" Little Joe clapped his hands in delight.

"Then get back into bed," Thomas said. "What would you like to hear?"

"Little Boy Blue." Joe handed his father the book of poems by Eugene Field.

Thomas pulled a chair beside the brass bed and opened the book to the marker. He started to read.

> "The little toy dog is covered with dust,
> But sturdy and stanch he stands;
> And the little toy soldier is red with rust,
> And his musket molds in his hands.
> Time was when the little toy dog was new
> And the soldier was passing fair,
> And that was the time when our Little Boy Blue
> Kissed them and put them there."

He stopped and looked over at Joe. A large tear was running down his cheek.

"Go on, Papa," he said. "You haven't finished."

"But if it makes you sad—"

"I like it. It's my favorite poem."

"Very well." Thomas continued.

> "'Now, don't you go till I come,' he said.
> 'And don't you make any noise!'
> So toddling off to his trundle-bed
> He dreamed of the pretty toys.
> An angel awakened our Little Boy Blue,—
> Oh, the years are many, the years are long,
> But the little toy friends are true."

Joe sniffled. Thomas put down the book.

"There's more," Joe said.

"So there is." Thomas read the final verse.

"Ay, faithful to Little Boy Blue they stand,
Each in the same old place,
Awaiting the touch of a little hand,
The smile of a little face,
And they wonder, as waiting these long years through,
In the dust of that little chair,
What has become of our Little Boy Blue
Since he kissed them and put them there."

He laid the book on the bedside table and turned out the light. "Shall I hear your prayers, son?"

"Mama already heard them. Oh, I forgot something." Joe closed his eyes and folded his hands. "And God bless Little Boy Blue and please bring him back to his toys."

He kissed his son on the forehead. "Sleep well, little Joe."

He had almost said Little Boy Blue and caught himself just in time. It was a morbid poem and he did not think Joe understood the meaning, but obviously it was upsetting to him. He wondered why his wife kept reading it to the child. He must speak to her about it.

"But he likes it," she said. "He keeps begging to hear it.

"Does he understand that Little Boy Blue has died?"

"I think so. I told him that Little Boy Blue became an angel in heaven."

"Well see if you can't find something else to read him. At four years old he shouldn't be thinking about death. Pretend you've lost the book."

"But—"

"Those are orders. Where's the evening paper?"

"I'll get it."

She returned in a few minutes with the *Oil City Blizzard* and handed it to him, then sat down and opened a magazine. After a while Thomas looked up. "What are you so engrossed in?" he asked.

She held out Lippincott's Magazine. "The second installment of *The Light that Failed*. It's a good story."

"Who wrote it?"

"Rudyard Kipling."

"Never heard of him."

"It's his first novel," Ardith said. "I think he's going to be an important writer."

But Thomas had already resumed reading the newspaper.

CHAPTER SIX

In future years the fifth of June would be known as the "Great Fire and Flood of 1892."

It all began on Saturday, June fourth. Several days of heavy rains had washed out the dam at Clear Lake, thirty miles up Oil Creek, and that evening a flood and fire hit Titusville. The high waters had been pouring through Oil City for almost twelve hours before they broke a tank of benzine at McClintockville. The highly volatile liquid rode the yellow torrents until it passed under the Pennsylvania Railroad bridge on upper Seneca Street.

Then the inevitable happened.

The sparks from a locomotive engine on the bridge fell into the creek. There was a violent explosion, quickly followed by two more.

In the Good Hope Evangelical Lutheran Church Pastor Reimann was in the middle of his morning sermon for Pentecost Sunday. The force of the explosion turned him completely around in his pulpit and his carefully-prepared sermon remained unfinished as the terrified congregation fled the building.

What they saw was like a scene out of Hell.

The whole creek bank, from the shanties near the tunnel to the New York Hotel, was a mass of flames and below there was a line of fire to the Moran House. Blackened and charred bodies hung on fences and out of windows where they had been blown by the explosion of the gas.

"Run for your life!" a man shouted, as a sheet of flames rose seventy feet above the railroad bridge. Frantic people scrambled to get away, bearing down women and children in their path. The horses from William Swyer's barn ran loose in the street and several men made their escape on them. Smoke from the burning oil was so thick that the crowd ran in darkness, relieved only by flashes of lurid flame. Some, their clothes and hair on fire and screaming in pain, threw themselves into the river and drowned.

Thomas and Ardith were just walking home from church with Elizabeth when the blast came, throwing them all to the ground. Elizabeth started to cry. Thomas quickly helped up Ardith, who was eight months pregnant, and dried his daughter's tears, as they all looked down at the river and the mass of flames.

"What could have happened?" Ardith asked.

"I don't know. Go in the house and gather the children together. I'll try to find out what's going on."

It looked as if every building in town was on fire. He saw everything he had worked so hard for being swept away in an instant.

"No, Papa, don't leave us!" Elizabeth screamed.

Ardith grabbed his arm. "She's right."

"It won't go far."

"But suppose—"

"The fire won't come up here. We're high enough. Now get inside."

In the house Elsa and Marthe were babbling in German and three-year-old Sarah was with them looking terrified.

"Where's Joe?" Ardith asked.

The maids looked at each other and then at her.

"Get him," she said.

They came back a few minutes later.

"He is not in the house," Marthe said.

"Or the garden," Elsa added. "We cannot find him."

"But he must be close by." She remembered that Joe liked to coast down the hill on his new red wagon. She ran to the window and saw the flames burning all the houses along the river and she felt suddenly faint. He couldn't have gone to watch the fire all by himself. He was only five. If any thing happened to him. . .

Why had Thomas gone off and left them just when she needed him? He must have gone down to his office to try to save things. His work was always more important than his family, she thought bitterly.

"Call Joe again," she said, on the verge of hysteria. "He can't be far. We must find him. Here, watch the girls. I'll look myself."

And she ran out of the house.

                                    *   *   *

It had been fun to escape Marthe and Elsa, who were busy in the kitchen, and who treated him like a baby. He bet they wouldn't even notice that he had sneaked out, unless Sarah tattled on him, and he would be back before Papa and Mama and Elizabeth returned from church.

Joe started up the hill again pulling his red wagon. The wet sidewalks made the wagon coast faster and there was no one to say, "Don't go so fast, watch out, you'll hurt yourself." For three days he had been cooped up in the house with the rain, his nose pressed against the windowpane, wanting to go outside.

He turned the wagon around and was about to get in it when there was the loudest noise he had ever heard and another and another coming from the direction of the river, and then flames shooting up high in the sky. The last blast pulled the wagon from his hand and it started to roll down the hill. He ran after it but the wagon went faster and faster and he knew that he could never catch it.

Then there was billowing smoke and people screaming and the sky got dark like at night and he was scared.

A horse galloped by with a man clinging to it and the man's head was cut open and blood was pouring out.

"Mama!" he screamed. "Mama!"

He didn't know which way to go. The smoke was so thick it was hard to breathe and he started to cough. He didn't care about his wagon anymore, all he wanted to do was get home.

People were running up the hill, their eyes wild with fright, and the red-gold flames danced along the river and he heard a crackling sound of wooden houses going up and the roar of the wind.

He didn't think he was that far from his house but he couldn't even see it.

Then he heard a voice calling, "Joe, Joe, where are you?" It was his mother.

"Here!" he shouted. "I'm here!"

Her face had soot on it and her hair had come unpinned. She pulled him to her and he could feel the bulge of her stomach that she had told him was a new baby, but he didn't understand how it got in there or how it would get out.

"Joe!" she cried. "Hurry, we have to get back to the house."

"What happened? What' s going on?"

"I don't know. Your father is trying to find out." She took his hand.

Tears were running down her face now. "I was afraid something had happened to you. I don't know what I'd do if—"

"I was all right, Mama. Don't worry."

They were only a few blocks from the house but it seemed to take forever. Flying embers, fanned by the winds, flew over their heads.

"There's more oil coming down the river!" someone yelled.

"The whole town's going to burn! They can't stop it!" another voice cried.

They reached the house and ran in. A few minutes later his father appeared. He was out of breath and his clothes were covered with soot and dirt.

"The fire was headed for the Boiler Works, but the wind shifted just in time. I think they're getting it under control."

Joe noticed that his mother looked very pale.

"Are you feeling all right?" his father asked.

She nodded and clutched the stair railing.

"You'd better lie down. Joe, get Marthe and ask her to help your mother up to bed."

Later that night the water broke and her labor began a month early. The baby, a boy, was delivered in breech position and they almost lost him. He was tiny and red, barely five pounds, and they named him Stephen.

The next day the fire was out. It had claimed sixty lives in Oil City and left dozens horribly burned and eight hundred homeless.

But except for ashes in the rose garden, the Wyman home was untouched.

From the first Stephen was a difficult baby, cranky and colicky, as if protesting his premature entrance into life. Whenever Ardith picked him up he would stop crying, but the minute she put him down he would start again.

"The other babies weren't like this," Thomas said. "He just wants attention. Let him cry it out."

She tried it one night, but after two hours of hearing him scream, she could stand it no longer and went in to him. He was soaking wet and his face was the color of a persimmon. She changed him, rocked him to sleep, and crept back into bed beside Thomas.

"You're spoiling him," Thomas mumbled sleepily.

She lay there staring out the window at the horse-chestnut tree illuminated by the full moon and wondered: Is this all there is to my life— the endless childbearing? She loved her children, but there was something missing. Her music. It had filled her life before her marriage and now she scarcely had time to practice. No, that wasn't true, she could in the evenings while she was waiting for Thomas to come home, but then she was too tired and all she wanted to do was collapse on the bed.

And she was starting to get terrible headaches . . .

She watched Thomas sleeping. She had pulled away from him earlier when he wanted to make love and she knew he was angry. She was so afraid of getting pregnant again. She had thought of asking Thomas if they could have separate bedrooms but she knew that would make him even angrier. She liked having him hold her in his arms, but the rest . . . and then, nine months later, another baby.

Did most women feel this way or was there something wrong with her? She had no way of knowing how other women felt, since it was something that just wasn't discussed.

Finally she fell asleep and dreamed that she was Nellie Melba giving a concert to a hall full of admirers. Her voice soared, and then suddenly she could not remember the words of the aria.

A shrill cry penetrated her dream. It was Stephen waking up again.

Thomas lowered the pages of the *Oil City Derrick.* "A car that runs on gasoline," he mused, stirring his coffee.

"What did you say?" Ardith asked.

He pointed to an item in the morning newspaper. "Henry Ford has completed the construction of a gasoline engine for an automobile and given it a successful road test."

"Imagine that! Do you think it will be better than the electric one?"

"I don't know, but I'm certainly going to look into it." He tore the article out of the paper. "A car that uses gasoline — that's another use for petroleum. Mark my words, oil is going to control our lives."

CHAPTER SEVEN

S arah stood before him in a costume of blue gauze with two silver wings attached to her back, holding a silver wand with a star made of cardboard. On her long red-gold curls rested a silver paper crown.

"Do you like it, Papa?" she asked, twirling around in a circle for his approval. "Elsa made it for me. I'm the Blue Fairy."

"You look beautiful. But will you be warm enough?"

"If I wear a coat it will spoil the effect. We're not going far. Just around the neighborhood."

"Where are Joe and Elizabeth?"

"They're not ready yet. They're both wearing real spooky costumes. Elizabeth's a witch and Joe won't tell what he's going to be." She ran to the window and looked out. "It's almost dark. I'm going to light the pumpkin."

"Don't you light it. Get Elsa or Marthe to do it."

She looked crestfallen. "Oh, Papa, you never think I'm big enough to do anything myself!" And she ran from the room

Do I protect her too much? Thomas wondered. But she was only five years old and he didn't want her playing with fire. There was something special about Sarah, she was part of his heart, and he didn't know what he would do if anything ever happened to her. Someday she would leave him, go off on her own, get married, but now, while she was small, these years were precious.

He went back to reading the Wall Street reports. It was only a few minutes later that he heard the screams, screams so terrifying that his blood ran cold, and they were coming from the front porch where the children had placed the pumpkin. He threw down his newspaper and rushed to the hall and flung open the front door.

A small figure was running toward the rose garden, her gauze costume and fairy wings burning like a torch as she continued to scream. On the steps sat the pumpkin, the candle inside lighting up its grin with the crooked teeth and shining through its eyes and nose.

Thomas quickly took off his jacket. "Sarah!" he called, running after her. "Stop!"

The fire was consuming her, her costume was burned off and her red-gold curls were aflame.

She was heading for the pond in the rose garden with the fountain where the robins drank. If only she would stop so that he could wrap the jacket round her and try to smother the flames.

He ran faster. "Sarah, Sarah!"

She seemed not to hear him, she was a moth burning and her screams grew more terrible.

She collapsed as he caught her, a charred Blue Fairy, a burned puppet, no longer recognizable, as he wrapped her in his jacket and beat out the flames.

Ardith and the maids came running followed by Elizabeth and Joe.

"Bring blankets!" he shouted. "And tell Oliver to get the carriage ready. We must take her to the hospital right away."

Later, he would not remember the frantic ride to the hospital. Sarah, mercifully, was unconscious, as Ardith held the small pitiful form wrapped in blankets.

"Can't we go faster?"

"It's as fast as the horses will go, sir," Oliver said. "We'll soon be there."

Soon. Would soon be soon enough to save her? She was scarcely breathing.

"Let me hold her," Thomas said.

Sarah lived three days and then she died. She never regained consciousness.

It was after Sarah's death that he decided to build the marble mausoleum in the cemetery up on the hill overlooking the river. He had an artist from Italy design it after the tombs in Italian cemeteries and he had a statue carved in white marble for the top, a small girl with wings like an angel. It consumed him, this memorial to his beloved daughter. This was where all the Wyman family would lie when their time came.

"But why, dear God," he asked as he looked up at the sky, "why did it have to be Sarah?"

Seven months later Ardith gave birth again. She had hoped for another daughter, though she knew that no one could ever replace Sarah. Instead she was delivered of a son.

He was stillborn.

CHAPTER EIGHT

His partner wanted to return to Germany.

"My parents are getting old and I haven't seen them in over twenty years," Ernst said. "And Anneliese—she has never really adjusted to this country or learned properly the language. She misses Germany."

"Then you intend to go back permanently, not just for a visit?"

"Yes. I know that I have made my fortune here, but I, too, miss the old country. After all, I was born there."

"But you are still too young to retire," Thomas said.

"My family owns some property along the Rhine, a vineyard. I could work that with my brothers, and then my sons could take over. And also, there is another reason."

"What is that?"

"We both have seen the handwriting on the wall. The days are numbered for independent oil operators like ourselves."

"You mean the Standard Oil Company?"

"Exactly. John D. Rockefeller controls now ninety-five percent of the oil produced in the nation and he's ruthless. The independent oil refiners like us won't stand a chance. He'll wipe us out."

"Like hell he will!" Thomas said. "I'll fight him."

So Ernst went back to Germany with his family and Wyman & Ludwig became the Wyman Oil Company. But Ernst's prediction proved right. Standard Oil was determined to exterminate all competitors.

Thomas lay awake many nights trying to decide what to do. There seemed to be no way out.

"When I put a man on the road and he takes orders for several hundred barrels a week, before I am able to ship them, Standard Oil has already gotten there and forced them to cancel my orders," he told Ardith.

"And what if they refuse?"

"Then Standard puts the price of oil down to such a low price that they can't afford to handle my barrels."

"Isn't there anything you can do?"

"I don't know."

It was one thing to try to fight them if he had nothing to lose and no responsibilities. But he had his family to think of.

He did not have long to wait. A letter came from the offices of John D. Rockefeller at 26 Broadway in New York City asking to see him.

Thomas got on the train for New York, a fiery speech against Standard Oil forming in his mind.

He was shown into an office furnished in Spartan style where a man was sitting in a rocking chair behind a roll-top desk. He had a narrow, almost expressionless face with a heavy mustache over thin lips and eyes that were hooded and impassive. It was John D. Rockefeller.

"Please sit down," he said.

Thomas was surprised at the thin, reedy voice. At a closer range he observed the lines in Rockefeller's face and the slight tremor of his hands.

Crossing his long legs and smoothing the wrinkles in his pin-striped pants, Rockefeller began to speak, the saintly expression on his face a contrast to the cold, ruthless eyes. With great civility he explained how his plan would work to the benefit of all. Everyone was offered the opportunity to come in with Standard Oil. Those who refused to sell would be crushed, their property valueless. He controlled the banks and the railroads and he intended to buy out the few remaining independent oil refiners.

He rocked back and forth in his chair, never taking his eyes from Thomas. He seemed to be sizing him up.

Thomas was one of the last hold-outs, he told him, and he was giving him the same choice he had given the others—cash or stock in Standard Oil. Of course, if he valued his principles more than economic survival . . .

Thomas was furious. "What you and your associates have done to the independent oil men like myself is outrageous, Mr. Rockefeller! What choice do I have? Certainly I value my principles. I also have a wife and children to support and you are holding all the cards."

The chair rocked back and forth but the poker expression never changed. Like a spider who has lured a fly into his web, Rockefeller watched him.

There was a long pause. Finally Thomas said, "I will take stock in Standard Oil."

Now the narrow lips turned up slightly but the eyes remained blank.

"That was a wise choice," Rockefeller said. "You'll not regret it, I can assure you." Their eyes met. "I like your spirit, Wyman. You are not a yes man. It is just possible that I may have something for you. You'll be hearing from me."

And he did. Three months later Rockefeller offered him a job as assistant to the president of Standard Oil of Kentucky. Its headquarters were in Cincinnati, Ohio.

"Why Cincinnati?" Ardith asked. She was lying in bed with one of her migraine headaches.

"Because it's right over the state line from Kentucky."

"But we've just finished the summer cottage. And now if we have to move to Cincinnati—"

Thomas felt restless, cooped up. For several months he had occupied himself with building their summer place up the river in the Allegheny woods where several wealthy Oil City families had cottages. He had designed it himself of rough-hewn stone and wood surrounded by a large porch, and a flagstone path and steps led down to a dock for rowboats and canoes. There were five bedrooms on the second floor and an attic room for the maids. He named the cottage Llantarnam after the village in Wales where Ardith's parents were born.

"We won't have to move," Thomas said. "At least not now. I'll come home on weekends and part of the summer."

"But why do you have to work? We have enough money for you to retire, haven't we?"

How could he explain to her the sense of excitement it gave him to be back in the business world again? He needed the challenge of competition. He was not ready to retire for many years yet.

"You'll be so busy with the children you won't even notice that I'm gone," he said, patting her hand.

"Would you pull down that shade, please? The light hurts my eyes."

It was a different world, that of men and women. A man was the hunter, he had to go out and kill the bear, while a woman's role was to tend the home and raise the children. "You'll see as much of me as you do now," Thomas said.

Ardith did not reply. She had turned on her side and was pressing the pillow against her temple.

"Extra! Extra! Battleship *Maine* blown up in Havana harbor!" the newsboy shouted. "Two hundred sixty American seamen lost. Want a paper, sir?"

"Yes, give me one," Thomas said.

It was February 15, 1898. Only three weeks before the *Maine* had arrived in Havana on a friendly visit, though its real purpose was to protect American life and property in Cuba's revolt against Spain.

Now we'll be in it, Thomas thought. He was glad that his sons were too young to fight. Joe was eleven and Stephen seven. Elizabeth had just turned thirteen and they were all doing well in school, except for Stephen. Once more Ardith was pregnant and they were hoping for another girl. The baby was due the first week of May.

On April twenty-third President McKinley issued a call for one hundred and twenty-five thousand volunteers to fight in the war against Spain.

The first of May there was a naval engagement in Manila Bay between Spanish and American fleets, commanded by Admiral Dewey and ending with the destruction of the Spanish forces.

And also, on the first of May, their daughter Grace was born.

He had hastily come from Cincinnati when his wife went into labor. Like the others, it was a difficult birth, and afterward the doctor wanted to have a talk with him.

"Your wife must have no more children," he told Thomas. "She has had six pregnancies and they were all touch and go. She would not survive another."

Thomas nodded. Ardith was forty, no longer a young woman.

"You understand what I am saying, then?" He wanted to make it quite clear. "Your . . . ah . . . marital relations must cease."

"Have you told my wife?"

"Yes." The doctor did not say that when he explained this to Mrs. Wyman she seemed relieved. It was not unusual. He had observed this with many women, including his own wife. Well, there were places for men to go. "You have a nice family, two sons to carry on your name, and two daughters," he said. "And now I will bid you good day."

                           *   *   *

Ardith lay in bed nursing her baby daughter. She was a pretty little
thing with dainty features and delphinium-blue eyes with long lashes. She
was sorry she didn't have more milk to give her. Her milk was already
drying up and she would have to put her on a formula or else find a wet
nurse.

And my breasts aren't the only things that are drying up, she thought.
There were new lines in her face and she had found two gray hairs. Well,
at forty she should expect that. Odd how old forty was for a woman, while
Thomas, only a year younger, was still in the prime of life.

At least she wouldn't have any more pregnancies to tear her apart,
and those long months that preceded the births when her body grew
bloated and clumsy and she felt queasy most of the time. If men had to bear
children instead of women would they want so many, one after another?
She doubted it. She was glad the doctor had spoken to Thomas. She had
never cared for that part of marriage and she would not miss it.

CHAPTER NINE

In 1899, the Supreme Court of Ohio ruled that the Standard Oil Trust, which controlled ninety-five percent of the oil refining business, was in violation of the Sherman Anti-Trust Act. The trust was replaced by the holding device, Standard Oil of New Jersey, and Thomas was asked to be vice-president.

He thought that his wife would be happy about moving to New York, but she did not want to. Her migraine headaches had increased and she had become almost a recluse, sitting in her music room and playing opera records by the hour when she was not lying in bed in a darkened room complaining of the pain. The family doctor told him it was the menopause and that there was nothing he could do.

"She just has to go through it and then she'll be all right," the doctor told him. "It's not uncommon."

Thomas hoped so. Sometimes he wondered if she was using her pain to try to control him. Since Grace's birth their marriage had existed in name only and a large gulf now separated their interests. Or perhaps it was always there and he was just too busy to notice. He saw his children whenever he could, but business occupied most of his time. Elizabeth was in boarding school at Farmington, Connecticut, and Joe would be going to Groton in two years and then on to Harvard.

He smiled fondly when he thought of Joe. Nothing was too good for him. What hopes he had for him! They stopped nothing short of the White House.

And why not? Wasn't that the American dream?

He first saw her at the opening of the Horse Show in Madison Square Garden. He had been invited to sit in the Rockefeller box for the gala event, which brought out everyone social in New York. All eyes were on the beautiful blonde woman riding the black horse, aristocratic in her bearing, as she fearlessly took jump after jump to the applause of the crowd.

Thomas looked at his program for her name. It was Mrs. Edgar van Vechten.

"Claire's in fine form tonight," one of the women said.

"Isn't she always?" another remarked. There was a trace of envy in her voice and Thomas wondered if they hoped she would take a spill. He had never seen such horsemanship.

Nor had he ever seen such a woman.

Without trying to appear obvious, he found out everything he could about her. She was twenty-seven, her husband, a multimillionaire, was sixty. They had no children. There were rumors that the husband was impotent. There were also other rumors about Claire. She was supposed to have come from a town in upstate New York, but no one had met her relatives. There was an air of mystery about her.

Somehow, some way, he must meet her.

Several months later he was seated next to her at a supper party at Delmonico's following the theatre. She wore a low-cut green velvet dress that showed off her alabaster white shoulders and bosom and brought out the green of her eyes. Her blonde hair was piled high on her head in the latest fashion, caught with an emerald clip.

"You were magnificent in the Horse Show," he said.

She smiled. "Oh, were you there?"

"Yes. I've been wanting to meet you ever since so that I could tell you—" Tell her what? That he had fallen madly in love the first time he saw her?

"Yes?" She leaned forward and he could smell a perfume like lilies of the valley.

"How very much I admired your horsemanship," he finished lamely.

"Oh?" She lowered her eyes and opened her fan. "Do you ride, Mr. Wyman?"

"I ride." He speared a shrimp with his fork. "But not in horse shows." At the end of the table he saw her husband watching them. He was portly, with a red face from too much drinking, and had white hair and a walrus mustache. For the life of him Thomas could not imagine the two of them in bed together.

"Then you must come out to our place in Old Westbury one

weekend," she said. "You and Mrs. Wyman. Which lady is your wife? I don't believe I've met her."

"My wife is not here. She is at our home in Pennsylvania with the children." He felt a sudden surge of guilt. "She isn't very well, and she doesn't care for New York."

"I see."

"I go home quite often on weekends."

The next course was served and she turned to talk to the person on the other side of her. Thomas reluctantly did the same.

On the way back to the Waldorf in the hansom cab he decided to try and persuade Ardith to bring the children to New York. It was not good for a man to be alone in this city without his wife. There were far too many temptations. They could rent a house on Fifth Avenue, the children could play in Central Park and make new friends at school, Ardith could go to the Metropolitan Opera. Yes definitely, that was the thing to do. He would write Ardith a letter tonight.

A telegram was waiting for him at the front desk.

COME HOME AS SOON AS POSSIBLE. JOE IN HOSPITAL. ARDITH.

Not Joe, he thought. Please, dear God, nothing must happen to Joe.

He got on the next train to Oil City. It was snowing when he arrived and bitter cold. Oliver met him at the station and carried his suitcase to the carriage.

"Mrs. Wyman is at the hospital, sir," Oliver said. "I'll take you there directly."

"How is my son?"

Oliver paused. "Master Joe had a very bad accident on his sled, but he's holding his own. He's a strong little lad. I'm sure he'll pull through."

Pull through? As bad as that? He's got to pull through! Thomas thought fiercely. He heard the clip-clop of the horses' hooves on the hard-packed snow and the cold wind whistled up from the river as they sped along. Hang on, Joe! I'm coming.

They pulled up in front of the hospital and Thomas leapt out and ran up the steps two at a time.

"Which room is my son in?" he asked a nurse at the admitting desk.

"205 in the new wing, Mr. Wyman. I'll take you there."

It was the wing he had donated in memory of his mother. And now Joe was there, perhaps dying. I'll get the best doctors for you, son. Just hang on! Don't die, you mustn't die.

"Here we are," the nurse said.

The room was in semi-darkness and Ardith was sitting in a chair by the bed. Joe had bandages wound round his head and his right leg was in traction. His eyes were closed and his face was very pale. Thomas couldn't tell if he was asleep or unconscious.

Ardith saw him at the door and got up and ran to him. She was crying softly as she threw herself into his arms.

"Thomas! I'm so glad you're here!"

"I came as fast as I could." He looked at the still figure lying on the hospital bed. "Is he conscious?"

"He goes in and out. The doctor says he'll be that way for another day or two. He's been asking for you."

"How did it happen?"

"You know how he likes speed, the way he was as a little boy with his wagon? He was going down a steep hill on his sled and it went out of control and hit a brick wall. He has a bad concussion and three broken ribs and a dislocated hip. The doctor said. . ." She started to cry again.

"What is it, dear?" Thomas stroked her face. How worn out she looked and thin.

"The doctor isn't sure if he'll be able to walk normally ever again. They won't know for a year."

"We'll get another doctor's opinion. The best specialists. Joe's got to be all right."

She put her finger to her lips. "I think he's waking up."

They walked over and stood together beside the bed. Joe opened his eyes but they had a glazed look.

Thomas bent down and kissed him on the forehead. "I'm here, son."

There was no response.

"Papa's here, Joe," Ardith said.

The eyes were still blank. "Faster, faster," he mumbled.

The nurse came back in the room. "He still thinks he's on his sled," she whispered. She took his pulse, then wrote something on a pad. "There's a waiting room down the hall. Perhaps you'd like some coffee? I know your wife hasn't eaten anything. I'll be here with him and there's nothing you can do right now. Sometimes they go on this way for days. I'll call you if there's any change."

It was two days before Joe recognized his father and six weeks before he left the hospital on crutches. He was still in intense pain from the broken ribs and the doctor held out only a fifty-fifty chance that there would be no permanent damage to the hip.

"I'll take you fishing as soon as you're better, son," Thomas promised.

"That won't be till summer."

"That's right. By then your leg will be fine." He had let the pressure of business keep him away too much from his children and he vowed that he would spend all next summer at the cottage.

Grace was two years old now, a Dresden doll whom everyone wanted to pick up and hug. She could wind him around her tiny finger and it would be that way all his life.

"While you're home this time I want you to have a talk with Stephen," Ardith said. "I don't know what I'm going to do about him."

"What's he done this time?"

"He insulted Mademoiselle and she's threatened to quit."

They had hired a French governess two years before and both Elizabeth and Joe had been progressing splendidly. Even little Grace could say a few words in French.

"In what way did he insult Mademoiselle?" Thomas asked.

"He said a bad word when she asked him to conjugate an irregular verb."

"What bad word was that?"

"I'm not sure, but Mademoiselle turned red and told me that she was going back to France where children behaved properly and that she didn't have to work for *nouveaux riches* American families."

"Did you make Stephen apologize to Mademoiselle?"

"I tried to but he refused. And he's too big for me to turn over my knee and spank. If only you were home more. . ."

"I'll make him shape up," Thomas said.

CHAPTER TEN

During the long months while they waited for Joe to recover, Thomas wondered if there was a balance sheet in life that said: I will give you success but not personal happiness. You cannot have both. Choose.

He had achieved a business and financial success beyond his wildest dreams. But there was the other side of the coin. The early death of his beloved mother, for whom he wanted so much, the loss of Sarah, the stillborn baby, now Joe's accident. And his marriage an empty shell, wanting a woman he could not have. He buried himself even more in his work and went back and forth to Oil City on weekends to be with his family.

He did not see Claire again until one rainy April afternoon when they ran into each other accidentally at the Metropolitan Museum of Art. She was standing in front of a painting by Romney, wearing a plum-colored velvet outfit and a large white hat lined with the same color and topped with coque plumes. He walked over and stood beside her.

"You look as if you could have posed for it," he said.

She turned in surprise. "Why, hello. How nice to see you." She held out a gloved hand and there was a faint scent of lily of the valley. "Do you come here often?"

"Now and then. And you?"

"I come every Thursday afternoon."

"By yourself?"

"Yes." She smiled. "It's my escape."

"I shouldn't think you'd have anything to escape from."

She looked up at him and again he noticed the tiny gold flecks in her green eyes. "We all have," she said quietly.

"Shall we walk around together?"

"Yes, I'd like that."

They left the English gallery and headed for the French Impression-
ists.

"It gives me a sense of permanence to look at the works of the great
masters," she said. "To feel that beauty will endure, that even after we are
gone others will look at these paintings and be moved and inspired by
them as we are. Like that painting by Romney. I will get old and faded,
but she never will, she is frozen in time, eternally young and beautiful."

"You will never be old."

She laughed. "One day. Ah, here are the Monets. I'm trying to design
a garden like that at our place in Old Westbury. I can't seem to get quite
the same effect."

"I'm sure that whatever you designed would be beautiful."

"You make me feel better. I'm glad we ran into each other today."

"So am I."

"I haven't seen you around at any of the parties since that evening at
Delmonico's."

"I had to go home for a while. My son was in an accident."

Her tone changed quickly. "I'm so sorry." She looked genuinely
sympathetic.

"He's much better now."

"If I ask you something. . ." She stopped. "No, I'd better not."

"Go ahead."

"I don't know why, but I feel that your marriage is very much like
mine. That there is no communication, no closeness."

He did not answer. Was his unhappiness that obvious?

"Forgive me, I shouldn't have said that. It's not any of my business."

"You're right. About the first part, I mean. But there's nothing I can
do about it."

"I hope we can be friends," she said. "We both need someone to talk
to."

Friends, Thomas thought, and he had the feeling of skating on a pond
of thin ice. Could a man and a woman really be just friends? He did not
think so and he did not think that Claire believed it either. They were both
lonely. And what he felt for her was not friendship, it was much more than
that and he had known it from the first. It was love, a love that was
forbidden, a love that could only bring unhappiness.

But in the months ahead, as they felt themselves being drawn more
and more to each other, like all lovers, they lost sight of reality.

So they were unprepared for the tragedy that finally came.

His room at the Waldorf became their trysting place, and sometimes, when her husband was on a business trip, they went to her house at Old Westbury. Her passion both amazed and delighted him. He had always believed that a "nice woman" could not feel sexual desire, or was not supposed to.

At parties when he would see Claire's tall and willowy figure dancing with her husband or some other man, Thomas felt himself consumed by jealousy. It was hard to conceal his true feelings for Claire in front of others, but he must. If their liaison became public knowledge he did not like to think of the consequences. And divorce was out of the question.

Time passed, the affair continued.

Joe was able to walk without crutches and after a year the doctor declared his hip completely healed. So he would not be a cripple after all, as they had feared, and Thomas donated a new organ to the Oil City Presbyterian Church in grateful thanks.

On September 6, 1901, President McKinley was shot by an anarchist in Buffalo and died from the wounds a week later. Theodore Roosevelt was sworn in as the twenty-sixth president. And that same week Ardith received a letter from Edgar van Vechten informing her of her husband's affair with his wife.

"What exactly does this mean?" Ardith's hand was trembling and her eyes blazed with fury as she held out the letter to Thomas.

He blanched when he read it. "The man is crazy," he said. "I don't know what he's talking about."

"But you do know his wife?"

"Of course. I know them both. I've danced with her at parties, as have many other men. She's a very attractive woman and a good dancer."

"Then why did he write this letter?"

"Jealousy, I suppose. He's much older than she and I guess he imagines that every man who looks at her is having an affair with her."

Ardith was not convinced. "He wants me to know the truth so that I will do something about it."

"Well you can't do much about his imagination, can you?"

"All right, if that's what it is, I want you to swear something to me.

I want you to swear that you have not had . . . had relations with Mrs. van Vechten. I want you to swear on Joe's death."

"I won't swear any such thing!" Thomas threw the letter in the fireplace and lit a match to it. "That's what I think of that letter."

Ardith stood staring into the flames as they curled around the letter and turned it to blackened bits of paper.

If only the whole situation could be resolved that easily, Thomas thought. How had Edgar van Vechten found out? He must have employed a detective — that was the only possible explanation.

"There's something I'd like you to do," he said.

"What's that?"

"Come to New York with me."

"But—"

"I won't hear of any more excuses. Elizabeth and Joe are both in boarding school and it isn't as if the other two were still babies. Stephen is nine and Grace is three"

"What are you suggesting?"

"That we rent a house on Fifth Avenue and put Stephen in school in New York. There are good private schools there and maybe a change might help his grades. They couldn't be worse as it is."

"But what about the house here?"

"We'll close it up and bring Marthe and Elsa with us and Mademoiselle. She can take Grace to play in Central Park and pick up Stephen after school."

"Well . . ."

"It's all decided then? Good. I'll look for a house and you get everything packed up here."

"But what about the summer? It's hot in New York."

"We can come back to the cottage. Or take a trip to Europe. How about that? Go to the opera, take the children to the art galleries, the museums, see the historic places. I think that's a bully idea."

"Then there was truly nothing to that letter, Thomas?"

"Are you still thinking about that? Of course not!"

CHAPTER ELEVEN

And so they closed up the Victorian mansion in Oil City and moved to New York for the winter.

The affair with Claire was over. At least for the time being.

But for Thomas it was easier saying it was over than believing it. He saw her one night at the opera in a gauzy lilac gown with a long rope of pearls, her upswept bouffant blonde hair and swanlike neck turning from her husband to another man sitting in their box, a young handsome man he did not know. It was like a knife going through him. Caruso was singing *Pagliacci* and it seemed to him appropriate, the clown hiding his breaking heart. He knew Claire had seen him but she gave no evidence of it.

But during the intermission she came up to him and he introduced her to Ardith.

"She's very beautiful," Ardith said later. "I could understand why—"

"There was nothing to it!" he said angrily.

Several weeks later he saw Claire again at a supper dance at the Harry Payne Whitneys'. Ardith was ill with one of her migraines but urged him to go without her.

"I won't stay late," he promised. "I'll come home right after dinner."

But he stayed long enough to dance with his hostess.

And with Claire.

"Have you missed me?" Claire asked him, as they whirled around the oak-paneled ballroom embellished with gold ornaments and hung with Gobelin tapestries and old French and Italian paintings.

"Yes, very much."

"Then why haven't you tried to see me?"

"Because I have a wife and family whom I love and do not wish to hurt," he said stiffly.

"You're quite right."

"Who was the man I saw with you in the opera box?"

"Why? Were you jealous?"

"No. I just wondered."

"He was a houseguest from Boston."

"I must see you," he said. "Alone."

She smiled. "I was wondering how long it would take you."

"Where?"

"Tomorrow afternoon at Old Westbury?"

"But—"

"Edgar's leaving on a business trip in the morning. It's safe."

"You're sure?"

"Quite sure. Unless, of course, you're afraid."

"I'm not afraid."

He said goodnight to Gertrude and Harry Whitney and left quietly.

They lay in front of the fire, drowsy after making love all afternoon, and he knew that he could never give her up.

"Shall I fix us something to eat?" she asked.

"No, I'd better be getting back to town."

"When will we see each other again?"

"I'll get in touch with you. Do you still go to the Metropolitan Museum on Thursdays?"

"Sometimes."

"Our usual place then? In front of the Romney?"

"All right."

There was a noise. "What was that?"

She listened. "I don't hear anything."

"I thought I heard footsteps."

"There's no one here. The house is empty." Sheets still covered most of the furniture as it had been closed after the summer.

"I'd better go. Are you staying down?"

"Yes, I'll drive back in the morning."

"Till Thursday, then?"

Her golden hair was loose around her bare shoulders, her face flushed from the fire. "Till Thursday, my love," she said.

How beautiful she was, he thought. He did not know it was the last time he was ever to see her alive.

It must have happened shortly after he left.

MILLIONAIRE KILLS WIFE AND HIMSELF, screamed the headlines the next day. "Couple found dead at Old Westbury estate." There was a picture of Claire at a horseshow accepting a cup and another in a ballgown with her husband at the opening of the opera. According to the coroner they had been dead since the evening before. It was not a pretty sight. Claire had been shot through the head and then Edgar put the gun in his mouth and shot himself.

Thomas was in shock. So it must have been Edgar after all that he heard lurking around the house, coming back early from his business trip and spying on them. Or perhaps that was just a ruse and he had never gone. If only he had not left Claire alone there. But if Edgar had found them both together he also would have been killed. Edgar had a gun, there would have been nothing he could have done to protect her or himself. But Edgar was there earlier and chose to wait. For what reason? Because he wanted to take Claire from him forever and this was the only way he could do it.

There were no notes but the tabloids had a field day. They brought out the difference in their ages and that Claire was a flirt who liked attention from young men. There was also something mysterious about her background. She was supposed to have been the illegitimate daughter of a prominent society woman and a married French nobleman who was raised by an aunt in upstate New York.

The motive for the murder was given as jealousy. Edgar van Vechten had suspected his beautiful young wife of affairs with other men from the time they were first married. No names were mentioned, no doubt due to the libel laws.

Affairs, Thomas thought. So he was not the only one, but just one of many. And his pain at the loss of Claire was compounded by doubt and jealousy. If only she could rise from the grave and set his mind at ease, assure him that he. . .

If. What a futile word!

Claire was gone and she would not return. This time the affair that he had tried to end was truly over.

After a while, when the pain numbed, he was grateful for his family's sake that his name had not been dragged into the scandal. Only Ardith knew the truth. Claire's name was never mentioned again, but it lay like a sword between them and always would.

He tried to pull himself together. He decided to take his family to Europe for the summer.

And so he wandered through palaces and museums with Ardith and the children, seeing nothing. One country was the same to him as any other.

He could no longer stand New York. It held too many reminders of Claire. When they returned he resigned from his position as vice-president of Standard Oil of New Jersey. He would devote himself to business and civic affairs in Pennsylvania. That was where he belonged.

So they moved back to Oil City.

And as the years passed, Claire van Vechten became a dim memory.

CHAPTER TWELVE

In 1907, Joe was twenty and in his junior year at Harvard. The previous year Elizabeth had married Hubert Dillon, a young banker from Philadelphia. Stephen, at fifteen, had already been kicked out of two prep schools, and Grace had just celebrated her ninth birthday.

It was an evening in early May and Thomas was just about to go for his usual after-dinner walk when Marthe knocked at his bedroom door and told him that there was a man waiting to see him.

"What does he want?" Thomas asked.

"He said it was important business and that he must see you right away."

"Did you get his name?"

"He told me but I can't pronounce it."

"Very well. Show him into the library and I'll be right down." Marthe started to leave the room. "Oh, Marthe, where is Mrs. Wyman?"

"She's in the music room, sir, playing her opera records. Did you want to see her?"

"No, no that's all right. I just wondered where she was."

The man stood there in a shabby suit looking uncomfortable in the richly paneled library with the leather-bound books and Aubusson carpet. He appeared to be in his early forties with a square face and a nose that looked as if it had once been broken and set crookedly. He shifted his cap from one hand to another and Thomas noticed that his hands were rough and muscular with heavy calluses, a workingman's hands.

"Mr. Wyman?"

"Yes."

"My name is Krzyzynski. John Krzyzynski."

A Pole, Thomas thought. The Poles had come to Oil City with the

last wave of immigrants and did menial labor work in the factories and
lived on the other side of the railroad tracks. "If it's about work," he said,
"you can see me at my office."

The man looked angry. "It's not about a job. It's a personal matter."

A grudge, perhaps? Thomas put one hand on his desk drawer where
he kept a revolver and waited.

"It's about my daughter Mary that I've come."

Mary Krzyzynski? Thomas racked his brain. Had they ever employed a maid by that name? Or possibly a laundress? "I don't believe I
know your daughter."

"Your son does. He knows her all right, he does. He's got her in the
family way."

"I have two sons. Which one are you referring to?"

"Joe, he's the one. He's been seeing my Mary. He told her he was in
love with her. Then when she wrote to tell him that she was in trouble—"

"Are you sure you have the right person? My son is away at college.
Perhaps he does not feel that he is responsible for your daughter's
condition."

Krzyzynski's face turned red. "He was here at Easter vacation.
That's when it happened. My Mary is only sixteen and she's a good
Catholic girl."

"Mr. Krzy—"

"Krzyzynski."

"Mr. Krzyzynski, what is it exactly that you expect me to do?"

"I thought that you could make your son see his duty toward my
Mary."

"By duty do you mean — to marry her?"

"That's right."

Joe, with the daughter of this man? Joe, with all the things he had
planned for him? It was absurd. Thomas paused, choosing his words
carefully. "Even if what you tell me is true, I can't force my son to marry
someone he doesn't want to." Someone he's obviously tired of, he
thought. "Besides, he's too young. He still has another year of college."

"So where does that leave my daughter?"

Thomas opened a drawer of the desk and took out his checkbook. He
wrote out a check for a thousand dollars and handed it to the man. "This
should help with your daughter's medical expenses."

John Krzyzynski ripped the check in half and threw it on the carpet.

"You can't buy off my daughter!" he shouted. "Or me! Your son is responsible and he'll pay for it. You sit here in your fancy house thinking he's too good for my daughter. You'll be sorry, the both of you!"

And he stormed out, slamming the front door loudly as he left and cracking one of the stained glass panes.

The sound of the opera records in the music room had stopped. His wife appeared at the library door.

"What was that all about?" she asked.

Thomas wondered how much she had heard. "Nothing important," he assured her. "An employee I had to fire. Marthe shouldn't have let him in. I'll have to tell her to be more careful in future."

"He sounded as if he might make trouble."

"I don't think so. Don't worry about it."

But the next day Thomas hired a bodyguard, a man who had worked with him in the oil fields and who looked as tough as John Krzyzynski. And when Joe came home for summer vacation at the end of the month, Thomas promptly shipped him off to work in one of the lead mines he owned in Missouri.

That would take care of him for the summer, Thomas thought, and in September he would be back at Harvard.

Possibly he had slept with the girl, even told her in a weak moment that he loved her. But marriage? That was out of the question!

And in time the whole thing would blow over.

Three years passed and he heard no more from John Krzyzynski. He assumed that the girl had had the baby and given it up for adoption.

Then, one Saturday morning, he looked out the window and saw a young woman standing on the sidewalk outside the front gate holding a toddler by the hand and pointing to the house. He was suddenly struck by how much the little boy resembled Joe at the same age.

Was she planning to come in the house and speak to him or Ardith? His wife had never known anything about the affair and he could hear her voice now drifting up from the music room. She was singing the new hit song, "A Perfect Day" by Carrie Jacobs Bond.

Quickly Thomas put on his hat and took his walking stick and opened the front door. The girl and the child were still standing there. He would find out what she wanted. He walked briskly down the stone walk to the green wrought-iron gate.

"Can I help you?" he asked.

"You're Mr. Wyman."

"That's right." She was a pretty girl, Thomas observed, with fair hair and deep blue eyes.

"I'm Mary Krzyzynski." She pointed to the little boy. "And this is Joey. Joey, say how-do-you-do to the man the way I taught you."

The child hid behind his mother's skirts and smiled shyly but said nothing.

"He talks all the time at home," she said. "Go on, Joey."

Joey held out a mittened hand. "How do you do?"

Thomas shook it. "You're a fine boy," he said. He must get rid of them before Ardith saw them.

"How is Joe?" Mary asked. Her lower lip trembled slightly as she spoke his name.

"Fine, just fine. He's in law school. At Harvard," he added. Joe was dating a girl from a wealthy old Boston family and he and Ardith hoped that eventually they would marry. "Now, I'm just on my way to the post office. What was it that you wanted?"

Mary Krzyznyski drew herself up proudly. "We don't want anything from you, Mr. Wyman. I have a job as a seamstress and my mother helps take care of Joey. I just thought that you might want to see your grandson."

"Yes, well—" Thomas cleared his throat and glanced toward the window of the music room. "My wife is not in good health and she knows nothing about—" He looked down at Joey. "—All of this. It would upset her very much. So if there is anything I can do for you, I would like to ask you to come to my office in future and not to my home."

Tears gathered in her eyes and threatened to spill over. "I understand. Come, Joey. We must go home now. It will be time for lunch soon.'"

And the two of them walked off.

He even walks like Joe, Thomas thought. He wondered what would become of him.

CHAPTER THIRTEEN

Grace was sixteen and attending Mount Vernon Seminary in Washington. She had developed into a lovely young woman with many suitors. She also had a talent for art and wanted to go to Paris to study in the fall. Thomas was against it but his wife encouraged her.

"Let her go, Thomas. Let her see what she can do. Then she won't regret anything later. . ." She stopped.

"The way you did?"

"That wasn't what I meant."

"Do you regret marrying me? That you didn't go on with your singing?"

"No, of course not. But perhaps someday women will be able to have both a career and marriage, not have to give up one for the other."

"That will never happen, my dear," Thomas said. "A man wants his wife at home, not running around pursuing some career, and I don't think it's going to change."

"Maybe not in our lifetime, but one day it will."

Thomas had picked up the newspaper and turned to the stock market reports.

"But to continue about Grace," Ardith said. "There is a French countess — a widow — who runs a small exclusive school in Paris. I've looked into it and Grace would be very well chaperoned—"

"What's wrong with Mount Vernon Seminary? She still has two more years there."

"There's nothing wrong with it, Thomas. It's just that Grace feels that she would have a greater opportunity to study her painting in Europe. After all, the school is only a few blocks from the Louvre. And the girls are taken to the opera and on excursions to the countryside on weekends, such as the Loire Valley to see the châteaux, and to Versailles and Chartres. It sounds to me like the ideal school for Grace."

"Please, Papa," Grace pleaded at dinner. "I really want to go."

"Well, if that's what you want, we'll have to see what we can do about it."

"Thank you, Papa, thank you! I knew you'd agree."

But on the twenty-eighth of June, at Sarajevo, the Austrian Archduke Francis Ferdinand and his wife were assassinated, and Europe was plunged into war.

Going to Paris was now out of the question. Grace continued her studies at Mount Vernon Seminary.

Then on May 7, 1915, the steamship *Lusitania* was sunk without warning by a German submarine off the coast of Ireland. Among those drowned were a hundred and fourteen Americans. Indignation ran high, and Oil City, with its large German population, was divided. Everyone expected President Wilson to declare war. Instead notes went back and forth and Germany announced that properly marked ships of neutral countries could cross the seas unmolested by German submarines.

"We'll be in it for sure, sooner or later," Thomas told Ardith. He wondered what had happened to his old partner. For a while, after Ernst left, they exchanged Christmas cards, and then those stopped. If his sons had to go to war, they could be fighting against Ernst Ludwig's sons . . .

Joe graduated from law school and was promptly offered a job with a prestigious New York law firm. The romance with the Boston girl had fizzled out and she had married someone else. Joe did not seem perturbed about it. He had many girlfriends, but seemed in no hurry to settle down. Elizabeth and her banker husband were now the parents of two little girls and lived on the Philadelphia Main Line. As for Stephen, he was continuing his pattern as the black sheep of the family by being kicked out of Amherst. He was now taking flying lessons at the Burgess Flying School in Marblehead, Massachusetts.

Some Americans are going to France to join a flying group called the Lafayette Escadrille, Stephen wrote to his parents. *I may sign up.*

His mother was frantic.

"Let him go," Thomas said. "Perhaps it will make a man of him."

"Unless he gets shot down." She had always had a soft spot for Stephen and bailed him out whenever he got in a scrape. "If it were Joe you wouldn't encourage him to go."

Thomas did not reply. He knew she was right. But damn it, Stephen wasn't Joe. At twenty-two he had shown no interest in anything but drinking and having a good time. If he was going to amount to anything in life there was no evidence as yet. Joe was the one he was counting on, the one in whom he had invested his dreams.

So Stephen left for France and after a while letters drifted back. The Lafayette Escadrille was a great group of guys, he wrote. Their barracks was a villa at Bar-le-Duc on a hill with a winding stone stairway running up to the door and flower beds all around. He loved flying and had downed his first German Fokker.

"Sounds like he's living in a damned country club," his father remarked.

But it seemed that at last Stephen had found his niche.

The series of U-boat attacks continued and President Wilson threatened to sever diplomatic relations. The country was drawing closer and closer to war with Germany and on April 6, 1917, it finally came.

Joe immediately quit his job with the New York law firm and enlisted in the Army. Two months later he landed in France with the American Expeditionary Forces under General John J. Pershing.

For Thomas there was a name that would always be engraved on his heart.

Château-Thierry.

How could such a beautiful name be so ugly?

For it was there that Thomas Joseph Wyman, Jr. fell. Joe, the fair-haired boy of his future. Joe, who was going to carry on the torch of the Wyman dynasty.

End of hopes, of dreams.

Stephen came through unscathed.

After the armistice in November, Thomas brought his son's body back to Oil City to be buried in the family mausoleum. His shoulders were stooped and he felt on the point of collapse. Again and again he asked himself a question that had no answer: Why Joe?

His wife, weakened by the influenza that had swept the country, was unable to leave her bed to attend the funeral. It was Grace who comforted him, Grace who sat beside him during the long evenings when he had no desire for sleep, only for forgetfulness. He remembered Joe as a small boy, how he would put his small hand up to pat his face. Still, Thomas was unable to cry. It was as if his insides had turned to stone.

And then, one Sunday afternoon as he was going through Joe's things, he came across the worn copy of poems by Eugene Field and the marker fell open to "Little Boy Blue." Tears came, overflowing like a creek long dammed up, his sobs seemed as if they would tear him apart.

"Joe, Joe. My son . . ."

Thomas had hoped that Grace would marry one of her many beaux and settle down in Oil City, but none of them interested her and she appeared bored and listless.

"I want to go to Paris, Papa," she said. "The war is over now and I'd like to go on with my painting."

He tried not to show his disappointment. "I guess it isn't very exciting sitting here with your old father—"

"You're not old, Papa." She put her arms round his neck.

"I feel old. I'll be sixty my next birthday."

She didn't say anything. "Of course, if you want me to stay—"

"No, no, I'm all right. You have your life to lead and you should get on with it. It's just that I'll miss you."

"I'll miss you too, Papa. But I've got to find out if I'm any good."

So Grace went to Paris to study art. And then one day they received a letter from her.

Dearest Papa and Mama, it read. *I have met someone. His name is Julian Rodgers. He is from New Orleans and he is an artist. I know you will like him.*

"It sounds serious," Thomas said. "I'd better go to Paris and look this fellow over. For all we know, he may be just some fortune hunter."

But before he was able to get to Paris there was another letter from Grace. She and Julian Rodgers were married.

"How could she do this to us?" Ardith wailed. "Just to elope like that! There must be something funny about the whole thing. Why didn't she come home and have a proper wedding like Elizabeth? Why, Thomas?"

"I'm afraid I have no answer for you, my dear."

"What will we tell our friends? She must be pregnant to have gotten married so quickly."

That thought had been going through his mind too, but Thomas said nothing. Grace, his little Grace. You give your children everything and then they turn around and hurt you.

"Don't you think it's strange?" Ardith asked.

"I don't know what to think." He only knew that if this Julian Rodgers ever hurt his daughter he would kill him. Suddenly a scene flashed through his mind. John Krzyzynski standing in the library telling him that Joe had made his daughter pregnant. Now he appreciated how he must have felt.

How old would the little boy be now? About twelve. Ironic that his only grandson was one he could not claim. Elizabeth had only daughters, three of them now. Stephen had not married and seemed unlikely to. Perhaps Grace would have a son, one she would name after him.

"Obviously he's someone she knew we wouldn't approve of," Ardith said.

"Who?" Thomas was still lost in the past.

"This Julian Rodgers, whoever he is."

But Grace was not pregnant. She wrote to her parents that she and Julian had found a flat in Montmartre with a view that looked down on all of Paris. They were very happy. She was doing some watercolors and Julian had sold a painting. They were not to worry about her.

"It sounds like they're living on a shoestring," Thomas said. "A starving artist. I don't like the whole thing."

"But Grace says that he's sold a painting."

"Ha! Probably to a tourist for a few dollars. How long can they live on that?"

"But it seems to be what she wants."

"We'll see. Time will tell."

CHAPTER FOURTEEN

"So there I was all alone with a Fokker coming right at me," Stephen said. "I didn't have much ammunition left, so I had to conserve it for the right moment. Once I thought the damned fool would crash me in mid-air, but he didn't." Stephen picked up another glass to demonstrate. "Finally my chance came and I let him have it, rat-a-tat-tat! When I saw the flames I knew that he was hit, but I followed him down to make sure of my confirmation." His voice slurred. "And then he crashed, boom!" Stephen smashed the glass on the bar and sharp pieces of jagged glass flew everywhere.

"Let's get him out of here," the bartender of Gruber's Saloon said to another man, "before he breaks anything else."

"I haven't finished my story," Stephen shouted. "What did you do in the war?"

"The war's been over a long time, buddy. You can't relive it forever."

"Shut up!" Stephen swung at him, lost his balance, and stumbled against a table, knocking it over. Then he grabbed a bottle, waved it over his head, and threw it through the front plate glass window.

"Better call his old man to come and get him."

"Hell no, this time I'm calling the police," the bartender said.

"You're a bunch of yellow-livered cowards!" Stephen yelled. "All of you!"

Thomas got Stephen out of jail, paid the damage to Gruber's Saloon, and kept the whole thing out of the papers. He had a long talk with Stephen, but his speech went in one ear and out the other. Finally he lost control of himself and burst out, "Why can't you be more like your brother?"

"Because I'm not Joe!" Stephen shouted. "And that's the trouble, it's always been the trouble. Everything was for Joe. The sun rose and set on Joe. He was perfect. But he's dead, the hero is dead, and the black sheep son is alive. And that's what you can't forgive!"

His mother, as usual, defended Stephen.

"He's a sensitive boy," she told Thomas. "He saw so many terrible things during the war, his friends shot down in flames. Most of the members of the Lafayette Escadrille were killed, even the man who talked Stephen into joining."

"I expected you to make excuses for him. You've always mollycoddled him. No wonder he's a weakling."

"Stephen's not weak! He was a brave pilot. He won medals—"

"If he's such a great pilot why doesn't he get a job with the mail service? They're looking for fliers." He already knew the answer. They wanted men who were reliable and sober, not reckless drunks. "There's never been a drunkard in my family," Thomas said. Then he remembered his own father, the bottles of Allegheny rye for the pain in his leg during the cold Pennsylvania winters. Another victim of another war. A drunkard must always have an excuse.

"I'm at the end of my wits with that boy," he said. "Mark my words, he's going to come to a bad end."

During the summer of 1923 there was disturbing news from Paris. Grace was pregnant and her marriage was not going well. She wanted to come home. Alone.

"I'm sure there's plenty she's never told us," Thomas said, "and probably never will. Just wait till I get my hands on that fellow!"

He sent Grace the money for her passage home and went to New York to meet the ship.

Grace looked pale and drawn with deep circles under her eyes as if she had been crying the whole voyage. The baby was due in two months. She refused to talk about her marriage, only telling her father that she wanted to think things over.

"You should have done the thinking before you married that bounder," Thomas told her.

"Please, Papa. I'm not up to a lecture. How is Mother?"

"Your mother's fine. She has your room all ready."

"And Stephen?"

There was a brief silence.

"The same?"

"The same. He can't seem to find himself."

"That happens to a lot of men, Papa."

"Not the ones with any gumption. Why when I was seventeen I walked all the way from Franklin to Pittsburgh with just a few cents in my pocket looking for work—"

"You've told us."

"Well it's the truth. Those who want to find work can."

Grace said nothing. Her eyes looked very sad and far away. "Not always, Papa."

Thomas reached over and took her hand. "It's good to have you home again. I've missed you."

The baby was born the twenty-sixth of September, a girl with brown eyes, olive skin, and dark brown hair.

"She doesn't look like any of the Wymans," Thomas said.

"No, she doesn't," Grace replied. "She looks exactly like Julian."

"Too bad."

"He's a very handsome man, Papa."

"Have you decided on a name?"

"Yes. I want to name her after Mother. Ardith."

"Ardith Rodgers. It's a pretty name. And it will make your mother very happy."

"I knew she'd go back to him!" Thomas shouted.

"She still loves him, Thomas," Ardith said. "And there's the baby—"

"What kind of a life can he give them? A starving artist! And we still don't know why she left him in the first place, but I'm sure there was a damned good reason."

"Maybe he's changed. That's possible."

Thomas shook his head. "Men don't change, my dear. It's only women who think they will."

Thomas opened the *Oil City Derrick* to the sports page. "Well, here we are. It's not a bad photograph of the team." He handed the paper across the dining room table to Ardith.

"Familiar names are in this gold team that represented the Wanango Country Club at a match in—"

"You don't need to read the whole article aloud," he said. "Here, let me have it."

He looked at the article again and then another photograph on the same page caught his eye and a story with it. "Former *Derrick* Carrierboy Wins Scholarship." Joseph Krzyzynski, who was captain of the football team at Oil City High School and valedictorian of the class of 1925, had been awarded a football scholarship to Notre Dame University.

Joe's son. His grandson.

Ardith buttered a piece of toast. "You seem to be in a bad mood today."

"Sorry, my dear, I didn't mean to speak to you so sharply. It's just that my rheumatism has been bothering me."

"Why don't you see the doctor?"

"You know how I feel about doctors." He looked at the photograph of Joseph Krzyzynski again. A good-looking boy. Not only tops in sports but valedictorian of his class. He recalled the shy little boy who had hidden behind his mother's skirts that day in front of the house. He was doing all right.

The article said that Joseph had been an altar boy at Assumption Blessed Virgin Mary. So he had been raised as a Catholic, Thomas thought. He frowned. But of course, Poles were Roman Catholics. It was just something that had not occurred to him before. And besides being a carrierboy for the *Derrick,* which meant getting up each morning at five-thirty, he'd also had a *Saturday Evening Post* route to earn extra money.

The boy has ambition, Thomas thought. He takes after me. "I wonder . . ."

"You wonder what?" Ardith asked.

"Oh, nothing." He didn't realize that he had spoken aloud. "It's not important."

BOOK TWO

1928

CHAPTER FIFTEEN

For the rest of her life the sound of church chimes and the scent of roses would bring Ardith Rodgers back in memory to the old Victorian mansion up on Third Street.

Her grandfather's house — the house where she was born. She could hear his step on the marble staircase and the tap of his cane. The ornate brass carving on the handle made the cane a weapon and he slept with a loaded revolver under his pillow at night. A fierce police dog, Alaska, ran the length of the house on a long chain.

She would never forget the night they took her baby pillow away and gave her a grown-up one.

"You're five years old and big enough for a regular pillow now," her mother said, closing the door.

Her room was near the back stairs. It had floral wallpaper, a brass bed, a marble-topped commode, and a white wicker chair. There was a print of "The Broken Pitcher" by Greuze in a gilt frame above the bed.

"I want my pillow back," she sobbed, but no one came. She lay there unable to sleep, hearing Alaska running up and down on his chain. He had knocked her to the ground once when she tried to pat him and she had been afraid of him ever since.

The damp mist drifted up from the river, cold with the smell of winter in it.

She heard the sound of the train across the river. Always she hoped the train would bring her father back, but it never did. Why doesn't he come? she wondered. It had been a long time since that afternoon she had said goodbye to him in New Orleans.

He had taken her for a ride on the riverboat up the Mississippi. The river was such a muddy color and her father had looked so sad. Her mother was not with them. She said she wanted to look at some antiques on Royal Street in the French Quarter and would meet them later.

Her father had been trying to tell her something, but he seemed unable to say it. They went to the French Market afterward and had doughnuts. She drank milk and her father gave her a sip of *café au lait*.

He looked so handsome. He was tall and typically Creole with black hair and brown eyes. Everyone always told Ardith she was the image of him.

He bought her a rosary and had it blessed by a priest at the Saint Louis Cathedral.

"Always keep this," he said.

They walked by a pavilion where a band concert was playing. The song was Irving Berlin's "Remember."

Remember the night — the night you said — "I love you" — Remember?

Ardith looked up at her father. He was holding her hand tightly and there were tears in his eyes.

"Your mother will be wondering what happened to us," he said quickly.

Later, at the railroad station, he'd kissed them goodbye. "See you in a few weeks in Oil City," he said.

That was a year ago. Whenever she asked about him, people changed the subject. Finally her mother said, "Your father did something that hurt me very much. When you are old enough to understand, I will explain it to you."

Whenever they went in a store and some saleslady asked, "Where did you get those beautiful brown eyes?" (her mother had blue eyes and was very blonde) she noticed her mother got a strange look, the same look she'd had that day at the railroad station in New Orleans.

Ardith got out of bed and tiptoed along the hall toward her mother's room. And then she heard the voices. They were coming from her grandfather's room. The door was ajar.

"For God's sake, Grace, why did you marry that bum?"

"You've no right to call him that, Papa."

"I told you he was no good, but you wouldn't listen to me . . ."

She crept back to her room.

What did my father do? she wondered. And why doesn't he come back?

She heard the whistle of the train and the music in the pavilion in New Orleans.

You promised that you'd forget me not — But you forgot to remember.

She clutched the rosary with white beads and cried herself to sleep.

Right after Christmas they moved to Washington and bought a house on Kalorama Circle overlooking Rock Creek Park. She started first grade at the Potomac School. Everyone had made friends by then and she was "that new girl."

"Ardith — what a funny name!" said a girl whose name was Peggy. Peggy's father was something important in Hoover's cabinet.

"It's Welsh," Ardith said. "I was named after my grandmother."

Peggy was the most popular girl in the class and lived in a big house on Tracy Place around the corner. Ardith wanted desperately to be liked by her. Maybe Peggy would invite her over to go rollerskating or to play hop-scotch. Whenever Ardith went for a walk with Mademoiselle and passed Peggy's house there were children playing games. If only Peggy would ask her too. . .

Peggy was staring at her. "You're odd," she said. She giggled and walked off with another girl.

The promenades continued with Mademoiselle. Usually they walked down Massachusetts Avenue past the embassies and met other children with their nurses at Sheridan Circle. The nurses sat and gossiped while the children played and tried to climb on top of the statue of General Sheridan sitting astride his horse. They were mostly children of the diplomatic corps. Ardith made friends with the daughter of the Venezuelan ambassador. She was a stranger in Washington too.

Spring came. Forsythia bushes were in bloom and a cardinal sang in the dogwood tree. Ardith sat at the piano playing a Beethoven sonata while Miss Clovelly tapped out the time with a pencil. Miss Clovelly came every Wednesday after school, and on Tuesday Ardith would practice frantically to make up for the whole week.

"Land's sake, child, how do you expect to play this if you don't practice? And don't tell me you don't have time. Now, start over. One and two and . . . less pedal, please . . ." Miss Clovelly sighed. She was plump and fifty and would be out of breath and puffing after walking up the steep front steps. Her first request was always for a glass of water with lots of ice. Now she sat there like a huge toad crunching the ice. Today she was wearing a beige suit with a shocking pink chiffon scarf at the throat and two pink cabbage roses in her frizzy gray hair. Two brown bead bracelets and a gold bracelet with a medallion clinked on her right arm and a large amethyst ring glittered. Her left arm had another gold bracelet and a signet ring on the index finger. Her costume was complete with gold earrings and flat, brown suede shoes. Each piece of jewelry had a story and was collected on her travels in "better times."

Mademoiselle came in with tea and little cakes.

"Well, I really shouldn't," said Miss Clovelly, stuffing a chocolate éclair in her mouth.

The lesson was over. Ardith got up. "Now do your homework," Mademoiselle said. As she left the room Ardith heard Mademoiselle regaling Miss Clovelly with the latest gossip.

She seldom saw her mother. Her mother was always going out with different escorts. Some of them would bring Ardith presents and pat her on the head. Sometimes, when her mother was waiting for her escort to call for her, Ardith would notice her staring out the window with a wistful, far-off expression.

She loved to go in her mother's dressing room and try on her hats and look at the beautiful brocade and satin ball gowns and furs. Her mother had rows of shoes all dyed different colors to match her dresses.

"I'll be so glad when I'm grown up and can wear pretty dresses and jewelry," Ardith said.

"Don't be in too much of a hurry to grow up, baby," her mother said.

Ardith sat curled up in the window seat listening to the music drifting across the park from the Shoreham Hotel. The house was quiet. Her mother was at an election night party, and Mademoiselle, not interested in American politics, had gone to her room.

The searchlight from the Shoreham swept the park in large circles as the electoral votes came in from all over the country. Green for Hoover, red for Roosevelt. Ardith was determined to stay up till the end. She had never stayed up this late before. The green light swept round again above the bare branches of the trees. Another green . . . then a red. It gave Rock Creek Park a fairyland quality. She watched, fascinated.

Once she had taken a shoe box and made a woodland scene in it. With cardboard she cut holes in a wheel and covered it with cellophane paper in red, green, blue, and yellow, and attached an electric light bulb to it. By turning the wheel the setting changed to different times of day and seasons.

She pressed her nose against the icy windowpane. The lights were mostly green . . . no, there was a red one. When all the votes were in the searchlight would remain fixed. She hoped she could stay awake that late. Her eyelids were getting so heavy. Another red light, then more green ones.

She walked over to her bed and put her robe on over her long flannel nightgown. Then she took a blanket and pillow and tucked herself in the window seat again. She yawned. Red, green, green, red . . . she had lost count by now. I must stay awake, she thought. She felt so sleepy. . .

She jumped in terror. Her eyes suddenly flew open. Fingers were digging into her shoulder blades. Mademoiselle was shaking her and the whole sky was filled with a red glow.

Roosevelt had been elected.

CHAPTER SIXTEEN

They were spending the summer in Pennsylvania at her grandfather's summer cottage on the Allegheny River.

Ardith lay in a hammock on the porch reading *The Garden of Allah*. She had seen it on one of the bookshelves in the living room and asked her mother if she could read it.

"When you're older," her mother had replied. "It's not a suitable book for a child of ten."

Maybe not, but it was much more exciting than *The Wind in the Willows*. She was carried away by the love story of Domini and Androvsky. Would she love like that someday? she wondered. It was very romantic.

"The cool wind of the night blows over the vast spaces of the Sahara and touches her cheek . . ." she read on, transported. *'Come,' he said. 'Domini.' And he drew her in through the tent door almost violently."*

Suddenly Ardith heard the tap of her grandfather's cane on the stone walk leading up to the cottage from the river. He was returning from his after-dinner walk. She quickly hid the book under the pillow.

Her grandfather appeared, immaculate in blue seersucker suit, white shirt, and tie even in the woods. On the small finger of his left hand he wore a gold ring set with a pigeonblood ruby. What a distinguished figure he was, Ardith thought, with his white hair and heavy mustache and blue eyes that never missed anything behind the rimless glasses. Though he was in his seventies he stood straighter than men half his age and had twice their energy.

"Good evening, sir," she said, standing up.

He had a police dog with him. This one was named Rex. Someone had shot Alaska one night. Ardith liked Rex better, anyway. At least he didn't knock her down when she came near him, even though he looked fierce.

Her grandfather nodded, scarcely noticing her, and sat down in the wicker armchair with the high back. Rex lay panting at his feet. Her grandfather took a Corona-Corona cigar from his pocket and lighted it. Then he picked up the *Oil City Derrick* and started to read.

Ardith watched him. The sun had gone down now behind the hills and she could hear the splashing of oars on the river and frogs croaking in the bulrushes down by the dock. Crickets were starting to chirp and there was the smell of honeysuckle.

Suddenly her grandfather's face turned the color of the pigeon blood ruby. He looked as if he were going to choke. He threw down the newspaper and muttered one word:

"Roosevelt!"

He said it as if it were a curse word.

"That man is ruining this country," he fumed. "No wonder we're in the midst of a Depression."

Franklin Delano Roosevelt was her grandfather's favorite topic of conversation. She had listened in silence during dinner while he presided at the head of the long table on the porch as if he were at a board meeting talking about "that man in Washington," the N.R.A., and other subjects she did not quite understand. She was used to listening. "Children should be seen and not heard," was one of her grandfather's frequent remarks.

Someday I'll say all the things I want to say and you won't stop me, Ardith thought rebelliously.

It was a good dinner. Fried chicken, corn-on-the-cob, salad, hot biscuits with buckwheat honey, and huckleberry pie. She had a second piece of pie.

"That man should be impeached!" her grandfather roared, pounding the table with his fist.

Her mother and Uncle Stephen agreed. Roosevelt was a horrible man.

Ardith didn't quite understand about the Depression, either. It seemed that there were breadlines all over the country and people were starving. However, they seemed to have plenty to eat and her grandfather had a new Packard with a chauffeur who looked like a thug because he was also a bodyguard.

She looked at her grandfather again. He had folded the paper over to the financial page and was reading the stock market reports.

Ardith picked up her sweater from the hammock and slipped *The Garden of Allah* under it. She was starting down the stone steps when her grandfather looked up from his newspaper and cleared his throat.

"Where are you going?"

"I thought I'd go for a row before it gets dark."

"Fine. But don't go near the rapids."

"I won't."

Why was this warning repeated every time? she wondered. The rapids were up at the river bend near a big overhanging rock. It was hard to tell where they began, the water was so blue-green and peaceful . . . then suddenly there were the ripples. They frightened her but at the same time she felt drawn to the danger, wondering what it would be like to be caught in them.

Ardith took the oars from the dock and put them in the rowboat. Then she untied the boat and jumped in. She loved the river, especially in the early evening. She rowed down to the Boat Club and back, passing the summer cottages with their docks. A freight train came along the tracks across the river. It passed every evening at this time on its way from Corry to Oil City. She waved to the engineer and the man in the caboose and they waved back.

She felt so lonely most of the time. She tried not to think about her father. He never wrote or sent presents for Christmas or her birthdays. It was six years since she had seen him.

But you forgot to remember.

That song could still make her cry whenever she heard it.

Was this the way love ended? she wondered. In the fairy tales the handsome prince married the beautiful princess and they always lived happily ever after. But in *The Garden of Allah* and other grown-up books she was not supposed to read, the love affairs ended unhappily. She had already peeked at the last page of *The Garden of Allah* to see what happened. Domini was alone with her little boy and Androvsky gone.

Like my mother, she thought.

In the book, Androvsky was a Catholic priest who had left his church and finally returned to it. What had her father done to want to leave them forever? Did he, too, carry some terrible guilt about something?

That day at the station in New Orleans he had asked, "How much do you love Daddy?"

She had put her arms around his neck and hugged him.

"I love you more than anything in this world," he had said. There was such pain in his eyes.

Then why did he go away?

Someday she would find him, she promised herself.

That was the last summer they spent in Pennsylvania. They went abroad after that and rented a villa at Cap d'Antibes on the French Riviera. It was while they were there that her Uncle Stephen shot himself. The papers hushed it up nicely. "Son of oil magnate T. J. Wyman accidentally killed while cleaning his shotgun." They did not mention that Stephen had been found in his pajamas at three in the morning with an empty bottle of whiskey nearby and that it was not the hunting season.

Mary Krzyzynski put down the *Oil City Derrick.* Another tragedy in the Wyman family, she thought, a second son dead. And something fishy about it at that. It was ironic that all their money couldn't bring them happiness.

Not that she wished them any ill, she had put all that behind her long ago, or tried to. She was forty-three now and time had streaked her fair hair with gray and etched fine lines around the blue eyes, but the merry twinkle was still there and the sweet expression. She still did dressmaking in the little house on Innis Street that Joey had bought for her after Pop died.

Joey. . . she must remember to call him Joe now that he was a lawyer and running for the Oil City Council. How proud she was of him! He had graduated with honors from Notre Dame, then worked his way through Georgetown Law School. It hadn't been easy, especially in the midst of such bad economic times with so many people out of work.

She had never told Joey who his father really was, only that he was someone she loved very much who was killed before they could be married. Someday she would tell him the truth. Strange how respect for a woman was based on that narrow gold band that signified that a man wanted her for his wife, his possession. She'd had offers of marriage over the years, but she could give herself only to a man she truly loved. And that love would always belong to one man alone.

Would there be a black wreath hanging on the door of the mansion at Petroleum and Third Street, the way there was when Joe was killed? She had gone by the house then and stood there in the rain, watching people go in and out to pay their condolences. And afterwards she had walked slowly home, the rain streaking her face, not caring that she was soaked to the skin, only grieving for a lost love that would not come again.

It was a lonely life sometimes, but she had her son and her church. And her memories. No one could take those from her.

Someday Joey would be an important man, even more successful than his grandfather, the grandfather who had never acknowledged him, Thomas Joseph Wyman. It was not just a mother's faith that believed it, it was something she was sure of. There was a reason for everything, and God had his reasons for wanting Joey to be born. He was a man of destiny.

Mary picked up her sewing again and started stitching. This dress must be finished by tomorrow.

CHAPTER SEVENTEEN

Ardith crossed off another day on the calendar she had made in the back of her homework assignment notebook. Twenty-eight more days till Christmas vacation, she thought. It seemed forever.

This was her second year at Miss Putnam's, a boarding school in Connecticut just outside of Hartford. At fifteen she felt far less sophisticated than the other girls, all of whom were terribly boy-crazy. But her mother had been eager for her to attend Miss Putnam's and meet girls from the best Eastern families. She was the only girl from Washington. The others were mostly from New York, Philadelphia, and Boston, and spoke with affected broad a's.

She gazed out the classroom window at the red maple tree. There was the smell of burning leaves in the air. . .

"I will explain this once more," Frau Glavis said, "and it is for the last time. In German the indirect object precedes: *Er gibt der Mutter die Rose,* unless the direct object is a personal pronoun. *Er gibt sie der Mutter.* You understand? *Ja?"* Frau Glavis had reddish-blonde hair wound in braids around her head and her face looked as if she had been standing over a steam kettle. She snapped the grammar book shut. "For Monday you are to read another chapter of *Immensee a*nd review your verbs. Class dismissed."

Everyone filed out into the hall.

"What a language!" Carol Sears groaned. "It seemed easy in the beginning. Now I wish I'd taken Latin instead."

"My father says there may be another war," said Buffie Witherspoon. She lowered her voice. "I hear Frau Glavis has a son in the Hitler Youth. No wonder she looks worried."

"My brother was in Germany last summer with a group of Harvard boys," Carol said. "He told us that all those bicycle factories are really munitions plants. They've been rearming for years. Daddy says that all Germans are naturally militaristic and we should never allow them any weapon stronger than a pea-shooter."

"Well, just as long as America doesn't get dragged into it," said Buffie. "I don't care what happens in Europe. I don't want anything to spoil my coming-out party."

Carol laughed. "Come on, let's go get our mail."

Ardith listened to their conversation in growing disgust. She had looked forward to boarding school, partly because of stories she had read in books and her mother's glowing accounts of her own days at Mount Vernon Seminary. "They were the happiest days of my life," her mother often told her. "So carefree . . . with no responsibilities."

Maybe these girls were right. At least they seemed to have fun. But didn't it matter what happened in the rest of the world?

Last summer in Switzerland she had met a Jewish girl who was staying at the same hotel. She said her family had to move from Berlin and that terrible things were going on in Germany that America wasn't even aware of. Many Germans pretended not to know or chose not to see. It was just beginning and it would get worse . . .

"You think too much, Ardith," her roommate was always telling her. "You're much too serious about everything."

She tucked her books under her arm and walked along the path back to her dormitory. The leaves crackled under her feet.

Chattering girls ran past.

"Is Jack coming for tea tomorrow?"

"I met the cutest boy — he goes to Choate."

"Guess what? Patsy was invited to Yale!"

More giggling.

She walked on. Perhaps I'm just jealous because I don't have any invitations or boys writing to me, she thought.

She remembered a dream she had the night before. She was a beautiful, elegantly-dressed woman dining with a handsome, dark stranger in the Court of Two Sisters in New Orleans. She had dreams like this quite often until they seemed almost real . . . but there was always the awakening to plain, shy Ardith Rodgers who was a wallflower at dancing school, who had no callers on Saturday afternoons when the other girls had beaux from nearby prep schools for tea.

But this dream was different from the others.

As the waiter approached them she suddenly realized that he seemed familiar. He had white hair and a white mustache and his eyes were a cold blue behind his rimless glasses. It was her grandfather — except that he was short. Very short. He held out the menu to her dashing escort who looked, oddly, like her father. "What will you have, sir?" the waiter asked, bowing. Then she awoke.

Often she wondered why none of the Wymans was happy. Her grandfather was a great success in the financial world yet he was grim and humorless, totally lacking in affection. He and her grandmother had bedrooms at opposite ends of the house and she grew up thinking this was normal. She thought of her grandmother who always looked sad and was afraid of dying, her Uncle Stephen who found escape in the bottle and then in suicide, her mother who filled her hours with a frantic social whirl. None of them found happiness.

What was happiness, anyway? She was happy when she listened to music, when she took long walks through the woods . . . and then there were the other times when she was filled with an aching loneliness, reaching out for. . . what? She did not know.

Something in her wanted to run from everything she was supposed to be, everything that was expected of her.

And there was no place to run. . .

Sunday. A gray, drizzly day. The wind whipped the leaves from the trees and scattered them along the paths.

She buttoned her raincoat and tied a scarf around her head. From her bureau drawer she took her rosary and slipped it in her purse. In a few minutes she would be going in to Hartford for Mass with the French teacher and the other Catholic girls.

She loved High Mass with the chanting and the incense and the lighting of candles, but she found that most Catholics preferred to attend the shorter Mass. The Drunkard's Mass, her grandfather called it. He was furious when he found out she'd been taking instructions in the Catholic faith. "What's wrong with the Presbyterian Church?" he roared. "Why in thunderation do you want to join a church that's controlled by Rome?" It was useless to argue with him. "Damned bunch of hypocrites," she overheard him say to her mother. "They think they can do anything and then go to confession and be forgiven. Say a few Hail Marys and then go out and do it all over again!"

There were some things that she herself found difficult to accept, but she would never admit it to her grandfather. One day she asked the priest for an explanation of something she did not understand. "My child, you must have faith," he said in a shocked voice. "We must not question these things."

From then on she remained silent.

The Catholic Church gave her something to cling to. It was a refuge from the storm. Always she was filled with an inner turmoil, a feeling of being pulled in different directions, caught between two worlds. Sometimes, when she saw the calm, peaceful look on the faces of nuns, she felt a kind of envy, but she knew she could never be like them. She could not shut herself away in a convent and give up the world.

Life beckoned with a strange excitement. . .

CHAPTER EIGHTEEN

T he house they had rented at Newport was called Wisteria Lodge, and from her bedroom, through masses of lavender blossoms and vines, she could see the surf spraying against the rocks and smell the salt air. It was said that during the hurricane two years ago the waves had come as high as the second story, and for a while it appeared as if the house would be swept out into the Atlantic. The experience was so terrifying for the owner, an elderly widow, that she had not been back to Newport since.

It was the summer of 1940 and her mother was busy making plans for Ardith's debut. She would be seventeen in September and going to The French School in New York for a year, since Miss May's in Florence was out because of the war in Europe. Next June it would start. There would be a tea at the F. Street Club in Washington to meet the older people, the diplomatic and social group, a ball in Newport during Tennis Week, then in November another ball at the Sulgrave Club in Washington. Meyer Davis had been engaged to play at both dances and her mother was busy with lists of the "right people."

The whole idea filled Ardith with terror — of being manipulated as a puppet to gratify her mother's unfulfilled ambitions. Was she never going to be able to do what she wanted — to study singing and have a career, to pick her own husband? Or would he be chosen for her from this list of Van Rensselaers, Goelets, Duponts, Wanamakers? Her mother's bible was the thin black book known as the *Blue Book*, and she was determined that Ardith would not repeat her own mistake, of marrying beneath her. Love was not enough, as her own life had proved. Family background was everything and the worst name anyone could be called was *nouveau riche*. That her own father was *nouveau riche* compared to the old New York and Boston families who summered in Newport, did not occur to her mother.

Her grandfather was arriving that afternoon for a week's visit (her grandmother had died the winter before of pneumonia) and after lunch the chauffeur would drive them to Providence to meet the train. Her mother did not drive, and besides, everyone else had a chauffeur. His name was Smith, and he was teaching Ardith to drive. They would take the Cadillac on the winding road out beyond Bailey's Beach where there was no traffic. "Easy on the gas, Miss Ardith," Smith warned her, turning pale.

She took riding lessons and would race around the ring, flying over the jumps, and tennis lessons at the Newport Casino from the pro, and two mornings a week Smith drove her to her singing lesson with a former opera singer. That was the part of her life that seemed real to her, when she stood by the piano in Emma Beldini's simple house and sang *"Mi Chiamano Mimi"* from *La Bohème*.

Most of Emma Beldini's pupils came from poor families and it was a struggle for them to scrape together enough money for singing lessons. Ardith felt self-conscious arriving in a car driven by a chauffeur. Several times she asked Smith to park the Cadillac around the corner and let her walk the rest of the way. No, that was silly, she told herself, she knew she had a good voice, that she could really sing, and she practiced as hard as the rest of Emma Beldini's students, why should the others resent her? It was not her fault that she had been born to the background she was. Would she always have to prove herself, or would she have to stay in the narrow, stuffy world to which she was born?

They stood at the Providence station waiting for the New York to Boston express. There it was. She noticed her mother's tense expression around the mouth, as if she both looked forward to and dreaded this visit. Her mother was his favorite, yet they always fought.

Her grandfather seemed to have aged since she had last seen him. He stepped onto the platform and kissed her on the cheek. His mustache tickled and there was the smell of cigar smoke. T.J. never understood how anyone could find the smell of a good cigar objectionable.

They drove through the Rhode Island countryside and her grandfather started on his favorite subject again: Roosevelt. The Democratic Convention two weeks before in Chicago had renominated Roosevelt to run against Wendell Willkie.

"He doesn't have a chance against F.D.R.," her grandfather said, lighting up a Corona-Corona. "No Republican does. This country is going

to the dogs. Generations to come will pay for what that man is doing in
the White House." He picked up the microphone and spoke to the
chauffeur through the glass partition. "Drive faster," he commanded.

"Papa, I don't like to drive eighty the way you do," her mother said.
"They're very strict about speeding in Rhode Island. You may be able to
fix any tickets in Pennsylvania—"

"I don't like to crawl like a snail," her grandfather said, blowing out
a cloud of black smoke. Ardith coughed and her mother rolled down a
window.

"How do you like Newport, Ardith?" he asked.

"Fine."

"Yesterday she went sailing with the Van Pelt boy," her mother said.
She looked at T.J. for approval. "You know, Reginald Van Pelt's
grandson?"

"Oh yes. I saw Reggie the other day at the New York Yacht Club.
What's the boy like?"

"He's a jerk," said Ardith.

"Now dear, I wouldn't say that. He seems very nice to me." Her
mother's voice had a warning edge.

"He's stupid. It's taken him six years to get through Groton. I think
his tutor's much more attractive."

Her mother quickly changed the subject.

"We're having dinner tonight at the Clambake Club, Papa."

"Good." T.J. pulled out the gold watch that was presented to him by
the Venango County Republican League. "I'll have time for a few holes
of golf first."

They were driving down Bellevue Avenue. "Place looks the same as
ever," he said.

"Bailey's Beach has been completely rebuilt since the hurricane,"
her mother said.

Bailey's Beach was where everyone gathered at eleven for a swim
followed by a buffet lunch and then one went sailing or played tennis.
Only servants swam in the afternoons at Newport. Bailey's Beach had a
fascinating collection of people. There were the two elderly Grosvenor
sisters with their parasols and gloves and Pekineses (it was said butlers
served the Pekineses filet mignon on Royal Doulton china), old Mr. Rice,
whose wife had died several years before and who lived in a marble palace
on Bellevue Avenue with a "niece" whom people said was really his

mistress, the former star of a Broadway musical who had married into the social register and given up her career, whose hair was obviously peroxided and caused dowagers to whisper cattily whenever she appeared. The titled Austrians and Hungarians, who had fled Europe leaving their money behind and were looking for wealthy American girls to marry, the sub-deb and debutante group and young men, tanned and blasé, the children building sand castles while their governesses watched. This was Bailey's Beach.

Ardith was fascinated by the list posted inside the entrance of members who owed dues, while the same members' names could be seen on the society pages as having given an elegant party the night before.

They were entering the driveway of Wisteria Lodge. The house was completely hidden from the road and sat out on a point. There were many fruit trees and formal flower gardens surrounded by low hedges and a gardener's cottage was by the entrance gate. The house itself was like an Austrian inn with overhanging wisteria vines.

The chauffeur pulled the car up to the front door where a butler and maid were waiting. The butler took out T.J.'s suitcase and golf clubs and carried them in. Ardith started up the stairs.

"She's turned into quite a beauty, Grace," Ardith heard her grandfather say to her mother. "She was a strange child, moody, I never knew what she was thinking. I still don't. She's not like us." It seemed to puzzle him. "She's not like any of the Wymans," he repeated.

No, I'm not like any of you, Ardith thought. I don't want to live in gloomy mansions and spend all my time rewriting my will, tying things up in trusts to be passed from one generation to another, never touch the principal, always the threat of disinheritance if one steps out of line, living in a cocoon, hands reaching out from the grave, voices saying: "You mustn't think that, you must believe the way I believed, or else not a penny!" To be strong enough to say, "I don't care, I'll make my own money." How? When one has lived wrapped in cotton, protected from the world, how does one escape? Like walking into a thunderstorm dressed in a nightgown. Why don't you stay in your own world, little girl? The year-round residents of Newport who hated the summer colony, they looked at her the same way. But I'm not like them, she thought. Am I? Am I?

She picked up a silver comb and ran it through her long dark hair. It was strange now, she thought, to hear people call her a beauty after being told for so many years that she was plain. Almost overnight it seemed that everything had changed. Boys were calling her for dates, though her mother only let her go out with a selected few and she had to be home by eleven. Two days ago Bob Ewing had asked her to go to the movies with him. She walked in her mother's room and found her turning the pages of the thin black book with a perturbed expression.

"I can't find him," she said. "Where did you meet him?"

"The other night at the Blue Moon," Ardith said. The Blue Moon was a nightclub near the docks frequented by sailors, where the summer colony went slumming on occasion. Ardith had never been there.

Her mother gasped.

"Turn to the A's, Mother, and I think you'll find him under Auchincloss. His mother's remarried."

"Oh yes, here he is. His mother was a Widener from Philadelphia. I went to Mount Vernon Seminary with one of the Widener girls. Do they have a house here?" Bob's pedigree established, her mother closed the book and put it on her night table.

"He's visiting the Goelets for Tennis Week."

"Where does Bob go to school?"

"He's starting Princeton in the fall."

"How nice. Maybe he'll invite you to one of the football games." Her mother picked up a nail file. "What movie are you going to see?"

"Bette Davis is playing in *The Great Lie*. I think we'll see that."

Her mother was busy with her nails and seemed not to have heard. "Cynthia Widener," she said. "Yes, I'm sure that must be Bob's aunt. I wonder how Cynthia is these days . . . I heard she was living in Rome. I must ask Bob when he picks you up."

Ardith looked at her mother and suddenly felt very sorry for her. Grace Wyman Rodgers was still pretty and very chic and could have a life of her own, but she preferred living vicariously through others. At forty-two she still had suitors but she apparently wasn't interested in any of them. "Women are fooled by their emotions," she once said, and that was the closest she had ever come to talking about her marriage. It was like a diary that she kept locked with the key on a chain around her neck, and maybe opened late at night when no one was looking. For Ardith knew her mother had trouble sleeping and bottles of yellow capsules came frequently from the drugstore. Often in the mornings her mother had a vacant look as if she were in another world and her coordination was poor. Once she spilled a cup of coffee all over her new negligee from Bergdorf's. It was probably lucky she didn't drive and had a chauffeur.

If only I can get my own license soon and have a car of my own, Ardith thought. Then I won't need Smith to drive me everywhere. It was a good idea to know how to drive anyway. She thought how horrified her mother would be if she could see some of these boys she thought so nice after the Saturday night dances at Bailey's Beach. She felt she was taking her life in her hands to get in a car with them and she would be saying her prayers all the way home. Last week Ricky Van Pelt had parked the car on a dark side road and she had to slap his face. She hadn't told her mother about that. Ricky had a bad case of acne and perspiring, roving hands, and his big passion in life, besides wrestling with girls, was playing the trap drums. He was always going up to the orchestra leader at parties and asking if he could play the drums and his date never saw him until the end of the evening. She couldn't stand him. She didn't care how many millions he was going to inherit.

But she liked Bob Ewing. He was attractive, and nice.

Bob had cut in on her Friday night at the Frazier's party and he kept cutting back. He was dancing with her when they played the last dance.

"Well," he said. "I guess I'd better take you back to your date. Who's the lucky guy?"

At that point there was a loud crash.

"Hey, Ricky just passed out," someone said.

"That *was* my date," Ardith said, as two boys carried Ricky in from the terrace and laid him on a sofa.

"So you're with Van Pelt. Well, I see he hasn't changed. Don't worry, I'll see that you get home."

They said goodnight to the hostess and got in Bob's car.

"I went to prep school with Ricky," Bob said.

"All six years?"

Bob laughed. "He did flunk a grade or two. Ricky's not exactly a candidate for Phi Beta Kappa, but with all that money I guess he's not too concerned."

"What do you want to do when you finish Princeton?"

"I'll probably go in my Dad's brokerage firm. That is, if I don't have to go to war first."

"Do you think we'll get in it?"

"I don't know how we can stay out."

They were turning in the driveway of Wisteria Lodge.

"Look, I'd like to take you out while I'm here. Do you think I'll pass your Dad's inspection?"

"My father—" she paused a second, — "is dead." Yes, it was easier to say that. Much easier. It was a lie that she started in boarding school and now she almost believed it.

"I'm sorry," Bob said. He looked uncomfortable.

"I'm sure my mother will let me go out with you," she said quickly. She smiled and held out her hand to him. "Thank you for taking me home."

"My pleasure. Maybe we can go to a movie Sunday night?"

"I'd love to."

"Good. I'll call you."

"Fine. Goodnight, Bob."

Darn, she thought, he's the only really attractive boy I've met this summer, except for the Van Pelt's tutor. Why does he have to be here for just one week?

The next day Ricky sent a box of orchids from his family's greenhouse with a note of apology. Ardith gave the orchids to the maid. "And when Mr. Van Pelt calls, tell him I'm out."

"Now, dear, don't you think you're being a bit silly?" her mother said. "After all, a girl can't have too many beaux."

Ardith went to the tennis matches at the Newport Casino with Bob and in the afternoons they went sailing. It seemed they were just getting to know each other when the week was over.

"If you're going to school in New York this winter I can get in to see you and you can come to Princeton for the football games," Bob said. "That's a little over a month from now. And I'll write to you."

"Nice chap, that young Ewing," her grandfather remarked after Bob left. He was leaving himself the next day and going to New York on business and then back to Oil City. Ardith noticed his hands had a slight tremor and sometimes he would repeat himself. But after all, he was eighty-one, and he still got out and played golf and beat much younger men. She felt an almost overwhelming desire to talk to him, she wondered what he was like when he was a boy dreaming of success someday, of making money, of his early days in the oil business. What was he like when he courted her grandmother, was he always so stiff and austere? Did he ever unbend and laugh, really laugh? She had never seen him. What was this thing that the Wymans had about not showing their emotions? Was this what it meant to be proper, to have breeding? What was breeding, anyway? He had started out in life with nothing. "The only point in having money is to make others happy with it," he said. Others, she thought, but not us. Not us.

Would she have tried harder to know him and to understand if she had known that this was the last time she would see him alive? But we can never know. If only a voice could whisper to us and say, "This is your last chance to understand, to communicate with someone who is leaving this life. Soon it will be too late." She did not know that for years after she would seek the answers to questions she could have asked him and did not.

She kissed him goodbye at the Providence station. "See you at Christmas," she said.

CHAPTER NINETEEN

O n her seventeenth birthday her mother gave her a real pearl necklace and a silver fox jacket. Her grandfather sent a check. She and her mother went to New York several days before school started to shop. They stayed at the Plaza and Bob Ewing had tea with them and took Ardith to see her first Broadway musical, *Louisiana Purchase*. Afterward they went to the Stork Club and Sherman Billingsley sent over two green *crème de menthe* cocktails on the house. Ardith had never had one before but she sat there and pretended to sip it so Mr. Billingsley wouldn't be offended. The color was pretty, anyway, and it made her feel very sophisticated. She noticed a man staring at her several tables away and Bob told her he was Cholly Knickerbocker.

"Maybe you'll be in his column," Bob said.

And she was — the next day.

She had spent the day shopping with her mother and they returned to the Plaza laden with packages from Bergdorf-Goodman and Henri Bendel. Mrs. Rodgers picked up the New York *Journal-American* in the lobby and, barely glancing at the world news, turned to the society page.

"Well, dear," she said in a pleased voice, "you seem to have made quite a hit with Mr. Knickerbocker." She showed Ardith the paper. "I'll get a few more copies before they're sold out."

There was a picture of Ardith taken arriving at Bailey's Beach and the caption said: NEW GLAMOUR GIRL. She read on. "Cholly's candidate for the number one glamour girl of the coming debutante season is beautiful Ardith Rodgers, granddaughter of Standard Oil magnate T. J. Wyman. She has everything it takes to be a huge social success: looks, money, poise. Dark and striking in the Brenda Frazier tradition, she will be presented to Newport society at a ball next August by her mother, Mrs.

Wyman Rodgers. Then in November she will have another ball at the Sulgrave Club in Washington. She will also attend the debutante parties in New York and Philadelphia of her classmates at the exclusive Miss Putnam's School in Connecticut. This winter Ardith will attend The French School on Park Avenue, where she can pursue her interests in music and languages — she speaks several fluently. Her favorite sports are sailing and tennis. My spies tell me that both Ricky Van Pelt and Bob Ewing are quite smitten with her."

Ardith read the article over again. This is me? she thought. She wondered who Cholly's spies were. He had certainly gotten a lot of information in one day.

Her mother returned with a dozen copies of the *Journal-American* and they waited for the elevator. Her mother seemed to be walking on a cloud. She acted as if everyone in the elevator should turn around and ask for Ardith's autograph. A grim-looking man next to them was reading the headlines: ALL MEN 20 TO 36 MUST REGISTER FOR DRAFT.

The next day they went to The French School. It was a duplex at the corner of Park Avenue and 79th Street and they only took twenty girls.

Madame Duval greeted them.

"Bonjour, Ardith." She turned to Mrs. Rodgers. *"Vous parlez français, Madame?"*

"Oui, un peu."

Madame Duval smiled. "Tomorrow morning we start. No English. You say *bonjour* and if that is all you can say, you remain silent until you can say it in French. One learns rather fast that way. Some of the girls already can speak French fairly well, others . . ." She shrugged. "They will learn. Come, I will show you your room. Your roommate is from Boston, Katherine Peabody. We do not allow nicknames here. The girls may wear a light lipstick but no nail polish." She glanced at Ardith who was wearing Elizabeth Arden's Cyclamen. "Mia!" She called the maid and pointed to the bags. "Mia is Finnish. She speaks no English — or French. We use sign language. *C'est la guerre.*"

They walked up the stairs to the second floor. Ardith's room looked out over 79th Street and was decorated in chintz. It was quite a change from Miss Putnam's where she slept on an iron cot in a room that resembled a jail cell. This looked more like a home.

Katherine was already unpacked. Madame introduced them. "Now you girls get acquainted," she said. "Because tomorrow," she waved her arm, "everything will be *en français.*"

"Well, darling," her mother said, "I'll run along now." She kissed Ardith. "I know you're going to just love it here."

"Goodbye, Mother. I'll write often."

"And if there's anything you need, dear, just pick up the phone and call. Reverse the charges." She looked around the room for a telephone.

"The only phone is in the hall," said Katherine, "and we aren't allowed to call long distance except in an emergency."

"Oh?" Grace Rodgers looked as if she thought this a very silly rule. "Well . . . I guess that is wise." She kissed Ardith again. "Goodbye, dear."

Ardith hung her coat in the closet and opened her suitcase.

"Where did you go to school last year?" she asked Katherine.

"Westover. What about you?"

"Miss Putnam's." She put her sweaters in a drawer.

"Did you like it?"

"I hated it," Ardith said. "But I think I'll like it here. It's kind of exciting being in New York. I can't wait to go to the opera."

"Do you like that stuff?"

Ardith nodded. "I'm studying singing. Mother's arranged for me to have lessons with a woman who has a studio in Carnegie Hall."

"I'm taking art," said Katherine. "Come on, let's meet the other girls before we have to say everything in French. It was my worst subject at Westover!"

Saturdays, if they weren't going away for the weekend, the girls were allowed to go shopping or to the movies without a chaperone as long as they stayed in certain boundaries. They were not to go east of Lexington Avenue, south of 35th Street, west of Fifth Avenue, or north of 85th Street.

That limited them to Loew's Lexington and the Plaza at 58th and Madison, and it seemed that most of the movies they wanted to see were over on Broadway. Ardith liked to see foreign films and she would tell Madame she was going to the Plaza and then go to one of the German movies on 86th Street. This section of town was considered especially dangerous. One afternoon she was trying to talk a girl into going with her to see a Viennese film. It was a love story with music set in the era of Franz Josef and had gotten very good reviews.

"Don't you know why we aren't supposed to go to that part of town?"

Mary Ogden asked, horrified when Ardith told her that she was going alone. "Or to Broadway?"

Ardith shook her head. "It's just another of their silly rules."

"No." Mary lowered her voice. "It's because of the white slavers."

"White slavers?"

"Yes. A man can sit next to you and put a needle in your arm and then you pass out and when the usher comes to see what's wrong he says, 'It's all right. This is my sister—she's fainted.' When you come to you're in a brothel in Mexico City or South America where no one can ever find you again." Mary was breathless.

"I don't believe it," said Ardith.

"Well, it's true."

The next time she went to a movie in the German section she noticed a strange-looking man watching her. It's just my imagination, she thought nervously. But when he changed seats and moved next to her, she got up quickly and left the theatre. After that she decided to stay within the boundaries.

She was in Nancy Larimer's room one evening and her eyes kept going to a photograph on Nancy's bureau. It was of a young man, fair and very handsome, and she had never seen him before, yet somehow she knew that he would be important in her life. It gave her the strangest feeling. She wondered who he was. Was he a beau of Nancy's?

Nancy noticed her glance and said, "That's my brother Doug. He goes to the University of Virginia."

Doug Larimer. She said the name over to herself. Why should that name have a vibration different from all the others? Someone in a photograph, someone she didn't even know.

"I'll introduce him to you at my coming-out party," Nancy said. Nancy was from Warrenton, Virginia, and had attended Chatham Hall. Horses were her great interest in life and she won cups at all the horse shows. Every Saturday she went riding in Central Park. She had a great sense of humor and was always playing practical jokes, not always appreciated by Madame Duval. "I think Doug would like you," said Nancy. "Usually I can't get him to look at any of my friends — he likes older girls. But you're different."

It was more than eight months before she would meet him, and many things would happen during that time.

CHAPTER TWENTY

Thomas sat in the library, his German shepherd lying at his feet, as he listened with growing despondency to the election returns. At first Willkie had made a good showing, but now it was becoming obvious. Roosevelt was going to be re-elected for a second term. He turned off the radio and glared into the fire. The dog whined and looked up at him.

"Another administration under the Democrats," he mumbled. "More spending and waste. Don't you agree, old fellow?"

Rex wagged his tail and looked adoringly at his master.

"Good old boy." Thomas leaned over and patted him. Rex was showing his age. His eyes were bad now and he didn't hear the way he used to. But neither do I, Thomas thought. "We're both old now, Rex," he said. "We've outlived our usefulness."

The dog stood up and put his head on Thomas's lap.

How faithful dogs are, Thomas thought. More so than most people. They ask for so little, just that you feed them, give them a home, some love and attention. And in return they give you their complete devotion, they are always glad to see you, they never judge you.

They never judge you.

How many people never judge you? You are judged from the day you are born until the day you die, if not by others, by your own expectations for yourself.

I'm eighty-one, Thomas thought. I suppose by most men's standards I would be considered to have led a successful life. And he had not just taken, he had given back what he earned. He had donated generously to charities, built a wing for the Oil City Hospital as well as founding a sanatorium for the treatment of tuberculosis. He had improved the Pennsylvania roads and played an important role in the preservation of

Cook Forest. He had contributed time and money to the Republican Party. He had obtained the Carnegie library for Oil City and built a public swimming pool. He had tried to lead a life of useful service.

But on the other side was his personal life. Had that been a success? His children had all disappointed him, in one way or another. And there was no one to carry on the Wyman name. He had no grandson, only granddaughters.

No, that was not quite true. He had a grandson.

Joseph Krzyzynski, now Congressman Joseph Kreskie, Democrat from Pennsylvania. Joe's son.

Was it pride that had kept him from getting in touch with him during all these years? Once he had thought of doing so, but then something stopped him.

"I never knew my father," Congressman Kreskie said in a newspaper interview when he was running for election. "He died before I was born. Everything that I am I owe to my sainted mother. She never lost faith in me."

Mary Krzyzynski had never married, held her head high, and raised her son alone. She died of cancer in 1937.

If Joe had married her, my grandson would bear my name, Thomas thought. The Wyman name would go on. Years later he discovered that Joe had really loved the girl. Then why didn't he have the guts to stand up to me? Thomas wondered. Was I that intimidating? Or was Joe really weak?

No, now he remembered. He had threatened to disinherit Joe if he ever saw Mary Krzyzynski again.

Was it too late now to try to make amends? He recalled the scene in this very library long ago. John Krzyzynski tearing up his check in a fury and storming out of the house, slamming the front door so hard that one of the stained glass panes had to be replaced.

And then the scene in front of the house with Mary Krzyzynski and little Joey. How proud she had been, so disdainful of his money. All she wanted was his love, something he had been unable to give.

Was it too late now?

He would get in touch with Joseph Kreskie and ask him to come and see him. He would make up for past neglect. He would do it tomorrow.

Rex was looking at him, wagging his tail.

"You want to go for a walk, don't you, old boy? All right." Thomas stood up and pulled out the gold watch given to him by the Venango County Republican League at a testimonial dinner on his eightieth birthday. No point sticking around listening to any more election news. Willkie had lost. "Let's go, Rex. A walk will do us both good."

He went to the front door and picked up his walking stick with the ornate brass carving on the handle. He refused to think of it as a cane, that denoted infirmity.

Yes, tomorrow I will write to Joseph Kreskie, he told himself, and the thought made him feel good. Tomorrow. . .

But for Thomas Joseph Wyman it was already too late.

For tomorrow would never come.

CHAPTER TWENTY-ONE

"Ardith, Madame wants to see you," Katherine called up the stairs. "She's in her office."

"What about, do you know?"

Katherine shrugged. "You've got me."

I wonder what rule I've broken now, Ardith thought, as she knocked on the door to Madame Duval's office.

"*Entrez.*"

Madame was sitting at her desk with an especially grim expression, but then she had looked grim ever since her beloved Paris was occupied by the Nazis.

"*Voulez-vous me voir, Madame?*"

"Yes, Ardith. And you may speak English. Sit down, please."

Madame Duval picked up a telegram. Telegrams were never given directly to the girls in case they contained bad news, but were always opened in the office. Bob Ewing hadn't realized this when he sent a telegram several weeks ago saying: "I hope those old bags will let you out to go to the Princeton-Yale game and prom the weekend of November 8th."

Madame Duval fingered the telegram nervously. "I regret that I have sad news to tell you. Your grandfather passed away last night of a cerebral hemorrhage." Her stern face looked kinder. "The funeral is on Friday in Oil City. I am so sorry, my dear. If there is anything I can do. . ."

Ardith shook her head. I can't go to Princeton this weekend, she thought suddenly, and was shocked that this was her only reaction. She hoped it didn't register on her face.

"Thank you, Madame," she said. "I'll go pack now."

* * *

And now they were all gathered, family and friends, in the First Presbyterian Church in Oil City, to say their final farewell. Ardith glanced at her mother beside her dressed in black with a heavy veil and a diamond bar pin glittering at her throat where her mink coat fell open. What was she thinking now? She was the only member of the family who had ever dared oppose him.

The minister closed his prayer book and the organist softly played her grandfather's favorite hymns as the mourners filed past the open casket. He had been a 33rd degree Mason and two men in uniform stood guard on either end. Only the Masons would attend the final burial rites at the marble mausoleum up on the hill.

He lay there with his hands crossed on his chest, a shrunken, wax-like figure in the satin-lined gray coffin with its sheath of white chrysan-themums. She had never seen someone dead before and it filled her with horror. Why did they display anyone this way? The person was not there, only an empty shell. It was better to remember him as he was.

She started to tremble. He had such power in life . . . Now it was all gone. Ashes to ashes, dust to dust. What did my father do, Grandfather? Now I will never know.

"Doesn't he look well?" a voice behind her whispered. "So peace-ful."

Why do people say such stupid things? She wanted to scream and fought for control of herself.

Photographers' bulbs flashed as they came out of the church. The hearse and the long black cars were waiting. Crowds stood on the steps and policemen cleared the way. Two small boys in bare feet and patched clothes stared and pointed.

"It's that rich old guy who lived in the big house on Third Street," one of them said.

Ardith noticed that her mother seemed on the point of collapse. Crowds had always given her claustrophobia. The family lawyer took her arm and steered them to the limousine. Another flashbulb exploded.

The procession wound slowly through the streets of the town. The late afternoon sun glittered on the frozen Allegheny River and the oil derricks on the hill were silhouetted against the blue-gray sky. Fleecy white clouds floated above and Ardith remembered how as a child she would try to find shapes of animals in their ever-changing forms.

Her mother fumbled in her purse for a bottle of smelling salts and took a strong whiff. She dabbed at her eyes with a lace handkerchief. Her face was pale and drawn.

The cars were pulling up in front of the house now. Everyone went inside. It seemed strange not to see him, for one could feel his presence everywhere. His black umbrella was still in the stand by the front door as if waiting for the next thunderstorm. She wondered what had happened to his cane. Was it buried with him? She had not seen it.

The maid had tea and cinnamon toast prepared on a silver tray and sherry for those who preferred something stronger. Her Aunt Elizabeth was there from Philadelphia with her stuffy banker husband and her three cousins, whom she seldom saw. The mayor, a state senator and his wife, judges, presidents of oil companies, and old friends and neighbors dropped by to leave cards and express their sympathies.

"So sudden . . . such a great loss to the community."

"He always stood for what was right."

"We disagreed on certain issues, but I always respected him. He was a real fighter."

The butler placed a stack of newspapers on the hall table. T. J. WYMAN DIES, were the headlines of the *Oil City Derrick.* "Oil industry pioneer and the first citizen of Oil City and of northwestern Pennsylvania for half a century, dies of a stroke. . ."

"I'm so sorry, my dear," said the president of Quaker State Oil, pressing Ardith's hand. "A great man . . . everyone loved him."

"Thank you." Everyone loved him, she thought. Prominent political figures, businessmen, strangers who benefited from his philanthropic deeds, hospitals he endowed, so many anonymously, why then was he so cold to his own family? Was he so busy with his other affairs that he hadn't had time for them?

Before her grandmother died, Ardith once overheard her complaining to one of the maids that her husband left her alone all the time. Above the white marble mantle there was a portrait of her grandmother painted by Sargent. She was young then and smiling and gay.

What would happen to this old Victorian mansion now? Ardith wondered. No one wanted it, yet her grandfather had poured a fortune into it. It would be sold, no doubt.

She could not foresee that the house would be sold to a dentist who would use the upstairs for living quarters and this room for the waiting room in which to receive his patients. And that the music room, in which the golden voices of Caruso and Galli-Curci soared on the victrola she played as a child, would reverberate to the sound of the dentist's drill.

The guests were leaving now and only members of the family remained. Her tea was cold. From the hall there came an icy draft.

"It was a lovely service, Grace," her Aunt Elizabeth said, pouring herself another glass of sherry. "Just the way Papa would have wanted it."

Her mother said nothing. She acted very depressed.

Uncle Hubert cleared his throat. "We may not all be together again like this for some time, so this might be an appropriate time to discuss . . . er . . . ah . . . a few business matters." He took a small white pill from a silver case and swallowed it with a gulp of sherry. Her uncle was portly and suffered from asthma and heart trouble. He was always wheezing and gasping for breath. "Now Elizabeth and I have made up a list of the things we'd like from the house . . ."

Her mother's face froze. She had never been close to her sister and she considered her brother-in-law a stuffed shirt. Her father was not yet cold in his grave and they sat there like vultures dividing the spoils.

"Children," she said, "I think you'd better go upstairs."

Ardith followed her cousins up the circular staircase. Through the open door of her grandfather's room she could see the great black walnut bed with its high carved headboard.

Would she always feel like an outsider in this family? she wondered. Maybe they had mixed up babies in the hospital. But she wasn't born in a hospital — she was born here in this very house.

"We've all been reading about you in Cholly Knickerbocker, Ardith," her cousin Cordelia said. "You must have a press agent." Cordelia was fat and had halitosis. "Grandfather used to say that a lady's name should only be mentioned in the newspapers three times: when she's born, when she's married, and when she dies."

When she was small, Ardith recalled, Cordelia used to tease her about her dark coloring and tell her that Creole meant having Negro blood. She thought of a nasty remark she could make. No, it was better to forget it.

They went in the room that had belonged to her grandmother. It looked much the same. The dresser set of Kirk's repoussé on the marble-topped commode, the pitcher of cranberry glass, the bisque shepherdess that always reminded her of her mother, the brass bed, the wicker armchair where her grandmother used to sit while the maid brushed her long gray hair. It came below her waist and she had never cut it, but wore it in a knot at the back of her head. She had always seemed so old and sad-looking.

Ardith looked out the window. The horse-chestnut trees were gone now . . . there had been a blight several years ago. There was where Alaska had run on his chain, no wonder he was fierce, always on a chain. Am I on a chain too? Like Alaska, only allowed to run so far? Poor Alaska, are you happy now wherever you are?

There was the walk where she used to ride her tricycle, where she picked dandelions with her governess. She was told to blow the dandelion petals away and make a wish. Her wish had never come true. Why did she suddenly feel like crying? It was not for her grandfather.

Cordelia had not finished her speech. "Don't think you're anything special because of all this publicity," she said. "It's only because of Grandfather. Everything we have, or will ever have, we owe to him."

Suddenly she wanted to get away. "Excuse me," she said. She ran in the hall bathroom and locked the door. It was the same as she remembered. The porcelain tub on legs, the old basin, the tank-type toilet with a long chain that led to the skylight.

She could hear a train, far off, though she knew it was only in her memory.

Tears flooded her eyes and she cried uncontrollably. She stayed there for over an hour. They knocked on the door but she wouldn't open it. She couldn't stop sobbing.

Finally her mother came.

"I think the funeral was too much for her," she heard Cordelia tell her mother. "She's very high-strung."

"Ardith, dear," her mother said, "please don't grieve this way. After all, your grandfather led a full and useful life . . . ."

They didn't understand. None of them understood.

She unlocked the door and went in her room and lay down on the bed. They called a doctor and he came and gave her a sedative.

"She'll be all right tomorrow," he said.

CHAPTER TWENTY-TWO

There was something depressing about New York in January when the skies were gray and there was slush in the streets. Even the buildings looked dirty and dingy and it seemed that spring would never come.

Her grandfather had been dead for two months now and her mother and her Aunt Elizabeth had not spoken to each other since the day of the funeral. It was a feud that promised to continue long after the will was out of probate. "Your aunt is the most selfish person I've ever known in my life," her mother told Ardith during Christmas vacation. "I'm just now finding out some of the things she's done. If Papa . . ." The sentence was left unfinished.

Ardith was fighting a cold. She sat at her desk with a box of Kleenex and chewed on the end of her pencil.

"I never did understand Wagner's Ring series in English," she told Katherine. "I always got Siegfried and Sieglinde and all those characters mixed up . . . and now having to write a ten-page report on *Die Götterdammerung* in French . . ." She sighed.

"Maybe you'll be lucky and miss going," Katherine said. "I thought you were the one around here who liked opera."

"I do — the French and Italian ones."

Last week there had been a beautiful production of *Louise* with Grace Moore and Ardith was learning the leading aria, *"Depuis le jour,"* with her singing teacher. And in two weeks Lily Pons was doing her very favorite, *La Traviata*. She could hardly wait for that.

Every Monday evening they went to the Metropolitan Opera in a chartered bus with Madame Duval. The French School had two boxes. The week before Madame would tell the girls the story of the opera they were going to hear. She stressed the fact that one "heard" an opera and never to make the *faux pas* of saying that you had "seen" an opera. Everyone took notes and then wrote a ten-page report of the plot and the leading arias in each act. The report had to be handed in to Madame the Thursday before. So even if they were not familiar with the language of the opera, they at least understood what was going on — and in great detail.

Even worse than saying one had "seen" an opera was to carry packages home from a store. Madame said ladies never did this. One was always to say to the salesgirl at Saks or Bonwit Teller or wherever, "Please send this." Ardith thought that this was a very stupid rule, especially if it was some thing you wanted right away. But Madame was most firm. Carrying packages was not done.

She had just had a difference of opinion with Madame about what she was going to wear to the opera. She had bought a pink satin gown at De Pinna's trimmed in maribou feathers and she had a cluster of pink feathers on a comb to wear in her hair. A black velvet cape and long white gloves completed her costume. Madame Duval informed her in no uncertain terms that *jeunes filles bien élevées* did not wear feathers in their hair. This was Madame's favorite expression and Ardith had come to loathe it. To be a well-brought-up lady, she thought, meant to lead a very dull life indeed!

She had some photographs taken by Hal Phyfe, the leading society photographer. One was published in *Town & Country* and told about her coming debut; others were sent to the Washington newspapers. The glamour girl build-up had started.

She had her choice of invitations. She went to a football game at Princeton with Bob Ewing and another at Harvard with Ricky Van Pelt. She debated whether to accept Ricky's invitation but she wanted to go to the Harvard-Yale game and she knew she wouldn't have to be alone with him.

"And you might meet someone else there," Katherine said. "Someone divine. You never know."

Yes, she told herself, it was important to meet new boys and have enough beaux to take her to all the different parties next season. Her wallflower days at dancing school still loomed with terror in her memory. Since being a debutante was inevitable, she was determined to be a success at it.

I'll go through the year and do all the proper things, she thought, and then I'll tell them all to go to hell and do what *I* want.

Her mother came up to see her and they went to Bergdorf-Goodman and ordered the gown for her ball in Newport. It was to be white tulle and was being especially designed by Nanty, who designed Queen Elizabeth's clothes. They wanted it early so *Town & Country* could photograph her in it for their June issue which went to press in March. The invitations were ordered from Tiffany's, the orchestra hired.

One day she was surprised to get a letter from the advertising agency that handled Camel cigarettes. They were using prominent society women and debutantes to endorse Camels in their current campaign, full-page color ads on the back of leading magazines, and they offered her five hundred dollars to pose.

She was flabbergasted. Five hundred dollars just for her endorsement? It made her feel like a celebrity.

The money seemed like a huge sum to her. Her allowance was five dollars a week, though she was able to charge things on her mother's account. Still, it wasn't the same as having five hundred dollars you had earned yourself. She had never earned a cent. In fact the whole subject of money was something that was never discussed by well-bred people. It was just there.

She looked at the letter again. Why would the fact that she, Ardith Rodgers, smoked Camels, make a difference to anyone? But the offer was tempting and the ads were done in very good taste. She had seen one on the back of *Vogue*.

Madame Duval would have a fit, she thought, and that was almost reason enough to do it. She could just hear another of Madame's speeches about what was proper for a *jeune fille bien élevée*.

She went in to see the woman who handled the account. Ardith noticed that there were social registers from every city prominently displayed. She was offered a cigarette and out of habit she started to refuse.

"You *do* smoke, Miss Rodgers?"

"Oh, yes." She took one and tried not to cough.

"Camels, of course?"

"Naturally." The smoke was filling her nostrils and the back of her throat and her eyes were starting to water. How do people do this all the time? she wondered. She looked for an ashtray and tapped the ashes in what she hoped looked like a natural manner. Please open a window, she thought.

The woman was still watching her. "Of course, since you're a minor, your mother will have to give her permission." She handed her some papers to sign.

This was something else. She doubted that her mother would permit her to endorse a cigarette. No woman in the Wyman family had ever smoked. But for five hundred dollars. . .

"I'll give you the five hundred dollars *not* to endorse Camels," her mother said. "The very idea! Your grandfather would turn over in his grave. No lady smokes."

And that settled that.

She was allowed, however, to endorse Woodbury soap and pose in a car. *Life* magazine asked permission to cover her Newport ball. They wanted to use her on the cover and write an article about her.

All this attention both flattered and frightened her. She didn't feel she deserved it. If she had done something really important it would be different. But to be fussed over this way just for being a debutante. . .

And it was all so insincere.

One day she went in a small dress shop on Madison Avenue where she wasn't known. She had seen a dress she liked in the window. It was raining and she had on a raincoat and a scarf tied round her head. The salesgirl brought out the dress. Her manner was very condescending.

Ardith looked at herself in the long dressing room mirror. It was a pretty dress but she couldn't quite make up her mind. And the salesgirl's attitude annoyed her. Was this the way they treated people they thought might not have enough money?

"Thank you very much. I'll think about it," Ardith said, handing the dress back to the salesgirl.

The following Saturday she decided she wanted it and went back to the shop. In the meantime her picture had been in the paper. The same salesgirl greeted her. This time her attitude was quite different.

"That was a beautiful picture of you in the *Journal-American,* Miss Rodgers," the salesgirl said. She rushed to get the dress.

But I'm still the same person, Ardith thought. Only now she thinks I'm somebody she has to be nice to. She felt like walking out of the shop and saying that she had changed her mind, but she really wanted the dress. She hadn't been able to find another she liked as well.

"This dress looked so lovely on you, Miss Rodgers," the salesgirl gushed, "that I just *knew* you'd be back for it. Do you want to take it with you?"

She remembered Madame's rule about carrying packages. "No, please send it," she said. "The French School, 903 Park Avenue."

"We'd be so happy to have you open a charge account with us," the salesgirl said. "Please come back soon. We have some lovely things coming in that I'm sure you'll like."

The rest of the year passed very quickly, and before she knew it, it was graduation day at The French School.

Madame Duval gave the commencement address in English, since the parents were there and not all of them understood French. Her words would haunt Ardith for many years to come. All the bitterness of having to teach spoiled and wealthy American girls the social graces while her own country was occupied by the Nazis was between the lines she spoke. If America had come to the aid of France at the beginning of the war she would not have been defeated, her grim expression seemed to say.

"Young ladies," she said, "you are starting down the road of life, as I did, in a year when the world is at war. Who knows what your lives will be? . . . But one thing is certain . . . they will not be easy."

There was a note of triumph in her voice.

CHAPTER TWENTY-THREE

"And now, one of Oil City's own, a graduate of this school, will address you, the graduating class of 1941." The principal of Oil City High cleared his throat. "It gives me great pleasure to introduce the distinguished congressman from Pennsylvania, the Honorable Joseph Kreskie."

There was applause from the students in the high school audience. Joe Kreskie looked out at the eager young faces before him. What could he say to them that would make a difference in their lives, inspire them to make the right choices? Some would succeed, in spite of odds, others would fail. How could you pass on a formula to anyone? It was a matter of hard work, of being in the right place at the right time and then another quality, one he saw lacking in many young people today: faith.

He had always known that he was going to succeed, even when he was a carrierboy for the *Oil City Derrick*, his first job. To hawk the *Derrick* meant getting up at five-thirty every morning. The paper sold for three cents and he made a penny on each copy. On a good morning he earned twelve cents, sometimes fifteen. After picking up his papers in the mailroom he would head for one of the four corners of Seneca and Center Streets. At six-fifteen he would be there waiting with his papers when the Transit Company buses arrived bringing workers for Oil Well Supply in Siverly or the refineries near Rouseville and the transfers to and from Franklin and Reno. The trick was to catch the men making transfers, and he soon knew who wanted a *Derrick* and had his regular customers lined up. There were other newsboys selling papers but they didn't do as well and he wondered why. Then one day one of his customers told him, "I like to buy a paper from you because when I do you always say 'thank you'."

After school he sold the *Blizzard*. His first stop was always Luigi's shoe-shine parlor, then a quick dash into Lee's bowling alleys and after that Smith's Department Store. Then Hansen's soda parlor and McGuigan's poolroom, where he could read the latest baseball scores chalked on a big blackboard. Sometimes he could make a sale in the lobby of the Arlington Hotel, even though the hotel had the same paper at its desk. And people waiting at the Pennsylvania Railroad's depot always wanted a newspaper. During the winter the steam-heat of the train station was a welcome relief before trudging home in the snow.

Then supper with his mother and grandparents, who always said the blessing in Polish, and several hours of homework before falling exhausted into bed.

As he saw it, there was no easy route to success.

Congressman Joseph Kreskie glanced at the prepared speech he had written, then put it down and started to talk.

Every Memorial Day weekend he returned to Oil City from Washington to put flowers on his mother's grave. Now Joe Kreskie knelt in the rain by the simple white tombstone that read only:

MARY KRZYZYNSKI

1891-1937

He had shortened his name when he decided to run for Congress to make it easier to spell and pronounce. He crossed himself, closed his eyes, and said a brief prayer. His mother had led a hard life and she was at peace. For that he was grateful. But he missed her.

Just before her lingering death from cancer four years ago she had told him who his father really was. "Don't hold it against him, Joey, that he couldn't give you his name," she said. "I don't."

But he did. He was still bitter about the way his mother had been treated.

At the other end of the cemetery was the Wyman mausoleum. Just as they had lived, he thought ironically, at the other part of town.

His mind went back — his first memory, dimly recollected. Standing in front of a Victorian house with a large porch and turrets and surrounded by an iron fence, the biggest house he had ever seen, for he and his mother and his grandparents lived in a small sooty house near the railroad tracks that shook when the trains went by. In the big house on Third Street on that long-ago morning he had heard a lady singing and years later he heard the same song and goose pimples ran up and down his arm and he broke out in a cold sweat.

He remembered holding his mother's hand and hiding behind her skirts when the tall thin man with glasses and the severe expression came up to them. The man had not smiled, he was not happy to see them. That was his grandfather, his other grandfather, Thomas Joseph Wyman, but he didn't know it then. His mother had made him shake hands with the man and he hadn't wanted to.

The man was dead now and lay in that ornate mausoleum. He read about his death in the newspapers and it gave him a strange feeling. His grandfather.

A grandfather who had never recognized him.

"Forgive him," his mother begged. "If you ever meet him, forgive him." His mother had been a saint, a devout Catholic who went to Mass every morning without fail, until the very last days when she could hardly drag herself out of bed, and then the priest had come to her. She died in terrible pain, believing herself to be a sinner because of her illicit love affair with his father.

His mother was a pretty woman and through the years there were men who wanted to marry her. He remembered one especially, a house painter named Karl Mueller. Mr. Mueller would often stop by after work, still in his white painter's uniform, and have a beer in the kitchen. Sometimes he came for Sunday dinner with them after church. He was a Catholic, too, but he went to a different church. He had liked Mr. Mueller. He was jolly and laughed a lot, he played ball with him and took them out on Saturdays and Sundays. He wondered why his mother didn't marry him and one day he asked her. "Karl Mueller is a good man and I like him very much. But I am not in love with him," she had replied.

He missed having a father. The kids at school used to make cracks about it and he was always getting into fights. His parish priest suggested he go out for football in high school. It was a good idea and it won him a scholarship to Notre Dame. But he didn't get it for athletic prowess alone. He studied hard. No one was going to call him a dumb Polack who could only run down a field with a ball.

There were girls during those years, a lot of them, but he didn't want to be tied down to any one girl. When he got married, it would have to last. He was ambitious and he intended to do something important with his life. It would be a long time before he would be able to support a wife and family.

In the Polish community during the Depression any son or daughter who went to college did so with the idea that the boy would become a priest and the girl a nun. He knew the life of a priest was not for him. He liked women too much. He wanted to study law and go into politics. That way he could serve as well. After Notre Dame he had his choice of several law schools. He picked Georgetown because he wanted to be in Washington, and he worked on the side to pay for his tuition. It was a hard grind, but he made it.

And he made it on his own.

Now, at thirty-three, he was one of the youngest congressmen on the Hill. And his plans did not stop there. He had his eye on the Senate.

But there was one score he hadn't settled. He looked over at the Wyman mausoleum.

Forgive and forget.

It was easier said than done.

CHAPTER TWENTY-FOUR

T he whirl had begun and there was no turning back. In a moment of panic, Ardith considered marrying Bob Ewing. He had asked her one weekend at Princeton just before school finished. She knew he was in love with her, but she wasn't so sure about her own feelings. Was it because this was her first proposal of marriage and she was secretly afraid no one else would ever ask her? Or that she was afraid she might not be the great social belle her mother expected? If she was married no one would know if she was popular or not. A girl she knew at Miss Putnam's had eloped just before her coming-out party after the invitations were already out. It caused quite a commotion and all kinds of rumors. "There's always something funny when people elope," her mother had said. "Imagine doing that to her family after all the trouble they'd gone to."

The tea at the F. Street Club introduced her to all her mother's friends and a lot of people she had never seen before. She stood in a receiving line with her mother and shook hands with everyone. They seemed to be looking her over as if she were on the block in a slave market. No doubt some of them had eligible sons, whom she would meet later.

A fat woman in a floral chiffon mopped her brow with a handkerchief and kept an eye on all the guests as they were announced. She appeared to be mentally checking them off and she was. She was Mrs. Matheson, the social secretary, and she made out the lists for all the parties, hired the caterers, addressed the invitations, many of which came back because of her illegible scrawl. She became a social secretary right after the stock market crash when her broker husband jumped out a window, leaving her with two sons to raise. Everyone in Washington feared her and curried her favor. To be scratched from Mrs. Matheson's list meant to be socially ostracized. It wasn't too difficult — a boy who had too many drinks, a girl who wore a dress that was too décolleté, someone who failed to speak to her at a party. Suddenly the invitations stopped and they wondered why.

Names kept on being announced. The Argentine Ambassador and Senora Vargas, the Secretary of State and his wife, the second secretary of the Turkish Embassy, who was a bachelor, Mrs. Breckinridge, an elderly dowager, who lived around the corner.

It was a warm June afternoon and Ardith's long white kid gloves felt sticky after shaking so many hands. Violin music was playing softly and there was the strong scent of carnations and tuberoses from the many baskets of flowers. She would have to write thank-you notes for each one.

People were wandering around with glasses of champagne, and the many voices sounded like the buzzing of bees. Soon most of them would be taking off for their summer places, for the hot humid weather was beginning. June in Washington was known as the "little season" and in the fall the social activities really started. Thanksgiving weekend the debutante balls began and they continued until after New Year's. Ardith's ball was set for the Friday after Thanksgiving and would be at the Sulgrave Club.

"Yes, we're going to Newport in two weeks," her mother was saying. "I hope you'll visit us there."

Ardith's feet were beginning to hurt and she wondered if she dared kick off her shoes. She was wearing a long organdy gown, so no one would notice. No, she'd better not. Mrs. Matheson was watching her from across the room.

I'll just have to suffer through this tea, she thought. At her ball there would be mostly young people and then she could dance and have fun.

The society editor of *The Washington Post* was going through the line now. They were doing a full page lay-out on Sunday of her called "A Day in the Life of a Debutante." She had posed for the pictures last week, playing tennis at the Chevy Chase Club, lunching at the Mayflower with another debutante, doing charity work at Georgetown Hospital, and dinner-dancing with a beau in the evening.

This weekend she was going to Warrenton for Nancy Larimer's coming-out party. She did not know that it was a weekend that would change her life.

The Larimer estate in Warrenton, Virginia, looked like a scene from a Venice carnival. A pink marquee had been erected on the lawn with poles striped in gold and blue. Venetian lanterns illuminated the tent and the tables around the dance floor were covered with cloths of amethyst, turquoise, orange, and blue, each centered with varicolored frosted candles on Venetian gold stems. Meyer Davis and his orchestra were dressed in gondolier costumes.

Ardith was having a whirl, and unlike her hideous dancing school days, getting a rush from the stagline. It's probably because I'm a new face on the local scene, she thought.

Suddenly a tall, handsome young man cut in. He was blond with very blue eyes, and though he looked familiar, she couldn't place him.

"I'm Doug Larimer," he said. "Nancy's brother."

Of course. The photograph on Nancy's bureau at school.

Another boy quickly tapped him on the shoulder and then another cut in. Doug cut back.

"Look, let's get some champagne," he said. "That's the only chance I'll get to talk to you." His voice had a faint Southern drawl, not the twang that many of them had, but just enough to be pleasant and restful. From her childhood, another voice like his . . . half-remembered . . . New Orleans . . . the Mississippi.

They walked over to the punch bowl.

"Nancy told me about you," he said, "but you know how a guy feels about his little sister's friends."

"And you were afraid of getting stuck with me?"

He grinned. "That shows what an idiot I was. You could have been my dinner partner. But I'm tired of being fixed up with someone's roommate who turns out to be the captain of the hockey team. Girls have no idea of what's attractive to a guy."

"It works the other way too."

"I guess.

"Besides I'm terrible at hockey — I loathe it!"

They both laughed.

"Would you like to see the gardens?" he asked. "I think I see someone coming to ask you to dance. Unless you'd rather go back . . . "

"No."

The sunken rose garden was illuminated with pink and green lights. They sat down on a wrought-iron bench. Fireflies glowed in the dark. The strains of "Falling in Love with Love" drifted from the marquee.

"It's a beautiful party."

"Yes," he agreed, "it turned out pretty well. I guess Nancy's been waiting all her life for this night."

"Have you always lived here?"

"Yes . . . and my grandfather before that. This house dates back to the Civil War. The old slave quarters were down the road there. Come on, I'll show you."

The driveway was lined with huge old trees. A rope swing hung from a weeping willow tree.

"I used to have a swing like that," she said.

"Sit down, I'll give you a push."

An aged black man in a white coat passed carrying a tray of mint juleps. "Evenin', Mistah Doug," he said.

"That's Jesse. He's been with our family since my father was a boy."

"It must have been wonderful growing up on a place like this. I mean knowing everyone around the countryside and feeling part of everything."

"It was. Nancy and I had our own ponies when we were children, and there were ducks on that pond over there. In the winter we could go ice-skating and toast marshmallows in the fireplace afterward. It was a great life."

"You must have had such a feeling of permanence," she said. A shadow suddenly swept across her face.

"What is it?"

"Oh . . . I was just remembering when I was little . . . how I used to cry when it was time to take down the Christmas tree. I loved sitting under it and looking at the beautiful lights and colored balls. I wanted it to stay there forever. Even when I was told that the tree was a fire hazard and was shedding pine needles all over the carpet, I still couldn't understand why they had to take it away."

"Nothing is permanent," Doug said. "When I was eight I had a beagle with big brown eyes — his name was Mischief — he slept at the foot of my bed and we took long walks together through the woods. One day he ran out in front of a car and was killed right before my eyes. I thought I'd never get over it. I swore I'd never have another dog as long as I lived. But I did. Wounds heal, and life renews itself. You learn that in medicine."

"I didn't know you were in medical school."

"I'm not . . . yet. I've another year at the University of Virginia and then I'm going to medical school. It may sound strange to you, but I want to be a country doctor — not just take care of the rich, horsey set, but there are a lot of poor people who live around here who can't afford decent medical attention for themselves or their children. They're the ones I'd like to help." He smiled. "Sounds pretty idealistic, doesn't it?"

"No, I think it sounds wonderful."

"Well, I've been pretty selfish taking up so much of your time. I guess I'd better take you back to the dance floor or they'll be sending out a search party."

Bob Ewing was waiting for her. "I've been looking all over for you," he said. He glared at Doug. He took Ardith's arm and led her over to the buffet table where a midnight supper was prepared. A butler served them scrambled eggs and slices of Virginia ham with corn bread.

"I don't want all that, Bob. I'm really not hungry."

He seemed not to have heard and led her to a table on the terrace away from the others.

"What were you doing all that time?" he asked. "You must have been gone for over an hour with that guy."

"Just talking," she said. The orchestra was playing "Music of the Spheres." She felt as if she were floating. "Besides, it wasn't that long."

So this is how it happens, she thought. All of a sudden and without warning. As if I'd been waiting all my life for this moment. It does exist, and not just in novels. You meet someone and everything is different, the whole world is transformed. She felt like singing and whirling around the dance floor. . .

Bob was looking at her intently and saying something.

"I'm sorry, Bob. What did you say?"

"I said I thought we should get married next summer and announce our engagement at Christmas."

Dear Bob, she thought. He was really very sweet. He would make a very good husband—for someone else.

"I. . ." She stopped.

"You don't have to decide tonight," he said. He squeezed her hand. "I'll wait. Whenever you're ready, I'll be there."

It won't do any good, Bob, she thought. I'm in love with someone else. I just met him and I don't even know how he feels about me. I know it's crazy, but I don't care!

CHAPTER TWENTY-FIVE

The next day Bob drove her back to Washington and she did not see Doug again. Nancy came in town to shop the following week and asked Ardith to have lunch with her.

"Guess who likes you?" Nancy said, stirring her vichyssoise. They were at La Salle du Bois.

"Who?"

"My brother."

So he was interested after all, she thought. Then why hadn't he called? "I haven't heard from him since your party," she said, in what she hoped was a casual tone.

"That's because he doesn't want to get serious about any girl and he's afraid he could about you. He has another year of college and then he's going to medical school."

"Yes, he told me. But what does that have to do with anything?"

"He just doesn't want to get emotionally involved, so he's staying away from you on purpose."

Ardith looked disappointed.

"Doug's very serious about becoming a doctor and he doesn't want anything to interfere with his plans. Or maybe I should say anyone. But don't worry," Nancy smiled knowingly. "He'll call."

They went to Newport a week later and she still had not heard from Doug. She tried to dismiss him from her mind and busied herself with plans for her debut. It was to be held at the end of Tennis Week on August sixteenth. "A small dance," the invitations said, though five hundred guests had been invited to Wisteria Lodge.

She was looking forward to making her debut now, and she found she enjoyed being the center of attention and seeing her picture in the papers.

Every time she went to Bailey's Beach or the Newport Casino a photographer snapped her picture, and she began to feel like a celebrity. Already she had almost enough press clippings to fill a scrapbook.

She wished that the newspapers would stop continually referring to her as the granddaughter of the late Standard Oil magnate, T. J. Wyman. Was she never to have any identity of her own? she wondered. She recalled her cousin Cordelia's remark at her grandfather's funeral: "Everything we have or will ever have we owe to him." Did she herself have nothing to offer as a person? It gave her a terrible sense of insecurity. Would people always be after her because of a false image and not what she really was? What was she really? Could she ever feel completely close to anyone? She never had. It seemed she wore a mask . . . the glamour girl with the painted-on smile. . .while underneath there was still the plain, lonely girl who had wandered through the Pennsylvania woods picking wildflowers, listening to the river sounds, and searching for a love that was lost.

The sound of foghorns awoke her and the cries of seagulls. She lay there watching the sun rise and the sky turn from gray to pink. There was a clammy feeling of terror in the pit of her stomach. It was the sixteenth of August. Tonight was her debut. Suppose her party was a dismal flop after all this publicity? How could she face anyone again? She wanted to stay in bed and pull the covers over her head.

She thought of the house on Bellevue Avenue known as "the haunted house," with broken windows and paint peeling, its once beautiful gardens grown over with tangled brush and weeds. The story was that it had belonged to some people who came from California and tried to crash Newport society. They gave a ball and sent invitations to everyone in Newport, but no one came. The orchestra played to an empty ballroom and they stood there in a receiving line waiting for guests who never arrived. After that snub they were so angry that they packed up and returned to California. They swore revenge. The house would remain as an eyesore, a monument to Newport snobbery. That was over twenty years ago. Their children still owned the house, so it could not be sold or torn down, and on quiet nights some swore they could hear ghostly music playing in the dilapidated ballroom.

The maid came in with her breakfast on a tray.

"Your mother says you're to eat all of this, Miss Ardith," she said. "And stay in bed until the people from *Life* arrive. There's nothing for you

to do and your mother wants you to look rested tonight." She handed
Ardith the *New York Times* which had been folded over to the society
page.

There was her photograph and underneath it the article said: "Mrs.
Wyman Rodgers will give a Blue, White and Silver Ball for 500 guests
tonight at Wisteria Lodge to introduce her daughter, Miss Ardith
Rodgers . . ."

She spread strawberry jam on an English muffin and sipped her
coffee. "Meyer Davis and his orchestra will play," the article continued.
"Striking floral and electrical effects have been arranged, including
illumination of trees on the estate."

She heard the sound of trucks in the driveway and hammering.
Electricians were stringing wires through the trees and carpenters were
finishing the steps leading down to the marquee several terraces below.
The doorbell kept ringing with deliveries of flowers. Rest? she thought.
She was starting to get a headache. She took two aspirins and washed and
set her hair.

Her mother came in with a sheath of telegrams.

"I've never seen so many gorgeous baskets of flowers," she said. She
looked out the window. "I hope those steps are secure. I'm so worried
about someone falling after too much to drink . . ." She peered at Ardith.
"Darling, you have circles under your eyes. Did you get enough sleep?"

"Yes, Mother. Besides, a little pancake make-up will cover them."

The maid appeared with a box of flowers.

"One of the electricians would like to see you, Mrs. Rodgers. He's
having trouble with the lights." She handed the box to Ardith. "These just
came, Miss Ardith."

Ardith opened the box eagerly. Nestled in the green wax paper were
two dozen pink sweetheart roses and the card was signed: *Doug Larimer.*

The photographer from *Life* arrived at eleven with a lady reporter.
They posed her in bed in a lace negligee reading her telegrams and
surrounded by flowers.

"How do you feel about your debut, Miss Rodgers?" the lady
reporter asked, as a flashbulb exploded. Her name was Miss Quinn and she
was waspish and wore horn-rimmed spectacles. "Were you excited when
you woke up this morning?"

"Well . . . yes . . ." Her head was starting to ache again.

Miss Quinn scribbled something in a notebook and looked around the room. Ardith had the feeling she would like to go around opening all the closets.

"Now don't let us disturb you," Miss Quinn said. "We'll just go around snapping pictures and we want them to be informal. Except for the one for our cover. We want to get one in your ball gown just before the guests arrive."

Ardith and her mother stood in the receiving line before a flower-banked fireplace in the candle-lit living room. Her gown was a bouffant white net with a tight-fitting bodice and a cape effect decorated in ruchings fell from her bare shoulders. She carried a bouquet of gardenias and a single gardenia was pinned in her long dark hair.

She thought how pretty and young her mother looked tonight in her gown of pale blue marganza and aquamarine necklace and earrings. Her blonde hair was piled high on her head and she looked like the Duchess of Tower in *Peter Ibbetson*. Mademoiselle had taken her to see it as a child and she had never forgotten the love scene between Ann Harding and Gary Cooper and his line as they parted: "I will love you in this world . . . and the next." It was so sad and romantic and everyone in the theatre was weeping. Even Mademoiselle, whom she couldn't imagine ever loving anyone, took out her handkerchief and blew her nose.

The receiving line was endless. Ardith tried to catch all the names as the butler announced them, but after a short time she gave up and just smiled and shook hands.

"Thank you . . . I'm so glad you could come."

"Yes, wasn't it lucky the fog cleared."

She realized it didn't matter what you said because no one listened anyway. At a large wedding reception recently, just to prove this point, a man went around saying conversationally and with a big smile, "The Germans have just bombed New York."

"Yes, it's a beautiful wedding."

After a few more attempts he gave up. No one had heard a word he said.

No wonder you could see people for years at parties, Ardith thought, and never know anything about them.

No one listened to anyone.

The Archduke of Something was being announced. She wished all the guests would come so she could dance and enjoy her own party. A Viennese waltz drifted in through the open French doors. Just then Peter Ogden came in from the terrace.

"I've been waiting for you to come onto the dance floor," he said. "Can't I steal you away from this receiving line now? You've been here for over an hour."

"Go on, dear," her mother said.

Peter took her arm and they went down the blue-carpeted stairway to the marquee. The trees and shrubbery sparkled with blue and green lights. Four apple trees flanked the stairs and the illumination made the apples look like thousands of bluish-green orbs. Smilax covered the poles of the blue-and-white tent and there were masses of white gladioli, snapdragons, lilies, lace flowers, and blue delphinium.

Meyer Davis nodded to her and raised his baton. The orchestra started playing "Music of the Spheres" by Josef Strauss. It was the piece she always requested at parties and now, whenever she came on the dance floor, he played it automatically.

The tent had a revolving mirror on which colored spotlights played, and it was as if they were whirling around in a rainbow. The stagline started to cut in and she was only able to dance two or three steps with the same partner.

"Fabulous party, Ardith."

"Thank you.

"What a dramatic effect with that blue stairway."

She whirled from one to the next. Time flew and it all became a blur of music and colored lights. The *Life* photographer was going around snapping pictures. She was conscious of faces and snatches of conversation and she felt like the ballerina on a music box, wound up and twirling in circles.

Finally all the guests had gone and the party was over.

Ardith went to her room and slipped off her silver sandals. Her feet were swollen and aching and there was a pain in the muscle above her left collar bone from holding her head erect. She felt exhausted, but too keyed-up to sleep.

Her mother came in and kissed her. She looked very happy.

"It was a huge success, darling," she said. "Beyond my wildest dreams. And I received so many compliments about you. The Archduke Otto wants to call on you. Do you remember dancing with him?"

"You mean that funny little man with the black mustache?"

Her mother nodded. "He's quite charming. I had a long talk with him and his mother."

"But he's so old."

"I'd hardly call twenty-eight old. Besides, he's the heir to the Austrian throne."

Ardith unzipped her dress and threw it over a chair. It was a shame, she thought, that this beautiful dress could just be worn one evening. Like a wedding gown.

"There was another young man who was a house guest of the Van Pelt's," her mother said. "He's from a very wealthy Boston family — I believe his name is Kennedy. Of course, they're Democrats, but he seemed very nice."

"Oh, yes, the one with the bushy hair. He's a very good dancer." She looked at the pink roses from Doug Larimer in a vase on her night table. If only he had been there.

"I'll let you get some sleep now," her mother said, kissing her. "See you in the morning."

After she had gone, Ardith took one of the pink rosebuds from the vase and put it on her pillow. In the dark room her ball gown looked like a fluffy white cloud. She could hear the surf crashing against the rocks and she still seemed to be whirling around the dance floor to colored lights.

It was a long time before she was able to fall asleep.

CHAPTER TWENTY-SIX

Congressman Joseph Kreskie read with disgust the accounts of his cousin's Newport coming-out party, and then wondered why he even bothered to read them. It was the name Wyman that jumped out at him from the newspaper print and from the story in *Life*. Of course, no one knew she was his cousin and their paths had yet to cross. She was a beautiful girl from the photographs, but like a wax doll. He was sure he wouldn't like her.

He tossed the paper aside. He had too many other matters to attend to that were more important than this social crap.

He picked up the morning's mail and started to go through it. There were several letters from Pennsylvania citizens asking him to work for flood control of the Allegheny and another letter from a Seneca Indian group worried that they would be evicted from their lands if the proposed dam were built. The mother of an Oil City boy, who had received his draft notice, had written asking him to intervene. *After all,* she wrote, *it's not our war, and I don't see why my son should be called up.*

Hitler had occupied most of Europe and yet there were still people who thought we could look the other way and not become involved. America danced while the guns of war rumbled at our shores. It was only a matter of time.

Joe Kreskie leaned back in the brown leather chair and stared at a painting of Cook Forest on his office wall. The sunlight slanting through the tall trees of the Pennsylvania woods, the dark greens and gold and russet against the blue river and sky, gave him a feeling of peace when he was troubled. He had walked through those woods many times as a boy.

He picked up a yellow legal pad and wrote: *I can sympathize with*

*your feelings as a mother, but there is nothing I can do to help your son
avoid. . .*

He put down the pad and pressed the buzzer for his secretary. Helen
Flanagan was a pretty redhead with blue-green eyes who had just started
working for him. Now she stood at the door with an expectant expression
and her shorthand pad in her hand.

He suddenly realized he was turning into a workaholic with no social
life to speak of. He wanted say, "What are you doing tonight, Miss
Flanagan? How about dinner, and then perhaps a nightcap at my place
afterward?"

But instead he said, "Would you answer these letters for me, please?
I've made some notes about what to say."

The remaining weeks of August passed, and after Labor Day Ardith
and her mother returned to Washington. She had fittings at Garfinckel's
for the ball gown for her debut at the Sulgrave Club in November. She had
designed it herself. It was to be of white Duchess satin with a hooped skirt,
and around the neck and down the back of the dress was an openwork
pattern of camellias edged with rhinestones. A white satin muff would be
trimmed with real camellias.

The war news was getting worse and many people thought America
would be in it soon. Roosevelt gave orders to attack on sight any German
or Italian vessel met in United States defensive waters. Several boys she
knew had been drafted into the Army.

But the Washington social whirl went on.

She attended debutante lunches and served on charity committees.
She played tennis at the Chevy Chase Club and went riding in Rock Creek
Park.

And Doug Larimer called.

By now she had almost given him up. She had written him a thank-
you note for the roses and heard nothing after that. And here he was on the
phone as if she had seen him yesterday.

"Hi," he said. "I was in town for the day and I was hoping you'd be
free to have dinner with me."

"Tonight?" She had a date, but maybe she could get out of it
somehow.

"You're probably busy and it's very rude of me to call at the last
minute like this, but I would like to see you."

The lazy Southern drawl . . . like the voice long ago that made her feel safe, before her world turned upside-down. She would break her date. She'd think of some excuse. "I'd love to have dinner with you."

"Great." He sounded very happy. "Is seven too early?"

"No, that will be fine."

"See you then."

"Goodbye, Doug."

She hung up the phone. Would she find him as attractive as she had three months ago? she wondered. Perhaps she had just built up something that wasn't there. Nancy's party, the moonlight walk, the music . . .

She ran her bath and poured in some bath oil. Suddenly she remembered that she must get out of her other date. She called his number, rehearsing her speech. "I'm terribly sorry about tonight, Jack, but could we postpone it? I think I'm coming down with something. . ." Well, that wasn't a complete lie.

Jack was very understanding. Or at least he sounded so.

"I'll call later and see how you're feeling," he said.

"That's very sweet of you, Jack, but I'll probably just have some hot soup and go right to sleep. Call me tomorrow, will you?" He doesn't believe me, she thought. Oh well, it couldn't be helped. She had to see Doug tonight.

She was waiting in the library when Doug arrived. Carrie, their maid, showed him in. He seemed pleased to see that she was ready on time and he looked even more attractive than she remembered. His tan emphasized his blond hair and deep blue eyes, and he was wearing a gray flannel suit and a white button-down shirt and striped tie.

He held out his hand and smiled.

"I've been keeping up with your activities," he said. "That was quite a spread in *Life*."

"Oh . . . yes." She never knew quite what to say when people said, "I saw your picture in the paper."

"But the cover didn't do you justice. You're much prettier."

"Thank you."

"It's a beautiful evening for a drive. How about having dinner at the Olney Inn? Do you think it's still open?"

"I think so. That's a good idea." Also, she wasn't likely to run into Jack there. "I'll get my coat."

She thought of offering him a drink . . . no, it was better to leave before her mother came down and started quizzing him on his family history. Her mother had such a subtle way of doing it. "Larimer?" she would say and pause. "I believe I knew a family by that name years ago . . . they lived in Virginia. Are you related by any chance?" Then they would be trapped and Doug might feel he had to invite her mother to join them for dinner.

She walked quickly past her mother's room.

"Goodnight, Mother," she called.

"Are you leaving so soon? Why don't you ask the Larimer boy to have a drink and I'll be down in a few minutes."

"He's already made a dinner reservation for seven-thirty," Ardith said, hoping her mother wouldn't ask where.

"Oh." Her mother sounded disappointed. "Well, have a good time, baby. And don't be too late."

Baby. I was eighteen last week, she thought, and I still don't have any freedom. Her mother was always checking on her and waited up for her until she came home. I guess it's because I'm all she has, Ardith thought, as she went down the stairs with her coat over her shoulders. But I wish she had a life of her own and didn't just live vicariously through me.

The Olney Inn was still open, but in late September not many people were there. They sat at a table overlooking the gardens. A rustic bridge crossed a running brook and the moon hung like a golden torch above the trees. Fireflies flickered in the darkness.

Doug looked at her across the candle-lit table. A yellow cut-glass vase was filled with bronze chrysanthemums. "I was afraid I might find you engaged to an archduke after the whirl you were having at Newport," he said.

She laughed. "Oh, that silly item in Cholly Knickerbocker! I don't know where he gets his information. I've never even had a date with the archduke. I've just danced with him at parties."

"But you like all these parties, don't you?"

"Yes . . . and no. They're fun, but most of the people are so unreal, and deep underneath they're unhappy and trying to escape boredom in a frantic kind of gaiety."

"Then you do see that? Because I've had several seasons of going to these deb parties and there's a terrible let-down for the girls after it's all over. It gives them the idea that life is just one long dance with Meyer

Davis playing their favorite song. A lot of them end up drinking too much and after three or four divorces taking an overdose of pills. They can't seem to get off the merry-go-round."

"I can see how it happens. Only last week I was offered a screen test just because of that write-up in *Life*. Isn't it ridiculous? The only acting I've ever done was in school plays."

"Are you going to do it?"

"I was, but Mother had a fit. She said that all movie people were moral degenerates. Of course, she's never known any, so she can speak with great authority."

"In a way she's right. Not all, of course. You can't make broad, sweeping statements about any group. But you've led a very sheltered life. You've never been up against it and seen the rough side of life. People act differently when they're fighting for survival, and they resent those who've had it easy. It's only natural."

"I guess so." She looked past him out into the gardens. "I suppose I have had what most people would call an easy life — at least I've never known what it is to go hungry or to worry about being thrown out in the street because we couldn't pay the rent. But sometimes I wonder what it would have been like to have a mother and father together, to have had someone to talk to as a child besides my dog, who couldn't answer, or my governess, who didn't care . . ."

"Where was your mother?"

"Out at some party. Or else sitting in her room lost in an unhappy dream world. I don't remember her ever taking me to the zoo or to a circus . . . I always went with Mademoiselle."

"Where was your father?"

"He died when I was five."

"Do you remember him at all?"

"Yes . . . very clearly." She looked at Doug for a minute and thought: Shall I tell him the truth? "He isn't dead," she heard herself saying, and noticed the surprised expression on Doug's face. "It's a convenient lie. The truth is that I don't know where he is because he just disappeared." She paused. "But somewhere he is alive . . ."

"I'm sorry if I touched on a painful subject that you'd rather not talk about."

"No, I don't mind. I'm glad I told you. I've bottled it up for so long."

"That's not good," he said gently. "I guess it hasn't been easy for you." He reached across the table and touched her hand. "You're very sweet. I tried hard to get you out of my mind, but I wasn't able to. You know what I said to myself the night we met?"

"No . . . what?"

"That's the kind of girl I'd like to marry. And suddenly it scared the hell out of me." He grinned.

Everything Nancy told me was right, she thought.

"Oh, not because of you," he quickly added. "But marriage to anyone was something that didn't enter into my plans for quite a few years. I have medical school ahead of me and that's a long hard grind. It doesn't leave any time for a wife."

"So you decided to stay away?"

He nodded. "Then I read about that whirl you were having with all those guys . . . and that archduke. I got worried. I had to see you again."

"I'm glad."

"Will you be in Washington from now on?"

"Most of the time. I have to go to New York on Monday to pose for some pictures for *Harper's Bazaar,* but I'll be back the end of the week."

"Good. I can drive up from the University of Virginia for the weekend. That is, if you're not too busy to see me."

She smiled. "I think I can manage."

"And perhaps you'll come down for a football weekend and prom. On second thought, I don't know about that. Most of the guys do a lot of drinking and it gets pretty wild sometimes, so I hesitate about asking a nice girl. We'll see."

"Who do they usually have?" She was curious.

"Oh . . . there are girls around the campus," he said vaguely. He took her hand and smiled. "No one like you."

CHAPTER TWENTY-SEVEN

The Chevy Chase Club was just over the Maryland state line and resembled a Southern plantation with its wide veranda that looked out over sweeping green lawns and huge trees. A short walk led to the swimming pool and beyond were the tennis courts and golf course. It was the only cool place to escape from the heat and humidity of Washington's unbearable summers for those few lucky enough to belong to its select membership. Newcomers to Washington waited for years at the end of a long list to be approved by the board when there was a vacancy. This was only when a member died or moved away.

"Good evenin', Miss Rodgers."

"How are you, Todd?"

"Tolerable, tolerable." He gave her a wide grin showing gleaming white teeth. The same black man had been at the door ever since she could remember and he knew all the members and their children. He had been in the hospital during the summer and now walked with a limp.

"Just wait a minute, Doug," Ardith said. "I'll be right back."

She walked over to the guest register and signed: *Douglas Larimer, Warrenton, Virginia, guest of Mrs. Wyman Rodgers*. She glanced quickly at the other names. The Saturday night dances were very popular and Sidney's orchestra was just tuning up.

Nearby, two senators were discussing the world situation with grim expressions. The headlines during that first week of October 1941 were hardly optimistic. NAZIS EXECUTE 58 MORE RED HOSTAGES, REDS RIP LENINGRAD LINE, R.A.F. BOMBS GERMANY, NORSE IN REVOLT, CZECH PREMIER EXECUTED, NEW JAPANESE CABINET FORMED, AMERICAN ARMY NOW IN ICELAND.

"How can we stay out of it?" she heard one senator say to the other, who was a member of the America First Committee. "Hell, we're in it now and we don't know it."

Mrs. Breckinridge had spotted her and came sailing over like a battleship. Long ropes of pearls swung around her neck and an enormous ruby and diamond brooch was like a headlight on her black velvet gown. Her white hair had a deep blue rinse — either her hairdresser was color blind or Mrs. Breckinridge liked it that way, Ardith could never figure out which.

"Ardith, how lovely you look! I had the nicest lunch with your mother the other day at the Sulgrave Club."

Doug came to her rescue.

"Mrs. Breckinridge, may I present Doug Larimer?"

Mrs. Breckinridge peered at him through her lorgnette. "I don't believe I've met you before. But then I can't keep up with all of Ardith's beaux. I like you, young man. You must have Ardith bring you to one of my Sunday brunches."

"Thank you," Doug said. "I'd like to."

Mrs. Breckinridge snapped her fingers at a passing waiter. "Would you please find Mr. Breckinridge and tell him I'm ready. I believe he's in the bar." And she swept on regally.

"Mrs. Breckinridge lives around the corner and she's on the symphony board with Mother," Ardith explained. "She practically keeps it going with her donations."

They were passing the ladies' cloak room.

"I'll just leave my wrap." Ardith handed her silver fox jacket to the maid. She noticed several girls looking at Doug with interest.

They went up the broad stairs to the dining room.

The same people came here week after week and year after year and any new face caused a stir. In a corner by the window were the Wilsons and the McKnights, leaders of the young married set. Moira McKnight was pregnant again and wearing maternity clothes. She had three boys — the oldest was four — and she had hopefully relined her bassinet in pink dotted Swiss. Georgia Wilson had one boy and said she didn't intend to lose her figure having another. She was from Atlanta and her husband was a radio executive with NBC. She was a very pretty brunette and always looked chic in Hattie Carnegie clothes. It was rumored that she really bought her dresses at a little shop on Connecticut Avenue and sewed Hattie Carnegie labels in them, then hung them inside out in her closet.

Ardith couldn't imagine anyone going to so much trouble. The Wilsons were always giving dinner parties that were written up in the society pages, but when it came to giving a donation to the Red Cross or the Community Chest or some other charity the Wilsons were suddenly unreachable. "I'm so sorry, Mrs. Wilson is having her hair done at Elizabeth Arden's. May she call you back?" the maid would say. If one managed to trap her at home, Georgia was prepared. "I'll have to ask Keith and he's at the White House now arranging a broadcast with President Roosevelt." The Wilsons changed their politics conveniently to be in with whatever party was in power.

Georgia Wilson looked up as Ardith and Doug entered and whispered something to her husband.

Washington was really like a small town, Ardith thought, and especially the Chevy Chase Club on Saturday night. She was beginning to wish she hadn't asked Doug to come here, but there was really nowhere else to go. The District blue laws closed every place in town at midnight.

They had dinner and went downstairs. She stopped in the ladies' room and ran into Ann Garrett and Courtney Ellis. They were debutantes also and were coming out during Christmas week. Ardith was glad hers was the first party of the season because by the end of December everyone was tired of parties and one dance seemed the same as any other, especially since they were all held at the Sulgrave Club. She didn't want people coming to her party and saying, "Oh, I'm so tired of going out . . . I wish I could stay home tonight and have a nice bowl of cornflakes."

Courtney was putting on a fresh coat of lipstick. It looked almost black. She was overweight and had squeezed herself into a tight mauve taffeta.

"Who are you with tonight, Ardith?" Courtney asked. "He's cute."

"Doug Larimer. He goes to the University of Virginia."

"Is he coming to your party?" Ann asked.

"I guess so." She ran a comb through her hair. She thought of all the times she had come here through the years. Those awful, awkward years of twelve and thirteen especially, when she felt so unattractive and self-conscious, when she used to watch the boys and girls on the tennis courts and in the pool and envy their relaxed manner and wish she could be like them. She was sure then that no boy would ever like her. Or at least, no one she liked, and who wanted some jerk? It was amazing how in a few years everything could change.

"I can hardly wait for the parties to start," Courtney said. She took a bottle of Schiaparelli's *Shocking* from her purse and dabbed some behind her ears. "Yours is the first, isn't it, Ardith?"

"Yes, November twenty-eighth. Right after Thanksgiving."

"I'm so glad they're changing Thanksgiving back to its usual time this year," Ann said. "Honestly, that Roosevelt! I wonder what he'll do next?"

"Last year we had to celebrate Thanksgiving twice," said Courtney. "My brother goes to Saint Alban's and they gave them 'Frank's Giving' off, then a week later I came home from Westover because Connecticut didn't recognize the new date and the cook had to prepare a turkey dinner with mince pie and everything all over again. It was a mess!"

The orchestra was playing "The Very Thought of You" and Ardith could hear the music above their chatter. "I'd better get back to my date," she said.

Doug's lips brushed her hair as they danced. He was six feet-two and she was glad he was tall. She liked looking up to a man and she always felt strange dancing with boys who were the same height she was. That was one of the painful things about dancing school — the girls were usually taller than the boys. She could never imagine herself being attracted to a short man.

"What are you thinking about?" Doug asked.

"That I like dancing with you."

He smiled and held her closer. "I'm afraid I see some competition coming."

Orhan Baydar, the second secretary of the Turkish Embassy, walked up and tapped Doug. He released her reluctantly.

Speaking of short men, Ardith thought. Orhan came up to her shoulder. She remembered a costume party at the Sulgrave Club when everyone had to come as a song. Orhan came in a straw skirt. "I'm 'Turkey in the Straw,'" he explained. He won first prize.

Orhan was supposed to be quite a ladies' man. He had called several times for dates but she always had an excuse ready. It was not easy to discourage him.

"There is a party at the Brazilian Embassy Thursday evening," Orhan said, "and I would be so happy if you could go with me. It should be quite an elegant affair."

"Oh, I'm so sorry, but I'm going to be in New York next week," she said.

"Then I will call you upon your return. If you're not otherwise engaged." He glanced in Doug's direction.

The music stopped and Doug came back to claim her.

"Thank you," Orhan said. He bowed and smiled, showing several gold teeth. She had heard that he was very attentive to some of the married women whose husbands were away frequently.

Doug took her arm and they walked out to the porch. Several groups of older people were playing bridge. They seemed very serious about it. Ardith wondered what it would be like to be that old with most of your life behind you, wondering what suit to bid while the young people danced. She had tried to learn bridge but it bored her. Later, maybe. No, she couldn't ever picture herself sitting around with "the girls" playing bridge at a country club, exchanging snapshots of grandchildren, talking about the "good old days." But once these same people had been young. It was a depressing thought.

"Let's go sit on the stairs," she said.

"Yes, it does look a little like the old folk's home," Doug agreed.

"The weekends pass so quickly," he said.

They were sitting in Doug's car in front of her house. He had to drive back to Virginia Sunday morning to study for an exam on Monday.

"I know. You hardly arrive before you have to turn around and go back."

He stroked her hair. "I'll miss you. It gets harder and harder to leave you."

I never thought I could be this happy, she thought, and suddenly it frightened her. It was too good to last. She wanted him to hold her close this way forever. Nothing else mattered.

It had started to rain and she could hear the drops on the roof of the car and smell the wet leaves in the street.

"I'd better take you in," he said. He kissed her. "Till next weekend, darling."

CHAPTER TWENTY-EIGHT

They had their first fight two weeks later.

He had invited her to come down for a football game and dance the first weekend in November, and then decided it wasn't a good idea after all and that he would come up to Washington instead. She was furious and told him so over the phone.

"But, sweetheart, I didn't think you'd care that much. It just gets too wild and I don't want to expose you to all the drinking and everything that goes on. I asked you against my better judgement—"

"But I've told everyone that I was going to the University of Virginia that weekend. I've never been there and I want to come!" She was aware that she sounded like a spoiled child determined to have her own way, but she didn't care. Boys didn't realize how important such things were to a girl.

"It isn't as if I were standing you up or something. We can still be together and go out to Chevy or somewhere Saturday night."

"I'm tired of going to Chevy. I want to go to the game and the dance."

"Well I don't know where you'd stay. I called up Mrs. Pitts and her rooms are all filled. You mentioned a chaperone and she's the only one I know of."

"I see."

"As I think I told you once before, these weekends at Virginia are drunken brawls and you wouldn't have a good time."

She took a deep breath. "You don't need to explain further. It's quite obvious that you don't want me to come down. As a matter of fact, I have an invitation to go to Princeton that same weekend. He's very amusing and I think I may accept."

"If that's the way you feel."

"It is." She hung up.

Now why did I say those stupid things? she thought. Her old feeling of being rejected had arisen and one word led to another. Well, he'll call back, she assured herself.

But he didn't.

She tossed and turned that night unable to sleep. Had he gone and gotten drunk at the fraternity house? Or worse yet, picked up some girl for consolation? She remembered him saying, "Oh, there are girls around the campus. No one like you." What kind did he mean? Prostitutes?

Someone had told her that he used to date a girl who went to Sweet Briar. He had invited her to the dances at Virginia. She had heard that boys used a crude expression to describe a girl who was fast. "She's a one-two-three-bang type." Was this girl from Sweet Briar one of those? The more she thought about it, the more upset she got. Tomorrow he would surely call and say he was sorry and everything would be fine.

He did not call the next day and she refused to swallow her pride and call him.

The third day there was a telegram.

VERY SORRY BUT REFUSE TO HAVE YOU DOWN FOR DANCE. YOU HAD BETTER ACCEPT YOUR INVITATION WITH PRINCETON VERY AMUSING.   DOUG

She tossed the telegram on the bed and burst into tears. How could he act like this? To hell with him! Let him take out that tart from Sweet Briar. She wanted nothing more to do with him! No, that wasn't true. She loved him and she felt utterly and completely miserable. She stayed in her room and refused to eat any dinner.

The next morning another telegram arrived.

FORGET TELEGRAM. IF NOT TOO LATE EXPECT YOU FOR DANCE. MAY DRIVE TO WASHINGTON TO GET YOU. LET YOU KNOW LATER. I AM NOT CRAZY. ALL MY LOVE.   DOUG

That evening there was a special delivery letter.

Darling,

I suppose you think I'm perfectly nuts for confusing the issue about coming down. At first I didn't want you to see Virginia at its worst, or best, as the case may be. But I want to see you so much that nothing will stand in the way.

As I told you on the phone, Mrs. Pitts's rooms are all filled, so I've got you a room at the Farmington Country Club, which is on the outskirts of Charlottesville. It is quite a nice place and you won't be disappointed.

We will have a good time—I hope. Two girls from New York, Elaine Russell and someone Sloane are coming; so if they're good sports you perhaps may be able to stand it.

If I get through classes early enough on Friday I will come up to Washington and drive you down so you won't have to take the train, which is slow, dirty, and smells.

Let me know if everything is satisfactory.

> *All my love,*
>> *Doug*

She put down the letter. She had gotten her way this time and everything had worked out, but somehow she had the impression she had better not try it again. Doug wasn't the kind of person to be pushed against his will. Why did she feel so insecure? She wanted love and yet it frightened her. Was it because of what she had seen it do to her mother? Once her mother had been in love and happy and then love had vanished, leaving her an empty shell. She knew that people did not live happily ever after and she wanted to run before love hurt her as badly as it had hurt her mother.

But that was silly, she reasoned with herself. Why should she be afraid? Doug loved her and they were happy together. Nothing could destroy that. Nothing.

It turned out that Doug wasn't able to drive up in time to get her so she had to take the train. He was standing at the Charlottesville station waiting for her. There was a touch of frost in the air and he had the collar of his overcoat turned up.

"Hello, sweetheart." He kissed her and took her suitcase from the porter. "My car's right over there."

They walked along the platform. "I'm sorry I couldn't drive you down," he said, "but they threw an exam at us at the last minute, so I was stuck."

"The train ride wasn't too bad, in spite of your description of it," she said.

They both laughed.

"There's a cocktail party at the Zeta Psi house and then we can have dinner afterward with my roommate and his date. You haven't met Chuck, have you?"

"I don't think so."

"You'd remember if you had. He usually makes quite an impression with the girls. 'The bacon heir,' we call him. He's from Lake Forest and his family's in the meat packing business. He may be back there soon because I think he's about to flunk out. Too many extra-curricular activities," Doug grinned.

They were driving through the campus.

"I'll give you the real tour tomorrow," he said, "but I wanted you to see something of the college before it got dark."

She admired the red brick Colonial buildings and the serpentine walls. It was the most beautiful campus she'd seen.

"You should see it in the spring when the dogwood's out and the apple trees in blossom."

"Maybe someone will invite me down then."

"Maybe." He smiled. "If you're not going to Princeton. I hope your friend there wasn't too disappointed."

"All right," she said.

"I won't mention him again. Promise."

"Doug, we mustn't ever fight again. I was so miserable for two days."

"So was I. I've never heard you mad before, and you were really mad at me."

"It all seems so silly now. And to think we could have broken up over it."

"No," he said. "I wouldn't have let you get away from me."

The next evening he asked her to marry him. "In June, after I graduate," he said. "That will give us time for a honeymoon before I have to start medical school."

They planned to keep their engagement secret until spring and announce it at Easter vacation.

By then he would be twenty-one and come into a small trust fund his grandfather had left him. They talked of where they would go on their honeymoon. Hawaii, maybe? They would have two children, a boy and a girl . . . but not for several years.

"I'd like a little girl who looks just like you," he said, kissing her.

"Girls usually look like their fathers," she said. She suddenly wondered who would give her away.

"Are you going to tell your mother when you get home?"

She thought of her mother in the midst of preparations for her ball at the Sulgrave Club. That was only three weeks away. It all seemed like a waste of time now since she had already met the man she was going to marry. "I think I'll wait until after my party," she said.

"I kind of feel sorry for all those guys who will be getting their hopes up when they meet you. It will be such a shock when they find out you're not on the market."

"What an expression! But that's really just what a debut is. Available as a wife to the highest bidder. Anyway," she smiled, "maybe I won't tell them."

She felt very sure of herself now that everything was all settled. Doug loved her and they were to be married in June. Life was beautiful and she was completely happy. How wonderful to be eighteen and have one's life all planned!

But suddenly, for some unexplained reason, she felt restless . . .

"But it amounts to a declaration of war!" shouted the congressman from Virginia.

A debate was in progress in the House of Representatives over a ship-arming bill.

"Our unarmed Merchant Marine ships are being sunk by German submarines. Should we just stand by and do nothing?" Joe Kreskie asked, angry at the group of Southern Democrats opposing the bill.

The defenders of Moscow were still holding off the German armies and the State Department had just announced a billion dollar lend-lease loan for Russia. At home, with winter fast approaching, the nation's biggest concern was the threatened coal strike.

On November thirteenth the ship-arming bill finally passed, but barely, by a very narrow vote.

And on the fifteenth of November the Japanese envoy, Saburo Kurusu, landed at the Washington Airport to join Ambassador Nomura in peace talks with Secretary of State Cordell Hull. Thrusting a microphone before him, the newsreel men asked Kurusu for his message to the American people.

Peace, he assured them, grinning broadly, looked good.

CHAPTER TWENTY-NINE

Nancy Larimer came up to Washington for the day and Ardith had lunch with her at the Mayflower.

"Doug told me," Nancy said. "And I'm so thrilled! I don't know how you'll be able to keep it a secret till spring."

She was sorry Doug had said anything but she knew how close he and Nancy were and that they confided in each other. It must be nice to have an older brother to talk things over with and ask advice from. Unfortunately, Nancy wasn't very good at keeping secrets.

"Please don't tell anyone, Nancy. I haven't even told my mother yet and I don't want her to hear it from someone else."

"Oh, I won't say a word to a soul. Cross my heart." Nancy smiled archly. "Besides, I have some news of my own."

"You're getting married too?"

"Well, I want to but there's a bit of a problem with the family. They think he's too old for me and he's been divorced. If it weren't for the war in Europe I think Mother and Daddy would send me off on one of those trips to get him out of my mind. A year at a pension in Florence or something. But that wouldn't do any good anyway. I've had a crush on him since I was fifteen."

"Do I know him?"

"I don't think so. He lives in Middleburg. Oh, there's nothing wrong with his family. First Families of Virginia and all that. I said to Mother, 'At least I didn't run off and marry my horse trainer like your friend Mrs. Randolph did after her husband died.'"

"Why do they object?"

"Oh," Nancy shrugged, "Daddy thinks he's a playboy and that he drinks too much. And then the fact that he's been divorced. Well, he explained all that to me. It was one of those things when he was in college and it just lasted a short time — it could happen to anyone. Parents are so unreasonable!"

"I suppose we'll be that way when we're their age and have children of our own."

"I hope not. Anyway, Clint likes all the same things I like—"

"You mean horses?"

"Well, that's been my whole life ever since I can remember."

"Have you asked Doug to talk to them?"

"Listen to this: *they* had Doug talk to *me*. It was all very subtle. They thought it would be nice if Doug brought some of his college friends home for a weekend. Oh, Doug's on my side, but he's kind of caught in the middle."

"I hope it all works out for you, Nancy. I'm sure it will."

Nancy sighed. "I hope when I'm old like they are I won't have forgotten what it's like to be in love. They just can't understand."

The waiter came over with the French pastry cart.

"May I serve you some dessert, ladies?"

It all looked so good, Ardith thought. Chocolate rum cake, strawberry tarts, lemon chiffon pie . . .

"I will if you will," Nancy said.

"All right. I'll have a Napoleon."

"And I'll have . . . um . . . it's so hard to choose. . . I'll have a piece of lemon chiffon . . . no, a strawberry tart."

The waiter served them, looking as if he expected Nancy to change her mind again, and quickly rolled the cart on to the next table.

"Let's go down to Garfinckel's after lunch," Nancy said. "I have to find a dress to wear to your party."

Feathery white and gold chrysanthemums lined the paneled walls of the Sulgrave Club and festooned the glittering crystal chandeliers. The huge mirror in the ballroom was massed in green smilax and reflected the young couples dancing to the music of Meyer Davis. In their tulle and satin dresses the girls looked like gaily-colored butterflies as they whirled around the dance floor.

Little did they dream how soon it all would end.

At the top of the curving stairway Ardith and her mother greeted the guests as they arrived. Nearby, as usual, hovered Mrs. Matheson with a watchful eye. Guests were checked off on a list at the door, but there was still the chance of a crasher. Mrs. Matheson was peering suspiciously at someone now, but decided he passed inspection.

A tall dark man with a mustache was coming up the stairs. He was all alone and for a moment Ardith caught her breath. It couldn't be . . . no, he wouldn't come, and besides, she wasn't quite sure what he looked like now, she had only seen the photograph in her mother's dressing room and that was taken years ago. But she had had so much publicity, and wherever he was he must have seen it and known about her debut. How could he stay away all these years without even a card on her birthday?

She remembered a scene in a movie she had seen as a child with Mademoiselle. Mademoiselle loved movies, the sadder the better, and she saw all kinds of films. "Now don't tell your mother we saw this," Mademoiselle would threaten as they came out of a theatre when they were supposedly at the zoo. The movie was called *A Bill of Divorcement* and Katharine Hepburn was about to get married when the long lost father, John Barrymore, suddenly appeared on the scene. He had escaped from an insane asylum where he had been hidden by the family. She asked Mademoiselle all kinds of questions on the way home. "What is an asylum?" "Is that where my daddy is?"

"Of course not," Mademoiselle had answered crossly. "Stop asking such stupid questions. And do not tell anyone you saw this movie."

For months afterward it troubled her and there was no one she could ask about it.

Once she stood at the top of the pantry stairs and heard Mademoiselle and the French cook talking about her. Their voices were low and all she could make out was *"pauvre petite."*

Poor little one. Why did they feel sorry for her?

The tall dark man with the mustache was approaching. Her hands felt like ice in the satin muff covered with white camellias. She wanted to swallow and couldn't. And then she heard the butler announcing him:

"His Excellency, the Argentine Ambassador."

Of course. She should have known. But he looked so much like the photograph on her mother's dressing table.

Would she always be seeking him in every man?

Across the room Doug caught her eye and smiled. Doug loves me, she thought. I'm happy now. Why do I keep wondering about the past? It cannot touch me.

* * *

They had been for a walk in Rock Creek Park. It was a beautiful Sunday afternoon, cold but clear, and they were holding hands and laughing as they strolled along. They passed Henry Morgenthau's house on Belmont Road and noticed that his chauffeur was sitting in the car with the radio on and they heard something about Japanese planes. Then Mr. Morgenthau rushed out of the house carrying a briefcase and looking very solemn and they drove off.

"I wonder what that's all about?" Doug said. "He was in a hell of a hurry."

"Oh, probably another meeting with F.D.R. The Morgenthaus rented this house from friends of Mother's and he had a special line put in right away. A couple of weeks ago some people in the block were having tree work done and a large branch fell and knocked down all the telephone lines, including Mr. Morgenthau's private one to the White House. He was furious!"

They turned at Kalorama Circle and walked up the steps to Ardith's house.

"Do you think your mother will be surprised about us?" Doug asked.

"No, I kind of think she suspects something."

Grace Rodgers opened the front door.

"Mother, Doug and I would like to talk to you. We have something important to tell you. We—" Ardith stopped at the expression on her mother's face. "What is it? Is something wrong?"

Her mother was nervously twisting the pearls at her throat. "Oh, children, terrible news. It's just come over the radio. The Japanese have bombed Pearl Harbor."

Ardith looked at her in stunned silence.

"Half our fleet has been sunk," her mother went on. "They attacked without warning. We're at war." She looked as if she was in a state of shock. She had not thought that America would be drawn into it. "We're at war," she repeated in disbelief.

War. Ardith thought what the word meant. The horror, the fear, the dying. Of broken bodies on foreign battlefields, of bombed-out cities. Would they bomb Washington and New York the way they bombed London and Coventry?

She lay in bed looking out at the bare trees in the moonlight thinking she could hear the sound of planes. War. It was not real. It was something that belonged to another generation but not to hers. And now it had come.

When she was a little girl the Sunday papers had published pictures in the brown rotogravure section of the dead from World War I. "Lest we forget," read the caption. That was the war to end all wars, yet we were at war again. She remembered how she had tried to avoid looking at the pictures and had been drawn to them with horrified fascination. Afterward she was ill and couldn't eat her lunch.

There were pictures of dead bodies fallen at ChâteauThierry. Was one of them her uncle, the uncle she had never known, the one from whose death her grandfather had never recovered? "War always takes the best," her mother told her. Yet horrible as war was, there was something exciting and romantic about it. She used to read the poems of Rupert Brooke and Alan Seeger's "I have a Rendezvous with Death," and one she especially liked was "The Spires of Oxford." She thought of the words:

> I saw the spires of Oxford
>   As I was passing by,
> The gray spires of Oxford
>   Against the pearl-gray sky;
> My heart was with the Oxford men
>   Who went abroad to die.

And now our boys would be going abroad to die. Doug. No! she wanted to cry out. Not like those horrible pictures in the rotogravure section. But they weren't all killed. Many came back. Wounded. No, she would not think of that.

Only this afternoon they had been so happy. They had made plans for their future, they had laughed, while all the time fate was laughing at them and they did not know it. Now everything was uncertain. Any moment Doug might be drafted. Or else volunteer. He looked very serious when he left to go back to the University of Virginia.

"Maybe you won't be called right away," she said hopefully.

He had not answered. Already an ocean separated them. What a difference a few hours could make. I was too happy, she thought. It was all too perfect.

Now, perhaps he wouldn't want to get married. Or else wait until after the war was over, however many years that took. A sudden chill went through her. I don't want to wait that long, she thought.

She could see herself waiting for news from the front, waiting and wondering: Is he all right? For that was all that women could do. Wait.

Mademoiselle's fiancé was killed in World War I. It was hard to picture Mademoiselle as a young girl in a little French town, falling in love and waiting for the soldier who never came back. Mademoiselle had always looked like the typical, dried-up spinster, her hair drawn back in a knot, two deep furrows in her forehead between her heavy, unplucked brows, her mouth in a tight line. Yet once Mademoiselle had loved a man and he had loved her and they had plans and dreams together.

Just the way Doug and I have, she thought.

She got up and walked over to the window. There were a few stars in the sky. The air was frosty like snow. She felt hungry. She went down to the kitchen and poured herself a glass of milk and took some graham crackers from the cupboard. At Miss Putnam's they always put out milk and graham crackers for the girls at bedtime. It was one of the few pleasant memories she had of Miss Putnam's. Was it possible that was only a few years ago?

Everything she had known seemed far away and the future filled her with fear. She felt suspended in space.

She went back to her room and pulled the covers over her. But sleep was worse than being awake. She was crawling through long dark tunnels with no air and she could not see the end and she could not go back. And then she was walking across a desert and the sands were burning hot on her bare feet. She was wearing the white gown she had worn at her coming-out party at the Sulgrave Club and it was torn and blood-stained. She was carrying her muff with white camellias and they were brown around the edges and the sun was a red ball of fire and through parched lips she called, "Doug, Doug!"

But there was no reply.

On a distant sand dune she could see row after row of white crosses. She felt as if she couldn't walk another step. Then she heard the sound of planes. She looked up. They had swastikas painted on them. Bombs were exploding all around her. There was no place to run for cover. She threw herself on the ground. The sand was in her mouth and her eyes and her hair. She couldn't breathe. She was suffocating. . .

Her mother was sitting by her bed in her dressing gown. She looked worried.

"You were having a nightmare," she said. "Here's a fresh nightgown. You're wringing wet."

Ardith sat up in bed and stared straight ahead. She was shaking.

"It was just a bad dream," her mother said. "Everything's going to be all right."

CHAPTER THIRTY

She awoke with a throbbing headache. The sun was coming through the half-open Venetian blinds and she could hear the radio in her mother's room across the hall broadcasting the latest news. She propped herself up on one elbow and listened. It was not reassuring. Casualty lists were coming in from Pearl Harbor, President Roosevelt had asked Congress for a declaration of war and would speak later in the day, a stunned and angry nation was trying to pull itself together after the surprise attack.

She got dressed and went in her mother's room. Her mother had her coat and purse on the bed and appeared to have been up for hours. Usually she never arose before ten.

"Good morning, Mother."

"Oh, baby, I was going to have Carrie bring you a tray." She kissed Ardith on the cheek. "How do you feel? You look feverish."

"I'm all right. Are you going out?"

"Yes, Madge Breckinridge is picking me up in a few minutes and we're going down to Red Cross Headquarters. Everyone will be needed. We must all pitch in."

Ardith could picture Mrs. Breckinridge directing the war effort with great gusto. This was just her cup of tea.

Grace Rodgers put on her coat and picked up her purse and gloves. "Just to think that those horrid little Japs were having peace talks with Cordell Hull only a few weeks ago, when all the time they had this attack planned. And don't think Roosevelt didn't know about it! Madge Breckinridge told me—"

"Oh, Mother, Mrs. Breckinridge is a terrible gossip."

"Well, she lives right next door to the German military attaché and she told me when she phoned this morning that the lights have been burning at his house till all hours of the night the past week and they have been burning trash in their yard continuously."

"Does Mrs. Breckinridge spend all her time hanging out the window?"

"Ardith, you're being very unfair. She does a great deal of good around town. And she practically keeps the National Symphony going. But I think it's quite obvious if the Germans knew about this plan to attack Pearl Harbor, Roosevelt must have known and deliberately kept the information from our military leaders. Imagine having almost our entire fleet bottled up like sitting-ducks for the Japanese. It's just luck that they didn't get any of our aircraft carriers."

The doorbell rang.

"There's Madge. I'll see you later, baby." Grace Rodgers swept out with a determined air. It was the first time Ardith had noticed how much her mother resembled her grandfather.

She went down to the dining room and looked at the headlines in *The Washington Post* while she drank her orange juice. Carrie came in with scrambled eggs and bacon.

"Awful, ain't it, Miss Ardith?" she said, glancing at the newspapers. "All them poor boys killed. Lordy!" She shook her head.

Carrie had been with them for several years and was like a member of the family. They had gone back to having colored help after all the difficulties with the foreign ones. At one time they had a French cook and a German maid and Ardith had a marvelous time practicing her languages, but the two hated each other like poison. There were continual fights in the kitchen and the sound of pots and pans being thrown around, until her mother had to dismiss them both.

Then there was the Finnish butler-chauffeur. He had been with them for a brief time while Ardith was going to Miss Putnam's. She came home for vacation and a tall, handsome blond Finn opened the door. He looked like a movie star. A few weeks later her mother returned from luncheon with a friend and, thinking she had forgotten her key, rang the bell. No answer. She rang again. Finally she discovered the key in the bottom of her purse, went in, looked around for the handsome Finn, and found him. He was in the cellar, dead drunk.

She shook him until he opened his eyes and said two words that he had no difficulty understanding: "You're fired!"

His next position was at the Egyptian Embassy. One day, so it was told, the Egyptian Ambassador was called by the police.

"Your car is bring driven zig-zag down Massachusetts Avenue. Do you mind?"

Carrie came back with hot buttered toast.

"Your mother says she's going to work in a hospital," Carrie said, with a look of disbelief. "Be a nurse's aide or something."

Ardith couldn't imagine her mother as a nurse. For years she had served on the board of the Children's Convalescent Home, but she never went near the hospital. The sight of blood made her ill.

When she was eight Ardith had fallen in Rock Creek Park and a twig had pierced her leg. She remembered the scene in the bathroom afterward with her mother and Mademoiselle and how she had screamed in pain when they tried to pull out the twig.

"If you're going to carry on over a little thing like this, you'd better never have a baby," her mother said, and then seemed to be sorry she had spoken. Ardith found out later on that she had been a high forceps delivery and her mother had almost died. It filled her with guilt, even though it wasn't her fault, and she had a terrible fear of childbirth.

She finished her breakfast, wrote a letter to Doug, and walked to the mailbox on the corner to post it.

Everything looked the same as usual. But it isn't the same, she thought. We're at war. She looked up at the sky, half expecting to see Nazi bombers. She passed the house of the German military attaché and it looked very quiet with the blinds drawn. She wondered what they were thinking now. Frau Koester was a pretty blonde and there were twin girls with blonde braids and rosy cheeks. Ardith had always smiled and said hello when they passed on the street. Now they were the enemy, waiting to be interned somewhere for the duration of the war.

That house had a history of unpleasant events. When they first moved to Washington it was owned by the Wellers. Billy Weller was in her class at Potomac School and her mother became friends with the parents and often went to their home. One day Billy was not in school and there were mysterious rumors as to the reason.

When Ardith returned home after school Mademoiselle was wringing her hands and saying, "*Comme c'est terrible! Pauvre monsieur.*"

"What's terrible? What has happened?"

"Mr. Weller . . . he was found this morning hanging from a beam in the attic. He has killed himself. *Ah, mon dieu!*" Mademoiselle crossed herself.

Her mother had rushed over to comfort Mrs. Weller as soon as she heard the news. She was still there.

Why? Why had he done this and in this awful way? No one knew. She heard the servants whispering at the back stairs.

Finally, her mother came home. She looked drained.

Ardith rushed to her. "Mother, what happened? Why did Mr. Weller kill himself?"

Grace Rodgers threw Mademoiselle a withering look. What did you tell the child? her glance said.

Mademoiselle quickly went upstairs.

Mrs. Rodgers went in the living room and sank down on the green damask sofa. Ardith followed her.

"To think he tried to get money from me, too," she said. "But there was something about him I didn't trust. Something about his eyes. And his wife buying shoes at thirty dollars a pair in the midst of the Depression when everyone else was cutting down . . ."

"You mean Mr. Weller?"

"No, his best friend. He was swindled by his best friend, a stockbroker who took everything he had. Everything. He was left without a penny. And he tried to get my stocks, too. to invest."

"Who?" Ardith was puzzled. None of it made sense.

"Henry Curtis."

"You mean Jimmy Curtis's daddy?"

"Yes, that dreadful man! That crook!" Her mother's voice rose hysterically.

Jimmy Curtis had also been absent from school today. His daddy had caused Billy's daddy to kill himself. And he had tried to get her mother's money, too. She didn't see how anyone could do anything so awful. Robbers were bad men who stole and were put in jail, but not Mr. Curtis who was their friend and seemed so nice.

Her thoughts returned to the present. She looked again at the brick house where the Wellers had once lived. Do some houses bring bad luck to their occupants, she wondered, like the Hope Diamond, that brought tragedy to everyone who wore it? Or is it just chance?

A blind was raised and a small bewildered face peered out of an upstairs window. One of the Koester twins.

Now the enemy.

It's not your fault, poor little thing, she thought. I wonder what will happen to you? She walked quickly on.

"Mr. Vice President, and Mr. Speaker, and Members of the Senate and House of Representatives . . ."

Franklin Delano Roosevelt looked like a man who had not slept for the past twenty-four hours, Joe Kreskie thought, but the resonant voice was firm and unwavering.

"Yesterday, December 7, 1941 — a date which will live in infamy— the United States of America was suddenly and deliberately attacked by naval and air forces of the Empire of Japan."

Joe was in Pennsylvania when the attack on Pearl Harbor came, and he hurried back to Washington immediately for the special meeting of Congress.

"The attack yesterday on the Hawaiian Islands has caused severe damage to American naval and military forces," President Roosevelt continued. "I regret to tell you that very many American lives have been lost. In addition, American ships have been reported torpedoed on the high seas between San Francisco and Honolulu."

There was a pause. The President's face was grim. "Yesterday the Japanese Government also launched an attack against Malaya. Last night Japanese forces attacked Hong Kong. Last night Japanese forces attacked Guam. Last night Japanese forces attacked the Philippine Islands. Last night the Japanese attacked Midway Island."

Why had the military commanders been given no warning? Joe wondered. What was our intelligence doing that we could be caught this way with our pants down? He made a note to look into it.

"As Commander in Chief of the Army and Navy I have directed that all measures be taken for our defense."

A little late, Joe thought.

"No matter how long it may take us to overcome this premeditated invasion, the American people in their righteous might will win through to absolute victory."

Tremendous applause swept the hall.

"With confidence in our armed forces — with the unbounding determination of our people — we will gain the inevitable triumph — so help us God."

There was another burst of applause. President Roosevelt raised his hand.

"I ask that the Congress declare that since the unprovoked and dastardly attack by Japan on Sunday, December 7, 1941, a state of war has existed between the United States and the Japanese Empire."

Joe looked at his watch. The President's speech had taken exactly six and a half minutes.

The vote that followed was unanimous in the Senate and, with one exception, in the House. Representative Jeanette Rankin was the only dissenting voice.

War had been officially declared on Japan.

CHAPTER THIRTY-ONE

Grace Rodgers decided she would be more useful as a Gray Lady than a nurse's aide, especially when she found out the jobs a nurse's aide had to do—emptying bedpans and so forth. She took the course at the Red Cross and became chairman of the Gray Ladies at Walter Reed Hospital. In her gray cotton uniform and crisp white collar and cuffs and white starched cap with flowing gray veil, it was hard to recognize the woman who had lived for parties and social events. She was at the hospital every day from early morning till late afternoon. From ward to ward she went, doing what she could do to help the wounded.

Some of the boys they brought in were so young. If I'd had a son, she thought, as she sat beside the cot of a soldier whose eyes were bandaged, he might be this boy. I've lived through one war, why must there be another, this terrible suffering that goes on and on, is there no end to it? She was glad she had a daughter, yet her daughter loved a boy who any day would be going to war and perhaps return like these. It was all too horrible.

Just yesterday she'd had to write a letter for a boy to his fiancée telling her that both his legs were amputated. He wanted to break the engagement. A good-looking boy, only twenty-three. What plans they must have had . . . and now he felt his life was finished. It wasn't fair. But then, is life ever fair?

She thought how she had tried to protect Ardith. Maybe too much. It is impossible to protect anyone, she told herself. There is only one way to learn and that is by experience. My father tried to protect me and I was headstrong, too. But I couldn't bear to have Ardith suffer the way I did.

She looked at the boy with bandaged eyes. He would never see again.

He was talking about the farm in Iowa where he was raised. How in the spring . . . She couldn't bear it.

"You have a nice voice," he said. "Different from my mom's, but nice. Where are you from?"

"Pennsylvania." She had not thought of herself as being from Pennsylvania for a long time.

"Will you come back and see me tomorrow?" he asked.

"Yes," she said. "I'll be back."

Some of the nurses had fixed up a little Christmas tree in the ward and the choirboys from Saint Matthews were coming to sing carols later. It was starting to snow but it did not seem like Christmas.

Ardith had returned from the Blood Bank and was in the library reading the *Evening Star.* She still had on her blue cotton canteen uniform with the red cross on the pocket and *Volunteer,* sewn above it.

"Wake Island has fallen," she said, handing her mother the paper. "The Japanese have captured everyone." She looked worried. "Doug is thinking of enlisting," she said. Her lower lip trembled. "I think I'll take a hot bath before dinner." She got up and quickly left the room.

She appeared at the dinner table an hour later wearing a tweed skirt and cashmere sweater and looking more composed. Carrie brought in the soup.

"Cream of tomato? After working all afternoon at the Blood Bank? Honestly, I don't see how doctors can eat after operations," Ardith said.

"I see what you mean. But try and drink a little. It's hot and nourishing. How's everything going?"

"Oh, all right. I can make coffee in a fifty-gallon urn, but I don't know how to make it for two people." Ardith laughed. "And I've learned that men are more likely to faint after giving blood than women. Today I had given a husky truck driver a glass of orange juice and when I came back with his coffee a minute later, I couldn't find him. I finally looked under the table and there he was — stretched out cold! The head nurse said it happens all the time."

"The stronger sex."

"Yes, so they tell us. Anyway, I didn't faint. I decided not to look at the bottle and I couldn't feel a thing."

"You mean you gave blood?"

"Yes, when I finished working. They weighed me and asked if I'd had a cold recently and I said no and that I was in good health—"

"No wonder you look pale. You must go right to bed."

"Really, Mother, I'm fine. I didn't think I'd have the nerve to do it and it wasn't anything at all."

Carrie came back.

"Yes, thank you, Carrie, we're through with the soup. And could we have something other than tomato from now on?"

Doug came up to Washington the next day. Nancy had eloped with the man his family disapproved of and they were very upset.

"Mother's really taking it hard," he said. "I guess she thought it would break up, but when Nancy sets her mind on something there's no swaying her. I did my best to talk some sense into her. I found out some things about him around Middleburg that would make your hair curl, but Nancy said it was all a pack of lies and that people just didn't understand him." He shook his head. "I hope it works out."

Ardith noticed he had not said anything recently about their marriage plans. Had he decided against it now because of the war? Everything seemed so uncertain.

"I guess with all the furor about Nancy this isn't the time to enlist. I'll be drafted soon enough, anyhow."

"But they'll let you finish college, won't they?" That would give them until June and maybe the war would be over by then. No, she knew it would last a long time. Possibly ten years, some said. Ten years! I'll be old then, she thought. Twenty-eight. She saw herself as a spinster like Mademoiselle and the idea terrified her. Because she knew she would never love anyone but Doug. Never. They must get married right away. Now. Before anything happened.

"Who knows?" he said. "I could be called up tomorrow. He stroked her cheek with his fingertips. "This really throws a monkey wrench into all our plans, doesn't it?"

"How do you mean?"

"I couldn't marry you and then go off to war right away. It wouldn't be fair to you."

"But maybe you wouldn't have to go for a while." Maybe you wouldn't have to go at all, she thought. Maybe you could get a deferment as a medical student. No, she wouldn't respect him if he shirked his duty. She mustn't let him see how frightened she was.

"We'll play it by ear," he said. He kissed her. "You know I love you. I always will."

It's as if he's saying goodbye, she thought. Remember that if I never see you again, I'll always love you.

"Hold me close," she said, and her arms tightened around him.

From the library they heard the hall clock strike one, then two o'clock.

"I'd better go," he said. "And I almost forgot. I have something for you. It's in my overcoat."

He went out in the hall and returned with a small package wrapped in gold foil and tied with a green bow.

"Since tomorrow is Christmas Eve, I'll let you open it now," he said, smiling. "Besides, I want to see if it fits."

She unwrapped the package eagerly and gasped when she saw the emerald ring in an old-fashioned gold setting.

"Oh, how beautiful!"

"It belonged to my grandmother. I can have it reset in something more modern if you'd like."

"Oh, no. I love it just the way it is."

"Let me put it on." He took her left hand. "Perfect. It's as if it was made for you."

"Oh, Doug . . ." She threw her arms around him. "I'm so happy! In spite of the war, in spite of everything. Is that wrong? I always felt I didn't have the right to be happy. I do, don't I?"

"Of course. And we will be happy — in spite of the war."

She held her hand so that the moonlight coming through the window caught the emerald and it seemed to give off green sparks, and then the whole world shimmered in an emerald glow.

BOOK THREE

1942

CHAPTER THIRTY-TWO

In February, after Doug's twenty-first birthday, they announced their engagement. The wedding would take place in June after his graduation. But the Army did not intend to let him finish college. In March he was drafted and sent to Fort Benning, Georgia.

He was now a private in the infantry.

Ardith continued to work at the Blood Bank and wrote him every day. Bataan Peninsula fell and the "Death March" began. Stories of Japanese atrocities filled the newspapers. It now seemed incredible to her that at this time last year she was at The French School and planning her coming-out parties in Newport and Washington. So much had happened during that year.

She lived for the mail.

Darling, (Doug wrote)

I've been selected for Officer Candidate School. It appears they need more 2nd Lieutenants to replace the ones they've lost —(this was not a consoling thought) *anyway, the ninety-day course starts the first week in May and we get several days leave before so will see you then. Tried to call you the other evening but here was such a long line of guys waiting for the phone that I finally had to give up.*

Am writing this in the dark with a flashlight. Miss you terribly and wish we were together. It won't be long.

All my love, sweetheart,

Doug

She looked at the emerald ring on her finger and wondered about the woman who had worn it before . . . his grandmother . . . she had died when Doug was a small boy. What was her life like? Was she happy with his grandfather? Why did she always wonder about people so much? As a child she had once overheard an older person say that happiness was the acceptance of life as it is. But how could you accept what you did not know? She got out her blue notepaper with the silver monogram and started another letter to Doug.

It seemed strange to see him in uniform. His hair was cut much shorter and he had lost weight.

"Private Larimer reporting," he said, kissing her.

She wound her arms around his neck. "Oh, Doug, I've missed you so."

"Me, too."

For a few minutes they held each other without speaking. Then she stepped back. "Let me get a good look at you. I can't believe you're really here."

"I almost wasn't. They were going to cancel our leave, but the C.O. changed his mind and decided to give us a break."

"You're much thinner. Are they feeding you enough?"

"Oh, sure. But Fort Benning isn't exactly a country club." He grinned. "We don't have the chef of the Salle du Bois cooking our meals. But you can get used to anything."

She led him into the library.

"I thought we'd have dinner here at the house tonight. Carrie has roast beef with Yorkshire pudding and her special lemon meringue pie."

"Great. My mouth's watering already."

"Mother's working at Walter Reed Hospital. She should be home soon."

"How is your mother?"

"She's a changed person these days. You wouldn't know her, Doug. It's as if — well, as if she's finally found some purpose in life. You'll see."

"How's the Blood Bank?"

"Oh, fine. And I'm working at Red Cross Headquarters too. We serve lunch there for the officers stationed nearby, much more inexpensively than they could get in a restaurant. I can now prepare food for masses of people. And once a week we go in the mobile canteen to Fort Myer."

"I bet you look pretty cute in that Red Cross uniform."

"Doug . . . how long do you think the war will last?"

He shrugged. "Who knows?"

"Let's not listen to a radio or look at a newspaper for the next couple of days. Let's pretend the war doesn't exist."

"That's fine with me."

"I know it won't change things . . . but I want to be happy while you're here and not think about tomorrow. We have such a short time together and I've looked forward to it so much."

"So have I, sweetheart. I've counted the days."

"We're together again and it's spring and nothing else matters."

"Nothing else matters," he said.

But they both knew and it hung over them like a dark cloud. The scent of lilacs mingled with the smell of gunpowder. . . .

"Bring me the copies of those messages on Pearl Harbor, will you, Miss Flanagan? The ones to Admiral Kimmel and General Short."

Joe Kreskie frowned as he studied the reports again. There was something fishy about the whole thing, something that had been withheld from the commanding officers. And it appeared to come from high up. As high up as the White House? They had been strangely uncooperative about his investigation.

"There's a message to Admiral Block as well. Is it here?"

"The Commandant of Pearl Harbor?"

"Right."

"I'll get it."

Obviously Roosevelt expected war, knew, because we had broken the Japanese code, that an attack was imminent. Then why had he not alerted the military commanders at Pearl, leaving them unprepared? General Short had taken precautions only against sabotage and Admiral Kimmel had been given no information which would justify interrupting a very urgent training program.

And then came the attack.

AIR RAID ON PEARL HARBOR. THIS IS NOT DRILL.

Nineteen ships sunk or damaged, three thousand American lives lost. Among them was a boy from Oil City, a sailor on the *Arizona*. He had gone to school with his brother.

It could have been prevented. That was the thought that kept nagging him. Someone was covering up something, and he intended to find out just who it was and why.

*   *   *

The Stage Door Canteen opened in Washington and the local debutantes were recruited to be hostesses. Ardith had her picture taken with
Ann Garrett for the Sunday society section of the *Times-Herald* greeting
the servicemen as they arrived.

It was a new experience for her. She talked to boys whose backgrounds were totally different from hers, who came from towns all over
the country. Soon most of them would be going overseas. She danced with
boys from Pueblo, Colorado, and she learned that there was a Pittsburg,
Kansas. A sailor from Oklahoma taught her to jitterbug and a soldier from
Laramie, Wyoming, who was part Indian, gave her a small photo he
wanted her to have for good luck.

"Don't you have a girl?" she asked.

"No," he said. "I want you to have it." He was nineteen and had never
been away from Wyoming before. He was terribly homesick.

Their lives had been uprooted and they were all so brave. The same
ones were seldom there for very long, and when they did not come back,
she knew they had been shipped out. When she read the headlines she
wondered if any of the boys she had danced with and talked to were in any
of those battles. Especially the Marines. They were really having a tough
time in the Pacific and their casualties were very high.

She was glad that Doug had not joined the Marines, but the infantry
was almost as bad. She prayed that he wouldn't have to go overseas right
away and would be stationed at some Army post for a while. They planned
to be married in early August as soon as he finished Officers' Candidate
School.

He wrote of the rugged training they were having at Fort Benning, of
long marches through mosquito-infested Georgia swamps, of the unbearable heat and humidity. *Looks like they're preparing us for jungle
warfare*, his last letter said. They used live ammunition in the mock battles
and there had been several accidents. *It's the tough ones who survive*, he
wrote. *The more rugged the training, the better chance for all of us*.

No, war was not for the weak, she thought. Only the strong would
survive. And the lucky.

But Doug never appeared concerned about himself. "Don't worry,"
he'd say. "I'll come through. I've got too much to live for. I'll be an old
man someday boring our grandchildren with stories of what I did in the
war."

She had laughed at the thought of Doug as an elderly gentleman with a cane. Somehow she could not picture it.

"And you," he said, "will always be beautiful, with snow-white hair and a shawl . . . green, maybe, to match my ring, and your brown eyes will still have a twinkle. And we will always be in love. That is the one thing that will never change."

They were married on the sixth of August in the garden of the house on Kalorama Circle by Father Murphy from Saint Matthew's. Doug did not want to become a Catholic (his family had been Methodists from way back) but he signed papers saying that any children they had would be raised as Catholics.

Ardith wore an ivory lace gown with a mantilla and carried a bouquet of white roses and lilies-of-the-valley. In one hand she clasped her rosary with the white beads and silver crucifix. An old friend of her mother's gave her away.

It was a small wedding attended only by Doug's family and a few close friends. Nancy was matron of honor, her green organdy dress cut full in front to conceal the fact that she was pregnant, and she carried a sheath of pink roses. Ardith had heard that the marriage wasn't going too well, but Nancy was doing her best to appear happy.

Doug looked very handsome as he slipped the heavy gold wedding band on her finger. The afternoon sun glittered on the shiny new gold bars on his shoulders. Her mother dabbed her eyes with a handkerchief.

The priest murmured a benediction in Latin and motioned to Doug to kiss her. It was over.

Now I'm Mrs. Douglas Larimer, she thought. Forever and ever. Doug was smiling at her tenderly.

The butler passed champagne around on a silver tray and then they went in the dining room and cut the cake. I will never be happier than I am right this minute, she thought, as they posed for the typical picture of the bride feeding the groom the first piece of cake.

"For our grandchildren," Doug whispered, as the flashbulb exploded.

"Where are you going on your honeymoon?" one of the guests asked.

"You don't expect us to tell, do you?" Doug laughed.

CHAPTER THIRTY-THREE

They lay on the hammock listening to the sounds from the river. The croaking of frogs, oars splashing in the water, the chirping of crickets. Tall pines near the cottage rustled in the breeze and honeysuckle filled the air.

"Happy, darling?" Doug asked. His arms tightened around her.

"Completely."

A bird started to sing and another answered. Then another. Suddenly there was a symphony of birds' voices.

"Listen . . . they're serenading us."

A chipmunk darted across the moss-covered stone walk and stopped for a moment, then disappeared into the ferns.

"I love this time of evening," Ardith said. "Twilight . . . it's always seemed to me to be kind of enchanted somehow."

A hummingbird lit on the pink rhododendron bush and they watched him, as with wings fluttering, he drew honey from the flowers.

She felt drowsy and content. If only they could stay here forever. . .

That night she had the dream again. The awful dream. She awoke trembling. Doug was holding her and stroking her hair.

"What is it, sweetheart? Are you all right?"

"Hold me. Don't let me go."

"I'm right here."

"Keep me safe."

"What were you dreaming about?"

"It's all right now. Hold me close."

They had breakfast on the porch. It was bright and sunny, but chilly. A chipmunk sat on a large rock watching them.

"There's our friend," Doug said. He took a piece of bread and threw it to him.

"Isn't he cute?" Ardith said. "I always wanted one as a pet. But they do an awful lot of damage when they get in the cottage during the winter. They really have strong teeth."

"How do they get in?"

"Down the chimney." She poured Doug another cup of coffee. "One year they practically chewed up everything."

"Your Red Cross training has come in handy. This is mighty good coffee, ma'am."

"Thank you, sir."

"And I think I'll have some more of those blueberry flapjacks. We don't get them like that at Fort Benning."

She smiled. "I've been practicing. More coming up right away."

"Give me a kiss first." He pulled her to him.

"You'd better watch out. I may forget about the flapjacks."

"That's all right. They can wait."

Later, she said, "I'll pack a lunch and show you where we used to go on picnics when I was a little girl."

"All right. And I'll get my camera and take some pictures."

She put on blue jeans and a pink-checked shirt.

They walked up the path back of the cottage to the road. A toad was sitting on the path. Ardith shuddered and carefully stepped around him.

"He's harmless," Doug laughed. "Toads don't really give you warts. Old wives' tale."

"I know — but they're so repulsive. One day I was walking up this very same path carrying my favorite doll — she belonged to my mother and she had the most beautiful Dresden china face and long curls. Suddenly, from behind a tree, jumped my cousin Cordelia holding a horrid toad. She was laughing and she tried to put this toad on me, all the time screaming that I would get warts all over me. In trying to get away from her I tripped and dropped my doll. Her beautiful face lay smashed in a million pieces all over the path and I was inconsolable for days. My aunt punished Cordelia and bought me another doll, but she wasn't the same. I felt as if I'd lost my only friend."

They had reached the dirt road. Ardith pointed to another path leading up the hill.

"That goes all the way to the top," she said. "There's a big cave up there and my grandmother's maids used to tell me that a black grizzly bear was sleeping in the cave. I never dared look in the cave to see if it was true."

She started down the road.

"We're not going to have our picnic in the bear's cave, I gather," Doug said.

She shook her head and smiled. "We're going to Horse Creek."

"Is it far?"

"No. You go past the Boat Club and turn down another road until you hear oil pumps and then you come to a wooden bridge that goes over the creek. Then the woods get very dense and there are the picnic grounds." She glanced at Doug's camera. "I don't know if there's enough light in there to take pictures, but it's so beautiful and peaceful. You'll love it."

"Why did they name it Horse Creek?"

"Years ago the Seneca Indians used the creek as a watering place for their horses."

Goldenrod and Queen Anne's lace grew by the roadside and Ardith discovered a blackberry bush. She stopped and picked one of the berries.

"Um . . . they're ripe. Here, try one."

"Good."

"Let's pick some on the way home. I'll make a blackberry pie."

"You're spoiling me."

"I'm so glad we came here," she said. "This is the one place I was truly happy. I wanted to show it to you. All the rest—Newport and Washington and all that phony society world never seemed real to me. But this place is real. Here I'm myself. I feel part of nature and — oh, I don't know — at the center of things. Does that make sense?"

"It makes very good sense."

Ahead they could see the bridge and hear water bubbling over the rocks. There was a cluster of Black-eyed Susans and the sound of oil pumps and the buzzing of bees. Birds sang in the tall trees.

"To think that Indians used to roam these woods," she said. "Led by Chief Cornplanter. That was the original name of Oil City when it was a Seneca village less than a hundred years ago."

They stood on the bridge and looked at the rainbow patches of oil and small fish swimming in the green water. Black-and-yellow butterflies hovered above the wildflowers in the bright sunshine.

"This would be a good place to take some pictures," she said.

"Because it's very dark in the picnic grounds with just a few patches of sunlight coming through the trees."

"Fine." He adjusted the camera. "Why don't you lean against the rail —not too posed — great, that's perfect."

He took a few more shots and then they followed the path into the forest. Fallen leaves and pine needles crackled under their feet. The sound of rushing water and chirping of birds became louder.

"You're right, it is dark in here," Doug said.

The trees seemed to reach almost to the sky and only a few shafts of light penetrated the heavy foliage. Then they saw the long wooden picnic tables and benches and a stone barbecue.

"Let's put our things here," Ardith said.

They left the picnic basket and Doug's camera on a table and walked over to the creek.

Here it was open and the sunlight sparkled on the moss-covered rocks and water. At one place a log had fallen across the creek. There were still, quiet pools with tiny pebbles at the bottom and other places where waterfalls cascaded over rocks. Ferns grew along the edge.

"It's beautiful," Doug said.

"I feel as if time has stopped here," she said.

"Time has stopped," he said, drawing her to him.

CHAPTER THIRTY-FOUR

The next day they took a canoe and paddled up the river past the summer cottages. Green wooded hills rose on either side of the Allegheny and fluffy white clouds floated in a turquoise sky. Ardith lay back with her head on a cushion, one hand trailing in the water. She had unfastened the straps of her yellow bathing suit and was trying to get a suntan.

They rounded the river bend and there was the big overhanging rock that she remembered from her childhood and she saw the ripples in the water and felt her blood pound with the feeling of danger and a strange excitement.

Stay away from the rapids, she could hear her grandfather warning her.

The ominous roaring sound became louder. She started to say something to Doug, but he had read her thoughts.

"Don't worry," he said, "I'm an old hand at this. I didn't tell you about the time I was a counselor at a boys' camp in Maine, did I?"

"No. When was that?"

"The summer I was sixteen. We paddled all the way up Crooked River in a canoe. It was a whole day's trip and we pitched tents on the banks and cooked our dinner over a campfire. It was a great experience."

As he spoke he was steering the canoe to the other side of the river.

"We learned sailing and I'm an expert at lifesaving. Squalls would come up on Lake Sebago without any warning and I would have to rescue someone whose sailboat had overturned."

They had passed the rapids and the river was calm again.

"I've never been up this far before," Ardith said. She looked around. There were no cottages, just dense woods, with tall cattails and wildflowers growing along the river bank. They came to a small secluded cove.

"Let's pull in here," Doug said. "We can eat our lunch and take a swim afterward."

He tied up the canoe and Ardith took out the fried chicken and sandwiches and a thermos of lemonade. They sat on a large rock and spread out the lunch on a blanket. Pink and white butterflies fluttered in the sunshine and in a shallow pool there were tadpoles swimming around.

"I used to fish off our dock," Ardith said, "and one day I finally got a bite. I reeled in my line and there was a little bass wiggling on the hook. But he was too small and I had to throw him back." She laughed. "I never had the patience to fish after that."

"I used to go fishing with my dad," Doug said. "And if we have a son I'm going to take him fishing and hunting with me."

"Not hunting for rabbits or deer. I don't want him to do that." She looked horrified.

Doug smiled and patted her hand reassuringly.

"That's a long way off," he said.

Dark rain clouds had gathered in the sky.

"Looks like a storm coming," Doug said. "We'd better start back."

They gathered up the picnic basket and blanket and put them in the canoe. Ardith sat in front with a paddle and Doug got in the back and gave the canoe a shove. As soon as they left the shelter of the cove there was a stiff breeze. They paddled faster. The breeze was blowing them in the direction of the rapids.

"Keep paddling," Doug said. "Don't worry, we'll make it."

Lightning streaked across the sky and there was the rumble of thunder. The sky looked almost black. They passed the rapids and then they felt the first raindrops and another roar of thunder. Lightning crackled and the air was filled with electricity.

Her whole arm and shoulder felt stiff from paddling against the strong breeze. At times it seemed the canoe was going to tip over.

"Steady," Doug said. "At least we're going down river. We have the current with us."

She remembered tales she had heard as a child about the Allegheny. It was supposed to be one of the most treacherous of all rivers and the captains of the old steamer packets considered the Allegheny a feat of navigation. And here they were in a canoe.

They turned the bend and the cottages came in view. "We're almost there," Doug said. The rain was filling the canoe. "I'll keep paddling, you bail out the water."

"With what?" She looked around helplessly.

"Use the thermos." He laughed. "I see you were never a Girl Scout."

A golden prong of lightning lit up the dark gray sky. The rain was coming down in torrents.

She pushed a wet strand of hair out of her eyes. "It's filling up faster than I can bail it out."

"There's the dock. We can always swim for it."

She was amazed at his calmness. Storms had always terrified her. She remembered going to the circus once with Mademoiselle and there was a strong wind and the tent poles were swaying. She was afraid the whole tent would fall down on top of them. Mademoiselle had laughed at her.

A sudden gust of wind swept them toward the dock. Doug held out his paddle to keep the side of the canoe from being bashed against the cement and the paddle broke in two. He jumped out holding the rope and pulled Ardith with him.

"Run for it," he said. "I'll be right up."

He pulled the canoe out of the river and turned it over to empty out the water. Ardith dashed up the steps and ran up the slippery, moss-covered flagstone path to the cottage holding a towel over her dripping hair.

When Doug came in she was sitting in front of a fire in the living room drying her hair. Suddenly she sneezed. "Better take a hot shower," he said. "I'll put some coffee on and be right up."

After dinner she was looking through the books on a shelf near the windowseat and suddenly she exclaimed, almost to herself, "Why, it's still here!"

She looked at the mustard-colored cover with the brown camel caravan etched on it and slowly turned the yellowed pages.

"*Don't let us miss anything, tonight,*" he said. "*All my life is tonight. Tomorrow — who knows. . . .*"

She read on.

"*Let us forget everything, everything that we ever knew before Beni-Mora, Domini.*"

Doug came over and looked over her shoulder.

"What are you reading?" he asked. She handed him the book. "*The Garden of Allah.*" He glanced through it. "Published in 1904."

"I guess it was my grandmother's." Did this sad, lonely woman read this romantic desert tale, she wondered, as a kind of compensation while her busy husband left her alone to attend his many business affairs?

"I read this one summer when I was ten," Ardith said.

"Ten? You must have been pretty precocious."

"Oh, I didn't understand it really. But I loved the beautiful descriptions of the desert and it all seemed so romantic and mysterious. I remember wanting to change my name to Domini." She laughed. "In my daydreams I used to pretend I was Domini and imagine all kinds of scenes until they seemed almost real. I've never forgotten this book." She put it back on the shelf.

Doug put his arms around her. "What a strange, lonely little girl you must have been."

"Didn't you read adventure stories as a boy?"

"Oh, a few. We had to read *Call of the Wild* and *Moby Dick* in school, but mostly I was interested in sports. And then, I always wanted to be a doctor. I used to pore through medical books. The only novels I read were required reading for English lit classes."

Outside they could see the rain dripping on the ferns and rhododendron. Pine logs crackled in the huge fireplace.

"Let's toast marshmallows over the fire," she said.

"Fine. I'll put on some music."

He walked over and turned on the radio.

"A fierce battle is still raging in the Solomons. Imperial Headquarters in Tokyo claims that twenty-eight U.S. warships and transports have been sunk or damaged."

"U.S. Marines on Guadalcanal are meeting considerable resistance. . ."

He switched to another station.

"Nazis push British back in desert fighting. . ."

Ardith had returned from the kitchen with a box of marshmallows. She stood frozen on the spot, as if awakened from a lovely dream to face an unpleasant reality.

"It's all war news," he said.

"Then turn it off. I don't want to listen. We only have a few more days before we have to go back."

She went over to the fireplace and picked up a long stick and placed a marshmallow on the end. Doug knelt beside her with another stick and they turned the marshmallows slowly over the low red-gold flames.

It was as if she could see words written in the fire.

"You know that saying of the Arabs about forgetting everything in the desert?"
"Yes, Domini, I know it."
"How long shall we stay in this world of forgetfulness?"
"There's all I want here."
"Let us stay here."
"But some day we must go back, mustn't we?"
"Why?"
"Can anything be lifelong — even our honeymoon?"

And she thought how all lovers say the same things to each other. There are no new words. Will you love me forever? And forever fades, like a flower one has pressed between the pages of a book, and time moves on and then there are only memories. . . .

Suddenly she noticed that her marshmallow was burned to a crisp.

"Oh, darn! I'll try another."

"Here, take mine. It's just right. What's the matter? You're shivering. You didn't get a chill, did you?" Doug looked worried.

"No, I'm fine. Really." But she continued to tremble.

"I'll get you a sweater."

"No, I don't need one."

"Then what is it?" He put his arms around her. "You're like ice."

"I feel warm when you hold me. Keep me safe." She buried her head on his shoulder. "Oh, Doug, I love you so much. Don't ever leave me."

He kissed her hair. "I'll always be with you," he said. "Wherever I am."

The fire turned to embers and finally the rain stopped. In a far-off tree an owl hooted.

CHAPTER THIRTY-FIVE

She looked out the car window at the Pennsylvania countryside with its fields of corn and red barns and cows grazing in a meadow near a stream. It did not seem possible that they were on their way back. The week had passed so quickly.

"I'd better get some gas," Doug said.

He stopped at the next service station and pulled out his gas coupon book. "I won't be needing this at Fort Benning," he said. He was wearing his uniform again and he appeared like a different person.

"Fill her up, please," he said to the attendant, who looked about sixteen. The other was a man in his fifties. It turned out he was his father and eager to make conversation.

"We don't get as many folks by here since gas rationing started," he told Ardith as she drank a Coke. He glanced at Doug's shiny gold bars and infantry insignia. "Is your husband on his way overseas?"

The word sent a chill through her. "We don't know. He's awaiting orders. We're just returning from our honeymoon," she added, hoping this would shut him up.

"My older boy's on Guadalcanal. He's a Marine," he said proudly. "Just a minute, I'll show you his picture."

He returned with a snapshot of a Marine private. It was one of those taken in a photograph booth and was slightly blurred.

"He sent us this from San Diego," he said.

"He's very good-looking."

"Yeah. Takes after his old man." He grinned.

"Darling, we're ready," Doug called.

"All right. I'll be right there." She put the empty Coke bottle in the rack and turned to the man. "Goodbye," she said.

"Goodbye, little lady." He waved to Doug. "Good luck, Lieutenant."
They got back in the car.

"You were having quite a conversation," Doug said. "What was he telling you?"

"Oh, he was sweet. He was so anxious to talk to someone. His older son's on Guadalcanal. He showed me his picture. He didn't look more than eighteen."

"Poor bastards."

"Why do you say that?"

"They're really getting it from the Japs."

He pointed to the headlines in a newspaper he had just bought, and she realized that they hadn't even read a paper in almost a week.

She picked up the newspaper and read the front page. None of the news was good. "I wonder if your orders have come through," she said.

"We'll soon know."

They crossed the Pennsylvania state line and headed into Maryland. Two sailors with duffel bags were trying to thumb a ride. A truck ahead of them slowed down and picked them up.

"Maybe you'll be stationed in Washington for a while," she said hopefully.

Doug shook his head. "From the training they've been giving us at Benning, I don't think they're preparing us to sit around the War Department sharpening pencils."

"You want to go overseas, don't you?"

"It isn't a matter of wanting to or not wanting to," he said slowly. "It's something that has to be done. I couldn't sit at a soft desk job and let other men do my fighting. And I don't think you'd want me to."

"No." She looked out the window at the passing landscape. The war will be over eventually, she thought, and then we can be together all the time. I mustn't let him see how frightened I am. Nothing will happen to him. It can't.

He reached over and took her hand. "Don't worry. We'll have the rest of our lives together. That's a long time."

They could feel the sticky August heat as they approached Washington. There was not a breath of air and steam rose from the pavements, even though it was late afternoon.

"It sure hasn't cooled off in our absence," Doug said, as they turned down Massachusetts Avenue. People were trying to elbow their way into an already overcrowded bus. They looked tired and hot.

"At least the house is fairly cool," Ardith said. Her mother had insulated the attic with rock wool several years ago. "And we get the breeze from Rock Creek Park."

They came to Kalorama Circle and Doug pulled up in front of the house. "You go in and I'll put the car in the garage and bring in the bags," he said. They had decided to leave his car in Washington. Tonight he would be taking the train back to Fort Benning and she would be sleeping in her old room. Alone.

Grace Rodgers had heard the car and came running down the stairs. She was still in her Gray Ladies uniform. Carrie was at the door with a big grin.

They were so happy to see her and she felt a sense of desolation to be back.

"Darling, did you have a good time?" her mother asked, kissing her.

"Yes. Everything was perfect." She put her purse on the hall table. "Doug's coming up through the garage."

"What time is his train?"

"At nine."

"Then we'll have dinner at seven, Carrie."

"Yes, ma'am." Carrie went back to the kitchen.

"He'll have to allow plenty of time to get to Union Station and it's not always easy to get a taxi."

Doug appeared with the suitcases and tennis racquets. Somehow they had never gotten around to playing tennis.

"Hello, Mother Rodgers," he said, kissing her on the cheek. "I'll just take these upstairs."

"Fine. Put them in Ardith's room."

Ardith started up the stairs with him.

"Oh, children, some more wedding gifts came while you were gone. They're in the guest room."

As Doug put the suitcases down, Ardith looked around the room. Her mother had arranged fresh bouquets of flowers to welcome her home and suddenly she remembered how her mother always had flowers in her room when she returned from boarding school. She had always taken these things for granted. In fact, she had never paid any attention to the running of a house before, as if it ran itself. She saw now that her mother had always gone to a great deal of trouble to have everything nice for her.

Doug laid his jacket on a chair and loosened his tie. "I think I'll take a shower," he said. "What time's dinner?"

"Seven."

"Good. Then we don't have to go down right away."

Her mother was waiting for them in the living room. She had changed from her Gray Ladies uniform to a powder-blue linen with pearls and her blonde hair was pulled back in a chignon. She was sitting on the sofa under the Gainsborough portrait sipping an Old Fashioned and looking at the *Evening Star*.

"How about a drink before dinner?" she asked, putting down the newspaper.

"Fine," Doug said. "A Scotch-and-water would taste pretty good after that long drive. I'll fix it. What about you, darling?" He turned to Ardith.

"I'll have a little Dubonnet, please."

"Mother Rodgers, can I fix you another?"

"Well . . ." She hesitated, then held out her glass. "Just sweeten this a little, please."

Doug walked over to the bar.

"The flowers in my room are so pretty, Mother," Ardith said.

Grace Rodgers looked pleased. "I'm glad you like them, dear. There isn't much in the garden right now."

Ardith noticed white gladioli in a tall silver vase on the piano and yellow roses on the coffee table. Her mother must have gotten up very early to arrange them.

Doug came back with the drinks.

"Thank you, Doug." Her mother raised her glass. "To many happy years."

Carrie came in and announced dinner.

"Let's just take our drinks in to the table."

Kirk's repoussé and crystal gleamed on the Belgian lace tablecloth and the centerpiece was an epergne of silver and cranberry glass filled with white roses, green grapes, and trailing ivy.

Carrie brought in chilled cups of vichyssoise, followed by a tossed salad with Roquefort dressing, roast beef with Yorkshire pudding (Doug's favorite), small green peas with onions, and a chocolate soufflé for dessert.

"This is delicious, Carrie," Doug said. "We could use you at Fort Benning."

A broad grin spread across her black face. "Thank you, Mistah Doug. I'll teach Miss Ardith how to make that soufflé for you."

"Yes, I'll have lots of time to practice my cooking this week."

"She's getting pretty good," Doug said loyally.

"Well, I'm improving, anyway," Ardith laughed. "A month ago I didn't know how to boil water."

The grandfather clock in the entrance hall chimed.

"I've ordered your cab for eight," Grace Rodgers said. "That should give you plenty of time."

They went back to the living room and Carrie served coffee.

"I'll put my suitcase by the front door," Doug said. Ardith watched him leave the room. Keep smiling, she told herself. Save the tears for afterward.

She poured herself another cup of coffee and put cream and sugar in it. The doorbell rang.

"Taxi's here, ma'am," Carrie announced.

"He's early," Ardith said.

"Tell him to wait, Carrie," Grace Rodgers said. "They're very independent these days."

Doug came downstairs and she said goodbye and tactfully left them alone.

Doug held Ardith close. "Goodbye, sweetheart. I'll call you as soon as I know my orders. Take care."

"Don't worry about me. I'll be fine," she said brightly. "I'll learn all kinds of delicious dishes to cook for you and I can finish all my thank-you notes. Oh . . . we forgot to open the presents that came while we were away. I'll do that tomorrow."

The taxi honked. Over Doug's shoulder she could see the driver sitting there with the door open and the meter running.

"I'd better go." He kissed her again.

"Yes. Goodbye, darling."

And she watched him walk down the front steps and get in the white cab with the red diamonds painted on the doors. She stood there waving until the taxi disappeared from sight.

CHAPTER THIRTY-SIX

She found it difficult to keep her mind on her thank-you notes. *Dear Mrs. Breckinridge,* she wrote in her round Miss Putnam's finishing school script, *The beautiful silver chafing dish that you sent us...*

She stopped and gazed out the window. From her desk she could see clouds lazily drifting across the tree tops in Rock Creek Park and hear birds chirping. She wondered what Doug was doing right now. It had seemed so strange not to find him next to her when she awoke this morning. They had been apart less than a day and already she missed him unbearably.

Well, back to the thank you notes. It was so difficult to find something different to say to each person. She looked at what she had written. That wasn't very original. Let's see . . . she thought a minute . . . *I know that my shrimp remoulade will taste much better in your beautiful silver chafing dish* . . . no. She sighed.

Her mother tapped on her door. She was in her uniform.

"I'm off, dear," she said. "Oh, good, you're getting at your notes. They don't have to be long but it's so important to be prompt. I think it's perfectly awful the way some of these brides don't even bother to thank you at all these days! I ran into Courtney Ellis's mother the other day at Camelier and Buckley and I said, 'Did Courtney ever receive the silver tray?' She was married over six months ago, you know, and she should have had plenty of time, but I haven't heard a word from her and the store said they delivered the tray. 'Why yes, my dear,' Mrs. Ellis said, 'and she just loves it. Hasn't she written you? I must speak to her about it.' Then she laughed and said something about 'these young people.' Frankly, I think it's inexcusably rude." Grace Rodgers shook her head. "I'd better go. Just let Carrie know what you'd like for lunch."

"Fine, Mother, I will."

"Fine, Mother, I will."

Ardith crumpled up the note and started again.

Dear Mrs. Breckinridge, she wrote, *I am so thrilled with the perfectly beautiful silver chafing dish and I know that Doug and I will enjoy...*

When will we enjoy it? When the war is over and we finally have our own home? How many years from now? She could picture herself traipsing down to Fort Benning with a silver chafing dish. No, she thought, I won't think about that. I'll imagine how lovely it will look in our own dining room in our house in the country. We'll entertain our friends on the weekends and have delicious buffet suppers and the children will come down in their pajamas looking like little angels to say goodnight.

I'll get a scrapbook, she thought, and cut out pictures of rooms I like from *House & Garden* and different magazines and plan our house. And I'll collect recipes in another scrapbook. The idea gave her a feeling of great exhilaration. She could hardly wait to look through some of those home magazines that she had never paid any attention to in the past.

She finished her note to Mrs. Breckinridge and checked her off. Then she looked at the next name in the wedding book. The Venezuelan Ambassador and Senora Perez: crystal bowl. She took out another sheet of monogrammed paper and started to write. Before she realized it the morning had passed.

After lunch she decided to take a walk. She took her letters and posted them in the mailbox on the corner. Across the street was the 18th Century house that had been transported from New England. Even the old wallpaper had been taken off and put back again. She remembered watching in awe when the house was moved in and it was quite a conversation piece in the neighborhood. She had never been inside but she was told it was like a museum filled with priceless antiques. The only trouble was that the house belonged in New England with property around it and not squeezed into a small corner lot. It must have cost the owner a fortune to have it moved and it was in completely the wrong setting.

Like some people, she thought.

She walked on up Kalorama Road past the big stone château that was the French Embassy. On the opposite corner was the old Siamese Legation, and on her promenades with Mademoiselle she remembered being fascinated by the children with slanting eyes that she glimpsed playing in the gardens.

"Are they Siamese twins? Why aren't they joined together?" she had asked.

She came to Connecticut Avenue with its large apartment buildings and walked down the hill past Saint Margaret's Church in the direction of the shops. She browsed slowly along looking in the shop windows. At Dupont Circle she turned and started back up Massachusetts Avenue. She passed the embassies and the large homes and she remembered the time the Austrian Embassy caught fire and the excitement of watching the fire trucks and the firemen with hoses and long ladders and the red flames coming out of the roof. It was the first fire she had ever seen.

She continued past Sheridan Circle, the Egyptian Embassy, and the Venezuelan Embassy, with its white marble sparkling in the August sunshine, which she still thought the most beautiful embassy of all.

At Belmont Road she turned and was glad for a slight breeze from Rock Creek Park. She glanced at the house that had been occupied by the German military attaché and his family. The week after Pearl Harbor, a large moving van appeared and they were moved to White Sulphur Springs for the duration. Some new people had the house now, but she hadn't met them.

On the next corner was the house where the old witch lived, or that was what the children in the neighborhood used to call her. She was an elderly widow who lived all alone and screamed at anyone who set foot on her lawn. She was always out front sweeping leaves off her walk with a broom. Once Raffles had lifted his leg on one of her azalea bushes and she chased him away waving the broom and yelling words Ardith had never heard before.

Old Lady MacDougal, that was her name. She had a gray cat and one Halloween some boys in the neighborhood soaped up her windows and tied tin cans to the cat's tail.

She could feel sorry for her now, Ardith thought. Poor old recluse, hating the world and everyone in it, except her cat. But as a child she had been scared to death of her.

She missed Raffles. She remembered the hours she used to spend talking to him and he would cock his head on one side as if he understood. Last year the vet said it would be more merciful to put him to sleep. He was fourteen years old, half blind, and could scarcely walk. She had suggested to her mother that they get another dog.

"Oh, dear, I don't want to go through all that again," her mother said. "You get so attached to them."

She was back at Kalorama Circle and she walked up the front steps and went in the house. From the library she collected all the copies she could find of *House Beautiful, Ladies' Home Journal, House & Garden,* and *Good Housekeeping* and took them up to her room. She lay on her bed and slowly poured over them, cutting out pictures of rooms that she liked and every now and then a recipe that looked tempting.

The cover of *Good Housekeeping* had a photograph of an adorable rosy-cheeked baby and she tore it off and put it with her clippings. She wondered what a child of theirs would look like. If she had a baby she wouldn't be so lonely when Doug went overseas, and she was almost certain that he would have to go. They had talked about having children, but not right away. Especially if she had to follow him around to different Army posts. Everything was so uncertain these days.

She picked up another magazine. There was a poem that seemed to reflect the times they were living in. It spoke of lovers parted in their youth, their songs silenced, their worlds cut separate by a sea. She looked at the author's name. A woman. It would have to be a woman, she thought, because a man did not feel this way. To him a battle was an adventure and all his life he prepared for it. The small boy playing with toy soldiers and guns, while a girl played with dolls.

The poem told of the feelings of all women in wartime. The waiting under station clocks. The loneliness. The lamp in the window. The waiting.

She read the final lines:

Thus from my world, which knew your touch and breath
You are not gone . . . in war . . . or even death.

Doug called that evening from Fort Benning. Long distance had a different ring and she rushed eagerly to the phone.

"Hello, sweetheart." His voice seemed muffled.

"Darling . . ." There was a buzzing on the line. "I can scarcely hear you."

"Hello . . . hello . . . operator . . ." Doug's voice faded out.

The operator cut in. "Ma'am, would you hang up please, and ah'll try to put this call through again." She had a thick Southern drawl and whether the call got through tonight or next week appeared to make little difference to her.

Ardith hung up the receiver and waited. In a few minutes the phone rang again. This time the connection was better.

"Finally," Doug said. "Can you hear me now?"

"Yes, fine. How are you, darling?"

"Oh, all right, I guess. I didn't get much sleep on that damn train. They were standing in the aisles."

"Did you get your orders?"

"We go on maneuvers around here in a few days. Some new games the general wants us to learn. That's all they've told us."

"But when can I come down and join you?"

There was a pause. "Sweetheart, there's no decent place for you to stay, and if you did come down you'd hardly see me, anyway."

"But I want to be with you."

"I want to be with you, too. But you'd only see me for a few hours a week."

"That would be better than nothing. I don't care what it's like there, just so we're together."

"Let's see what happens after these maneuvers are over." He changed the subject. "What did you do today?"

"Oh . . . I wrote some thank-you notes and took a walk and missed you horribly."

"I miss you, too." There was a click on the line. "Look, darling, I wish we could talk longer, but other guys are waiting for the phone. I'll write you. Take care."

She felt more dejected after the phone call than before. Somehow she had hoped that Doug would have found living quarters for them and that she could join him right away. Now it looked as if it would be several weeks before they saw each other. At this point that was an eternity.

He had been distant over the phone, too. But then, he was never one to carry on lengthy phone conversations, she reminded herself, and besides, he'd mentioned that other men were waiting, probably within earshot.

Tomorrow she would start working at the Blood Bank again and just keep herself busy. Then the weeks would pass faster.

CHAPTER THIRTY-SEVEN

"Is something the matter?" Joe Kreskie asked. His secretary looked as if she had been crying. "If there's anything I can do—"

Helen Flanagan took out a handkerchief and blew her nose. "I'm sorry. It's just that I'm so worried about my fiancé. I haven't heard anything from him for several weeks."

"What ship did you tell me he was on?"

"He's on an aircraft carrier. The *Hornet*."

The *Hornet* was in the Pacific somewhere off Guadalcanal. He tried to sound cheerful. "You know what they say about no news being good news."

"I keep telling myself that, but it doesn't do any good."

He had heard something about the *Hornet* on the radio this morning. "I'm sure you'll be getting a letter from him any day now," he said.

She brightened a little. "Do you think so?"

"You'll probably get several letters together."

"I hope so."

"In the meantime, if you'd like, I'll see what I can find out about the *Hornet*."

"Oh, would you? I'd appreciate it so much. I can't help worrying when I don't hear from him. I know it's silly, but—"

"Now, let's get to work. Have you typed up that speech I'm giving in Pittsburgh tomorrow?" He was in the final weeks of his campaign for senator and his opponent was starting to hit below the belt. He'd have to get tough if he hoped to win.

"Go in there and play fair and square," his football coach used to tell them before every game. "And win for Notre Dame."

The rules were clear in sports, but politics was another game. It was a dirty business and the higher you got, the bigger target you made. You started out with ideals, but it was hard to hang on to them. Someone was always out to knife you.

"Dirty Polack!"

"You ain't got no father!"

"Bastard!"

For a moment he was ten-year-old Joe Krzyzynski again, dodging stones and snowballs on his way home from school. He winced at the memory.

He had a clean record and he intended to keep it that way. He'd made no deals. But he saw the temptations and he wondered if he would be able to hold out. Power corrupts.

And he wanted power.

"I'm Mrs. Larimer," Ardith said to the nurse at the desk. "I have an appointment with Doctor Bradley at eleven."

"Just sign your name here." The nurse indicated a pad with a list of names. "Doctor Bradley will be a little late. He had an unexpected delivery." The telephone was ringing. "Excuse me." She reached for the phone. "Doctor Bradley's office . . . No, Doctor's at the hospital, but I expect him shortly . . . Yes . . . I see. Well he should be walking in here any minute. I'll have him call you." She hung up the phone and sighed wearily. It promptly rang again. "Doctor Bradley's office. . ."

Ardith looked around the waiting room. It was filled with women in various degrees of pregnancy. A wan-looking girl with large frightened eyes and stringy, mouse-brown hair pulled back with a ribbon nervously twisted her shiny wedding ring. She wore a print smock and a tan corduroy skirt with a cut-out for her bulging stomach. Her legs looked like sticks and she had on scuffed brown loafers.

Across from her was another woman, quite overweight, with cheeks like a chipmunk and wiry red hair. She wore a purple smock and her ankles looked swollen. Next to her was a small boy in blue jeans licking a green lollipop and at her feet a toddler played with a toy truck. Both had flaming red hair.

Ardith smiled at them and sat down on the sofa next to the little boy with the lollipop. He stared solemnly at her. "Hello," she said. She picked up a copy of the *New Yorker* from the table and noticed that it was three months old.

The little boy moved closer to her and continued to stare.

"Now, Davy," his mother said, "don't get that sticky lollipop on the lady's dress."

"Oh, that's all right," Ardith said. "How old is he?"

"Three last week." She pointed to the one crawling on the floor. He was about to empty the ashtray on the carpet. "Bobby is sixteen months." There was a crash as he pulled a lamp over.

His mother rushed to him. "Oh, bad lamp! Did it hurt Bobby?"

Bobby started howling at the top of his lungs and the nurse came over and put the lamp back on the table.

Two more women came in and signed the book. The phone rang again. "Doctor Bradley's office . . . Excuse me, I can't hear you," the nurse said, glaring at Bobby.

"Bobby, stop it!" his mother said. "You're not hurt. Here, play with your truck." She handed him a small yellow truck which he promptly threw at his brother, just missing a seascape on the wall above the sofa.

"Yes . . . and how far apart did you say the pains were?" the nurse asked the voice on the phone.

"If I don't have a girl this time," Bobby and Davy's mother said, "I'll commit hara-kiri." She rubbed her ankles.

"I want to go to the bathroom," Davy announced.

"Can't you wait till we get home?"

"No."

"Oh, dear. Well, come on." She turned to Ardith. "Would you mind watching Bobby for me while we go down the hall?"

"Not at all." Ardith smiled pleasantly at Bobby who had grabbed the *Saturday Evening Post* and ripped the cover off. Are all children like this? she thought in horror. "Come here, Bobby," she said. She picked him up and started to show him the pictures in a magazine.

The girl with the mouse-colored hair continued to twist her wedding ring. I *am* married, she seemed to be saying. See.

Another woman waddled in. The two arrivals before her looked surprised to see her. "Not yet?" they asked in unison.

"Nope. I think I'll go home and scrub the kitchen floor or something. This is getting to be a bore." She glanced at a magazine. "One of the things I like about coming here is that Doctor Bradley always has the latest magazines. I read this one last spring." She lowered herself with difficulty into a chair. "I've said it before but this time I mean it. This is my last."

"Oh, come on, Ethel, you'll be back here again next year."

"Not on your life!"

"If I had babies as easily as you do I wouldn't mind, but I was in labor over twenty hours with my last."

Ardith looked up from the magazine she was showing to Bobby.

"A breech," the woman went on with relish. "If men had to have them it would be a different story. All they do is pass around the cigars afterward and listen to congratulations. For what, I'd like to know?"

The red-haired woman came back with Davy. "Thank you so much," she said. "I hope he wasn't any trouble." She took Bobby on her lap and gave him a kiss. At this Davy reached out and punched his brother on the jaw.

The nurse was on the phone again. "Just a minute," she said, "I think I hear Doctor Bradley coming now."

The hall door opened and Doctor Bradley walked into his office and sat down at his desk. The nurse handed him a sheaf of messages. "And Mrs. McKosker is on the line," she said. "She insists it's urgent." The office door closed and the nurse came out. "You may go in one of the treatment rooms," she said to the girl with the mouse-brown hair. "And Mrs. Gilpin—" She turned to the mother of Davy and Bobby, "You may go in the other one. Just a second — have we weighed you?"

"Oh dear," Mrs. Gilpin giggled, "I hoped we could skip that today." She got on the scales apprehensively. "I really have been trying not to eat —but the children make me so nervous."

The nurse frowned and wrote something on a pad.

"I want to go home," Davy said. He yanked Bobby's hair.

"Now, boys, be good. Mother's almost through."

The nurse turned to Ardith. "Mrs. Larimer, I believe you wanted to talk to Doctor Bradley first?"

"Yes, please."

"You may go in his office now."

Doctor Bradley was close to sixty with a ruddy complexion, twinkling blue eyes, and a shock of white hair. Ardith had gone to Potomac School with his daughter Lucy.

He rose as she entered and reached across the desk and shook her hand. "Ardith," he said. "What a pleasant surprise. How's your mother?"

"Mother's fine, thank you. Busy working at Walter Reed as a Gray Lady." She glanced in the direction of the outer office. "And I see your business is booming."

Doctor Bradley smiled. "Always. I had a young doctor as my assistant but the Navy took him last month." The phone rang. "There's no let-up. Excuse me."

She looked out the window while he talked. A streetcar clanged down Connecticut Avenue. On the corner a newsboy was shouting: "Extra! Aircraft carrier *Hornet* sunk in Pacific! Extra! Read all about it!"

Doctor Bradley hung up the phone. "These women are all so afraid they're not going to get to the hospital in time just because they've read about some woman having her baby in a taxi. Well now, what can I do for you?"

"I think you have another patient. At least I'm pretty sure I'm pregnant."

Doctor Bradley looked at her card. "We'll soon find out," he said.

The treatment room was a sterile white with a short table with stirrups and a sink and a table covered with frightening-looking instruments. Doctor Bradley entered followed by the nurse and washed his hands and pulled on rubber gloves. The nurse handed him one of the instruments.

"I suddenly remembered a previous engagement," Ardith said, half-rising from the table.

"This won't hurt, child," Doctor Bradley said. The nurse took the cap off a tube of ointment. Somewhere she had heard that a nurse was always present during examinations to protect the doctor from being accused of improper conduct. She couldn't imagine anyone trying to seduce old Doctor Bradley, who looked more like Santa Claus than Don Juan.

"How's Lucy?" she asked. Lucy was Doctor Bradley's only child and the joy of his life. He had been past forty when she was born. His wife had been an invalid for a number of years and there were rumors that she was dying of cancer.

"Lucy's in San Francisco, but her husband is due to be shipped out any day now, so she should be home before long. You two girls must get together."

"Fine. I'd like to see her."

"Where's Doug now?"

"In Georgia, at Fort Benning. Ouch!"

"Just relax, child. I'm almost finished." Doctor Bradley handed the instruments back to the nurse. "I'd say you're right, but we'll know for sure when we get the test back from the lab. Call us in a week. In the meantime, get plenty of fresh air and exercise. Do you like to walk?"

"Yes."

"Good. I'll prescribe some vitamins and I'm very strict about weight —I don't want you to gain more than twenty pounds. It's easier to keep it off in the beginning. I say that to all my patients, but no matter what you tell some of these fool women, they can't wait to leave my office and dash to the nearest drugstore for a malt." He shook his head in disgust. "Anyway, I know you have more sense." He held out his hand to her and smiled. She noticed how tired he looked. "Goodbye, child."

And he was gone.

She got dressed and picked up the prescription he had written for her at the nurse's desk. Two women were staring at her and one whispered something to the other.

"Don't you know who she is?" Ardith heard her say to her friend. "She's that debutante—you know, the one whose picture's been in all the papers and on the cover of *Life*. She's . . ." The rest was garbled.

They both looked her over from head to toe as she passed.

As she closed the door she heard the voice say, "I suppose *she'll* have her maternity clothes designed by Hattie Carnegie."

She walked quickly down the hall in the direction of the pharmacy, stunned by the hostility in the voice. She had not thought of herself as a debutante for a long time.

CHAPTER THIRTY-EIGHT

There was a letter from Doug on the entrance hall table when she returned home. She ripped it open eagerly. All leaves had been cancelled, he wrote. It looked ominous. She read on. If she didn't hear from him for a while she was not to worry. He would let her know as soon as he could where to write. He loved her.

It was short and appeared to have been written in great haste. He's on his way overseas, her intuition said, and she was paralyzed by a nameless fear. She read the letter over again, trying to read between the lines.

Now there was nothing to do but wait.

She went up to her room and lay down on the bed. Waves of nausea swept over her. The pattern of the chintz curtains danced before her eyes. The birds' chirping made her want to scream. She pressed her face into the coolness of the pillow with its faint scent of lavender. She had the sensation of being whirled around in the rapids. Cool and quiet. Cool green hills. Cool blue water. If only the throbbing would stop.

She staggered into the bathroom and wet a towel with cold water and put it on her forehead. Then she lay down again and tried to picture the tall pines in the Pennsylvania woods rustling in the breeze and hear the waters of Horse Creek bubbling over the rocks.

A fire engine shrieked up Massachusetts Avenue. Next door the dog started howling. More sirens followed.

She put the pillow over her head, but that made her feel as if she were going to suffocate. Carrie knocked on the door. "Lunch is ready," she announced.

"Come in," Ardith said weakly.

Carrie peered at Ardith lying on the bed. "Chile, you look mighty poorly. Looks like you need a doctor."

"I'll be all right." If only this awful nausea would pass. I hope it doesn't last for the entire nine months, she thought.

"How about some nice broth and crackers?" Carrie asked. "That would be good for you."

"Thank you, Carrie, but I don't think I could keep anything down right now. Maybe a little later. But there is something I would like — could I have some cracked ice in a towel, please?"

"I'll bring you some right away, Miss Ardith." Carrie went out shaking her head. Ardith could hear her heavy steps on the back stairs and the pantry door closing.

She turned on her other side and stared at the tinted engraving of "Miranda" by John Hoppner on the wall beside her bed. Miranda stood next to a cliff with the angry waves at her feet, her white robe and cerise cloak billowing in the breeze. There was a blue ribbon in her long, tangled dark hair that matched her blue sash and the blue of her eyes, and one arm was outstretched imploringly.

Ardith thought of the many weeks she had lain prisoner in this bed with bronchitis during the winter months of her childhood, covered with mustard plasters and coughing and gasping for breath, and now whenever she looked at the picture of Miranda it gave her a tightening in her chest. She turned and looked at her mahogany bureau on the other side of the room with the lace runner and set of Kirk's repoussé that had belonged to her grandmother and the photograph of Doug in his uniform and beside it her wedding picture in a silver monogrammed frame.

"Doug," she whispered, "where are you?"

And she cursed the war that had torn him from her, the war that would keep them apart for months, or even years. He should be with her now when she needed him, when she felt sick and frightened and lost, and instead he was on a troopship going farther and farther away with every passing minute. She didn't even know where to write to him. He didn't even know about the baby. She would have to tell him in a letter. She had looked forward to telling him when they were together, when he was holding her, when she could see the happy expression in his eyes . . . and she was sure he would be happy about it, even though he had once said that they should wait a few years before starting a family. It was better to have children when you were young, she thought, and have them grow up with you, to enjoy doing things together as a family, all the things that had been lacking in her own childhood. Her children would never know the loneliness she had known because there would be so much love and warmth in their home.

"I'll always be with you," Doug had said. She would just have to imagine that he was beside her through all the lonely months ahead. People could do that, she had read somewhere. They could send thoughts to each other across oceans. But as a child she had sent thoughts to a man who was far away and he had not heard her calling him, he had not come when she wanted him. All her life she had gone through things alone. Was this the pattern of her life?

She walked over to the bureau and took Doug's picture and put it on the pillow beside her.

Several days later a letter finally came with a return address c/o Postmaster, New York. There was no indication of where he might be. He spoke of how much he loved and missed her, he thought of her constantly and hoped she was keeping busy because that would make the time pass faster until they were together again.

She wrote him every day and lived for the mail. October turned into November, and with the cold weather she felt better. She decided to wait a few months to tell him about the baby so he wouldn't worry about her. It wasn't due until early May, so Christmas would be soon enough to break the news.

During the first week of November there was a call from Doug's former roommate at the University of Virginia, the "bacon heir." He was in Washington for a few days and would like to take her out to dinner.

She was somewhat hesitant, knowing Chuck's reputation with women, but after all, he was Doug's friend and would respect her status as his wife. It was boring sitting in the house night after night and she was sure Doug wouldn't mind, and besides, it would seem most inhospitable of her not to at least offer Chuck a drink at her house. Maybe she could find one of her unmarried friends to introduce him to. No doubt that was what he hoped in calling her.

During dinner at La Salle du Bois she was sorry she had accepted Chuck's invitation. She had forgotten the way he had of looking at every woman as if he were mentally undressing her.

"Doug sure is a lucky guy to have gotten you," he said, staring at her neckline.

Her dresses were getting tighter on top, and while the black dress she was wearing would certainly not be considered décolleté, she suddenly wished she had worn something else.

"I certainly miss him," she said.

"You must." He moved closer, never taking his eyes from her. She remembered something Doug had once told her about some men who couldn't even walk in a bank to cash a check without making a play for the cashier. "Like Chuck?" she had suggested. Doug had laughed. He seemed to find Chuck's escapades amusing. "All these girls fall in love with Chuck," he had said. "I've watched him at parties concentrate on a certain girl across the room and he never failed to score."

"God, but you're beautiful," Chuck said. He touched her knee, then quickly withdrew his hand at her icy look. "Sorry, I couldn't help myself. Forgive me?" He had a hurt, little-boy expression. Maybe that was what he played on — the maternal impulse in women. He was of average height and skinny with narrow shoulders and a concave chest and his dark hair was already thinning. Certainly he could not be called good-looking. Was it his intense enthusiasm for life? He was brimming with vitality and ideas of fun things to do and places to go. "You know what I'd love to do?" he said suddenly. "Buy a hotel in Jamaica and invite all my friends for a house party. I've always wanted to be a beachcomber." For Chuck the war did not exist, apparently. For him all of life was one long house party.

Several tables away two British naval officers were watching them and she realized that Chuck was the only man in the restaurant not in uniform.

"It would be fine — if your draft board doesn't object." She realized this was not very nice and maybe Chuck had flat feet or something that kept him out of the Army, but she was getting a little tired of the "bacon heir."

"Well, that's one of the reasons I'm in Washington," Chuck said. "The draft board has finally caught up with me, and it's not that I don't want to do my part and all that, but why should I be a private in the infantry when I could be doing something more useful? After all, my family has been in the meat-packing business for several generations, and I thought the Quartermaster Corps would suit my talents better. Besides, I'm a lover, not a fighter." He flashed that little-boy grin that she suddenly found nauseating. "I've an appointment at the War Department tomorrow morning with a general who's a friend of my father's. But enough of that dull business. How about going dancing somewhere?" He reached for her hand.

She quickly pulled away and started to put on her gloves. "I have to be at the Red Cross the first thing in the morning," she said, "so I'd better be getting home."

"Oh." Chuck looked disappointed. "Well, some other time." He signaled for the check. "I wish we were in New York and I could take you dancing at El Morocco. I was there last night." He pulled a hundred dollar bill from an alligator wallet and put it on the plate. "Sorry, I don't have anything smaller," he said to the waiter. "El Morocco isn't the same these days," he said, as they waited for his change. "The characters they're letting in. Well," he shrugged, *"c'est la guerre."*

Yes, the war is inconvenient, isn't it, Chuck? she thought. And she wondered what Doug had ever found in common with this yellow-livered draft-dodger who was so totally different in every way from himself. Yet she knew if she ever said a word against Chuck, Doug would rise to his defense. That was the kind of person he was.

She was hoping they would have to share a cab, as was common in wartime Washington, because she didn't want to be alone with Chuck, and luckily an Army major was also waiting for a cab and was going to the Shoreham. Ardith noticed he had flier's wings and several ribbons. He said he had just returned from the Pacific.

A cab pulled up and they all got in.

"I hope you don't mind my sharing this cab with you and your wife," the major said to Chuck.

"Not at all."

Ardith started to say she wasn't Chuck's wife but realized that would make things sound worse. "We're going in the same direction," she said, smiling at the major.

"What part of the country are you from?" Chuck asked. The major spoke with a slow drawl.

"Montgomery, Alabama." He looked out the cab window at the embassies. "First time I've been to Washington. It's quite a place."

He had red hair and freckles and looked too young to be a major. "I'd like to bring my wife here some day for a visit," he said. "Bobbi Jo — that's my wife — she'd get a big kick out of seeing the White House and the Lincoln Memorial and all that."

"Where is your wife?" Ardith asked.

"Back home. We're expecting a baby any day now," he said proudly.

The cab driver turned down Kalorama Road.

"It's that house on the circle right by the lamppost," she told the driver. "And just hold the cab. The gentleman will be going on."

She noticed the surprised look on the major's face and a muscle in Chuck's cheek twitched visibly. What did he expect? To be invited in for a nightcap?

The cab driver opened the door and Chuck walked up the front steps with her. She had already taken her key out of her purse and held out a gloved hand to him.

"Thank you for taking an old married lady out to dinner," she said. Her nineteenth birthday had just passed.

"My pleasure," Chuck said. "Give my best to Doug when you write him." He had a sulky expression and it was obvious he was not used to being brushed off this way. Too bad, she thought. From now on she would stay home. It was less complicated that way.

Her mother had gone to bed. Ardith turned out the lights and went to her own room. She took Doug's photograph from the bureau and put it on her night table. She lay on her bed looking at it and thinking, I can't stand it any longer, I can't bear being away from him. How much longer do we have to be apart? She would tell him about the baby, there was no point in waiting now that she was sure. The second week in May, Doctor Bradley had said. That was a lovely time to have a baby, it would be warm and flowers would be blooming and maybe the war would be over by then and Doug would be home.

She took a sheet of V-mail paper and wrote:

Darling,

Some wonderful news—I wanted to wait until I was absolutely sure to tell you! (This V-mail didn't give you much room to say what you wanted, she thought. Also, she had to bear in mind that it would be read by the censor and who knows how many others before it reached Doug.) *We're having a baby the early part of May. I hope you'll be as happy about it as I am. I've seen Dr. Bradley and he says I'm fine and everything should go beautifully. I've never felt better.* (That was a lie but there was no need to worry him.)

Chuck was in town (here she hesitated, not knowing exactly what to say) *and he expects to be in the Army himself soon. He asked about you and sent his best.*

Darling, I miss you so much. I wish you were here with me right now. I love you.

She signed her name and sealed the letter. She put it on the table next to Doug's photograph and finally she fell asleep.

CHAPTER THIRTY-NINE

The next day she stopped at Garfinckel's on her way to the Red Cross and looked at baby clothes. She bought a tiny blue robe with a lamb embroidered on it and a matching receiving blanket. There was a bassinet trimmed in white dotted Swiss and blue ribbons and a white chifferobe decorated with Mother Goose characters and a yellow duck lamp. She ordered them all. She would fix up her dressing room as a nursery.

She figured she had another two months or maybe six weeks before she would have to start wearing maternity clothes and she wasn't anxious to get into them any earlier than she had to because the few she had seen all looked like sacks. She would squeeze into her own clothes as long as she possibly could. The Red Cross uniforms were loose and no one suspected that she was pregnant, except possibly that time she had fainted at the Blood Bank, and that could have been attributed to the heat. Doctor Bradley had said to keep on with her usual activities and she could continue with her Red Cross work until her condition became obvious. Then she could roll bandages or do some knitting. They needed wool helmets for men on the North Atlantic patrol and she was sure that wouldn't be too complicated. She could even knit some things for the baby. The main thing was to keep busy, she told herself.

She returned home in a very happy mood and was surprised to find Doug's sister waiting in the library. She had fixed herself a large drink and looked as if she had been crying.

"Nancy . . ." Ardith wondered if there had been news about Doug. She hadn't seen or heard from Nancy since Doug had left and she had been thinking of calling her.

Nancy got up and threw her arms around Ardith. Her eyes were red-rimmed and there was a strong smell of bourbon. This was obviously not her first and Ardith wondered how long she had been waiting.

"I hope you don't mind my just dropping in like this," Nancy said. "But I didn't know where else to go. I couldn't go home and face the family. I can't face anyone. I'm so miserable." Nancy threw herself on the sofa and burst into tears. "I've left him," she said through sobs. "I couldn't stand it any more."

"What happened?" Thank God it's not about Doug, Ardith thought. She had been terrified when she saw Nancy there and her heart almost stopped, and now she felt both relieved for herself and guilty that she wasn't more concerned about Nancy's unhappiness.

Nancy took a handkerchief from her purse and wiped her eyes. "Know-it-all Nancy," she said bitterly. "I thought I was so smart. That fancy finishing school we both went to didn't teach us anything about people. Oh, Daddy warned me about him. He even had a written report — he'd gotten someone to investigate Clint, but I told him it was all a pack of lies. I knew better. How could I have been so stupid?"

Ardith sat and waited. It was better to let Nancy do the talking and just listen.

"How can I face people? I can't bear the idea of seeing anyone in Warrenton or Middleburg."

"Nancy, whatever it is, I'm sure it isn't as bad as you think. And who cares what people say?"

Nancy stared at her in silence.

"I know we were brought up to think that way, but other people's opinions aren't really that important."

"But I feel like such a fool. You know, I met his first wife. She's a very nice person. She looked at me as if she felt sorry for me. Doug didn't like Clint either, but I knew better than anyone. I wouldn't listen."

"Most people don't when they're in love."

"Love!" Nancy spat out the word. "I hate him! I'm through with men. The only decent man is my brother. I'm going to devote my life to raising horses."

"You'll meet someone else and feel differently."

"Remember when I had that miscarriage? I didn't fall off a horse the way I said. I've never fallen off a horse in my life. I fell down the stairs. Clint pushed me. He said he hated children and he didn't want any."

Ardith looked at her in horror. "How awful!"

"He hates everyone," Nancy said. "The world. Most of all he hates himself. That's why he drinks so much. He's a spoiled mama's boy, he's never worked in his life. How could I have thought he was so wonderful? That's what I can't get over. What was wrong with me that I could have been attracted to such a person in the first place?"

"You said yourself that he was very charming. Everyone can make a mistake."

"The horrible part is that I think I still care about him. Oh, I don't know what I feel. I just know I can't go on living with him any longer."

"Nancy, stay here for a few days with me. I'd love to have you and it will give you a chance to get your bearings. But call your mother and father and tell them where you are so they won't worry."

"Oh, could I? I just can't go back to my family and listen to 'I told you so.' I think I'd go mad."

"You can stay as long as you want. I've been feeling pretty lonesome with Doug gone and it would be wonderful having you here."

At the mention of her brother's name Nancy's face brightened. "What do you hear from Doug?"

"Not too much. He's on his way overseas, that much I've figured out, but I can't tell where. Everything is censored."

"If only he were here," Nancy sighed. "He'd understand. I could always talk to him. Well, I think I'll have another little ole drink."

"Nancy . . ." Ardith hesitated. "Don't you think you'd better wait? We'll be having dinner soon, and then why don't we go to a movie? I think there's something good playing at the Ambassador."

"I don't think I could concentrate on a movie."

"Of course you could. It would take your mind off things. I think the new Rita Hayworth movie is playing." Ardith picked up the *Evening Star* and turned to the amusement section. "Yes, here it is. I'll call and see what time it comes on."

"Whatever you say." Nancy glanced at the front page. "I've been so busy trying to cope with Clint and his moods that I haven't even had time to keep up with the news. Not very cheery, is it?"

"That's why a movie would be good for both of us. Something light and gay like a musical."

"Fine with me." Nancy leaned back on the sofa. "I think I feel better already. If only I didn't have to face all those people in Warrenton. I can hear them gossiping already."

"Nancy, don't worry about them. If their lives are so boring that they have nothing else to do, feel sorry for them."

I'm a fine one, Ardith thought, giving all this advice to Nancy about what to do when I've been sitting here feeling sorry for myself. In spite of the situation that had brought Nancy to Washington, it was nice to have company and someone to talk to. Oh, there was her mother, but she was another generation and she couldn't really understand. That's why Nancy couldn't go to her own mother. When I have a daughter things will be different, she promised herself. We'll be close and she'll be able to come to me. She won't have to go running off to other people.

"Nancy," she said, "don't you think you'd better call your family now? When Clint discovers you've gone that's the first place he'll go and he'll get them all upset. Then he may go to the police and file a missing person's report and there could be things in the newspapers."

"You're right. I'll call right now," Nancy said. She stopped on her way to the telephone. "What will we tell your mother?"

"Let's see . . ." Ardith thought a moment. "How about this? Clint had to go to Kentucky to see a horse he wanted to buy and you decided to spend a few days in Washington while he was gone. Does that sound convincing?"

"Perfect." Nancy laughed. "Reminds me of the stories we used to tell Madame Duval."

"Oh, speaking of Madame, did you hear that the school had folded?"

"No. What happened?"

"I guess not enough girls wanted to learn French with the war on — and at those prices. She couldn't keep it going. Kathy Peabody was in Washington for a few days and she told me."

"Kat-rine, I do not find theese young man on the leest signed by your parents," Nancy mimicked Madame. "And ees that nail polish you are wearing?"

Ardith laughed. "I spent half my time trying to outwit Madame, but now I feel kind of sorry for her. Poor old thing."

"What's Kathy doing with herself these days? Does she have any special beau?"

"I don't think so. She's doing social service work in Boston and she's trying her darndest to get overseas with the Red Cross."

"I thought you had to be twenty-five to go overseas."

"Yes, those are the rules. But Kathy's trying through some friend of her family's. He used to be an ambassador and he has a lot of pull with Roosevelt."

Maybe it was this conversation that triggered the dream, Ardith thought the next morning. She was walking through the desert and it was somewhere in Africa. She was wearing her Red Cross uniform and there was a terrific sandstorm, she could feel sand in her teeth, the gritty, coarse feel of it, and her throat was dry and parched. Finally it cleared and she saw an Arab with a camel coming toward her. She found herself speaking to him in French. "Could you tell me where I will find the American cemetery?" she asked. He pointed to a small hill in the distance. There she saw row after row of plain white crosses. There was a sign but she could not read it.

She awoke with a terrific attack of nausea. Colored spots danced before her eyes. She staggered to the bathroom and took one of the pills Doctor Bradley had given her. "This won't last forever, child," he had said. "It's only in the beginning." If she could only stop worrying so much about everything. I must stay calm, she told herself. Everything is going to be all right.

After an hour she started to feel better and in the morning mail came two letters from Doug. She read them eagerly. If only the mail wasn't so slow in getting through. She wondered how long it would be before her letter about the baby reached him.

There was a tap at her door. "Hi," Nancy said. "I feel like a new person. Thanks for letting me sleep late."

"Have you had breakfast?"

"Yes, Carrie brought me a tray. What about you?"

"I wasn't very hungry."

"You look kind of green around the gills this morning. What's wrong?" Then it suddenly dawned on her. "Why didn't you tell me?"

"I was planning to."

"But that's wonderful! I'm so happy." She pranced around the room. "Aunt Nancy — yes, I like the idea." She saw the letters on the bed. "Oh, from Doug?"

"Yes." Ardith read her parts of them.

"I wonder where he is? There's no indication."

"They aren't allowed to say."

"No, I guess not."

Ardith started to get out of bed.

"Oh, don't get up because of me," Nancy said quickly. "Why don't you just stay there and rest?"

"I'm fine now." Ardith took a wool dress from the closet. "My clothes are all getting tight. Would you like to help me shop for some maternity clothes? And then we can have a sandwich at Pierre's or someplace."

That awful churning feeling had stopped and she felt much calmer. It would be good to get out of the house and have some fresh air.

"I'll be dressed in a few minutes," she told Nancy.

CHAPTER FORTY

It was the eighth of November and she had not heard from Doug for several weeks when all radio broadcasts were interrupted with a special bulletin.

"An Allied Expeditionary Force has landed in North Africa," came the announcer's voice. "Powerful American and British armies under Lieutenant General Dwight D. Eisenhower have already taken Algiers and are advancing on Casablanca and Oran. They are being supported by British and American battleships."

Doug. Doug was there with them. She did not know how she knew, but she knew. She got out the Encyclopedia Britannica and looked up the places on a map. During the following days she stayed close to the radio. She scarcely touched her food. Finally her mother became alarmed.

"Ardith, you must eat something. You'll make yourself ill."

"I can't."

"You have no proof that Doug is in North Africa. He could very well be in England or someplace."

There was no point in replying. She knew.

"If you aren't concerned about your own health, you should at least think of your child."

That did it. She forced herself to eat small amounts at a time and finally it became easier. The days passed and still no word.

Thanksgiving came and went. It was at this time last year, she thought, that I had my party, Doug and I were talking about marriage, there was no war. Yes, there was a war, but we weren't in it. That was what made all the difference. What doesn't touch you personally doesn't affect you. You may feel sympathy and say "I understand," but really you don't. In our safe world we watched the Nazis overrun Europe and thought we could stay out of it. She understood now Madame Duval's bitterness.

She started going to Mass every day and lighting a candle for Doug. She told herself that as long as the candle didn't go out he would be safe. She knelt before the statue of the Virgin Mary and looked up at the calm face with the blue robes.

"Watch over him, Holy Mother," she implored.

She asked Father Murphy to have a novena said for Doug's safety. She said her rosary over and over, but deep down she didn't really believe her prayers would be answered. She wished she could have a stronger faith. Now was the time it would really be tested.

Her dreams about the desert haunted her. But they were only dreams, she told herself.

One night when she was lying in bed she felt the baby move for the first time. It gave her the strangest feeling. I'm not alone after all, she thought. Part of Doug is here with me.

Finally a letter came. And while he couldn't say where he was, there was enough to tell her that he had taken part in the invasion. He was in action. But this is what he wanted, she thought. Doug was not a man content to stay in a safe post in the rear while others fought his battles. He had told her as much before he left and she admired that in him. He could have gotten a deferment . . . possibly . . . but could he have lived with himself afterward if he had? She knew he could not.

And what would he tell his son someday if he hadn't done his part in the war? Because by now she felt sure that the baby she was carrying was a boy.

She and her mother decorated the Christmas tree and she thought that at this time next year the baby would be in his playpen with stuffed animals, watching them. He would love the pretty lights, just as she had. The tree would be very gay, with every color. One year her mother had decorated the tree in just blue and silver balls. It was very artistic and her mother was pleased with it but Ardith thought it was cold, like an iceberg. She could still see that cold blue-and-silver tree and it made her shiver. After that, they had gone back to having the different colors again.

"Don't you get up on the stepladder, Ardith," her mother said. "You might fall. I'll get the high ones."

Grace Rodgers was pleased at the idea of being a grandmother. She talked as if Ardith and the baby were going to live there forever and not just until Doug came back. "We'll have to do something about these stairs," she said, looking up at the stairwell. "A small child could fall through the spokes in the bannister. It will have to be covered and have a gate at the top."

Ardith hoped by the time her baby was crawling, Doug would be home and they would be in a place of their own, but she did not say this to her mother.

"Of course, we could get a harness for him. I had a little white leather harness for you with bells. Maybe I still have it. I'll look for it."

A harness? I wore a harness? To keep me from going too far away? To keep me from being hurt? "My child won't wear a harness," Ardith said.

"Well, you can't take your eye off them for a second when they're small. I watched you all the time. That's why you never had a broken bone the way some children do."

Is that how you keep them from getting hurt? Don't you know that you can't keep anyone from getting hurt, Mother?

Her mother seemed to see her childhood now through a rosy glow of happy, safe times. She had conveniently forgotten all the times she left her with Mademoiselle. But of course, Mademoiselle was watching her, too, to see that she didn't hurt herself. Her cold eagle eye, her disapproving glance.

"Do you think I'll be pretty when I grow up, Mademoiselle?" the thin, sallow-faced little girl asked hopefully.

"Pretty?" A disdainful snort. "*Ça n'a pas d'importance. Le caractère, c'est tout.*"

But I don't care about having character, Mademoiselle. I want to be pretty! I know I'm ugly now and I want to be pretty. Tell me something nice. Please. . .

Ardith took a glittering gold ball from the box and hung it on the tree. "This was always one of my favorites," she said. "And this one." She held up a green glass elf with a laughing face and a red cap. My baby will love this one, she thought.

Grace Rodgers stared at the tall man with sandy hair and the shoulders of a fullback talking to General Marshall at the buffet table. There was something about him . . .

"Madge, isn't that—"

"Senator Joseph Kreskie. He's the new senator from Pennsylvania.

Haven't you met him before?"

"I don't believe so."

"He's very charming. Come, I'll introduce you. You'll like him —
even if he is a Democrat." Madge Breckinridge steered Grace through the
crowd.

"Hello, Grace." The general held out his hand. "It's good to see you."

"Hello, George."

"And this is Senator Kreskie," Madge said. "Mrs. Rodgers."

"How do you do."

"How do you do, Mrs. Rodgers."

"Please excuse me," Madge said. "I see some more guests arriving."
And she dashed off.

"I understand you're from Oil City, Senator Kreskie."

"That's right."

"So am I. At least I grew up there."

"It's a small world. Do you go back very often?"

"Not any more. Not since my father died. I wonder, by any chance,
if you ever knew him? His name was Thomas Wyman."

A peculiar expression crossed his face. "I met him only once."

"Oh? When was that?"

He hesitated. "It was a long time ago."

"He was quite an extraordinary man."

"So I understand."

"Is your beautiful daughter with you?" General Marshall interrupted.

"Unfortunately, I couldn't persuade Ardith to come." She turned to
Joe Kreskie. "My son-in-law is overseas with the Army and ever since the
invasion of North Africa Ardith has been glued to the radio listening for
news. She's sure Doug is with them." She looked at General Marshall as
if he could confirm or deny the fact, but his face was expressionless.

Madge came rushing back. "I'm going to have to steal Senator
Kreskie from you for a moment. Please excuse us."

"It's been nice meeting you, Mrs. Rodgers," he said.

Grace watched him as he walked across the room. Madge was right,
he was charming. But there was something else . . . and again she had the
feeling of *déjà vu*. She would have to find out more about Senator Kreskie.

"You're looking very serious about something, Grace."

"Oh . . . it's just that . . . George, how long do you think this terrible
war is going to last?"

"Until we win, Grace, until we win. And that, I'm afraid, is a long way off."

So that was my father's sister, he thought. She had looked at him curiously and for a moment he wondered if she had guessed anything. How would she have reacted if he had told her of their relationship? If, when Madge Breckinridge had introduced them, he had said, "Hello, Aunt Grace."

But it was not the time nor the place. The time would come when the Wyman family would know who he was.

But not yet.

BOOK FOUR

1943

CHAPTER FORTY-ONE

Ardith had always found history boring in school and had difficulty keeping the different battles and their dates straight in her mind.
Now she pored over maps of North Africa as new names cropped up in the
news: Tebessa, Thelepte, the Kasserine Pass. Someday all of this would
be history. Her children would read about General Rommel and General
Alexander the way she had read about military leaders in the past. On
Christmas Eve Admiral Darlan was assassinated in Algiers, and now, in
January, Roosevelt and Churchill were meeting in Casablanca to plan
future military strategy.

There were some who said the war might last five years or more.
Eventually, we would have to invade France and march on to Berlin. And
then there was Japan to deal with. In her concern with the North African
campaign she had almost forgotten the war in the Pacific. That would be
a long, drawnout affair.

And feeling her child move within her, like all mothers before her, she
thought fiercely: My son won't grow up to fight in another war!

Somehow, men and nations must learn to get along without fighting
and killing each other. She did not have the answer and it seemed no
generation had found it yet.

The winter passed and the first crocus appeared in the garden. She saw
a cardinal one morning sitting in the dogwood tree. Only two more months
to go, she thought. She felt as if she had been pregnant forever. It was
difficult going up and down stairs, and if she dropped something it was
hard to bend down. Now she knew how fat people felt. It was hard to
remember that she had once been slim and sylphlike when she caught sight
of her bloated image in a mirror. In a way, she was glad Doug wasn't able
to see her looking like this. When he returned she would have her figure

back again, she would greet him looking glamorous and like a femme fatale and present him with an adorable baby.

"Your son," she would say.

"But, sweetheart, you look marvelous, as if you hadn't had a baby at all. How did you do it?"

"It was nothing." She would toss it off casually.

Ouch . . . her back was hurting again and at night she had shooting pains in her legs that kept her awake. Sometimes she sat up half the night doing a crossword puzzle to keep her mind off things. This morning her eyes had been puffy with deep circles and her skin was looking strange. What was this glow that pregnant women were supposed to have? All she saw was that her complexion was muddy and sallow instead of the clear olive that it normally was and she felt awkward and ungainly. At least I haven't gotten those awful stretch marks across my stomach that Doctor Bradley warned me about, she thought. She had been very careful about her weight and it wasn't easy because all she wanted to do these days was eat.

In April, Ann Garrett gave a baby shower for her at her family's house in Georgetown. She sat in a comfortable armchair wearing a black cut-out skirt with a white pleated shirt and a gold and pearl pin at her throat to pull the attention away from her waist. Around her were piled packages wrapped in pink and blue, some tied with celluloid rattles or teething rings.

Ann passed her a package and the girls waited eagerly for her to open it. She was the first of her group to have a baby.

"Save the ribbon," someone said. "Then we tie it all together."

"Have you tried holding a gold wedding ring on a string over your stomach, Ardith?"

"What for?"

"You can tell whether it's a boy or girl by the way it swings. If it swings back and forth it's a boy and if it goes round and round it's a girl."

"Oh, come on, that's an old wives' tale."

"No, my sister tried it and it really worked."

Ardith had unwrapped the package. "Oh, how darling!" She held up a white knitted sweater with a matching cap and bootees. She read the card. "Thank you, Barbara. This is just precious!"

Barbara looked pleased with her choice. "It'll do for either a boy or a girl," she said.

"I'll pass it around," Ardith said. She opened the next package. It was a feeding dish divided into three sections and decorated with Mother Goose figures. Next was a yellow robe with a hood that zipped up the front.

"To bring the baby home from the hospital in," Ann said.

"This is so much fun! Maybe I'll have a baby every year. That is, as soon as Doug comes back."

"Where is he now?"

"Somewhere in Tunisia." She opened another package and held up a blue-and-white checked sunsuit. "Love from your Aunt Nancy," read the card.

"Oh, Nancy . . ." She was speechless.

"Well, my nephew has to have a proper wardrobe."

There was a Swiss embroidered pillowcase from Doctor Bradley's daughter Lucy. Lucy's husband was on an aircraft carrier "somewhere in the Pacific."

Ardith wrote each gift down in a book as she continued to open packages. There was a silver cup and a white kitten that was really a music box to tie on the crib, a tiny blue sweater with white ducks embroidered on it, and a yellow receiving blanket. Finally, she had opened everything.

"I'm overwhelmed," she said. "I've never seen so many adorable gifts for a baby. Thank you all so much."

"Have you decided on a name, Ardith?"

"Well, if it's a boy, naturally I'll name him after Doug. And I haven't been able to make up my mind about a girl's name. I'll wait and see."

"That won't be too long."

"No, around the eighth of May. At this point, it seems forever!"

CHAPTER FORTY-TWO

Later she would remember every detail of this day that began no differently from any other day.

She awoke early to find the late April sunshine flooding her room and there was a symphony of birds' voices in the garden. She heard a car go down the street and the beagle next door whimpered. On the carpet near the foot of her bed she noticed two patches of sunlight. She raised herself on one elbow and thought, I don't have long to go now. She had never been able to sleep on her back and that was the only position possible during these final weeks.

She had breakfast and read the newspaper. The Germans were on the run in North Africa and our troops were sweeping on through Tunisia in the direction of Bizerte. They hoped for a victory soon. Maybe after this Doug would be sent home for a rest. There had been no letters for two weeks and she always started to worry when she didn't hear anything. She wondered if he was with General Patton's troops, and she recalled when she had gone to Potomac School with Patton's niece and been invited to play at her house. There was a photograph on the piano of an Army officer in a helmet and riding boots with an arrogant, determined expression. "That's Uncle George," she was told. "He's a colonel . . . he's stationed in Hawaii." She gathered that "Uncle George" was considered quite a colorful character by his nieces and nephew and that they looked forward to his infrequent visits.

And now "Uncle George" was one of our greatest generals.

She finished reading the paper and went up to her room. Her mother left for the Red Cross with Mrs. Breckinridge—they were having an important meeting at headquarters. She washed and set her hair and wrote a letter to Doug. Then she walked to the mailbox and mailed it. She debated whether to walk over to Massachusetts Avenue and down past the embassies—it was such a beautiful day—no, she'd better not get too far away from the house. She had lunch and took a nap. It was three o'clock and she was just coming down the stairs when the doorbell rang. A letter, she thought hopefully. She opened the front door and froze.

There stood a Western Union messenger with a telegram.

He was very young with tousled blond hair and she could see his bicycle parked at the curb.

"Mrs. Douglas Larimer?"

She nodded.

He handed her the telegram.

She could feel her hands wet with perspiration. She knew. With a chilling finality, she knew. Slowly she opened it and the words swam before her eyes:

THE WAR DEPARTMENT REGRETS TO INFORM YOU. . . .

All was swirling blackness. . . and then green.

Green, she was in a green room and there were people with green masks. Once, when she was small, some children had told her a ghost story about a green room . . . was this it?

She was strapped to a table and in the corner was a hooded black figure with a cross.

"Holy Mary, Mother of God, pray for us sinners now and at the hour of our death."

A strange smell, they were gripping her shoulders, a black rubber mask went over her face. "Breathe it, it's oxygen."

"Let me go!" She formed the words with her lips but no sound came.

"It's all right, child." She recognized Doctor Bradley's voice.

And then a voice from the hooded figure. . . of course . . . the Mother Superior who was in every Catholic delivery room, the voice commanding, imperious, "Doctor, if there's any choice, you know what you are to do." A significant pause. "Save the child."

Save the child, save the child, the child will go to Hell, we are all born in sin. . . .

"We'll have to do a section."

"When she's in labor?"

"The husband will have to sign permission."

The War Department regrets to inform you . . .

"Oh." Another voice. "Her mother, then."

Buzzing, like insects, indistinguishable. A feeling like a feather across her stomach. They're cutting, she thought, but she could feel no pain. A cry, piercing the air. A slap.

"A boy," they said.

We have a son, Doug. We have a son. *The War Department regrets to inform you . . .* I need you. Where are you? Don't leave me alone, don't go off and leave me . . . like my father. In the end, they all leave you.

"Here's your baby. You have a nice little boy."

A red face with black hair in a white blanket.

Our son. Doug, we have a son. But you will never see him. *The War Department regrets to inform you.* God help me! And there is no help. There is no help. There is no God!

"She's delirious. Give her a shot."

The hooded black figure. "I'll call a priest to baptize the child."

Long corridors, an elevator, the clanking of metal bars. A stern-looking nurse in a starched white uniform. Her mother's voice drifting through a haze.

"Please, I'd like to stay here with my daughter."

"I'm sorry, it's against hospital regulations."

"But you don't understand . . . she's just had a great shock." Whispering.

"We can make no exceptions."

Please don't go, Mother. Don't leave me alone here. I hate hospitals!

"She's had very strong medication. She wouldn't even know if you were here. You may see her tomorrow — during visiting hours."

"I'll speak to Doctor Bradley about this. We asked for a private room."

"Doctor Bradley does not run this hospital and all the private rooms are filled. There's a war on. And now I must ask you to leave. I have other patients to attend to."

Noise in the streets outside. An ambulance siren. Cars going by. And then . . . numbness.

A light being shined in her face. A hypodermic needle. Clanking of metal bars again. And then the whirling blackness. Doug, where are you? I can't live without you, I can't . . .

A priest standing by her bed mumbling in Latin. Are they giving me the last rites?

The rapids are around the river bend. Stay away from the rapids. A roaring, rushing of water. . . I'm being drawn into them . . . I can't fight any more.

"Call Doctor Bradley."

Whispering. Footsteps coming down the corridor. More voices. "Blood transfusion."

Not that green room again. Not that awful green room!

"Her nails are turning blue."

"Quiet, she'll hear you."

"She's unconscious. . . she can't hear anything."

"Oh . . ."

"She's moaning. She's coming to."

"She's still out." Fingers on her pulse. "Very faint. Where's Doctor Bradley?"

"He's on his way."

Faces swimming above her. Blurry, as if under water. . .

"She's come to, she's trying to say something."

"I can't make it out."

"She's still in shock."

"Doctor Bradley's here."

An angry voice. "I gave instructions that she was not to be left alone."

"I just left her for a minute, Doctor. We're so understaffed here."

"Ardith . . . Ardith, do you hear me?"

"Oh . . ."

"You're going to be all right, child."

Morning. The city was awakening. Sunshine filtered through the partly open Venetian blinds. A pigeon came and sat on the windowsill. On the wall opposite her bed hung a wood-and-silver crucifix.

She felt her stomach. It was flat.

Oh. It was all coming back now. The door opened and a new nurse came in. She drew back the curtains separating the beds and Ardith was aware for the first time that there was another girl in the next bed. Had she been there all the time?

The nurse handed her a washcloth that had been dipped in warm water and a towel. "How are we feeling this morning?" she asked brightly. "Now wash your face and hands and I'll get your toothbrush. We'll be having breakfast very soon."

"When do they bring the babies in?" the other girl asked.

"Later in the morning. You aren't nursing, are you?"

"No."

The nurse looked pleased at that. Apparently the nursing mothers caused them a lot more work. She went out and in a few minutes another nurse came in. She had a black band around her cap.

"I'm Miss McCartney, the head nurse. Are you still having bad pains?" she asked Ardith.

"Yes." All the events of the day before were coming back as the heavy sedation wore off. Tears started to roll down her cheeks.

Miss McCartney patted her hand. "There, there . . ." She glanced at the chart. "You can't have a hypo oftener than every four hours. You have another hour to go."

"Was a priest here during the night?"

"Yes, Father Murphy came to see you. I didn't think you'd remember."

"Did they give me the last rites?"

Miss McCartney looked uncomfortable. It was obviously a question she preferred not to answer. "I wasn't on duty then. Now eat your breakfast like a good girl and it'll help you to get your strength back. Doctor Bradley will be in to see you before long."

Ardith lay back and stared at the crucifix on the wall. It was the only ornament in the room. I've got to go on living, she thought. Maybe it was a mistake about Doug, maybe . . . She buried her face in the pillow.

A nurse's aide came by with the morning newspapers. She was no longer interested. What did the war news matter now? The war had ended for her somewhere in Tunisia.

The morning passed. The other babies were brought to their mothers, but not hers.

"He's in an incubator," she was told. "Don't worry, he's doing fine."

"I want to see him."

"When Doctor Bradley comes we'll ask if we can wheel you down to the nursery."

"How much does he weigh now?"

"Four pounds, eight ounces."

The girl in the next bed had a baby girl. "You're lucky," she said. "This is my second girl. My husband wanted a boy."

Doctor Bradley arrived around noon. He had gone to his office after being up all night and he looked tired.

"How do you feel, child?" he asked. He checked her blood pressure and looked at her incision. "Sorry we had to do this to you, but the scar will fade after a while."

Wounds heal and life renews itself. Doug had said that to her once. Her eyes filled with tears. She still couldn't believe that he was dead. It was all a bad dream.

"When may I see my baby?" she asked.

"Let's see how you are tomorrow. Then perhaps we'll let you get up in a wheelchair for a little while. But you've got to start eating. I was told you scarcely touched your breakfast."

"I wasn't hungry."

"Then you'll have to force yourself. That's the only way you'll get your strength back."

"I'll try."

"Good girl. I'll see you tomorrow." He went through the door, almost colliding with a nurse who was carrying a bowl of white lilacs.

Flowers started arriving and soon the room looked like a florist's shop. There was an arrangement of tiny yellow roses and forget-me-nots in a ceramic baby boot, a basket of mixed spring flowers, a bowl of fruit, an azalea plant. The nurse put them on the bureau and handed her the cards.

Like a funeral, Ardith thought, as the overpowering sweetness filled the room. The nurse opened a window. "I'd better put some of these in the hall," she said.

"Why don't you put some of the arrangements in the nurses' office," Ardith suggested. "They might like them. And could I have that little one with the forget-me-nots by my bed, please?"

The Mother Superior who had been in the operating room came by, but the nurse had just given her another hypo to ease the pains, so she saw the black robes through glazed eyes. "Save the child." She would never forget those words, though they had denied afterward that it was said. She turned her face away from the Mother Superior. Leave me alone, she thought. She felt as if it would be a long time before she would ever be able to attend Mass again. What had once brought her so much comfort now seemed like complete hypocrisy.

Visiting hours in the maternity ward were from two to four and her mother brought her a pretty new bedjacket and a hairbrush and make-up. There had not been time to pack anything when they left for the hospital. Ardith put on the bedjacket over her muslin hospital gown and her mother brushed her hair. She felt like a little girl again when she used to have those sieges of bronchitis and her mother had taken care of her. Strange, when she was well, she recalled, her mother never had much time for her . . .

Now, again, she was the sick little girl who needed taking care of.

"I brought you some magazines," her mother said.

"Thank you, Mother." She was too drugged to read anything. The printed page all seemed a blur. "I'll look at them later."

"It's just too bad, dear, that we couldn't manage to get you a private room, after all you've been through." Grace Rodgers glanced at the drawn curtain between the two beds. "Just to put you in with anyone . . ." For an instant the woman who looked up everyone in the social register appeared again. "But I spoke to Doctor Bradley and if he can find a private nurse, I'm going to get you out of here as soon as I can."

Her mother chattered on, carefully avoiding any mention of Doug. The nurse to take care of the baby had not been engaged until the middle of May and she was booked until then. "But Carrie and I can pitch in," she said.

The nurse came in the room with another hypo. "Visiting hours are over," she announced, glaring at Mrs. Rodgers. She had a lot of things to do and visitors interfered with hospital routine.

"I'll see you tomorrow, dear," her mother said, blowing Ardith a kiss.

CHAPTER FORTY-THREE

She had a bad night and nothing they gave her could dull the pain. She awoke from a heavily-drugged sleep crying for Doug, only to become aware of the truth she still was unable to face. Doug was dead. Doug was dead somewhere in Tunisia and she would never see him again. Never again would he hold her in his arms, never again would they make love . . . no, no, it's a lie! everything in her screamed, he will come back to me, he must!

All the plans they had made together, all the dreams they had dreamed . . . it was not true that he was dead. A case of mistaken identity . . . yes, that was it. As soon as she got out of this awful hospital she would find that it had all been a mistake . . . there would be a letter from Doug . . . it would be explained. If only she could get out of this place. She shook the bars of the bed. They had her locked in like a prisoner. Help me . . . someone help me. She fell back exhausted on the pillow.

She drowsed off again. She was crawling across the desert and sand was blowing all around, it was hot and dry, her throat felt stuffed with cotton, if only she could have a drink of cold water, ice cold water, there was the sound of Nazi planes, she couldn't move, she heard a piercing scream. . .

There were voices and a light was shined in her face. Two figures in white stood by her bed.

"I can't give her any more sedation, Doctor."

"If we don't she'll wake up everyone in the hospital." It was not Doctor Bradley's voice. A strange doctor. Where was Doctor Bradley?

The sheet was pulled back and she felt a needle in her hip. She thought how she had always been terrified of shots and now they were like pin pricks compared to the pain that was inside her, and then the voices became indistinct and far away and she felt herself drifting . . .

She saw the river that wound through the green Pennsylvania hills of her childhood and she was back again in her beloved woods. In this place she was safe . . . here nothing could hurt her. She ran down the path from the cottage and she seemed to be floating. There was the scent of pine and honeysuckle and the sound of oars dipping in the water and the croaking of frogs. She felt the sunlight on her hair and watched velvety black-and-yellow butterflies hovering over the goldenrod and Queen Anne's lace. She knelt on the river bank among the bulrushes and made a boat of twigs with a leaf for a sail and watched it borne by the breeze across the water.

And then a figure came toward her with arms outstretched and she ran to him.

"There is no death," he said. "Remember that. I will always be with you."

"Then let us stay here forever."

He held her closer and did not answer. Suddenly she could feel him slipping away from her, the dream was fading, she was waking up.

"Doug . . . don't leave me!"

She was lying in her hospital bed gripping the sheet with both hands and she was soaked with perspiration. The room was hot, and then freezing cold. She tried to reach for the extra blanket folded at the bottom of her bed. It was too far away. She pushed the bell for the nurse.

Her teeth were chattering. Her hands and feet felt like ice. The nurse tucked the extra blanket around her and got a hot water bottle.

"Your body's adjusting to its normal temperature again," she said calmly. "You're fine."

She stared at the silver crucifix on the wall opposite her bed. She felt completely empty. Yes, I'm fine, she thought bitterly.

The girl in the next bed went home at noon and she was left alone. She asked to see her baby and was given a peculiar look. "Doctor Bradley will be here soon."

And then Doctor Bradley appeared with her mother and the expression on her mother's face was the same as the day she came home from school and found her canary dead on the floor of his cage, his feet sticking up in the air, his beautiful golden feathers a lifeless ball of fluff. They buried him under an azalea bush in a tin candy box decorated with violets and she cried for weeks. What made her think of that now?

Doctor Bradley pulled a chair over by her bed and took her hand. She noticed how large his hand was, you would never think that those huge hands could perform delicate surgery and yet he was so gentle.

"I'm sorry, child," he said. "Sometimes these things happen and we don't know why. Everything possible was done."

She stared at him blankly. The baby. Did he mean that the baby . . .

"When they're premature there's always a chance of this . . . and especially with boys."

He was holding a hypodermic needle. Her mother came over and put her arms around her. She had tears in her eyes.

Now I've nothing left, she thought. First Doug, and now our baby. There is no reason to go on living anymore. And then there was the needle and she felt herself sinking into a black whirlpool and in the swirling darkness she could hear Doctor Bradley's voice saying, like a phonograph record, farther and farther away until she could hear it no more:

"She's young . . . she'll get over it."

Days turned into weeks and one was the same as any other. She had a dim recollection of leaving the hospital and now she was back in her room at home. She lay back listlessly on the pillow. Nothing mattered any more. She was not yet twenty and her life was over.

Her mother had taken the crib and the baby clothes to the Children's Hospital and there was only a long red scar on her stomach to remind her that she had ever been pregnant. Slowly, that too was fading, but inside she still felt raw and bleeding. There had been a letter from Doug, written the night before he was killed, in which he seemed to have a premonition of what might happen. It arrived two weeks after she returned from the hospital and when she held the letter and read Doug's words and saw his handwriting the wound broke open afresh. This letter is alive but you are not, she thought, and again she could not believe it.

Father Murphy came by the house.

"We had a special Mass said for the baby," he said.

What good does that do now? she thought and she started to cry again. Her faith had left her completely.

"I know it's hard, my child, but we must accept the will of God." Father Murphy fingered his rosary. "We can be thankful that at least the little one was baptized, God rest his soul."

Or what would have happened, Father Murphy? Would my baby have gone to Hell? Or would he have drifted forever in that limbo to which the souls of unbaptized infants are condemned? Is that all you have to say of comfort? Tell me, what do I believe in now? She realized that she was staring at him with an angry expression and the thought crossed her mind that Catholics revered death rather than life. It was the next life that mattered to them, not this life. This life was not important and was meant to be endured in humility and suffering. "It is the will of God." Was eternal torment the will of God? Was this the religion she had chosen to escape from the loneliness of her childhood? Could it be that her grandfather had been right?

Father Murphy looked uncomfortable.

"I'll be going now," he said. "I hope to see you at Mass, my child."

Maybe I should become a nun, she thought, and drown myself in prayers and incense and lighting of candles. Shut out the world the way they do. Pray for the souls of others. Hope for immortality in the next world.

She went over to the window and curled up in the window seat. Everything was green and gray. The gray sky against the green of the trees. Birds' voices like a symphony tuning up. She saw Rock Creek Park . . . it was May now . . . and lovers would be wandering along its wooded paths and she thought: I can't live without love. I must have love to live!

And all was a gray emptiness. . . .

CHAPTER FORTY-FOUR

It was an evening in early June, and Ardith and her mother were sitting in the garden after dinner. The scent of roses hung in the humid air, and past and present seemed to mingle in the violet twilight. There was the sound of water splashing in the fountain and birds calling to each other.

Even they have someone, she thought.

Her loneliness and grief grew more intense as the weeks passed. There was nothing secure to hold on to and she was floating in a dark mist. Over and over again she asked herself: Why? Why both Doug and my baby?

And there was no answer.

"Time heals everything," they told her. But no one ever said how much time. Just time . . . stretching endlessly, a path winding through the woods that had no end, her arms reaching out to the night and returning empty, time that was measureless, that had no horizon, time that was unendurable.

Time had not healed her loneliness for her father.

Where was he now? The tall dark man who had held her hand by the banks of the Mississippi so long ago, the man who told her he loved her with tears in his eyes and then vanished forever.

She reached out and plucked a geranium from the bronze urn next to the wrought-iron bench on which she sat and turned it slowly in her fingers, stroking the velvety pink petals, and then she pulled the petals off one by one and scattered them at her feet.

"Mother," she said, "what happened to my father? Why did he go away?"

Grace Rodgers looked at her with a startled expression. A forbidden room had been broken into, one locked from prying eyes and covered with the dust of memory.

"You always said that when I was old enough to understand you would explain it to me and you never have." She picked another geranium. "Am I old enough now?"

"Don't do that to those flowers, Ardith."

"I want to know. I think it's time I knew the truth."

"All right." Her mother's face in the deepening shadows was filled with pain. She twisted the pearls at her throat and when she finally spoke, her voice came with difficulty.

"It was in Paris that I met your father. I was studying at the Sorbonne and he was in my art class. He wanted to be an artist and he was talented. Very talented." Her face softened and looked like a young girl's. "Julian Rodgers. He was from New Orleans and I thought I had never seen anyone so handsome. We went to little cafés and talked after classes and walked through the Luxembourg Gardens, and before we knew it we had fallen in love. He told me about his family. His mother was a d'Alvery, an old Creole family, and his father was a doctor who came down from the North in the midst of an epidemic and by chance walked into the house where a young woman lay dying. He saved her life and they were married. They had two daughters and then Julian . . . your father . . . was born."

Julian Rodgers. My father. Ardith listened in fascination.

"When your father was six his father had a sudden heart attack and died and his mother followed not long afterward. So he and his sisters were raised by his grandmother and a maiden aunt who lived in a gloomy old house in the Garden District. He had a very sad and lonely childhood, and later on when I tried to find some excuse for his behavior . . ."

The garden grew dark and fireflies came out. Ardith remembered when she had filled a whole glass jar full of them and it was like having a torch to see by. But where was my father during all that time? she wondered. Why did he leave us?

"Paris in those days was a very exciting place to be, filled with artists and writers. Many of the struggling ones we used to see in cafés are successful and famous now."

But not my father. Not Julian Rodgers.

Her grandfather had called him "that bum." She could still recall in vivid detail the night when she was five and had listened outside her grandfather's door. "Grace, why did you marry that bum?" But her mother had loved him. She still loved him, of that Ardith was quite sure.

"There is no lovelier place than Paris in the spring," her mother said dreamily, and as she spoke Ardith could see the chestnut trees in blossom along the Champs-Elysées, the barges on the Seine, and the white dome of Sacré Coeur high above the city. Her mother told of gathering wild violets in the Bois de Boulogne and walks in the spring evenings through the silvery-blue dusk of Paris streets and the smell of fresh bread and rolls in the bakeries.

"We had a flat in Montmartre with a big skylight . . ."

"Were you happy then, Mother?"

"Yes." Wistfully, "I was happy."

Then what happened? *"L'amour fait passer le temps, le temps fait passer l'amour."* She had seen that on a leather belt at Saks and she had wanted to say, "No, it's not true, time doesn't make love pass," and she looked at the other belts with sayings like: "My Kingdom for a Horse" and "Love Me, Love My Dog," and she bought the one with *"L'amour fait passer le temps, le temps fait passer l'amour"* because it was the prettiest and then put it away because it made her sad every time she looked at it and she couldn't understand why.

"We spent that winter in Paris and it was rainy and miserably cold and our flat had no heat. Your father was painting but he sold practically nothing and I had to accept money from your grandfather, which made him angry. He became increasingly moody and despaired of ever becoming a great artist. And then I became pregnant . . ."

With me, Ardith thought. She could see it all now between the things her mother did not say. The artist who didn't really want responsibilities, the trapped feelings, her mother caught in the middle, afraid to go home and hear, "I told you so." The freezing flat in Montmartre with the rain beating on the skylight. Love in a garret. The dreams slowly dissolving.

"We stayed in Paris through the spring and summer and your father was spending more time in cafés drinking Pernod than he was painting, though he said that was where he found interesting characters to paint. He grew a beard and sometimes he would appear with someone he had met during a drinking bout and demand that I fix dinner for them at some odd hour, even though there was scarcely anything in the flat to eat. Finally, in August, a month before you were due, it all became unbearable, and your grandfather sent the money for my passage home. That sobered him up . . . for a few days . . . and he begged me not to leave, that everything would be different. But it wasn't. One night he gave me a black eye and two days later I was on a ship for the United States."

"Where I was born."

"Yes, several weeks afterward, in Oil City."

So he wasn't there when I was born, Ardith thought. Her mother, chin high, having to face it all alone, the humiliation, her grandfather's icy blue eyes reminding her of her mistake.

"Your father wrote begging me to forgive him, that he couldn't live without me, and something about pride making a lonely bedfellow. We were both miserable apart and the following spring I rejoined him in Paris with you. I was determined to prove your grandfather wrong, I knew your father had talent, and I loved him. I thought love could surmount anything." Her mother gave a bitter laugh. "Women are fooled by their emotions."

"You've told me that before."

"Yes, to protect you. I didn't want you to go through what I did. You see, your grandfather was right. He was a better judge of men than I was."

"How long were we in Paris?"

"Until you were four. Do you remember it at all?"

"Yes. I remember watching a little boy in a sailor suit sailing a boat on a pond and graveled walks with flower beds and a marionette show. And bigger girls rolling hoops and wanting one. Where was that?"

"The Luxembourg Gardens. Yes, we used to take you there often. We had moved from Montmartre to the Left Bank by then."

"And there was a church . . . it had a square in front of it and there were a lot of pigeons. I used to feed them from a bag of stale bread crumbs."

"The Church of Saint Sulpice. We lived around the corner."

"There was a fountain with lions and statues of bishops." It was all coming back now, like a half-remembered dream. "And shops selling religious objects. Did I have a carved wooden statue of an angel?"

"Yes. Your father bought it for you. You saw it in a window and wanted it. You kept it by your bed."

"There was a narrow street with shops selling fruits and vegetables. And pastry shops." How clear it all seemed now. "And then we came to a river."

"The Seine."

"There were fishermen with long poles and weeping willow trees and a stone bridge." And something else . . . no, it was all a blank . . . there were empty spaces, as if something painful had happened. Voices, angry voices shouting at each other. Holding the wooden angel, trembling. The roofs of Paris in the moonlight. Glass breaking. "Go back to your oil millionaire father! I'll find myself a real woman." The sound of wood splintering. Music from a café. Sobbing. Then silence.

Lying in bed shivering, holding the angel. It was so cold. They had forgotten all about her. They wished she had never been born.

"You see, he felt inadequate, so he struck out at me. I felt so helpless. I loved him and I didn't know how to help. Finally I wrote to your grandfather and he offered him a job in one of his companies. That made him furious. He said he wasn't an ordinary man and he couldn't do that kind of work. He was an artist. If I wasn't happy I could go back and have my father support me. We decided to go to New Orleans. But his sisters had sold the family home and moved away, so we took a cheap apartment in the French Quarter. Things got worse. He was drinking more and more. He didn't really want the responsibility of a family. And yet the strange thing was that he loved us. He was so sweet and affectionate with you . . ." Her mother's voice broke. "Well, that was all a long time ago. But now maybe you can understand how hard it was for me to talk about it."

"But don't you ever wonder what's happened to him? Don't you want to see him?"

"What good would it do?"

"Perhaps he changed. He could have." Why did she still cling to this hope after all these years?

"Men don't change, Ardith. They're the way that they are."

There was the splashing of water in the fountain and fireflies flickered in the dark.

And then her mother said, half to herself, "You can't put the blossoms back on a tree after a storm."

CHAPTER FORTY-FIVE

They went to Newport in July, but it was a Newport changed by the war. Uniforms were everywhere and blackout was strictly observed. All the boys she had known before her marriage were in the service somewhere. Some of the P. T. boat heroes were allowed at Bailey's Beach as guests of members—"After all, it's the only patriotic thing to do," said one dowager—but mostly Bailey's Beach was populated by the elderly, pregnant women, and children. Nursemaids had given notice to join the WACs or WAVES and household help was hard to get, so many people had not reopened their homes. Ardith and her mother stayed at the Meunchinger-King, a cottage-type hotel in town.

General Patton invaded Sicily and Ardith thought that Doug would have been with them if . . . that small word that changed everything. One of his aides had written her a letter praising Doug's heroism and she had it in a small box with his medals and letters. And now she must try to forget the past and start a new life.

She went for long walks along the Cliff Walk, breathing in the sea air and watching ships on the distant horizon. She walked until she was in a state of exhaustion, hoping that then she could sleep at night without having to take a pill.

She thought of taking singing lessons with her old voice teacher, Emma Beldini, to find that Emma Beldini was off on a U.S.O. tour.

Mussolini resigned, U.S. bombers raided Romania's Ploesti oil fields and refineries, American troops landed in the Aleutians. The progress of the war seemed to have nothing to do with her anymore. Only time passing, time passing slowly and endlessly and the pain still there. She and her mother worked at the Newport Red Cross every morning for several hours and then went to Bailey's Beach. She still felt too weak from the

Caesarean to play tennis, so instead she walked, sometimes along Bellevue Avenue, sometimes along the ocean cliffs, and the solitary walks helped. Some of her friends tried to get her to go out on double dates with the officers stationed around Newport, but she declined.

Somehow she could not imagine herself ever going out with a man again, but everyone told her she would get over that. But she knew that she was not yet ready.

The summer passed, and after Labor Day they returned to Washington. Her birthday came and now she was twenty.

The leaves turned to red and gold and crackled underfoot. Nature went on, in spite of war and death. Was that what Doug had tried to tell her once? Was that the answer to the unanswered questions? Beauty remained, and it was stronger than ugliness and disillusion, the crocus coming after the snow, the birds returning after winter.

She found a book of poems by Tagore in the library and a line: "Faith is the bird that feels the light and sings when the dawn is still dark."

She started reading again. How strange to find people in other places, other centuries, who had the same feelings, the same hopes, the same doubts. She read lives of saints and philosophers and her suffering seemed small by comparison. Books, the friends of her childhood, were her only consolation. She read Emerson and Marcus Aurelius and Kahlil Gibran. She still had not gone to Mass and Father Murphy continued to call. Would they never leave her alone? That was what her grandfather had said about the Catholic Church . . . they hounded you, they filled you with guilt. Surely there must be some answer for what had happened other than, "It's the will of God, my child, and you must accept it."

With a punishing and vengeful God like that, she thought, who needs a devil?

The answer for her no longer lay in the Catholic Church, and she wondered if she had chosen it out of defiance. Or was it because it was her father's religion? But her father had not been a good Catholic. It had not solved his problems for him. Where was he now? What had become of him? It continued to haunt her, like finding a mystery story in an old magazine that was continued in the next issue and the next issue was nowhere to be found, leaving her forever in the dark.

"Ardith," her mother said finally, "why don't you see some of your friends? All this reading is going to ruin your eyes, and after all, you're still too young to shut yourself up like this."

"I don't care about seeing anyone, Mother. And I like to read."

"But it's not normal."

What should I do, Mother? Throw myself into an empty social whirl the way you did? Did that make you happy? I'd rather be alone.

"Ardith, you can't go on this way. It's been more than eight months since . . ." Her mother glanced at Doug's picture in the silver frame and then back to Ardith. "Ann Garrett is having a small dinner party Saturday evening at the Chevy Chase Club and she asked me to try to persuade you to go. They'll pick you up, so you won't have to go alone. Please say that you'll accept."

Ardith closed her book. "Well, I suppose I'll have to start sometime . . ."

"Good. That's my girl. I'll call Mrs. Garrett and say that you'll come. Now, let's see what you have to wear." Her mother rose from the edge of the bed and staggered suddenly, her left leg buckling under her. She grabbed the bedpost just as she was about to fall.

"What is it, Mother?"

"Oh, nothing, dear. Just this silly thing I've been having with my leg lately. It'll go away."

"You haven't said anything about it. Have you seen a doctor?"

"There's no reason to. It just happens when I get up in the morning and sometimes when I've been sitting for a while. There, it's gone." She walked over to the closet and started going through Ardith's dresses. "Why don't we go down to Garfinckel's and get something new?"

"I can wear one that I have."

"No, something new and pretty. It would cheer you up. Please, for me?"

"All right, Mother." What did it matter? she thought. She felt like a toddler again, being led on the white leather harness with bells.

As they drove up to the entrance of the Chevy Chase Club she felt a pang remembering the last time she had been there with Doug. It was strange to be arriving in a cab with Ann Garrett and two Army Air Force captains. She had kept up an animated conversation on the way out, and now suddenly she wanted to plead a headache and take the cab home. She didn't see how she could get through the evening.

Todd was still on the door at the Chevy Chase Club and his polished mahogany face beamed at the sight of her.

"Mrs. Larimer," he said, "it's right nice to see you again. It's been a long time."

"Yes."

"I was sure sorry about . . ." Words failed him, but his eyes conveyed his sympathy.

"Thank you, Todd."

Dear Todd, she thought, tears springing to her eyes. He's watched me come here since I was a little girl, he's seen me grow up. He was bent with rheumatism now but he still had the same cheery smile, as if to say, "All's right with the world." She couldn't imagine the club without him.

They passed the cloak room.

"We'll be right with you, boys," Ann said. "Isn't your date cute?" she whispered to Ardith. "And I can tell he likes you already."

They went up the stairs to the dining room and Ardith noticed the stares and whispering as she came in.

The Air Force captains were looking around the room with awe.

"Quite a lay-out here," Ann's date said.

"We like it," Ann said, waiting for him to pull out her chair.

"Nothing like this in Oklahoma," he said.

They sat down and ordered dinner.

Ardith turned to her date whose name was Harry. "Where are you from?" she asked.

"Nebraska."

They had both just returned from the Pacific and were awaiting further orders.

"What kind of plane did you fly?"

"A P-38."

She looked blank so Harry described it.

"Harry's quite a hero," his friend said. "He shot down three Jap planes."

Harry shrugged modestly.

"Tell them about it, Harry."

"The girls wouldn't be interested."

"Of course we would," Ann said.

"Well . . ." Harry put down his fork. "We were over Wewak — that's in New Guinea — and there were these Jap zeros coming at us . . ."

Ardith listened as his voice droned on. It was like the slow dripping of a faucet that one hears at night and is too tired to get up and shut off.

You keep hoping it will stop, and finally try to ignore it, knowing it will go on and on . . .

"We sure took care of those Japs," Harry said, putting a piece of steak in his mouth.

"See that medal, girls? That was given him personally by General Kenny."

"Aw . . ." Harry said, slicing another piece of steak. "This sure is good. Say, is that the orchestra tuning up?"

"Yes," Ann said. She had noticed how silent Ardith was during Harry's recitation. "Do you like to dance?"

"Sure do," Harry said, squeezing Ardith's hand. "How about you, honey?"

"Why . . . yes." She pulled her hand away, but Harry seemed not to notice.

"I sure got lucky tonight," he said. "You never know what you're going to get on a blind date. Remember those WACs, George?"

"Yeah."

They both laughed.

"I think they send all the ugly ones to the South Pacific," Harry said.

"My former roommate at boarding school is trying to go overseas with the Red Cross," Ardith said, "but they won't take anyone under twenty-five."

"There's a good reason for that," George said.

"Sure is," Harry winked.

"Half the WACs they sent to North Africa were sent home pregnant," George said.

Ann kicked him under the table.

There was an awkward silence while the waiter cleared away the plates. It's too soon, Ardith thought. I shouldn't have agreed to come on this date. Ann had changed the subject and was chattering nervously. The orchestra was playing "Moonlight Becomes You" and people were drifting out of the dining room.

"Do you like movies?" Harry asked.

"Oh . . . yes."

"Let's go one night."

"Fine." Ardith toyed with the chocolate sundae the waiter had just placed in front of her. If only this evening were over, she thought in desperation. She was not going out again for a long time . . . if ever. She knew that Ann had meant well in getting her out of the house but she would rather stay home with her memories of Doug.

Harry was asking her something.

"Pardon?"

"I said who's your favorite movie actress?"

"Oh . . ." She hadn't been to a movie in a long time, since before . . ."Ingrid Bergman," she said.

"Yeah, she's quite a woman."

The orchestra was playing "Comin' in on a Wing and a Prayer."

"There's our theme song," George said.

"Let's go down and dance, honey," Harry said, squeezing Ardith's arm.

They all got up and walked toward the door.

She caught snatches of conversation as she passed different tables. She always wondered why people never waited until you were out of earshot before they started talking about you.

"My dear, her husband hasn't been dead more than six months. In my day . . ."

"What do you expect her to do? Wear widow's weeds the rest of her life?"

"Of course not, but out having a good time. . ."

She tried to pretend she hadn't heard.

CHAPTER FORTY-SIX

There were other dates after that. Not with Harry, but with different men. And the different men were all the same. It did not matter whether they were Army Air Force or Navy or Marines. They all used the same dialogue and they were after the same thing. She got to know it by heart.

"Aw, come on, baby, it's going to be a long war."

"Who are you saving it for?"

"After all, you've been married."

"Honey, you need a man."

"What's the matter, are you frigid?" This was apparently how they summed up a woman who wasn't willing to leap into bed on a second date.

She gathered that most of the women they ran across were more than willing, including some of her own friends. She couldn't understand how they could let themselves be used so casually. Or did they consider that they were being patriotic? Wartime Washington was filled with men in uniform and she could have had a date every night. For a while she tried that and it only increased her loneliness and longing for Doug.

She decided to stay home and refuse all invitations, but she found that wasn't the answer either. What was? She couldn't imagine herself ever falling in love again. At least not the way she had been with Doug, and having known the best, she could not settle for something less. And the casual wartime affairs were not for her.

It was into this void that Frank Partridge came.

For three weeks she had spent her evenings reading and listening to the radio and playing her old opera records and her Nelson Eddy-Jeanette MacDonald operettas — she had seen *Naughty Marietta* thirteen times— but she was not eleven years old now, she was almost twenty-one. She was a woman, not a child who could escape loneliness with books and music.

She needed more in her life.

And the phone call from Frank Partridge was like a lifeline when she was drowning.

"Remember me?" he asked.

"Of course." Frank Partridge was one of the "older men" who had come to her debut and he used to cut in on her at the different parties. He was around thirty-five, tall, and wore horn-rimmed glasses. He was a beautiful dancer and Phi Beta Kappa at Harvard. She'd always thought him very nice, but not romantic or exciting.

"I was stationed in San Francisco," he said, "but I'm back here in the Navy Department for a while."

Frank was a lawyer before the war, she remembered, and was associated with one of the top law firms in Washington. Everyone liked and respected him and he was considered a most eligible bachelor. She wondered why he had never married.

"I'd like very much to see you again," he said.

"I'd like to see you, Frank. It's nice hearing from you."

"Could you have dinner with me Friday evening?"

"Yes . . . I'd love to." At least Frank is a gentleman, she thought, and I won't have to fight him off like some of these men who've been calling. These eager beavers out for a fast conquest so they could brag to their friends. Yes, it would be good to see Frank Partridge again.

Strange how timing affects our lives, how loneliness throws us into situations that normally we would walk away from. The fear of being alone, of having no one of our own. Is there any greater fear for a woman? Why does one panic at being alone for any length of time? Later on she would ask herself these questions.

The courage to wait without love for love. To stand alone, knowing that dawn comes after night, that spring will surely follow winter. For the heart must heal before it can care again.

She had felt numb for so many months and she had despaired of ever loving anyone again. For her, love was finished. But she wanted a shoulder to lean on, someone to take care of her, to be beside her in the dark. It could have been anyone.

But it happened to be Frank.

He was kind and considerate. He sent flowers, brought her books he thought she would enjoy. He took her to the theatre and concerts. He was understanding, he knew what she had been through and he made no attempt to rush her. It was a relief not to have to fight someone off and hear the same dialogue. He was there when she needed someone and he made no demands.

They went out together for several months and beyond holding her hand and kissing her on the cheek he had not made a pass at her. Then one night on the way home from a concert at Constitution Hall he said, "I guess you know that I'm very much in love with you."

She did not answer. She had supposed that was why he continued to see her, and yet she hoped they could just drift on in a kind of indefinite relationship with no commitment on her part. She needed a friend and she liked being with Frank, but she couldn't imagine ever caring for anyone but Doug.

"You don't have to say anything," he said, as if he read her thoughts. "I'll wait. I just wanted you to know."

She reached over and touched his hand and tears came to her eyes. "I . . ."

"I know you're not in love with me. But maybe later on you'll feel differently. I'd do anything in the world to make you happy. You're the loveliest woman I've ever known."

"Thank you."

"No, don't thank me. One doesn't meet many ladies these days. You're kind of rare."

And then he told her about the girl he was engaged to when he was going to Harvard Law School. She was a Boston debutante and very beautiful. He had her on a pedestal, he thought of her as kind of a goddess. Finally, he found out the truth. She was sleeping with half the boys at Harvard and no one had the heart to tell him. When confronted with the facts she said, "What do you expect me to do? I like to have fun and you always have your nose buried in a law book."

That was the end of the engagement and from then on he threw himself into his studies even more. He graduated at the top of his law class and was offered a job in a Washington law firm. He was glad to get away from Boston and its bitter memories. He was given a partnership in the law firm and he was on Mrs. Matheson's list of favorite bachelors.

His Boston goddess was involved in a hit-and-run accident not long after he came to Washington in which a child was killed. Her family's money got her off. Then she married one of the Harvard boys. It was rumored that she was five months pregnant at the time and wasn't quite sure who the father was. He tried to tell himself that she was good riddance, but his faith in women was completely destroyed. Or maybe it was his faith in himself for being such a fool. His ego. He would become an important figure in Washington, perhaps go into politics, he told himself. And then some day she would pick up *Time* magazine and read about dull Frank who was no fun and always buried in a law book and his revenge would be sweet.

But after a while he found he could hardly remember what the Boston debutante looked like. Oh, every now and then he would hear a laugh, a gay rippling laugh that was like hers, or see a girl who had a way of tossing her head that reminded him of her, and his palms would be wet with sweat and he felt like striking out at something, but that, too, passed. And he looked at women with contempt and thought: They're all sluts.

Until Ardith.

She was easily the most attractive debutante of her season, in fact of many seasons, and he had been on the Washington scene for some time now and danced with more debutantes than he could count. He had watched her from the stagline and at times she had an expression like a doe lost in a forest and he thought: She's frightened. She needs more time to grow up. She doesn't know what she wants. And then he heard that she was engaged.

So he had struck out again.

He got a commission in the Navy. His eyes kept him off sea duty, which he would have liked, and he found himself in Naval Intelligence. He was sent to San Francisco and was on the staff of the Western Sea Frontier for two years. He was often invited to the Burlingame Country Club for Saturday night dances and Sunday buffets. The San Francisco society matrons were delighted to have him take their daughters dancing at the Mark Hopkins and to Monday lunches at the Saint Francis. He had more invitations than he could accept.

And still he found himself thinking of Ardith.

He heard that her husband had been killed in North Africa. That she had given birth to a son who had lived three days.

He compared her in his mind to the San Francisco society girls, most of whom were just as willing to come to his room at the Fairmont Hotel as the waitresses in the Sir Francis Drake bar, and he wondered if the war had changed her.

And then he got orders to report to the Navy Department in Washington.

He found her even more beautiful than he remembered, but there was still suffering in her face and he knew that he must be patient. He was willing to wait. She was everything that he wanted.

BOOK FIVE

1944

CHAPTER FORTY-SEVEN

Joseph Kreskie and Helen Flanagan were married quietly on the first Saturday in May. The romance had grown slowly over the years. Several months after her fiancé was lost on the *Hornet*, Joe asked her to have dinner with him, and it became a regular thing. Still, he had no plans for marriage. He was content to go on having an affair. He was busy serving on the Armed Services Committee, as well as several others, and he felt that no wife would understand his work and the hours he kept. He had seen political marriages fall apart at the seams, though, of course, they stayed together, because divorce meant political suicide.

Helen came from a large Irish-Catholic family in Boston and she had gone to Katherine Gibbs Secretarial School upon graduating from high school. Unlike the other women he had dated, she understood his work.

But it wasn't until she told him that she was quitting that suddenly he realized how much he had come to depend on her. He could not imagine his life without her.

I'm in love with her, he thought in amazement. Me, Joe Kreskie, the confirmed bachelor.

And so he proposed. It was one of the smartest moves of his life, and he wondered why he hadn't done it sooner.

Ardith was in the garden when she first heard the bells from the cathedral. They continued to chime and as she listened she realized that there was something different about them. They were ringing out a hymn she used to sing in school. She tried to remember the words:

> "O hear us when we cry to Thee
> For those in peril on the sea . . ."

But why that particular hymn? And then suddenly she realized. The invasion! She rushed inside and turned on the radio. It had begun. The Allies had crossed the Channel at dawn and were landing on the Normandy beaches. The announcer read a message that General Eisenhower had given the men under his command:

"You are about to embark on a great crusade. The eyes of the world are upon you and the hopes and prayers of all liberty-loving peoples go with you . . .

"We will accept nothing less than full victory."

It was the first time she had been to Mass in a long time. Candles flickered and the priest intoned prayers and there was the sound of rosaries and women weeping. For all they could do now was pray for the safety of their men.

She looked at the worried faces around her and then up at the statue of Mary. Help them, O Blessed Mother, she prayed silently. Give them strength.

She remained on her knees for a long time and finally she left the darkened church and went out into the June sunlight. Newsboys were selling extras.

INVASION! read the black headlines.

An elderly man nudged another. "Say, Mac, it's started. And about time! I remember when I was at Château-Thierry during the last time. . ."

Château-Thierry. Her uncle had been killed at Château-Thierry during World War I. And her husband in Tunisia during World War II. Was there no end to this senseless killing? Would women continue to weep throughout the centuries for their men fallen in battle? And would history keep repeating itself with no lessons learned?

Would her son, if she ever had one, and the sons of her friends, have to fight in another war twenty-five years from now?

The old men were recalling with vicarious pleasure their days in France with General Pershing. Did men really like wars? Did it give many of them an escape from their mundane lives, an adventure they would not otherwise have? A sense of importance, a chance to play the hero and no one would really know the truth? To hear these men you would think that they had both won the Congressional Medal of Honor. She had found that real heroes were silent and did not talk about their exploits.

She walked down the street and boarded a streetcar. There were no seats and she hung on to a strap. Several men were sitting but no one got up.

The streetcar clanged up Connecticut Avenue, packing more people in at every stop. Finally she decided to get out and walk the rest of the way home. She pulled the bell and edged her way to the exit.

It was a relief to be in the fresh air again. She took deep breaths as she walked. She passed the apartment building where they had lived for three months when they first came to Washington, before they found the house on Kalorama Circle. The same doorman was still there. She waited for the light to change. To her right was the bridge going over Rock Creek Park known as "Suicide Bridge" because so many people had jumped off it. She and Mademoiselle used to walk across it often on their promenades. She had once peered over the edge and it was such a long way down it made her dizzy and she wondered about all the people who had become so desperate that they chose that way to end their lives. On the way down, as they were hurtling through the air, did any of them want to reconsider? And suppose they weren't killed, but instead landed on the concrete, smashed and bloody but still alive, invalids for life. She shuddered at the thought.

The light changed and she crossed Connecticut Avenue and walked down Kalorama Road past the French Embassy and then she came to Kalorama Circle and she was home.

Frank had called and asked her to have dinner with him tonight, but she preferred to be alone. She didn't feel up to making conversation with him, she just wanted to spend a quiet evening by herself. She thought of the women in church and how she, like them, had prayed to God for Doug's safe return and God had failed her.

But maybe we are not meant to understand life. There was a line she had found in a book by Santayana that Frank had given her — that the secret of life was not to understand it, but to live it.

Somehow, some way, she must release Doug and go on living.

Summer came and they went to Newport again. Frank came up on weekends and they played tennis and went to Bailey's Beach. Everyone liked him. He really would make a good husband, she told herself, and then he would do some small thing that would irritate her and she thought: No, it's impossible, I'm just not in love with him or he wouldn't get on my nerves the way he does. And then a huge box of flowers arrived or a gift that obviously he had selected with great care and she felt guilty. That feeling she used to have when Doug walked in a room, that excitement, was that just for the very young? The moonlight-and-roses thing that eventually died in every love affair, would that have passed with them if Doug had lived?

She felt very secure with Frank, he would take care of her and do everything to make her happy. Wasn't that mature love? And yet, something was missing. Perhaps it would come later.

Her mother liked Frank. "He's so devoted to you, dear," she said. "I hope you're not giving him false hopes. He's the kind of man who could be badly hurt. And sometimes that kind of man can be very vindictive when his feelings have been trifled with." Was this a warning? Frank was very jealous and constantly questioned her about other men at Newport who were calling her. In Washington he could keep better track of her. She had been able to stall him by saying, "I'm very fond of you, Frank, you know that, and I'd rather be with you than anyone I know, but I just don't know when I'll feel like getting married again."

I'm just not physically attracted to him, she thought.

With Doug it had been so different. It had been hard to wait and control her feelings until they were married. And when they were together everything had been so perfect. But that strong physical attraction had been there. From the very first. Frank was nice and she liked holding his hand and putting her head on his shoulder and she missed him when she didn't see him for a week. She tried to analyze her feelings. But that wasn't love. It was being fond of a dear friend. She couldn't imagine making love to him the way she had with Doug or doing any of the things . . . no, it was impossible, she must find some way of telling him without hurting him that . . . what? She just didn't feel any physical attraction for him and that was why she was holding out and not because she was a lady. But how do you tell a man that in a kind way? And if he was content to go on as things were, what was the harm? But she knew that she would be forced into a decision soon and it frightened her.

The decision came sooner than she expected.

Frank had been thinking things over while she was away, and as soon as she returned to Washington he decided to force the issue. He could not go on any longer the way things were, he told her, and he felt she had plenty of time to evaluate her feelings for him. He loved her and wanted to marry her. If she did not reciprocate his feelings he understood and he would always wish her happiness.

They were sitting in the library, the room where she had sat so many times with Doug and planned their future together. Her eyes avoided Frank's and she glanced at the bookshelves and the portrait of her grandfather over the mantle. If only someone could tell her what to do. She didn't want to stop seeing Frank, but she realized she wasn't being fair to him.

Frank was studying her. "A million thoughts are going through your head right now," he said. "What are they?"

"Oh . . ." She paused.

"Go on."

"I don't know what to say, Frank. You're one of the nicest people I've ever known and you've been wonderful to me. I'm very fond of you but . . ."

For a fleeting instant she saw a hurt expression on his face, and then he was the lawyer again. He stood up.

"It's very simple," he said. "Either you love or you don't. And apparently you don't. But if you ever need me, if you ever want anything, you just have to call me. I'll be there."

She couldn't say anything. She touched his arm. Finally she said, "I'm sorry, Frank."

"No, you can't help it. You're still carrying a torch. I understand." He kissed her quickly on the forehead. "Goodbye, Ardith."

And he was gone.

CHAPTER FORTY-EIGHT

She started dating other men and it was the same old story all over again. The same approaches, the fencing matches in cars and at the front door, the dialogue she had heard so many times. "What's the matter, are you afraid of men?"

And some of them got angry and accused her of leading them on. She found she missed Frank. She heard he had been seeing quite a bit of a divorcée around town, a woman in her thirties who had a reputation for being fast. He hadn't called. In the months that followed she thought about what he had said to her: "If you ever need me, I'll be there."

Could they be happy together? Was the fact that he loved her so much enough to make up for the feelings she didn't have? She missed his calls every day. She was tired of men trying to paw her. They were right, it was going to be a long war, and she was tired of being alone. Finally she came to a decision. She called Frank.

"If you still want me to, Frank," she said "I'll marry you."

And so they were married and moved into a house in Georgetown. But unlike the fairy tales, they did not live happily ever after.

You cannot throw yourself into another man's arms and say, "Take care of me . . . blot out the past." For the past arises like a ghost, pale and luminescent, gliding through the shadows. And she had not yet buried the past.

Seeing Frank several times a week was different from living with him day and night. She had not realized how fussy he was about so many things. Specks of dust, something not in its proper place, his morning egg must be cooked just so. . . he was almost old-maidish in his ways, from being a bachelor for so many years. The order that prevailed in his office at the Navy Department was carried over to his home. One month she mislaid the gas bill, and when a red final warning came in the mail, he had a fit.

"How can you be so disorganized?" he asked.

He was a perfectionist about everything. They gave small dinner parties fairly frequently and she would find herself tensing up as soon as she started planning the menu. It was like trying to please an overly critical father. A persistent pain in her lower back developed and she started going to a chiropractor for treatments. "What's causing all this tension?" he asked her one time. "Oh, the war and everything," she said vaguely. She was coming to him to adjust her back, not her personal problems, and she resented his probing.

After a dinner party Frank would compliment her and tell her how proud he was of her. The table was beautifully set, the food delicious, she looked lovely. Once he made her change her dress because it was too low-cut.

Everything ran on a schedule, including their lovemaking. That Frank was not an especially romantic lover she blamed partly on herself, because she had married him without being in love with him. If he noticed that she was merely submissive to his embraces, he said nothing. No doubt he thought this was how a lady should behave. She tried to be a good wife and pretend feelings she didn't have, but it was becoming increasingly more difficult. Several times she thought of consulting a psychiatrist. She couldn't discuss certain things with her priest and she needed some impartial person she could talk to. Other women talked all over town, this she knew only too well. Just last week when she was at Elizabeth Arden's having her hair set she heard a familiar voice in the next booth telling the hairdresser the intimate details of a mutual friend's marriage. No doubt the friend, distraught and needing someone to unload to, had confided her problems to what she thought were safe ears, and now it was being spread like wildfire all over Washington.

She had glanced in the booth on her way to the dryer to see who was talking, and there in a pink smock with purple foam covering the roots of her hair, was Georgia Wilson.

"Oh, hello, Ardith," Georgia said, completely unperturbed, and continued with her gossip.

Her marriage to Frank was a mistake, she had known that almost immediately, and she wondered how much longer she could go on pretending. Frank was always checking on her, he called home several times a day to see what she was doing, always under the pretense of concern. Sometimes he would appear unexpectedly for lunch when she had planned to go out and she began to feel like a prisoner in her own home. The thoughtfulness and attentiveness he had shown before marriage had turned into jealousy and possessiveness.

I'm trapped, she thought, I'm being smothered by a strangling kind of love that makes me want to escape. She thought suddenly of the sticky flypaper that hung from the beams of the porch at Llantarnam and how she felt like one of those flies, caught and unable to get free, being able to see the woods and the sunshine filtering through the trees and smell the honeysuckle — if only she could go back to where she had been so happy, to spend a week alone in the cottage, to wander once more along her beloved Allegheny and feel part of the woods and wildflowers, to be one with nature. I must get away, she thought, or I shall go mad!

It was the middle of March. In a few more weeks she would broach the subject with Frank.

The weeks passed and she rehearsed what she would say to Frank. She looked at her calendar. April twelfth. Tonight she would tell him of her plans. As soon as he came home.

"Roosevelt's dead." Frank had the evening paper under his arm. "Cerebral hemorrhage. He died at Warm Springs, Georgia."

"No!" She looked at the headlines in disbelief. The man who had been President practically all her life, "that man in the White House," cursed by some, worshipped by others, was it possible that he was dead?

"That means Truman," she said.

"Yes." Frank looked grim. "Roosevelt's been a very sick man for a long time. Far more so than was generally known."

"How will this affect the war?"

"It's not good."

They went in the library and Frank turned on the radio. The news was on every station. No, this was not the time to tell Frank about her plans. She would have to wait.

Frank thought they should have a baby.

"You have too much time on your hands," he said. "That's what's the matter with you."

She didn't even know if she could have another child. She thought of the tiny grave that she occasionally visited to put flowers on, the baby boy who had lived only three days, whom she had never even held in her arms, Doug's child. Would having another baby erase those painful memories? Could she fill her life with love for a child to make up for what was lacking in her relationship with Frank?

Sometimes a baby helped a marriage that was falling apart. She desperately needed someone to love. Was having a child the answer? Would it fill the empty spaces, the monotony of her life with Frank?

At times she felt as if she would explode from lack of excitement. But why was this necessary to her? She had a good husband, one who was faithful and loved her. Then why did he get on her nerves all the time? She felt guilty about her feeling and yet she couldn't help them.

She decided she would make an appointment to see the psychiatrist she had heard several of her friends speak of. She got out the phone book and looked up her number and address. Dr. Maida Ziedman.

Doctor Ziedman had a deep voice with an accent.

"Who referred you?" she asked brusquely.

"I . . . uh . . ." Ardith thought for a minute. She didn't want to give any of her friends' names. "My gynecologist spoke to me about you and suggested I see you. Doctor Bradley." Would she check to be sure?

"I have had a cancellation on Wednesday at three."

The phone clicked without waiting for a reply.

Doctor Ziedman's office was on the first floor of an old building. She found her name on the nameplate and went down a dark hall and opened the door to the waiting room. There was no receptionist or even a desk, just a small room with a chair and a table with some magazines. The room had a musty smell and it gave her a spooky feeling. There was a black-and-white framed drawing on the wall signed Picasso. She studied it. Was it a copy? No, it appeared to be an original, but with the fees she had heard most psychiatrists charged, no doubt Doctor Ziedman could well afford it. She tried to picture what Doctor Ziedman looked like from her voice on the phone. Voices were so deceiving. At Miss Putnam's before the boring Sunday evening sermons in the gymnasium, they would play a game and try not to look at the speaker while they formed a mental picture of him from his voice. It was always a shock to look up and find a short, bald man when one had imagined a tall, dignified one.

The door to the inner office opened and a heavy-set woman of about fifty, dressed in a mannish-tailored suit stood there. She held out her hand.

"Mrs. Partridge? I am Doctor Ziedman. Won't you come in?"

The earlier patient had gone out through another door. She had heard the psychiatrists did this so their patients wouldn't run into each other.

The room was pale green with a heavy mahogany desk and a brown leather chair. In one corner was a leather couch with a pillow and a straight-backed chair.

Doctor Ziedman indicated the brown leather chair in front of her desk. "Please sit down."

So she was not going to make her lie down on the couch right away, Ardith thought. That, no doubt, came later. Doctor Ziedman sat behind the desk and took out a pad and pencil.

"Now," she said in that deep voice, "how can I help you?"

"You mean what is my problem?"

"Precisely." Doctor Ziedman was staring at her under heavy black brows. "You are a patient of Doctor Bradley's?"

"Yes. That is, I was. He delivered my baby."

"You have one child?"

"No. That is, he died when . . ." She stopped, unable to get the words out. Doctor Ziedman had started to scribble furiously in a notebook. "I really don't know why I'm here . . . I mean, I don't have the neuroses that probably most of the people who come to you have . . . that is. . ."

Doctor Ziedman stopped writing. "Let's not talk about my other patients. We're interested in you. I see you don't like being called a patient."

"Well, I don't consider myself a patient. I just need someone to talk to, someone impartial who can give me some advice."

"You have no one close to you?"

Ardith shook her head. Her eyes were starting to fill with tears.

"Your husband?"

"No. That's one of the reasons I'm here. I feel so . . . trapped. I don't know where to turn." Suddenly she burst into tears.

Doctor Ziedman watched her. What was she writing? Ardith wondered. Patient on verge of nervous breakdown? She took out a handerchief and wiped her eyes. "I'm sorry," she said.

"Now suppose you tell me about it," the deep voice said gently. "When did all this start?"

When did it start? With Doug's death? No, she thought, it was long before. This feeling of being caught in the rapids, of being drowned in swirling waters, of trying to swim to the surface, the muddy waters cleared for a little while and then clouded over again, the Mississippi, brown and muddy, long ago, was that when it started? A man beside her holding her hand, and then vanishing forever. As love vanishes, even as you cling to it murmuring words like "forever" and "always." Love is in flight like the swallow, resting but for a moment, and then disappearing in the clouds.

"I'm afraid everything I love will leave me," she said. "As if I have no right to be happy. It fills me with terror."

"You love your husband?"

"No. That's why I thought I was safe. He couldn't hurt me."

"Safety. Is that what you want from life? A guarantee to be safe?"

"I don't know."

There was a modern painting in back of Doctor Ziedman's desk, garish orange and purple streaks splashed on canvas with small black figures. Were they meant to be people? It was ugly. Why would someone want to hang something so ugly on a wall? But Doctor Ziedman did not have to look at it. Only her patients.

"Does that painting disturb you?"

"No . . . it reminds me of . . . my father was a painter." Her throat felt tight, as if she couldn't swallow. "Could I have a glass of water, please?"

Doctor Ziedman was writing something again. She stopped, went to a room next to the office, and returned with a glass of water. Her eyes were like black beetles floating in a pond.

Ardith took a gulp of water. "Thank you." She pointed to the couch. "Am I supposed to lie down on that?"

Doctor Ziedman smiled. "Not if you don't want to. And many of my patients don't."

"What shall I talk about?"

"Anything that comes into your mind. You said your father was a painter. Tell me about him. What kind of paintings did he do?"

"I don't know. I never saw any of them."

And then she started to talk. Words flowed, like a river after the spring rains have swollen it, words tumbled forth and she was not conscious any more of Doctor Ziedman or the office or that hideous painting. She had just gotten to the part about Doug when Doctor Ziedman stood up.

"Is the hour up?"

"Yes." Doctor Ziedman smiled. "It went quickly, didn't it?"

"Yes."

"You did very well. It wasn't so difficult after all, was it?"

"No." She felt as if she could have gone on talking for several more hours.

Doctor Ziedman took out her appointment book. "Is next Wednesday at the same time all right?"

"Yes, fine."

Doctor Ziedman pointed to a door, not the one she had come in. "You may go out that way," she said.

CHAPTER FORTY-NINE

She found she looked forward to Wednesdays at three o'clock. In Doctor Ziedman's office she could say what she really felt. All her life she had had to conform to an image, to say what was expected of her. From the little girl curtseying, "Thank you so much . . . I've had a lovely time," when it had been anything but lovely, to the debutante whirling from party to party, to the perfect young wife and hostess. "So glad you could come, it was lovely, lovely, lovely. . ."

And then her escape into the Catholic religion.

"O my Jesus, forgive us our sins, save us from the fire of hell. . . ."

We are miserable sinners, miserable, miserable, miserable. Forgive us, even though we are not worthy. We are not worthy.

I am not worthy of happiness. That is why everything has happened. It was the will of God.

Doctor Ziedman was looking at her. "Tell me about your first marriage . . . about Doug. You were happy with him?"

"Yes . . . oh, yes. He was everything to me. My whole life."

"Was your life, then, so empty before?"

Empty? Yes, it was empty. At least, it was empty of love. "I wanted a normal life, the kind I didn't have, with a mother and father together . . . and children. A happy home with laughter and love. Doug and I would have had that, we talked about it, how wonderful it would be. And then he was killed. He went away and never came back. Like my father."

"You're bitter about that, aren't you?"

"Yes. In a way it seemed that the pattern of my life was repeating."

"Do you think life has a pattern?"

"Don't you?"

"It isn't important what I think. It's your feeling we're concerned with. Did you feel guilty when your father went away? Did you feel that you were in some way to blame?"

"Why . . . yes." She looked at Doctor Ziedman in amazement. "I did feel guilty and I couldn't understand why. I kept thinking that maybe I'd done something that made him angry. Or that he didn't really love me, in spite of what he said."

"And you missed him?"

"Terribly." Tears came to her eyes. "I seemed always to be looking for him. I stared at strangers in the street thinking maybe I would run into him and he would recognize me and put his arms around me and call me 'daughter.' But it never happened. I finally gave up looking."

"Did you?"

"No. No, that's not true. I sought him in every man I met. The image I had of him, the one I carried with me from my childhood."

"What was that image?"

"He was handsome and dashing . . . like the heroes in fairy tales. And he was warm and affectionate. All the Wymans were so cold."

"Your mother's family?"

"Yes. They were like ice, stiff and unbending."

"And is your mother like that?"

"She doesn't mean to be. At least, she tries awfully hard not to be. She can't help herself, I guess."

"Did Doug remind you of your father?"

She thought a moment. "Well, not really. He was blond and my father was very dark. But they were both tall and they were both Southerners. Doug's voice when I first met him made me think I'd heard it before. And they were both warm and tender, they could express their feelings, I felt they really cared about me. And then when I lost them . . . first my father, and then Doug and the baby . . . I felt that for some reason I couldn't understand, I wasn't meant to be happy."

"Do you still feel that way?"

"Yes. And now I feel guilty about Frank. I never should have married him."

"Why did you?"

"I couldn't stand being alone any more. I thought he would take care of me."

"And instead you feel like a prisoner."

"Yes. Yes, that's it exactly."

"What do you intend to do about it?"

"I don't know what to do. I hoped you could tell me."

"I can't tell you anything. You must come to see things for yourself."

"How long will that take?"

"That depends."

"On what?"

"On you." Doctor Zideman stood up.

"My hour's up?"

"Yes."

"I feel as if I'd only been talking for about ten minutes."

Doctor Ziedman smiled.

"I've heard this sometimes takes three years or more. I couldn't wait that long."

"Ah, my child, how impatient the young are. I wish I were your age again . . . and knew what I know now." For a moment the woman appeared, a woman who had known love and suffered its pangs and disappointments, and then a veil was drawn. Once more she was the doctor, efficient and sexless. "Next Wednesday at three," she said. The next patient was already waiting in the outer room.

"Why are you going to that head-shrinker?" Frank asked, when the bill from Doctor Ziedman came.

"She helps me. And I'll pay the bill."

"I'll pay the bills in my own home." He picked up the phone bill. "She's probably a lesbian. I don't trust women doctors. Is she married?"

"I don't know. I've never asked her."

She had often wondered about Doctor Ziedman's background. She knew that she was from Vienna, that she had left Austria when Hitler came to power, so probably she was Jewish. But beyond that she knew very little.

"All these psychiatrists do is try to break up marriages," Frank said, ripping open another bill and frowning as he totaled it. "You need a baby to keep you busy. You have too much time on your hands."

His favorite saying again. Time on your hands. She felt if she heard it one more time she would scream, but in a way it was true, she did have too much free time. She had thought of joining an art class. Now that the war in Europe was over, maybe she could travel before too long. But there was still the war in the Pacific to be won and that could go on for a long time, especially if we had to invade Japan. No, she didn't want to have a baby. She didn't want to be tied down to the house. Or was the real reason that she didn't want Frank's baby? Because she knew their marriage was doomed.

Frank walked across the room and straightened a picture that was crooked. "There, that's better," he said.

Everything he did irritated her. He was so fussy, almost like these effeminate old bachelors who were in demand as extra men by so many Washington hostesses, and yet Frank could hardly be called effeminate. He was always making remarks about pansies or "the boys" as he called them, he played golf and other masculine sports, he was well informed on all subjects, he read, and he liked good music. Here I am listing his good qualities again, she thought, as if I have to convince myself.

She watched a bee that was crawling up the window pane looking for a way out. How do *I* escape? she wondered. She went over and opened the window and the bee flew off. It's that simple, she told herself. Why can't I do it?

The summer wore on. It was the first summer she had spent entirely in Washington and she felt weak all the time from the heat. They went out to the Chevy Chase Club on Saturdays and Sundays and that helped break the monotony a bit. And then, on the sixth of August, the atomic bomb was dropped on Hiroshima, and in a little over a week, the Japanese surrendered.

The war that she once thought would never end was finally over.

There were wild celebrations and they went to a party on V-J night and she got quite high on champagne. That night she had her dream about the desert again, she was so thirsty, her throat was parched, she was dying of suffocation and the burning sun was beating down on her, her feet were bleeding, and then across the desert came a figure, an Army lieutenant, and she screamed, "Doug! Doug, you're back!"

And she awoke and there was Frank. He was beside her. He was real and the rest was all illusion. And suddenly she wanted to die. She wanted to go back to sleep and never wake up again.

But life does not end that easily. It goes on, and the black moments pass and others come.

The war was over. She was twenty-two. And life stretched ahead of her filled with blank pages, pages which she alone could fill. There was a calm now . . . and an emptiness.

Frank got out of the Navy in October and went back with his old law firm. Their life had changed very little. And she was seething with restlessness. Something was going to explode inside her if she didn't get away.

She persuaded Frank to let her go to New York and take a job. "I'll be home every weekend," she promised, "and besides, you're working on your law briefs every night, so you won't even know I'm gone."

"If you want to work, why don't you get a job in Washington? I'm sure there are plenty of things you could do here."

"Like what?" The idea of being in New York filled her with excitement, it made her feel alive again.

"What will people say?" Frank asked.

It was the question she had heard all her life, it was the creed which people of her background lived by. *What will people say?* "What people?" she asked.

"Everyone. Our friends. I could refuse to let you do it."

"Yes, you could." But I'd go anyway, she thought.

"Is this another of those crazy ideas of that headshrinker? Or have you stopped going to her?"

"It's my idea." She hadn't really consulted Doctor Ziedman about it. In fact, she had concluded that she had gotten about all she could from the sessions with Doctor Ziedman because they were becoming repetitive and she found herself saying the same things over and over again. Doctor Ziedman sat and nodded and agreed with her and every now and then would ask, "Why do you think that?" or something similar. Finally, she had asked in desperation, when she felt she had to get away from Frank, "But don't you ever feel that way in your marriage?"

"I'm not married," Doctor Ziedman said.

"But when you *were* married?"

"I've never been married," the deep voice behind the mahogany desk said, as if it were the most natural thing in the world to be advising people about something she had never experienced.

No, she had not told Doctor Ziedman of her decision. She was just going to call and say she was leaving town and cancel all future appointments.

"It was my idea entirely," she repeated.

CHAPTER FIFTY

S he felt the excitement and bustle of New York when the taxi came out of Pennsylvania Station and she wondered why in all the years she had lived in Washington it never gave her quite this feeling. She looked out the window at the milling throngs in the garment district as they slowly crawled across town, at the theatre signs on Broadway and the smart stores on Fifth Avenue, there was Saint Patrick's Cathedral and Saks and Bonwit Teller, and Bergdorf Goodman and F.A.O. Schwarz — how eagerly she awaited their Christmas toy catalogue when she was a child! And there was the fountain and the horses and carriages in front of the Plaza. Because of the shortage of hotel rooms in New York she had only been able to get a room for five days, but that would bring her to the weekend and she could look around for another place to stay next week.

The doorman opened the cab door and took her suitcase. She paid the driver and went up the steps. A strong breeze was blowing across Central Park and she held on to her hat. She registered at the desk and a bellboy carried her bag up in the elevator to her room. It was on the third floor and looked out on a side street. She would have preferred one with a view of the park, but there was no choice.

How lovely it was to be free, to do what she wanted for five whole days! "New York, I love you!" she sang, as she unpacked her suitcase. Maybe tonight she could get a ticket to *The Glass Menagerie* with Laurette Taylor and then there was *Carousel* — oh, there were so many things to do! She must call some of her friends and make lunch dates and she needed new clothes. Friday she had an appointment with *Vogue* for a job as assistant fashion editor. She had posed for them in her debutante days and it would be fun to help with the lay-outs and write some of the copy and actually earn a salary for it.

Why hadn't she done this before? And then she felt guilty about Frank.

But he had consented to let her come. Or perhaps he thought if he didn't oppose her she'd get it all out of her system and be glad to come back to Washington and Junior League work.

All my life I've lived for other people, she thought, I've done what was expected of me, and I've got to try something else or go mad. She couldn't spend the rest of her life running to Doctor Ziedman and pouring out her frustrations. Yes, I've done the right thing, she convinced herself.

The job on *Vogue* was to start Monday morning, so she would return to Washington Friday afternoon and take the Sunday afternoon train back to New York. She had been able to get a room at the Westbury Hotel at Madison Avenue and 69th Street and they agreed to let her stay there indefinitely. It was not nearly as expensive as the Plaza and the rooms were attractive and homelike. She could take the Madison Avenue bus to work, since it was too far to walk, and there were several nice little tearooms nearby if she got tired of eating at the Westbury.

She felt exhilarated about her job, but Frank did not quite share her enthusiasm. He complained of having to eat dinner alone all week, that she was self-centered and only thought of herself, and she could hardly wait to get away from him and back to New York.

He drove her to Union Station without speaking, and it was with relief that she boarded the train. She watched him through the window as the train pulled out of the station, standing there on the platform looking forlorn and filled with self-pity and she thought: Am I being selfish?

And again she felt torn the way she had all her life between the obligation to do what other people wanted and the desire to be herself.

She loved her job on *Vogue* and meeting new people who appeared to like her for herself and not for her family background. That they probably wouldn't have hired her if it were not for her society contacts never occurred to her. She was at the office bright and early every morning and worked as if her life depended on it. And in a way it did, because she had no time between setting up photographic sittings and writing copy and running all over town to worry about her problems and ask herself: Am I happy?

She had an interesting job and she was learning new things all the time. Eventually, she would have to make some decision about her marriage, but she preferred to put it off as long as possible. There was no one else in her life and she felt the future would take care of itself.

One day, rushing along Fifth Avenue, she ran into one of her classmates from The French School.

"Mary Ogden!" She remembered the time she had tried to talk Mary into going with her to a foreign film in the "forbidden" section of New York and how Mary had informed her about white slavers. Mary's hair was shorter and she had put on a little weight. Or else she was pregnant.

"Ardith!" Mary threw her arms around her. "It's been ages! Are you in town for long? We must get together."

"I'm working here. Assistant fashion editor on *Vogue*."

"How exciting! Where are you staying?"

"The Westbury. Madison at—"

"Sixty-ninth," Mary finished. "I know it well. The Polo Bar. We used to drop in there after weddings at Saint James Church across the street. Look let's have lunch. I've so much to tell you. I'm Mrs. Phillip Schuyler now and we have a little girl and another on the way. But a boy this time, we hope! Are you busy today?"

"Yes, I'm just dashing to a sitting, but what about Friday?"

"Fine. How about the Colony at twelve-thirty?"

"See you then." And she waved to Mary and crossed Fifth Avenue just as the light changed.

Mary was bursting with news. Her husband was in advertising and had gone to Princeton.

"I want you to meet him — I've told him all about you. We have an apartment at 530 Park Avenue. It's a great location and I can wheel Cecily in her stroller over to Central Park. It's so hard to get a decent nanny these days." Mary ordered a pancake filled with creamed chicken. "I'm supposed to keep my weight down. I probably should have a lettuce leaf with cottage cheese and grapefruit." She made a face. "Oh, well." She handed the menu back to the waiter. "Now, tell me everything about you. Oh, did you hear about Katherine Peabody? She was your roommate, wasn't she?"

"Yes. The last I heard she was trying to get overseas with the Red Cross."

"Well, it would have been better if she hadn't. She's in a mental institution somewhere outside of Hartford."

"No! What happened?" Katherine, who wanted to be a social worker, to improve conditions of those less fortunate, she had been so idealistic, so filled with hope, it could not be true that she had had a mental breakdown.

"She went overseas. She was under age, you know, but her family knew some senator and she was so determined to go, so they pulled a few strings and she was with a clubmobile in France. They were pretty close to the front and they went into Paris right after it was liberated."

"You mean the things she saw. . ."

"Well, partly. But after all, she had been doing social work in the poorer sections of Boston. Of course, war is ever so much worse, with the wounded men and all that, so it's not the same thing, but she wasn't a nurse, so she didn't see some of the horrible sights they did, well, I won't go into that during lunch . . ." Mary attacked her chicken pancake as if food was going out of style.

"What made her crack up?"

"She got involved with this Army captain . . . I heard he was very dashing . . . and he gave her a big line about being in love with her. The only thing he neglected to tell her was that he had a wife back in the States. She discovered that when she told him she was pregnant. He ran as if the Germans were chasing him. Katherine tried to kill herself and when that didn't work, she had an abortion. They sent her home and she went to pieces completely."

"Can she have visitors?" Ardith thought she would run up to Hartford to see her.

"What good would it do? They say she doesn't even recognize her family."

"Poor Katherine. I still can't believe it."

"I know. I probably shouldn't have told you."

"No." Ardith shook her head. "I just wish there was something that someone could do to help." She thought of their graduation day at The French School and Madame Duval's grim speech:

"Who knows what your lives will be? But one thing is certain . . . they will not be easy."

And she remembered all of them in their white dresses and bouquets of snapdragons and daisies, their eyes full of hope and dreams. The Class of 1941. And now, a little over four years later, they had all been touched by the war, they had all been thrust into a world for which they were little prepared.

The stern Frenchwoman's prophecy had come true.

"Whatever happened to Madame Duval?" Ardith asked.

"I've no idea. She closed the school and just disappeared." Mary waved to someone across the restaurant. "How about dessert?"

"I don't think so." She looked at her watch. "I'd better be getting back to the office."

"Oh, darn. I hoped you could come back with me and see the apartment."

"Another time." She took out her compact and quickly powdered her nose.

"I want you to meet Phil and Cecily. And I'd like to give a little party for you."

Mary was obviously curious about her marital situation and Ardith didn't feel like discussing it. She realized that Mary had done most of the talking during lunch, which was just as well, because there were things that she still found difficult to talk about.

Mary grabbed the check. "My treat," she insisted. "Next time you can take me."

CHAPTER FIFTY-ONE

The weeks flew by and before she knew it the Christmas holidays had arrived. The crosstown traffic was terrible and she barely managed to get to Penn Station before her train pulled out. She stood in line waiting to get into the diner and finally there was a place at a table with three other people. She ordered lunch and then gazed out at the New Jersey landscape whirling by. The sky was metal gray and there were patches of snow on the ground.

She was not looking forward to spending Christmas in Washington. Frank was becoming more and more critical of her job and the time she was away. Apparently he had hoped she would quit after a few weeks and come home. One weekend her mother had asked, "Is everything all right with you and Frank?"

"Why, yes. Did he say anything to you?"

"Oh no, dear. It's just that you're spending so much time in New York and people are beginning to talk."

"I'm sorry they have nothing more interesting to talk about. They must lead very dull lives," she had replied with irritation.

The fact was, she had thought about divorce more than once. But what charges could she use? She had to have a good reason and she had none. Frank was a good husband, even though his fussiness and constant looking for specks of dust drove her almost to distraction. If she were in love with him and they had a satisfactory sex life together, none of these things would be so important, but without that it was becoming more and more unbearable and she felt on the brink of an explosion.

It only needed the right person to push the trigger.

"Is everything all right?"

"What?" She looked up. The waiter was standing there. "Oh . . . yes, thank you, it's very good. I'm just not that hungry."

"Would you like some dessert?"

"No, just coffee. And would you bring the check, please?"

The man sitting directly opposite her was staring at her and she was sure she had seen him somewhere before but where? He looked so familiar and she wondered if she had met him at some Washington party.

"Do you mind if I smoke?" he asked, taking out a package of cigarettes.

"Not at all." Who was he? He was very attractive with sandy hair and blue eyes and rugged good looks.

"Would you like a cigarette?"

"No, thank you."

And then she realized who he was.

Joe Kreskie had been studying Ardith during the meal when she scarcely touched her food. She did not seem at all the way he had pictured her, the spoiled and arrogant debutante, but a young woman who was unhappy and vulnerable. Something was obviously bothering her and he wondered what it was. He wanted suddenly to reach out and touch her hand and say, "Don't look so unhappy. It's going to be all right." Odd that he should feel that way after the years of stored-up resentment.

The two other people at the table got up and left and he was alone with Ardith.

She was looking out the window again at the passing landscape. Was this the moment to say something, to introduce himself?

And then their eyes met across the table.

"You're Senator Kreskie," she said. "From Pennsylvania."

"That's right. And you're T. J. Wyman's granddaughter."

She looked surprised. "Were you a friend of my grandfather's?"

Friend? How would he define it? Certainly not friend. "Not exactly," he said.

"You knew him in Oil City, then?"

"In a way." He paused. "He played a very important role in my life."

She leaned forward. "Really? What was that?"

"He was responsible, largely, for what I am today."

"I don't quite understand."

"It's a long and complicated story. I don't want to bore you with it."

"I'd like to hear it."

"You would?"

"Yes, really."

Why not? he thought. It was as good a time as any other. And then, out of the corner of his eye, he noticed the head waiter bringing two more people down the aisle in the direction of their table. "Look, how about having a drink with me in the club car? There's still a line waiting to get in the diner and I think they'd like our places."

She hesitated just a minute. "Fine," she said. He signaled for the check. As he paid it he wondered what her reaction would be when she learned the truth.

They walked through several swaying cars till they came to the club car, and he found two seats in a quiet corner.

"What would you like to drink?" he asked.

"Dubonnet on the rocks, please."

He ordered a gin-and-tonic for himself.

"Now, tell me how you know so much about the Wyman family, Senator Kreskie. I'm curious."

"My friends call me Joe."

"Joe . . . that was my uncle's name. I never knew him, though. He was killed before I was born. He was my mother's favorite brother."

"I know." He paused. "He was my father."

Her eyes widened in surprise. "Did you say your father?"

"My father and your Uncle Joe were the same person. We're first cousins."

"But how—"

"When they were both very young, your Uncle Joe and my mother met and fell in love. But my mother came from a poor Polish family who lived on the wrong side of town, while the Wymans . . ." Suddenly all the bitterness that he had stored within him for so many years spilled out. "Anyway, to make a long story short, your grandfather didn't think she was good enough for his favorite son."

"I'm sorry."

"They treated my mother like dirt, tried to buy her off."

"By 'they' you mean my grandfather?"

He nodded. "T. J. Wyman."

"I don't blame you for feeling the way you do. I used to resent Grandfather a lot, too, when I was growing up."

"But why should you have resented him? You had everything."

"Everything—" she gave a bitter laugh— "and nothing. You see, I blamed him for my father's disappearance, though I've no definite proof of anything he did to cause it. It's just a feeling I have. Grandfather wanted to control everyone and if anyone in the family stepped out of line. . ."

No, he thought, she wasn't at all what he had expected.

"Someday I'm going to find my father. I know he's alive somewhere. And then I'll know the truth."

"Sometimes the truth can be unpleasant."

"I'm prepared for that. But anything is better than not knowing."

They were coming to the tunnels around Baltimore. It was dark and then suddenly light again.

"I'm glad that we finally met," she said. "And that we're cousins."

"So am I. You're not at all the kind of person I thought you'd be."

"Is that good or bad?"

He smiled. "It's good."

The train went into another tunnel. "Baltimore!" the porter called.

More passengers got on at Baltimore.

"Next stop Washington," announced the porter.

"I guess I'd better get back to my seat," she said. "Let's keep in touch. Will you call me?"

"I'll do that."

"And thank you for the drink." She leaned over and kissed him on the cheek. "Cousin Joe."

CHAPTER FIFTY-TWO

Ardith and Frank had dinner with her mother at the house on Kalorama Circle. There were icicles on the trees and the streets were like sheets of glass. Her mother was walking with a cane and the slight tremor that Ardith had noticed in the past was much worse.

"It's nothing." Grace Rodgers brushed it off.

"Don't you think you should see a doctor? Have you had a thorough checkup lately?"

"Now stop trying to treat me like an old lady. I'm fine."

"Here, Mother Rodgers, take this chair," Frank said.

Her mother sat down and Carrie brought in sherry and a Scotch-and-water for Frank. Her mother took a sip of sherry and her hand was shaking so that she almost spilled it. She put the glass down and cupped her right hand in her left to hide the trembling of her right arm.

There was no point in arguing with her, Ardith thought, but she made a mental note to see her mother's doctor and have a talk with him.

"It's nice having my wife back again," Frank said.

Ardith forced a smile. There had been a touch of sarcasm in Frank's voice. "It's nice being home again." She felt that she sounded horribly insincere.

Frank's law practice was going extremely well and she knew she should be here during the week to entertain his clients when he wanted her to. It was just that for the first time in her life she was beginning to feel free, to have some identity of her own. Was this wrong? She was being made to feel that it was. The narrow path she had to walk, the mold into which she was poured, the unyielding, rigid pattern she was supposed to fit.

"Frank's right," she heard her mother saying. "You should be in Washington during the week instead of New York. Why can't you stage some fashion shows for the Junior League?"

"Oh, Mother," she said with irritation, and then remembered that her mother wasn't well and that it was Christmas. "It's not quite the same."

"I don't see why not. It isn't as if you needed the money they're paying you at *Vogue*. I'm sure that barely covers your hotel bill."

Frank nodded in agreement.

She looked at the two of them. The lines were drawn. They had decided for her and she was supposed to go along. The path of least resistance. Conform.

"You don't understand," she said. And she wondered if she was looking for something that didn't exist. Would anyone ever really understand her? The longing for love that was deep within her, and fighting it, the need for an identity of her own. Must she sacrifice one for the other? Must she be a shadow of someone else?

There was no point trying to explain how she felt to either her mother or Frank.

"Dinner is served," Carrie announced.

The discussion was over for the time being, but she knew that it would come up again.

The night before she was to return to New York, Frank said he thought they should have a talk.

"Now, I've humored you in this crazy idea of yours to go and work on a fashion magazine. You can't say that I opposed you, can you?"

"No, Frank." She took off her earrings and put them on her dressing table. So now her parole was over. The warden had decided that she would be better off in prison. Safe from the temptations of the outer world. Already she could hear the keys rattling on a long chain.

"But enough is enough." Frank was pacing the bedroom as if he were in a courtroom. "I think that it's time that you started acting like a real woman again. A real wife. Not a part-time one."

He had been preparing this speech for some time, she thought, just waiting for the proper time to deliver it. She took her brush and started to brush her hair vigorously.

"Put that hairbrush down and listen to me!" Frank shouted. "This is important. It concerns us. You and me. If that still matters to you. Or did

I ever matter to you? Sometimes I wonder. I've had a lot of time to wonder lately — while you were in New York."

She made no reply. Let him say it all, she thought.

"You never express any affection toward me. Sometimes I wonder why you married me in the first place. Because you were lonely? Because there was nothing better in view?"

"You know that's not true." But it is true, she thought.

"I wasn't born yesterday," Frank said. "I don't believe you're just sitting in your room at the Westbury Hotel in the evenings by yourself. There's some other man in the picture and you might as well admit it, because I'll find out anyway."

This she was not prepared for. How could he think . . . but with his insanely jealous mind it made sense in a way.

"Who is he?"

"Frank . . ." She had to laugh. "You're being ridiculous!"

"I'm glad you find it amusing." He had her by the arm and was twisting it, a sadistic gleam in his eye.

"Frank, you're hurting me."

He released her and started to pace the room again.

In a flash she saw how one could be driven to infidelity by false accusations, how unreasonable jealousy could bring about the very situation that it feared.

"How do you think I feel when people in the office make sly remarks about how my wife likes working in New York?"

"I . . ."

"No, it never occurred to you, did it?"

"Well, since you mention it, it didn't."

"No, of course not. You always think of what you want to do. You never consider other people. It's been that way all your life. A friend of mine told me before I married you that you were spoiled, that you were used to being catered to."

Was the "friend" that older divorcée who was chasing you? she wondered. "Then why did you ignore your friend's warning?" she asked.

"Because I was in love with you. And I hoped that in time you would return my feelings. Apparently that hasn't happened."

Was this a question or a statement of fact? Did love ever grow if it wasn't there in the beginning? She had heard that sometimes it did. There were those who said that respect and mutual tastes and backgrounds were more important than romantic feelings. But she knew it was not true for her, and that was what was important. In marrying Frank she had not been true to herself.

"Frank, I think we're both unhappy in this situation." She must choose her words carefully. "Why don't we consider the next few months sort of a trial separation? And then—"

"Are you implying that you want a divorce?"

"It may be the only solution."

"There has never been a divorce in my family," Frank said stiffly. "My parents have been married for thirty-eight years. They may not be happy, but at least they are together."

She knew what he was implying by that and it made her angry.

"You may think them dull and stuffy if you like, but they kept our home together."

Suddenly she felt stifled by the kind of togetherness that forced people who hated each other to go on living together, and yet she knew how she had suffered by her parents' divorce. But in this case there were no children. No one would suffer. She and Frank would be far better off apart.

"So you can just tell this man, whoever he is, that there will be no divorce," Frank said. Apparently he still had the imaginary rival on his mind. "Now, let's go to bed." He took off his horn-rimmed glasses and started to undress.

CHAPTER FIFTY-THREE

She had been back in New York only a few days when Mary Schuyler called.

"Phil and I are having a small cocktail party Friday evening. Can you come, or will you be in Washington?"

"No, I'll be here and I'd love to come."

She felt exhilarated, as if suddenly something wonderful was going to happen, and she went out and bought herself a new dress. She loved beautiful clothes and it always gave her a lift to buy something new and glamorous. She wondered if this denoted a superficial flaw in her character. There were women who were very wealthy who didn't care what they put on and were almost dowdy in their appearance as if to say, "Our good works speak for us, we don't need to dress up." Some of the old Boston families especially, in fact Frank's mother was like that. She wrinkled her nose at the thought.

Her dress was deep red velvet and somewhat décolleté. Too much? She looked at herself in the mirror. No, she decided. She tried sweeping her hair on top of her head. It looked better down. She put on antique gold-and-pearl earrings and white gloves and her mink coat. It was snowing outside. She hoped there wouldn't be trouble getting a cab.

"Better wait inside," the doorman said. "I'll whistle for one and call you."

There were several people in long evening clothes waiting for a taxi ahead of her, two elderly ladies and one older man in white tie and tails. No doubt they were going to the opera. The ladies had on ermine capes, slightly yellow with age, and appeared to be sisters. She remembered seeing them in the elevator and they all exchanged vague smiles.

"Come, girls," said the man, and she noticed that he had a high-pitched, agitated voice and effeminate walk. "He's finally found us a cab."

Another cab pulled up right behind it and Ardith took that.

It gave her a strange feeling to be going to a party alone, unpleasantly reminiscent of her dancing school days, and she glanced in her purse mirror to reassure herself. It was snowing fairly hard now and she was glad they didn't have far to go.

The "small party" was jammed with people and she realized in terror that she didn't know a soul. For a moment she was sorry that she hadn't told the cab to wait. A maid took her coat and she looked around helplessly. Then she saw Mary in the middle of the room and at the same time Mary saw her and rushed toward her.

"Ardith! I'm so glad you could come. I want you to meet Phil. He was here just a minute ago . . ." She looked around. A couple came up to say goodbye. "Oh, must you leave so soon?"

The couple said they must, the commuter train to Greenwich, but it had been a lovely party, so much fun . . .

More people came through the door, it was like the subway at rush hour, but there was no strap to hang on to. Now which of these men was Mary's husband? She should know her host. If she just slipped out quietly, would anyone notice?

"Can I get you a drink?" a voice asked. "Come on, let's go over to the bar. That is, if you've decided to stay." He was tall and heavy-set, with hazel eyes and brown hair and a boyish grin. "I'm Stan Olson."

"Ardith Rodgers." She realized she had given her maiden name without thinking.

"I work at J. Walter Thompson with Phil," Stan said. "But I don't think I've ever met you at any of their parties."

"No, you haven't. I went to school with Mary and we ran into each other again a few weeks ago. I still haven't met Phil. Mary was trying to find him to introduce us when we were swept apart by the crowd." She smiled.

"Hi, Stan," someone called.

He waved back with a big grin that lit up his whole face. He wasn't handsome, she thought, but there was a rugged, masculine quality about him that made him very appealing. He had broad shoulders and a deep voice and a kind of animal magnetism. She couldn't place his voice. It wasn't New York or Boston and she couldn't figure out where he was from. It was as rich and resonant as a singer's voice, but he had said that he was in advertising. He seemed to know everyone in the room and from their attitude everyone liked him. He had a very easy-going, relaxed manner. She had heard that most advertising men were driving robots and had ulcers from trying to keep up with the constant pressure. Stan Olson looked as if nothing could bother him.

He got her a drink and they moved away from the bar. "Let's try and find a corner where we can talk," Stan said. They edged toward a window. "At least there's some air here," he grinned.

"Mary told me it was to be a small cocktail party."

"Just several hundred of their most intimate friends."

"Are you from New York? You know so many people here."

"Me?" He laughed. "No, ma'am, just a small town boy from Minnesota."

"You don't talk like a Midwesterner."

"That's because I was a radio announcer for a while. I had a twang to start with but I worked on it."

So it was a trained voice. She had been right about that. She tried to judge his age. Thirty-six? Around there.

"I worked at a radio station in St. Paul's for a while," he said. "I was just a kid, but full of confidence. I was going to lick the world. You know, Jack Armstrong, the All-American boy." He grinned. "We were in the midst of the Depression and I was lucky to have a job, but I didn't know that. I quit and hitchhiked to New York. I arrived with sixty cents in my pocket. I went to NBC and tried to convince them how lucky they would be to get me, but they didn't quite see it that way. So I washed dishes, was an usher at Radio City and quite a few other odd jobs, and kept looking for an opening in radio. Finally they realized what they had overlooked . . ." He grinned and waved to someone. "And from radio I went into advertising, and there you have it. The story of my life."

A bartender came by and Stan gave him his glass and ordered another Scotch.

"How about you? A refill? That's nothing but water."

"No, thanks. This is fine."

"Now that I've been doing all the talking, tell me about you."

"Well, let's see. I'm from Washington and I'm working as a fashion editor at *Vogue*." And I have a husband from whom I'm separated, but I don't think I'll mention him. Suddenly she wondered if Stan was married. He hadn't said anything about a wife and he seemed to be at the party alone. His next question dispelled that thought.

"Look, could you have dinner with me?"

She hesitated. Would that be wrong?

"Unless you have other plans."

She shook her head. "No, I haven't any other plans."

"Good. Then get your coat and let's duck out of here. We can talk in a quiet restaurant over a good steak. How does that sound?"

"Fine. Do you see our host or hostess?"

Stan glanced around the room. "We can call them tomorrow."

She got her coat and they slipped out. People were still arriving. It was one of those parties obviously to pay back business as well as social obligations, where the same guests would not have much in common at a dinner party but could all be mixed together at a large cocktail party.

"I love Phil and Mary," Stan said, as they rode down in the elevator, "but I hate a rat race like that. I have to go through that in business every day of my life."

"At least you knew people there. I didn't know a soul. I'm glad you came to my rescue."

He smiled and took her arm. "I thought we'd go to a little place I know over on Third Avenue. It has a lot of atmosphere and the best steaks in town. Unless, of course, you'd rather go to '21?'"

"No, let's go to your place. I love to discover new restaurants."

It had stopped snowing and the lampposts on Park Avenue sparkled against the powdery whiteness. The air was frosty and the stars were bright and clear with a new moon hanging like a golden caterpillar in the dark sky.

"Beautiful, isn't it?" Stan said.

"Yes." She looked up at him and felt a strange excitement and then thought how crazy it was because she had just met him.

"Here's my car," he said.

The doorman opened the door of a black Cadillac and helped her in.

I really don't know anything about him, she told herself, and yet it seemed as if she had known Stan all her life. And she thought how you can know someone for years and not know them and never feel really close to them, and then suddenly, in an instant, you meet someone and know that it could mean something. Just like that.

"Sometimes I think it's not worth keeping a car in New York," Stan said, "but on evenings like this when cabs are scarce, I'm glad I have one, even though I have to keep it in a garage three blocks from my apartment."

Stan shared an apartment with two other bachelors in an old brown-stone on East 67th Street. They passed it on the way and he pointed it out.

"It's not bad," he said, "and we're all seldom home at the same time."

She wondered if they had signals the way she knew men had who shared an apartment. A light in the window turned a certain way meaning, "Don't come home tonight, I have a guest."

"How long have you lived there?" she asked.

"A year."

He told her about his roommates. One was a photographer and the other was a salesman with a company that kept him on the road a lot.

"They're characters," he laughed. "You'll have to meet them."

She thought that she wouldn't like sharing an apartment with other women, with dripping stockings hanging all over the bathroom and sharing the closet and not having any privacy. But then men liked being together better than women and weren't as messy.

"Have you ever been married?" she asked. It seemed incredible that a man as attractive as Stan wasn't married, or at least going with someone, and he acted completely free. He hadn't even brought a date to the party.

"Yes, I've been married." His voice was bitter and she saw that she had better not pursue the subject. They were pulling up in front of the restaurant. "This is one of my favorite places," he said. "I hope you like it."

The restaurant was dark and lit by coach lamps and in a corner a man was playing the piano. The headwaiter and bartender greeted Stan happily and it was obvious that he came here often. The menu was written on a blackboard that was brought around to each table. It was simple. Your choice of steaks, a baked potato with sour cream and chives, and a mixed green salad.

"Nothing fancy, but I'm a meat and potatoes man myself," Stan grinned.

He ordered a martini and she had a Dubonnet. Stan raised his glass. "*Skoal.*"

"*Skoal.*"

"I know another toast." He smiled. "But I'll have to wait until I know you better."

So he intended to go on seeing her, that he seemed to take for granted. And she knew that she wanted to see him. For the first time since Doug's death, she felt alive.

"Olson," she said. "Is that Swedish?"

He nodded. "My father's parents were born in Sweden and they moved to Minnesota after they were married."

"Do they still live there?"

"My mother and a younger brother. My dad died when I was seventeen."

He told her about his boyhood and how he used to go hunting with his dad in the Minnesota woods. His father was a druggist and they knew everyone in the town. He mentioned the name but she had never heard of it.

"It's near St. Paul," he said.

He had a happy boyhood, the simple, smalltown life, the lakes and woods nearby, it was all very normal and uncomplicated until his father's death. Then he left the small town and went to St. Paul, and from there to New York. He was in the Navy during the war.

"Were you overseas?" she asked.

"No, I was stationed in New York the whole time." He grinned. "I fought the Battle of 90 Church Street."

He liked New York. There was an excitement about the advertising world. "I'd hate to get up every morning knowing exactly what was going to happen each day," he said. He took her hand. "Like this morning. When I woke up I didn't know I was going to meet you."

The piano player was playing "If I Loved You" from *Carousel.*

"Have you seen *Carousel?*" Stan asked.

"No, I haven't. I've been wanting to see it."

"Good. I'll get tickets for one night next week."

They ate their steaks and Stan told her about his early struggles in the New York advertising world during the Depression.

"For two weeks once I lived on cornflakes and peanut butter sandwiches," he said. "I haven't been able to stand either since."

I was at Miss Putnam's then, she thought, with a bunch of silly girls talking about their coming-out parties. How strange all that world seemed now.

"Well, here I've been doing all the talking and you've just been sitting there listening. What goes on behind those pretty brown eyes? A lot of things are going through your mind right now."

"Oh . . ."

"You'll tell me when you want to." He squeezed her hand. "Whatever it is, I'm sorry that you're so unhappy."

"I'm not unhappy." She paused. "Is it that obvious?"

He nodded. "I have a philosophy of life and it seems to work for me. Do you want to hear it?"

"Yes. What is it?"

"Enjoy each moment now. Don't worry about tomorrow or brood over yesterday. Live *now*. It never comes back."

"That's true."

"You're darn right. Most people are so busy worrying about what might happen in the future that they can't enjoy today."

Yes, but you can't just wave your hand and make things disappear. Like Frank, for instance. But worrying about it all the time didn't help either.

"Do you like violin music?" Stan asked.

"I love it."

"I thought you might. I know a little Viennese place not far from here. Let's drop by and have a drink on our way home."

Stan's New York was different from the one she had always known that consisted of the Stork Club and El Morocco and two or three other nightclubs and restaurants frequented by café society. His was more fun. His was not the world of inherited money and the feeling that one wasn't entitled to enjoy it. If Stan Olson had problems no one would know it, other than his brief references to his marriage. He loved every minute of living. He sparkled with enthusiasm. No wonder everyone was happy to see him.

He helped her on with her coat and they went to the Viennese Lantern.

Violinists serenaded them at their table and they drank champagne cocktails and she felt as if she never wanted the evening to end.

"I'm glad I went to that party at the Schuylers'," Stan said, holding her hand. "I almost didn't."

"Nor I. And I don't know when I've had such a lovely evening."

It was more than that and they both knew it. It was just beginning, and who could tell where it would lead? But she was not going to worry about tomorrow. She was going to take Stan's advice and enjoy today. To feel alive, to be happy again after all the empty years!

He kissed her goodnight in the lobby of the Westbury.

"I'll call you," he said.

CHAPTER FIFTY-FOUR

Once again her life had meaning. All colors, all sounds were intensified, she felt everything more deeply, it was as if she were awakening after a long sleep, there was excitement in the air and magic. She knew it was because of Stan. She was falling in love with him. It frightened her, yet at the same time, she knew that she could no more stop what was going to happen than she could divert a river from its course.

He called on Monday.

"I managed to get two house seats to *Carousel* for tomorrow evening, if you're free then," he said.

"Wonderful!"

"We can grab a quick bite at Sardi's beforehand."

She managed to leave the office a little early to have plenty of time to dress and she was waiting when he called from the lobby.

"I'm here."

"I'll be right down." She dabbed on some more perfume and threw on her coat.

He was waiting by the elevator doors.

"You look as beautiful as I remembered," he said, taking her arm and leading her to the car. "In a way, I hoped you wouldn't."

"Why?" So he was trying to fight it too.

"Oh, I don't know." He grinned that boyish grin and opened the car door.

And she thought how ironic it was that you could be attracted to a man not wanting to, knowing next to nothing about him, and how impossible it was to talk yourself into caring for someone—no, not caring—it wasn't as simple as that, because she did care for Frank. But what he said was true, she was cold with him, she did appear to just tolerate him in bed, and whether he made love to her or not made little difference. But with Stan she felt a wild excitement when he just touched her arm and she knew how it could be with them.

"What are you thinking?" Stan asked.

"Oh . . . that I was so glad you were able to get tickets to *Carousel*. I've been dying to see it. When I first came to New York, I tried to get a ticket to a matinee and they told me at the box office that they were sold out for months."

"It's no fun seeing a musical by yourself."

"No, you're right."

"Half the fun of things is doing them with the right person." He took her hand. "There are so many places I want to show you. When the weather is better I know an inn at Pound Ridge. It was built during the Revolution and has an old taproom . . . lots of atmosphere. You'd love it. We can go there some weekend."

He said it casually, as if he took it for granted that they were going to have an affair, and she wondered if he was used to inviting women on weekends and how naive he would think her if she told him that she had never stayed anywhere with a man other than her husband. She was told that she looked sophisticated and maybe that was what he took her for. A woman of the world.

Sardi's was packed and they were turning away people.

"Hello, Vincent," Stan said.

"Good evening, Mr. Olson. Right this way."

Vincent led them to one of the front tables where they could see whoever was coming in.

The waiter handed them a dinner menu.

"We'd better order right away," Stan said, glancing at his watch.

"The canneloni is very nice," the waiter said. "And I can have that for you in a few minutes."

"And fattening," Stan said. "Oh, well . . . if that's all right with you?"

"Fine," Ardith said.

"And a nice green salad?" The waiter stood with pencil poised.

"Good. And bring us a martini—very dry—and a Dubonnet on the rocks with a lemon twist."

She looked at the cartoons of different celebrities on the walls. Some of the people without reservations were being shown upstairs.

"I'm sorry, but everything is filled in the main room," Vincent was saying politely but firmly.

"Do you come here often?" she asked.

"Oh, pretty often. We have some clients who like to eat here."

The food arrived.

"I love food," Stan said, "and my doctor warned me the other day that I should lose at least ten pounds."

"You're not overweight." But she could see the beginning of a double chin and he had the kind of square, solid build that could turn into fat if he didn't watch it.

"I used to play golf," he said, "but I don't have time to any more."

"I guess your work keeps you pretty much on the go."

"It sure does." He grinned. "But it's never dull. That's the fun of the game."

She found herself wondering what his wife had been like. He had not mentioned her again after that brief reference the other night. Were there any children? She would make a lunch date with Mary Schuyler and work the conversation around in a subtle way without appearing too interested. In the meantime, maybe Stan would tell her.

"You said you went to school with Mary?" He had almost picked up her thoughts, she realized with a start.

"Yes, here in New York. We spoke French all the time. I don't know what ever happened to the school. I heard it folded during the war."

"And then what happened to you?"

"I went back to Washington and got married. He was killed in North Africa."

"I'm sorry."

"And then after a while I guess I got lonely, because I married someone else, and it was a horrible mistake. Oh, I don't mean because of him, because he's a very nice person, but I just wasn't in love with him. Anyway, we're separated . . . and I decided to come to New York and get a job."

"Do you like working on a magazine?"

"Yes, I love it. As you said about your job, it's never dull."

"It's a strange life, isn't it? I wonder what would have happened if I'd met you, oh say, ten years ago?"

She laughed. "I was twelve years old and had braces on my teeth. You wouldn't have liked me."

"I keep forgetting that you're so young." For an instant something seemed to be troubling him and then he smiled. "I'm glad we finally met."

"So am I."

"I guess we'd better be going. I have to pick up the tickets at the theatre by eight. We can have dessert afterward."

Stan glanced over at her as the house lights came on. She was dabbing at her eyes with a handkerchief.

"Did you like it?"

"Oh, it was beautiful! But so sad." She put her handkerchief back in her purse and looked at herself quickly in her compact mirror. "I'm a wreck!"

"I wouldn't say that." He helped her on with her coat and they walked up the aisle. People were humming the tunes on their way out. "It's a great score," he said.

"I think it's the best they've done."

"Look, why don't we go dancing somewhere? Would you like to?"

"Fine, I'd love to."

They dropped in at El Morocco and the headwaiter led them to a table on the edge of the dance floor. This was one of her old haunts and heads turned as they walked by. There were all the old familiar faces she remembered from her debutante days, only looking a little older and more jaded. The blank, bored faces looking for new thrills.

"We're going to Palm Beach next week. That's one of the few places that hasn't changed since the war. Of course, we had to give up the yacht . . ."

A man came over and kissed her hand. "Hello, beautiful."

"Oh, hello, Ghighi."

"I haven't seen you in here in such a long time."

"No. Mr. Cassini, Mr. Olson."

He went back to his companions and Stan said, "Is that the dress designer?"

"No, that's his brother, Oleg. Ghighi writes *Cholly Knickerbocker*."

Stan ordered champagne cocktails. The orchestra was playing "If I Loved You."

"There's our song," Stan said. "Let's dance."

They moved out onto the small crowded dance floor. He held her close and again she felt the tremendous excitement between them. It was the very thing that had been lacking in her relationship with Frank. She noticed Ghighi watching them.

"Your friend seems very interested in you," Stan observed.

"Oh, I'm last year's news," she laughed. And ironically she thought how true it was. Each year there were new debutantes and the old ones were considered on the shelf. Fame was fleeting. And she had had far more publicity than most of them, but that was five years ago.

The orchestra switched to a fast rhumba.

"I'm no good at those South American dances," Stan said. "I never had time to learn them. In fact, I never really learned to dance." He grinned. "I just shuffle along to the music. And it gives me a chance to hold you."

"You're a good dancer." He wasn't smooth like the Yale and Princeton boys she used to dance with but he had a sense of rhythm.

"No." He watched a couple next to them doing an intricate step. "And I sure can't fake that." He led her back to their table.

They sat down and he leaned toward her. "You're a very exciting woman to me," he said,

"Am I?" She sipped her drink.

"Yes, and I'm sure you know it."

She did not answer. I know what's going to happen between us, she thought. It's just a matter of time, but it's inevitable. She felt as if she were standing on the edge of a volcano. It was both frightening and exciting.

He pressed her hand. "Let's go," he said. "I was never much for these smoky nightclubs."

They drove back to the Westbury Hotel and he went up in the elevator with her. She opened the door and he pulled her to him. They stood kissing in the darkened entrance hall and then he led her through the living room toward the bedroom.

"No, Stan," she said suddenly.

"Why not?"

"Not . . . not yet."

"All right," he said. "I can wait if you can."

CHAPTER FIFTY-FIVE

It was Saturday afternoon and they were driving along the Merritt Parkway.

"The country around here is so beautiful in the fall when all the trees have turned," Stan said. "It reminds me of the woods in Minnesota when I was a boy."

"I've never been there."

"It's a great place to be from. Oh, it was fine when I was growing up, even with the Depression. We didn't feel it as much as those in the big cities. We had a nice house and plenty to eat. My dad owned the local drugstore. I went in heavily for sports in high school — baseball, football, track. Even had the lead in the play the dramatic club put on. I was King Lear." He grinned. "Fortunately, I decided not to make acting my profession."

"What made you leave?"

"After my dad's death I just wanted to get away." His face darkened for a moment. "Besides, you're pretty limited in a small town. The drugstore was sold and jobs were pretty scarce. I heard there was an opening for an announcer at a radio station in St. Paul, so I hitchhiked there and auditioned with everyone else and they hired me. I was only a seventeen-year-old kid and wet behind the ears, but I knew I was going to get that job."

"It must have taken a lot of courage to strike out that way on your own."

"No," he shrugged. "I'd go crazy in a small town. Whenever I go back there, which isn't often, and see some of the people I went to high school with, I wonder how they can stand it. But they seem content. My brother, for instance. He runs a gas station there. Happy as a clam. Doesn't care about seeing the rest of the world. He can't understand why I want to work in New York."

"It always amazes me how people can grow up in the same family and be so different."

"That's what makes the world. No two people are alike."

"But when you're little you so desperately want to be like everyone else. I know I did. I felt so strange and unlike every member of my family. As if I didn't belong. And I felt the same way at school too. It seemed that no one understood me."

"That's a common feeling. We all have it to some degree. And then we outgrow it when we find our niche in life."

"Does everyone have a niche?"

"Sure, but some never find it."

"I don't know what mine is."

"You're still very young. You'll find it." He pulled up in front of a rustic inn. "Here we are."

She looked around. The inn was painted red with white wooden shutters and two coach lamps were on either side of the front door.

"It used to be an old carriage house," Stan said. "I hope you like it."

They went in the dining room and ordered lunch.

"The other place I told you about is closed in the winter. But we'll go there in the spring when it opens."

Spring. It had been a long time since she had looked forward to spring. The past few years watching the dogwood burst into bloom and the daffodils and tulips and hyacinths, all the flowers that she had loved, had filled her with pain remembering her times with Doug, times that were dead and buried, memories that she must forget. She had been numb for three years and now she felt herself coming to life again. She looked at Stan across the table. He had such a strong face and powerful broad shoulders, he was so full of assurance and confidence, the very things she had always lacked, and she suddenly wondered what it would be like to be married to him, to sit across the table from him day after day, to hear his car in the driveway, to have him holding her at night. This feeling was different from what she had felt for Doug, for then she was a young girl, untouched by life, Doug was her first love, and first loves seldom lasted. Would she and Doug have outgrown each other if he had lived? She felt slightly disloyal at the thought. Her feelings for Stan were more intense, for Stan was a man, not a boy, he had known poverty and hard times and he had overcome obstacles along the way.

Stan was studying her. "I've never known a woman quite like you," he said.

She smiled. "Is that good or bad?"

"Good. I adore you. Everything about you."

And I never thought I could be happy again, she thought. I believed that love for me was finished. That's why I married Frank. How could I have been so foolish? She would ask Frank for a divorce. Surely he must see by now how impossible it was to continue their marriage, if it could be called a marriage. Then she and Stan . . . she was jumping ahead of herself, but she felt so completely right with Stan, and he talked of the future as if he planned to share it with her. It was all taken for granted.

"I'm thinking of moving out of the Westbury and taking an apartment," she said. "Maybe an unfurnished one that I can fix up myself."

"That's a good idea."

"Yes, I think I'll start looking around next week. I'm getting tired of hotel life and the food there is awful. And they won't let you do any cooking. I was going to get a hot plate but they said it was against hotel regulations."

"I know a broker who might know of an apartment. Why don't I call her on Monday?"

"That would be wonderful." She was filled with enthusiasm. Then she could fix dinner for Stan and they wouldn't have to go to restaurants all the time. It was a lovely idea.

They finished luncheon and drove around the countryside. "Let's go for a walk through the woods," he said. "Do you have on your walking shoes?"

"Yes. I wore these just in case." She pointed to her loafers.

The trees were bare against the winter sky and there were patches of snow that had not yet melted. They climbed over low stone walls and they came to a stream that ran through a pasture. Stan seemed familiar with the whole area, as if he came here often.

"I love the woods," he said. "When I'm out here it's as if everything's all right with the world."

"You don't appear to be the kind of person who has any problems."

He did not answer. Then he said, "Everyone has. But I guess I'm lucky because I can block out things I don't want to think about. Most of the time, anyway," he grinned.

They walked on. She stumbled over a branch across the path and he caught her. He held her in his arms for a moment. "I'd like to make love to you right now," he said softly.

"We can't here."

"No, but I'd like to."

They drove back to New York and had dinner at a little French restaurant on the West Side. There was a cold wind blowing across Central Park and in front of the Plaza Hotel a driver sat in a hansom with ear-muffs and his collar turned up, while his shivering horse stomped its feet to keep warm.

"Have you ever ridden in one of those?" Stan asked.

"No. I've always wanted to."

"Not tonight, but when the weather's warmer, I'll take you for a spin, m'lady. We can have dinner at that restaurant in the park. Now, how about a nightcap at your place?"

"All right." I've known him a little over a week, she thought, and my whole life has changed. How amazing and wonderful life is.

They walked in her hotel apartment and she got out the ice and two glasses. "What will you have?"

"I don't really want anything else to drink. Do you?"

"No."

"Come here." He turned out the light. "I love you," he said. "I really do."

They could hear the sounds of the city awakening and taxis honking and people in the streets far below. Then there were church chimes. It's Sunday, she remembered.

"Good morning, darling," Stan said. He pulled her closer and they made love again.

"Let's just stay here all day," she whispered.

"I wish we could."

"Why can't we?"

He got up and started to get dressed. "I have to go up to Wilton to see the kids."

"You have children?" She suddenly felt cold all over. She pulled the blanket up over her bare shoulders.

"Didn't I tell you?"

"No." So he *did* have children and Sunday was visiting day. And his ex-wife would be there, naturally. Of course. It had all been too perfect. I can block out things I don't want to think about. Wasn't that what he had said?

"What's the matter?" He was buttoning his shirt.

"Nothing."

"You have such a strange expression."

"Have I?"

"Sweetheart, I thought I'd told you. You know how it is when you promise kids something. They count on it."

And I thought we'd be together today, she thought. She tried to conceal her disappointment.

"How . . . how old are they? Your children?"

"Stan junior is nine . . . we call him Buddy . . . and Hilary is six. They're great kids." He beamed with fatherly pride.

"I'm sure they are." There was a great lump in her throat, as if she couldn't swallow.

"I wonder where my tie is?" He looked around. "I must have left it in the living room." He grinned.

She put on a dressing gown and sat on the edge of the bed.

He came over and cupped her face in his hands. "I wish I didn't have to leave you, darling. What will you do today?"

"Oh . . ." She really hadn't thought about it. "I might go to the Museum of Modern Art and look at some paintings. I hear there's a new exhibition."

"Good. That's a fine idea." He looked less guilty. "Well, I've got to be up there at noon. I promised Buddy that I'd go ice skating with him." He grinned that boyish grin again. "I haven't had a pair of skates on in years."

"Have fun." She smiled weakly.

"I'll call you tomorrow." He blew her a kiss from the bedroom door.

"All right."

He came back and put his arms around her. "I hate to leave you, darling."

But you are, she thought. You are.

"I'll be fine," she said.

And so the weeks passed and they continued to see each other and she tried not to mind that his weekends were claimed by his children. I admire him for being so responsible, she told herself, when Saturday approached and she knew she would not see him again until Monday. There were exceptions when the children had other plans and they were able to spend a weekend together, but those times were rare.

"I love you for being so understanding," he told her. "This has been so rough on the kids and their mother tells them such terrible things about me when I'm not there . . . I have to spend all weekend convincing them that I'm not such a bad guy and that I really care about them."

She thought of her own father and his silence over the years and how hurt she had been by his desertion. At least Stan wasn't doing that to his children. She *did* understand, but it didn't make the weekends any easier for her.

"It will all work out, sweetheart," Stan assured her. She believed him. She was madly in love with him and miserable when they were apart.

And she had her own problems to work out. Frank was still refusing to give her a divorce. Even her mother was on Frank's side.

"He's so much in love with you, dear. He just worships you. Can't you see his good points? I know he has some irritating mannerisms, but after all, no marriage is perfect."

"But I just can't go on living with him, Mother. It's all a complete lie."

"I could understand your wanting a divorce if there was another man in the picture . . ."

Does she suspect something? Ardith wondered. "No," she said, "I'm just unhappy with Frank."

It would all work out in time. She didn't care how long it took, but she knew she couldn't live without Stan.

One day in March, Mary Schuyler called and they met for lunch at Armando's. Mary's baby was due any day now.

"I may have to make a dash for the hospital in the middle of lunch," Mary laughed, "but I'm so tired of sitting around that damned apartment waiting for labor pains to start. Maybe this will hurry it up." Mary put down the menu and studied Ardith. "What's been happening in your life lately? You seem to have a new sparkle."

"Well, I've been busy working on the magazine—"

"That's not what I mean."

"And I've been seeing quite a lot of someone I met at your party. Stan Olson." She tried to sound casual.

"Oh."

"Why do you look like that?"

"Well . . . Stan's quite a ladies' man. We used to see Stan and Edna fairly often."

"Until they were divorced, you mean?"

Mary hesitated. "They're not divorced. Did he tell you they were?"

Not divorced? The dark restaurant and the noise and the smell of smoke suddenly made her feel as if she were smothering. Not divorced? Of course he was. He shared an apartment with two other men. Edna and the children lived in Connecticut.

"Oh, they've been separated for several years," Mary said. "But I don't think he'll ever get a divorce."

"Why not?"

"Because I think he's afraid of her, for one thing. She seems to have some kind of a hold on him. Oh, he's had affairs before, but he always goes back to his wife. That's why I hope you aren't too deeply involved with him."

"Is she attractive?"

"She used to be. She's older than Stan and she drinks fairly heavily, so that's starting to catch up with her. Her father was president of J. Walter Thompson when she and Stan were married. Oh, I don't mean that Stan got where he is because of nepotism. He's very talented and hard-working and he's well liked by everyone in the advertising business. Phil says Stan could sell iceboxes to the Eskimos," she laughed. "Anyway, just don't get in over your head."

But I already am, she thought, and suddenly she resented Mary for telling her what she had. She doesn't know Stan the way I know him, she thought. He is strong and good and I love him and he loves me. Who else can know what goes on between two people? Of course, he's probably had affairs with other women since he left Edna, but they didn't mean anything to him. He's serious about his feelings for me. He intends to marry me. Why, we've talked so often of all the things we'll do together, the places we'll go. She wanted to get away from Mary. It reminded her of the time when she was ten years old and she had saved her allowance and bought a bracelet for her mother at the Five & Ten. The bracelet had tiny lavender stones, and she had thought it so pretty until she showed it to a friend, who said, "But it's not real. It's fake." That had spoiled the bracelet for her and it wasn't good enough to give to her mother for her birthday, so she threw it away. Why did that awful memory come back to her now?

"I hate to eat and run," she told Mary, "but I'm due back at the office."

She was seeing Stan that evening and she would ask him. She would find out the truth.

Stan looked uncomfortable. "Sweetheart, I never said I was divorced."

"But—"

"You know I adore you and I'm trying to work things out in the best way for the kids. They're much better now and I think they're accepting the whole situation better than they were at the beginning. You've never had children, so you don't know what it's like."

A knife went through her and turned deep inside thinking about the baby who died.

Stan suddenly realized what he had said. "I'm sorry, darling, I forgot that—"

"It's all right."

"The kids keep asking me when I'm going to move back for good. It's real rough."

He looked very dejected and she thought: Maybe I am being unfair. After all, I'm still married.

He held out his arms to her. "Come here."

And they made love and nothing else seemed to matter.

Make me believe it, she thought. Make me believe that we have a right to be happy. "I love you so much," she said.

"I'm glad we were finally able to get you for dinner," Joe Kreskie said. "I left several messages, but I didn't hear from you."

"Frank never gave them to me," Ardith said. "He probably thought you were someone I was romancing." She laughed.

She had come down to Washington for the weekend and was staying with her mother at the house on Kalorama Circle. It was pleasant to relax and have a quiet evening with Helen and Joe. Their daughter Margaret had just celebrated her second birthday and they were expecting another baby in July.

"A boy, I hope," Helen said.

"I like little girls," Joe said, kissing her. "And I wouldn't mind at all having another."

They acted so much in love, Ardith thought, watching them, and she felt a sudden longing for Stan.

What was he doing now? she wondered.

CHAPTER FIFTY-SIX

So the months drifted by, and still nothing was resolved. Summer came and went, then autumn, and the first frost and then Christmas decorations appeared in the store windows along Fifth Avenue. She had known Stan almost a year now and the whole situation was making her on edge. She began to wonder if he really planned to marry her and she thought of forcing the issue and then she thought: He really is trying to work things out. I must be patient.

They were so happy together, it was only when they were apart that she had these horrible doubts and the future looked all so uncertain.

And so another year passed.

By now she and Frank had been living apart for two years and he solved that situation by asking her for a divorce. He had found someone else he wanted to marry.

It gave her a strange pang, and even though she had never loved Frank, she felt suddenly cast adrift. He had the papers drawn up and she signed them. She was finally free.

"Now you can marry that advertising man," Frank said. "If he ever gets a divorce. I understand he doesn't seem to be in any hurry."

She thought of letters she had read in columns to the lovelorn from women who had been going with a married man for several years who kept promising to get a divorce and never did. And the answer was always the same:

"Wake up and smell the coffee, sister! He doesn't intend to get a divorce."

But it's different in my case, she told herself. And she wondered if all those other women thought they were different, too.

If she stopped seeing Stan for a while . . .

No, she couldn't stand to be away from him. She would just have to give this relationship some kind of time limit. But when? She didn't want to pressure him, but things had drifted on long enough.

She would give it until spring, she decided.

Her mother was getting worse. On one of her visits to Washington the doctor finally told her the truth. Her mother had Parkinson's Disease and it was incurable.

"You must promise me that you will not let your mother know that I have told you," the doctor said. "She didn't want you to know. She didn't want you to worry."

"What should I do?"

"You must go on as usual or else she will suspect something."

"Does she know that . . ."

He nodded. "She knows. She's quite a remarkable woman, your mother."

"Yes." She sat there stunned and shaken and finally she said, "How long does she have?"

"It's hard to tell. Possibly several years. The palsy will get worse until she is completely confined to bed. For the time being she can get around with a cane, but she must be careful of falling."

"Is she in pain?"

He hesitated. "No . . . not yet."

She did not like the word "yet." "But there must be something, some cure—"

He shook his head. "Unfortunately, no. Like everything else, in time. . ."

"But what causes this disease?"

"We don't know. It comes from the brain and attacks the central nervous system."

"I see." But she did not see and she felt numb inside. She stood up.

"I'm sorry, my dear. I wish I could offer more hope."

"Thank you anyway for telling me the truth."

She stumbled out of his office in a daze. She must compose herself and be cheerful in front of her mother. She would make more frequent visits, not so it was obvious, but . . .

Oh, God, she thought, why? Why?

There followed a parade of nurses. One stole the silver, another drank, and all the while her mother protested that she didn't need a trained nurse, she wasn't an old lady yet and she refused to be treated like one. She was planning a trip to Europe and she would go in a wheel chair, if necessary. Ardith spent more time in Washington than in New York and between the situation with Stan and her mother's illness, she was a nervous wreck.

And then one day there was a long distance call. Her mother had fallen down the stairs. Her condition was critical.

She found her mother in a coma, too ill to be moved to a hospital.

"I don't know how it happened," the nurse said. "I only left her for a minute."

For three days she remained by her mother's bedside. On the third day her mother opened her eyes, looked at her and said, "Julian?"

"No, Mother. It's me . . . Ardith."

"Julian, you've come back. I always knew you would."

And then she smiled faintly and closed her eyes.

The funeral was in Oil City and her mother was laid to rest in the white marble mausoleum on the hill where all the Wymans were buried. It was spring and the lilacs and dogwood were in bloom. A breeze rippled the waters of the Allegheny. On the hill across the river Ardith could see the oil derricks standing like sentinels from days gone by.

"Goodbye, Mother," she whispered, and the years flashed past her and she wished that they had been closer and understood each other better. But does anyone really know what is in the heart of another? And she thought of the eternal loneliness of all human beings, and how, in the end, we are really all alone.

CHAPTER FIFTY-SEVEN

There were long sessions with lawyers and she was tied up in Washington for the next month going through papers and trying to decide whether to sell the house. She had no idea that the settlement of an estate and the taxes connected with it were so complicated. She was shocked at the size of the funeral bill and the lawyer's fees. Were they trying to take advantage of a woman alone? She had heard that they often did this. For the first time she felt the need of Frank's legal advice, but she did not feel she could call him. She had seen him one Sunday at the Chevy Chase Club with his new wife and he had nodded politely and coolly across the room.

And she couldn't call on Joe for advice because he had left for Europe with some other senators on a Congressional junket.

The strain of everything had drained her emotionally and Stan had been strangely silent. Finally, she reached him on the phone. He wanted to know when she was coming back to New York.

"I wish I could come down there and be with you, dear," he said. "I know what you've been going through, but we have this new account and I've been working on it day and night."

"I understand," she said. Was he really that busy? Right now she needed him so terribly. She felt lost and bewildered. She wanted his arms around her, to hear him tell her that he loved her. And then she thought that she was being selfish, because his work was important and a man's work should come first. But what about the weekend? Couldn't he come down then? No, these clients from the Midwest were in town and he had to entertain them.

"It's a bore," he said, "but you know how it is."

She felt close to tears. "It seems forever since we've seen each other. Since—" Since we've made love, she started to say. She felt drugged from all the sleeping pills she'd taken as a substitute the past month. "We've never been apart this long."

"I know, sweetheart. I miss you, too."

She stared at the telephone afterward with a drowning feeling and thought how dependent she had become on Stan. He was her world. That was the trouble with most women, she thought. They built their whole lives around one man, and if he disillusioned them their whole world fell apart.

She tried to think sensibly and logically, but she felt neither sensible nor logical, and one thought kept nagging at her over and over: If he really cared, he would be with her when she needed him, no matter what.

Was Stan the kind of man who ran in a crisis? Who avoided anything unpleasant? There were people like that. Was Stan one of them?

And then suddenly a story flashed through her mind that Mary Schuyler had told her about the death of Stan's father.

One fall, Stan and his father were deer hunting in the Minnesota woods, as they had done together many times. Stan had just taken aim at a deer and as he pulled the trigger of his rifle, his father, for no apparent reason, stood up directly in his path. Mr. Olson fell with a bullet in the back of his neck and died instantly. It was one of those freak, horrible things, like the man who accidentally backs over his own child in the driveway. Stan was seventeen at the time. He adored his father. It was shortly after his father's funeral that he left the little town in which he had grown up and took a job at a radio station in St. Paul.

"Please don't tell Stan I told you," Mary begged. "He told Phil this story one time when he'd had a few drinks. I guess he still feels guilty about it, even though it wasn't his fault. He may tell you the story himself sometime, and if he does, pretend you're hearing it for the first time."

But he never had told her.

That must be the reason he couldn't bear to be around death or funerals, she assured herself. It wasn't that he didn't care about her unhappiness. It was just that it brought back such painful memories for him.

And she determined to finish up things as quickly as she could and get back to New York.

Stan was glad to see her and he told her how much he'd missed her. "I wanted to be with you, dear, but this new account—"

"How's it going?"

"Oh, the usual problems. These guys can't make up their minds about what they want. We get one advertising campaign all set up and then they want changes. And you can't tell them anything. But they're the ones paying the bills," he grinned.

There was something different about him. It was as if he couldn't quite look her in the eye. I'm just imagining things, she thought. I'm unstrung by everything that's happened.

Later, when he was holding her, he said, "You've lost weight."

"Yes, I guess I have."

"We'll have to do something about that."

"It's so good to be together again," she whispered. "It's been so long."

"I'll say it has."

And they made love and the pain of the past weeks was blotted out.

But after a while, she wondered exactly what Stan intended to do about their relationship. Was he content to go on indefinitely this way? It would seem so. She felt restless and insecure and she knew she was heading for a showdown with him. Stan was having to work more and more in the evenings lately, and she found herself sitting by the phone waiting for his calls and never knowing when she was going to see him. She had invitations from other men but she didn't care about accepting them.

Still, Stan had not done anything definite about a divorce.

"I'm working it out," he told her. "The kids are finally getting used to the fact that we're separated, but it's rough on them. I think I've made everything clear to them and then Edna tells them that Daddy can move back any time he wants to. It gets them all confused again."

She had heard that there was a new secretary in the agency who had been making quite a play for Stan. "Common" was the way Ardith heard her described and she had been along on the trip to Bermuda.

"She's a little tramp, but after all, men are men," Mary Schuyler said. "Phil says she hangs around the office until Stan leaves. He can't get rid of her."

She wondered whether to ignore the situation and pretend she had heard nothing, but she knew she could not go on any longer the way things were. If Stan was that weak and wishy-washy, she was well rid of him. He was apparently not the tower of strength that she had thought. She was getting more angry by the minute when she added up all the inconsiderate things he had done. Why had she thought that he was everything that was good and fine?

Other things came back to her. "I fought the Battle of 90 Church Street." Stan grinning as he said it. He had obviously made no effort to get overseas during the war. Was Stan, deep down, a coward?

She saw it all in a flash, clearly and painfully. Stan never intended to get a divorce. She had fallen into the same trap as so many other women. How could she have been so blind and stupid? In spite of all the things Stan said about his wife, he still had an attachment to her. He needed her. She served as a buffer. When he got in too deep she would pull him out and scold him like a naughty little boy and then forgive him. Like a mother, in a way. Was this what men wanted who married women older than themselves?

Yes, Stan was a coward. He had never had the guts to stand up and fight for anything. Instead, he ran.

But he was so likeable and charming. He — no, she told herself, face the facts. Look at this whole situation the way it is, not the way you would like it to be, and then your common sense will tell you what to do.

She got out her note paper and started to write. It was short and to the point. She was giving him his choice. Otherwise, it was goodbye. She wrote Stan's name on the envelope and looked at it for a long time. At least she had made a decision. It was indecision that tore people apart and made them nervous wrecks. All her life she had been afraid of decisions.

Then she picked up the telephone and called the airport. There was a pause while she waited and then she said, her voice clear and steady, "I'd like a seat on the next plane to New Orleans."

CHAPTER FIFTY-EIGHT

She looked out the plane window and saw the swamps and bayous of Louisiana below and then she felt the landing gear going down and the NO SMOKING sign flashed on. The plane dipped sharply to one side and it seemed they were going to end up in Lake Pontchartrain and then the wheels touched the runway with a bump and sped along before coming to an abrupt stop.

"Please remain in your seats with your safety belts fastened until we have completely stopped," the stewardess warned, but no one appeared to have heard and people were crowding the aisle waiting for the cabin door to be opened.

The passengers were mostly businessmen with briefcases, an elderly couple, a woman with a baby . . . she glanced at them and thought: They have some destination, but I — why am I here? Do I really think I will find him after all these years? I don't even know if he's still alive.

She walked down the steps of the plane and into the New Orleans airport. It was an old wooden building, dirty and dreary, and she thought: This is one place where Huey Long didn't immortalize himself in cement, and she remembered the morning at Llantarnam when she had been sitting on the steps of the cottage playing with her doll and her grandfather opened the newspaper and exclaimed, "Well, somebody finally shot the son-of-a-bitch!" She didn't know who Huey Long was then and later she asked the maid what "son-of-a-bitch" meant. "Why, Miss Ardith, wherever did you hear that?" the maid replied in a shocked voice.

She waited for her suitcase and watched the Negro porters moving slowly around as if they had all the time in the world. They drove through the narrow streets past rows of houses painted pink, ocher, and umber, their balconies like black iron lacework, and every now and then she could glimpse a walled garden in back. It was like being in another century, she thought.

The cab turned down Royal Street with its antique shops and stopped in front of the Monteleone Hotel.

"Here you are, ma'am."

It was one of the oldest hotels in the French Quarter and she had a dim recollection of being there before. With her father, perhaps? It was all so long ago and yet the smell and sounds all seemed so familiar. She bought a copy of the *Times-Picayune* in the lobby and followed the bellboy to the elevator.

They were surprised that she had no reservation and at first she wasn't sure if she could get a room. But I only decided to come a few hours ago, she thought. No, that wasn't true. She had had this date for a long time.

She tipped the bellboy and he closed the door. She walked over to the window and looked out. Across the gabled rooftops she could see Jackson Square and the spires of the Saint Louis Cathedral glinting in the afternoon sunlight. Beyond was the muddy Mississippi with its ships piled with cargo. The cathedral bells chimed and a freighter leaving for a foreign port gave a forlorn wail.

How do I go about finding him? she wondered.

She picked up the phone book and went through the R's. Julian Rodgers. No such name. Unless he was using another name. Or was dead. But she was sure he wasn't. She was sure he was alive and somewhere in New Orleans.

She would walk around and see what she could find out. Maybe ask in restaurants or bars. Was he still painting? Did he have a studio around here? Because she was sure that this was where he would return. In the end we all return to our beginnings.

She started to walk in the direction of Jackson Square. There was the smell of coffee and pralines and oysters. She passed an oyster bar and she remembered having an oyster as a child and the slippery, horrible taste as it went down and feeling that she was going to choke and her father saying, "You're not a true Creole if you don't like oysters."

She stopped and watched some of the men eating plates of oysters and she thought: He could be among them now and how would I know? I'm not even sure what he looks like now. One of the men looked her up and down, nudged his companion, and she moved on in a hurry.

I'll have to stop staring at every man I see, she thought, unless I want to be picked up.

Two little Negro boys danced by and she smiled at them. A nun passed, her long dark skirts rustling slightly. Would the priest at the Saint Louis Cathedral know him? She took the white rosary out of her purse and thought: I wonder if the same priest is still here? But she didn't remember what he looked like, only a dim memory of a tall, kindly figure in black patting her on the head and saying, "Bless you, my child."

Had life blessed her? she thought ironically. She walked up the steps of the cathedral. Just inside the door a nun was selling rosaries and holy pictures.

Maybe she would know something. Ardith walked over to her. The nun smiled and held out a rosary. "These have all been blessed," she said. "Would you like one?"

"No, I already have one, thank you. But I'm trying to find someone and I wonder if you could help me. Julian Rodgers? Do you know him?"

The nun shook her head. "But Father Dubigny might. He's not in now, but his office is over there." She pointed to a door.

"Thank you." Ardith walked down the aisle of the ancient cathedral and knelt in front of a statue of the Holy Mother. A row of candles was flickering at her feet and Ardith dropped a coin in the box and took a taper and lit one.

"Help me to find him," she prayed. "I must find him. I can't stand being in the darkness any longer. I don't care what I discover about him, but only help me to find him."

She crossed herself and then she left the cathedral and walked over to Jackson Square.

She paused for a while before the statue of Andrew Jackson on his rearing horse and then she realized it was almost three o'clock and she had not eaten lunch. She walked back down Royal Street to the Court of Two Sisters. It was so peaceful in the courtyard with its old willow and fig trees and the splashing of the fountain. Birds chirped all around and there was the scent of magnolia.

She finished lunch and looked at her watch. Father Dubigny would be back at the cathedral now, and while there was only the slightest chance that he was the priest she remembered, still she must follow up every clue.

He was not the one. He had only been in New Orleans three years and he did not know her father.

"Perhaps he goes to another church?" he said hopefully.

"I'll try. Thank you, Father." But perhaps he had stopped going to church altogether. Though usually the Catholic Church had ways of finding you if they really wanted to. And she wondered again if he was still alive. For wouldn't he have tried to contact her in all these years if he were? She could go out to the Metairie Cemetery where all the d'Alverys were buried, and if she found his name on a tombstone she would know her search was over.

And then she would be as much in the dark as ever.

She walked over to Canal Street and boarded a streetcar to Metairie.

The d'Alvery family lot was on the other side of the cemetery and she walked past the raised tombs covered with moss and the marble statues, glancing now and then at the inscriptions. Most of them were very old and some had a line engraved in French. On a small tomb with a statue of a child above it was "*Ma Pauvre Petite Poupée*" and fresh flowers were in the vase beside it, though the grave was over fifty years old. And she thought of the grieving mother, probably an old lady by now, who had lost her child, and she thought of her own baby, who had lived such a brief time, and her eyes filled with tears and she walked quickly on.

There was a railing around the d'Alvery tomb and she walked in and looked at the names. She had never known her father's family, but now she stood surrounded by them. There was the name of the great-grandfather who had been a French planter on the island of Martinique and all the others. It was with relief that she found that her father was not among them.

So then, he must still be alive. She nodded to the caretaker at the entrance gate and waited for another streetcar.

It was late afternoon now and her feet ached from all the walking. She had no idea where to go now, but she was convinced she would find him.

And she wondered at the obsession all people have to know their beginnings. How awful for the adopted child never to know who his parents really were and have no way of finding out, for the records are sealed. Were they married, did they love each other, why did they give me up for adoption? Are these the questions that torture his brain, even though he knows that his adoptive parents love him and wanted him? And for a woman . . . she could imagine no worse agony than knowing that somewhere, someplace you had a child growing up, smiling at others, taking his first step, and knowing that you would never see this. Searching the faces of children the same age and wondering: Is it possible that this one could be mine? And never knowing. The never knowing — that is the real torture.

But was it not this same thing that had sent her on this search for her father?

For years she had sought him in every man, it motivated unconsciously her choice of a husband, for good or bad, and she must know why. What was this elusive quality in a man that she was seeking? And why had men always disappointed her?

Why did all the relationships that she began with such hope end in sorrow?

And so the first day passed, and then another, and she had been in New Orleans nearly a week and still she had not found him.

It was early evening and she found herself in Jackson Square again and she thought: I keep coming back to the same place, and it was like that game children play when something is hidden and they say, "Cold. Now you're warm. Very warm. No, cold." And you go around in circles and still you cannot find the hidden object. Usually it turns up right under your nose.

Right under my nose. Is someone trying to tell me something? she wondered.

She looked up at the aging cathedral. Flickering lights from the church's windows and half-open doors illuminated the shrubbery and gave the appearance to the brick buildings on either side of black lace thrown over a crimson shawl.

As if drawn by something, she left the square and walked along the alley next to the cathedral known as Pirates' Alley. She had passed this way many times before but this time she paused by a lamppost and her eyes were drawn to an iron balcony with green shuttered doors. Vines wound around the iron posts set into the curb and there were pots of red geraniums. She heard voices, a man and a woman, and they seemed to be having an argument, and then she thought she heard the name Julian. The shuttered doors flew open and a woman in a housecoat and gold sandals came out on the balcony.

Ardith started up the stairs, her hand on the railing.

The woman stared at her. Her hair was a brassy, reddish blonde and her face was flushed. Her toenails were painted a bright vermilion and she had a glass in her hand.

"Excuse me," Ardith said, "but I'm looking for Julian Rodgers. Do you know where he lives?"

"Leona . . ." A blurred voice came from inside the apartment. "Who's there?"

"Someone looking for you." The woman waved her hand and Ardith noticed that she had the kind of fingernails that curled over like parrots' claws. "In there."

A man was slumped in an armchair with a bottle of bourbon in one hand and a glass in the other. The studio, for that is what it was, was littered with half-finished canvases and half-empty cups of coffee. The ashtrays were overflowing with cigarette butts. Leona, whoever she was, was not exactly the world's best housekeeper.

Directly ahead of her was a large nude painting. Leona in her younger days, before the booze got to her. No . . . she looked again. The face was a coarser version of her mother's.

The man was staring at her with a shocked expression. He had not shaved in several days and his eyes were bloodshot and then tears started to roll down his cheeks.

Ardith was frozen to the spot. This can't be, she thought, and yet she knew it was. This sodden bum was her father. This was what they had been trying to spare her from all these years. Traces of the handsome rake he had been still remained, liquor had not completely destroyed his looks.

He came toward her and put his arms around her.

"Daughter," he said. "I knew someday you'd find me."

And now I wish I hadn't, she thought. She wanted to get away from this place, to have back the picture of the handsome man of her childhood memories, the man who was once her father. This man was not her father.

"Your voice is like your mother's," he said, "but you look just like me."

"So they used to tell me."

"Your grandfather." His voice had a sneer. "He never did like me. I couldn't measure up to his standards. I suppose the old boy's long dead now?"

"Yes."

"Leona, go in the back room. I want to talk to my daughter." He waited until the door had closed. "Leona's my model."

You don't have to explain her to me. I'm not a little girl any more. I get the whole picture. She thought these things but she said nothing.

"I read all about your debut in the newspapers, daughter. I saved all the clippings." He went to a drawer and pulled out a pile of clippings and the copy of *Life* with her picture on the cover.

So you did see them, she thought. But you never tried to get in touch with me. Not in all this time. Maybe it was just as well.

"How is your mother?" The words came with difficulty.

"She died two months ago."

He looked as if someone had struck him. "I didn't know." And then he said, as if in a trance, "I really loved her. I have never loved another woman."

She thought of her mother's dying words. She had never loved anyone else either, and Ardith felt sick at the way love could end, the emptiness of her mother's life, and his as well. Yet these two had once been young and in love, dreaming dreams as they strolled through the Luxembourg Gardens hand in hand under the blossoming chestnut trees of a Paris springtime. It was too cruel that it could have ended the way it did. What did it matter now how it all happened? Nothing could bring back the past.

She saw her father as he really was and not the way she had dreamed him. He was one of those handsome, weak men, of whom there are many, with charm and a certain amount of artistic talent, too sensitive to survive in the business world, yet lacking the discipline and dedication of the real artist.

There it was.

She glanced around the studio. The half-finished cups of coffee and the half-finished paintings. How indicative both were of his character.

And the blowsy Leona to complete the scene. A half-finished woman. He saw Ardith looking in contempt at the closed bedroom door and he said, "Don't judge me, daughter. A man gets lonely."

We all get lonely, Father.

"Try to understand. Your mother . . . well, she expected so much of me. I just couldn't be all the things she wanted. And Leona . . . she likes me the way I am. Everything I do is all right with her."

"I must go now." She had found him. The search was over. Now she knew the truth. She wanted to feel some pity for this man, and in a way she did, but a man should not be pitied. A man, a real man, should be respected. No, there was no substitute for that. She could see how her mother had fallen in love with him and she could also see how her mother had been unable to go on living with him. "Goodbye, Father."

"Ardith, you're not leaving? I need you."

And where were you when I needed you? When I listened for the train as I cried myself to sleep night after night . . . when I waited under the Christmas tree. Where were you then, Father?

And she left, running down the steps, hearing her high heels tapping, and the sound continued on the sidewalk and it seemed to be no part of her, something carried her on as if her feet were not attached to her body, she was walking faster and faster, she knew not where.

There were people's voices around her and the fragrance of unseen flowers and the lonely wail of a horn from the river beyond. The river. It seemed to draw her. It was like a warm bed waiting to embrace her.

The lovely warm waters of the Mississippi. The brown Mississippi, like the cup of *café au lait* that you let me sip at the French Market, do you remember, Father?

She was crying now, but there were no people around any more. Only the docks that loomed at the foot of Canal Street and bales of cotton ready to be loaded on a freighter in the morning. A freighter going to some far-off port. The whole world's a far-off port that we never reach, she thought, beckoning, promising . . . Her heel caught in the railroad track running alongside the platform and she pulled it free and walked on. She came to a wharf where huge green bunches of bananas were stacked. They looked almost artificial. Across the river she could see the lights of Algiers, where the ferry went. The dock seemed to be swaying on its wooden posts driven into the levees. Or was it that she was swaying? Everything was unreal.

She opened her purse and her eye fell on something white-and-silver in the bottom. Her rosary. "Always keep this." She laughed. What a lie! What a lie everything is! She held the rosary in her hands for a moment and then she let it slip through her fingers to the ground.

She walked on. What to believe in anymore? The stars were clear and bright, they sparkled like the lights on a Christmas tree. Once she had believed in Santa Claus, but he wasn't real either. It was her mother who brought the gifts.

She heard her footsteps on the wooden platform and then she stopped and the footsteps continued. Someone was following her.

She walked faster, she was running now. The footsteps sounded closer, she glanced over her shoulder and saw a man following her, he was big and black and looked like a dock worker, he was calling something to her. Where could she go? He could drag her into one of the wharves and rape her and then run a knife through her. She could hardly breathe, she was so terrified.

"Lady, come here."

He must have been on the dock where they were loading bananas, but she had not seen anyone around. She tried to run faster and it was like those nightmares where you find yourself running and the ground is like sticky tar. And then her spike heels caught in something and she lurched forward and fell. The black man loomed above her like a massive ebony statue and he was holding an object that glittered in his hand.

So this is how it ends, she thought, and it was ironic that she had been wishing for death, it had seemed like a welcome release after everything that had happened, to sleep endlessly, to have no more pain, no more bitter disillusion. Now, strangely, she wanted to live. Yes, she wanted to live. She saw now how people who knew they were dying fought so hard, clung with all their remaining strength to the slender thread of life that was slipping from them. If she pleaded with him . . .

He was looking down at her with a peculiar expression. "Lady, you dropped this," he said.

She was still too frightened to speak. The light caught the object in his hands and she saw what it was.

"Here." He held out her rosary. "You dropped this back there."

"Oh . . ."

"I thought you might want it. You didn't seem to notice that you'd dropped it. Here, let me help you up." He reached out his hand and pulled her to her feet. "I figured it could be something important to you."

"Yes . . . yes, it is. I . . . thank you very much."

"That's all right, lady. You shouldn't be walking down on these docks alone at night. It's not safe."

"No, I . . ." She reached in her purse to give him some money but he had vanished in the darkness.

And then she heard the chimes of the Saint Louis Cathedral. They sounded high and clear above the city. Hang on, they seemed to say, hang on. She was not as alone as she had thought. There was still hope, even when she had abandoned hope.

Was that what life was trying to tell her? Endure, do not give up, keep your head above the water. Whoever promised that life would be easy?

She walked, faster now, in the direction of the chimes.

BOOK SIX

1964

CHAPTER FIFTY-NINE

She walked along Fifth Avenue looking at the buildings, the crowds, feeling the cold in the air and thinking that New York had an excitement about it that no other city in the world had. She turned up the collar of her mink coat as an icy wind blew across from Central Park and she was just starting to cross 57th Street when someone grabbed her arm.

"Ardith!"

A man was smiling at her, a fat man in his fifties who looked somehow vaguely familiar. It couldn't be . . .

"Just a clean-cut American boy," he grinned, "only a little older."

"Stan." She held out her hand. "How nice to see you."

"You don't look a day older than when I last saw you. And you're more beautiful than ever."

"Thank you. It's been a long time."

"Fifteen years. That was quite a note you left me. It really shook me up."

Did it, Stan? But you didn't do anything about it. You never came after me. She was shocked at his appearance. Was this the man she had been so wildly in love with, that she had an affair with for almost three years? The man she once thought she couldn't live without? Life played funny tricks.

"Where are you living now?" he asked.

"Paris. I'm just here on a visit."

"Do you work there?"

"Yes, I'm an editor for a French publishing house."

People rushing by were bumping into them as they stood on the corner.

"We seem to be blocking traffic," Stan said. "Can you have a drink with me? I'd love to talk to you."

She glanced at her watch. She had to meet Marc in an hour, so that would give her time. "All right," she said.

"There's a little place I know right around here."

"Fine."

"It's sure good to see you. I can't get over it. So you're living in Paris?"

"Yes, in an apartment on the Avenue Foch. You've been to Paris, haven't you, Stan?"

"Nope. Never made it. Some day, if I can ever get away from this grind." He grinned. "Here we are."

In the restaurant, Stan ordered a glass of milk. "I'm on the wagon these days. An ulcer. I really need a vacation. My doctor says I've got to lose some weight and get the old blood pressure down." He pulled at the jowls on his neck.

"Are you still in advertising?"

"Oh, yes. But we sponsor some television shows now. I have to go out to the coast several times a year. Do you have television in Paris?"

"Three stations."

"We have this game show on CBS, strictly daytime TV for the housewives." The boyish grin appeared again in the middle-aged face with rolls of fat. Had she really been in love with this man, suffered because of him? It was incredible!

"We have these contestants," Stan's voice went on. "It's a pretty cute gimmick . . ."

What had it been? And she thought of those weeks when she returned from New Orleans and waited to hear from Stan, and there was only silence. She asked *Vogue* to transfer her to their Paris office and thought distance would help, but it had taken her a long time to forget. She used to find herself thinking of him constantly and there was pain in the remembering. And then she met Marc . . .

"So tell me what you've been doing all these years?" Stan asked.

She put down her cup of coffee.

"I worked for a while in the Paris office of *Vogue* — it was fun and I went to all the fashion showings. And I met some very nice people. After that I joined the staff of *l'Express* — it's a news magazine like *Time*. Then I got married. My husband is giving a speech at the United Nations tomorrow morning. That's one of the reasons we're here. He's with the French government."

"You married a Frenchman?"

Stan's face had a strange expression. Had he thought she would join a convent or something? Men were strange. They never thought a woman who had once loved them could get over them.

"He's a lucky guy," Stan said.

"I'm lucky, too."

"What's he like?" Stan pulled at the rolls of fat under his chin again. It was a nervous gesture that he had acquired. He seemed very nervous, she noticed. She had always thought him so calm. Also, he was getting bald.

"Oh . . . I think you'd like him." And then she realized that Stan wouldn't like him at all, they wouldn't have a thing in common. Except her. And she wondered how she could explain Marc. "He's tall and lean with dark hair that's gray at the temples," she started. How do I describe him? she thought. And she remembered their meeting at a party, how their eyes met across the room, and how fast everything happened after that. They had dinner at a little bistro and he told her about his family and the country estate near Chartres that he had loved so much as a boy. The Nazis occupied it during the war and then burned it to the ground and shot his father. His mother died of malnutrition and a broken heart. Marc joined the Resistance after France fell. They went on dangerous missions, bombed German supply lines, and he had been awarded the Croix de Guerre. He was strong, yet tender, he was an exciting lover, an understanding husband, she both respected and adored him. "Let's see . . . he has gray eyes, he smokes a pipe, well, I can't really describe him, but he's very attractive."

"Do you have children?"

"Yes, two. Nicole is eleven and Thomas is eight."

"Thomas — wasn't that your grandfather's name?"

"You have a good memory."

"I remember everything you ever told me. I remember everything about you, Ardith."

"And you — how are your children?"

"Fine." He pulled two pictures out of his wallet. "Pretty big now, aren't they?"

She paused. "And Edna? Are you still married?"

He shrugged. "You know how it is. The kids and all that."

So you never did get around to getting that divorce, she thought. How long I would have waited. How glad I am that I finally woke up. She looked at her watch. "I'd better go."

He paid the check and got out of his chair with difficulty. He suddenly reminded her of one of those melons that looks firm and solid until you squeeze it and then you find that it has soft, squishy spots.

"Goodbye, Stan," she said. "It was nice seeing you."

And she crossed Fifth Avenue and walked quickly across the square to the Plaza.

Marc would be waiting.

CHAPTER SIXTY

Along the Champs-Elysées the chestnut trees were in blossom, but 1968 was a spring unlike any other for the residents of Paris. A general strike gripped the country. Garbage was piled high around the opera house, postal workers had walked off their jobs, the subway was not running, and Air France had cancelled all flights. For the journalists covering the Vietnam peace talks at the Hôtel Majestic there were few taxis or buses. Grillework barricades were hastily put up at the United States Embassy and police posted at the bridges crossing the Seine.

On the Left Bank the air was filled with the stench of tear gas and smoke from burning cars. Rioting students had ripped up cobblestones from the streets to build barricades. *À BAS LES ORDONNANCES!* proclaimed posters on the Sorbonne's two main doors, and a statue of Pasteur was draped with a red flag.

"Down with decrees!" shouted the students.

"De Gaulle resign!"

"De Gaulle to the museum!" called a lycée student who had joined the crowd. Though she looked like one of the university students in her blue jeans and turtleneck sweater and long, straight blonde hair, she was only fifteen.

Her name was Nicole Saint-Céran.

"*Gouvernment Populaire!*" she yelled. "*Adieu, Charlot!*"

Her friend Claudette laughed and joined in. "*De Gaulle Démission!*"

Suddenly a cordon of police appeared, their black helmets with silver trim gleaming in the murky smoke, and blocked the entrance to the Rue Gay-Lussac.

"*Merde!*" Nicole muttered under her breath. "The C.R.S."

Some of the students grabbed lids of garbage pails to use as shields, others ran up apartment house staircases to continue fighting from the rooftops. As the special security police closed in waving their heavy clubs, some students threw rocks and Molotov cocktails.

"We'd better cut out of here," Claudette said.

"What for? It's just getting exciting."

The streets were littered with broken glass and firemen were busy putting out fires. By the iron fence of the Luxembourg Gardens stood two Red Cross ambulances and their attendants waiting for casualties.

"If your father ever finds out we were here—"

"So what?" Nicole tossed her blonde hair and her brown eyes flashed.

A rock went flying through the air. Far up the Rue de Rennes, near the old Montparnasse railroad station, students were setting fire to the street by filling gutters with gasoline and oil and lighting them. Flames belched from the sewers.

Along the Boulevard Saint-Michel students with saws and hatchets were cutting down the ancient plane trees to make street barricades. Another group of students, arms linked, were singing the Communist *Internationale*.

"If we aren't careful we'll be hauled off to the police station in their *paniers à salade* with the rest," Claudette warned.

"You wanted to come with me."

"I didn't know it would be like this."

"What did you expect? A tea party? Come on, let's go to the Place Denfert-Rochereau and see what's going on there."

Ardith had never seen Marc so angry. He waved *Le Figaro* in front of her.

"Have you seen this morning's paper?"

"Not yet. Why?"

"Look at this." He pointed to the front page with the latest news of the student uprisings. "Look carefully at this photograph."

It showed a group of students sitting in front of the Lion de Belfort statue on the Place Denfert-Rochereau listening to a speech by the rebel leader Daniel Cohn-Bendit. A self-styled anarchist whose aims were for the suppression of capitalist society, he was nicknamed by the press "Danny the Red." Ardith studied the photograph. Cohn-Bendit stood with fist upraised in the Communist salute. Male students sat at his feet, while in the back stood several girls listening with rapt attention and a look of adoration. One of the girls . . . no, it couldn't be. . .

She looked up at Marc.

"That's right. It's Nicole."

"I can't believe it."

He took back *Le Figaro*. "Where is she?" Without waiting for a reply, he shouted, "Nicole! I want to speak to you. This instant!"

Eleven-year-old Tommy appeared in the hall. "What has Nicole done?"

"Never you mind. Go back to your room."

"Yes, Papa? Did you want me?" Nicole looked worried.

"I want to have a talk with you. Come into the library."

He closed the door and handed her the newspaper. "Is this how you spend your time?"

She stared at her father with a sullen expression.

"I asked you a question and I expect an answer."

"What do you want me to say, Papa?"

"I don't care for your friends. In fact, I forbid you to see them. Is that clear?"

She shrugged.

"You are to come straight home after school. And the next two weekends you can spend doing some extra studying. If you expect to get into the university you'll have to bring up your grades."

"Yes, Papa."

"What I can't understand is—" he glanced again at the photograph in *Le Figaro* —"is what you could be doing around a rabble-rouser like this Cohn-Bendit, an avowed Communist—"

"He only wants to see that everyone gets a chance—"

"To do what? To riot? To wantonly destroy public property? Those ancient trees that were cut down will never grow back. And for what?"

"I wasn't involved in that, Papa."

"All right. You may go now. I've nothing more to say."

He walked over to the window and stood looking out over the rooftops of Paris and thought how difficult it was to raise a daughter in these times.

When he turned around Nicole had gone.

From inside the darkened bedroom she heard the sound of muffled sobs. Ardith hesitated, her hand on the doorknob of her daughter's room, then she knocked softly.

"Leave me alone!"

"Nicole, I want to talk to you."

There was no reply. She turned the knob. The door was locked. "Nicole—"

"I hate it here! It's like a prison."

I was rebellious at that age too, Ardith thought, remembering her boarding school days. But never like that. She had always wanted a daughter to be close to, to have the relationship she had never had with her own mother, and Nicole had been a delight as a small child, loving and affectionate, but now she defied her at every turn. Whenever she tried to kiss her she pulled away.

"Please, Nicole, let me in."

She waited. Then the door opened. Nicole walked back to the bed and threw herself face down, her blonde hair spread across the pillow. She looked like a little girl, Ardith thought. All she needed was her teddy bear to remind her of the child she once was, sleeping on her stomach, when she and Marc used to tiptoe in after a party and kiss her goodnight.

My little Nicole, how do I reach you? But she wasn't her little Nicole anymore, she was fifteen and a fully developed young woman. She suddenly wondered if Nicole was still a virgin. At her age she had never even kissed a boy, but today girls of Nicole's age and younger were sleeping with their boyfriends. What would be left for them later on?

It was hard to know how to handle daughters in these liberated times. She sighed. Marc was so strict with her and that was just making her more defiant.

Nicole turned over. "What did you want to talk to me about?"

"Nicole, your father and I both want the best for you—"

"*Merde*! That speech again."

And she had never used the language young people today used. "Nicole—" It was like a wall she couldn't penetrate. And yet she must. She had imagined them sharing confidences, laughing about things together, going shopping, all the fun things that mothers and daughters do. But the girls of this generation weren't interested in dressing up, they all wore blue jeans and shirts with slogans on them. It was sometimes hard to tell them from the boys.

Nicole glared at her. "I have a right to pick my own friends, and if Papa doesn't like them, that's just too bad!"

"Your father is only trying to protect you. He's seen a lot of the world and he can judge people better than you can." No, that was the wrong thing to say. She tried again. "He loves you very much, Nicole, and so do I."

"He has an odd way of showing it."

She wondered if Tommy would be as difficult. Boys were supposed to cause more trouble than girls when they reached their teens.

"Besides, Papa prefers Tommy to me," Nicole continued.

"Nicole, that's not true! Your father loves you both equally."

"I don't believe it."

This was getting nowhere. Maybe she should have left her alone after all. "You apparently want to argue tonight with everything I say. Perhaps you'll be in a better frame of mind tomorrow."

Nicole said nothing.

"Goodnight, Nicole." And she went out and closed the door.

When she was sure that her mother and father were both asleep, Nicole dressed and crept out of her room. It had started to rain, so she wore her poncho and boots. Where she was going she wasn't sure. And the buses and the Métro were not running because of the student strikes, so she would have to walk.

I don't care, she thought, as she pushed the button for the elevator. It will be an adventure.

CHAPTER SIXTY-ONE

"Mademoiselle Nicole is not in her room," Simone said. "I went to call her for breakfast and—"

Ardith rushed past her to Nicole's room. The bedcovers were pulled back, the bed empty.

Simone followed. "Perhaps Monsieur knows something," the maid said hopefully.

Marc had already left for the Elysée Palace for a meeting with de Gaulle, who had cut short a visit to Rumania and returned home. Nicole must have gotten up before Marc did, Ardith thought. But why? And where had she gone? Usually Nicole was a late riser, barely getting out of bed in time to dash to school. The school — she must telephone the school right away.

A frightening thought suddenly went through her head. Nicole couldn't have been kidnapped, could she? So many terrible things were happening now and Marc had an important post in the de Gaulle government.

Quickly she dialed the school, her heart beating faster.

No, she was told, Nicole was not there, but perhaps she was just late with all the problems, the strikes and so forth.

"Will you let me know the minute she arrives?" Ardith asked.

"Certainly, Madame."

Could she be with Claudette? She should have asked if she was in school but it had slipped her mind. Claudette was her best friend. Maybe they were playing hooky.

If only she and Nicole hadn't parted on such bad terms the night before . . .

Well, no point thinking about that now, the important thing was to find her. In the meantime, she must get control of herself. There was probably some simple explanation and she was getting herself all worked up over nothing.

She was due at the office of *Les Presses de la Cité* in less than an hour. Should she call the publishing house and say that she was ill? She hadn't been working there very long and it might make a bad impression. No, she would go to work as usual and have any telephone calls transferred there.

It was very naughty of Nicole to upset everyone like this, she thought, starting to get angry. Possibly she was doing this deliberately to get even with them, especially Marc, for punishing her.

What was the answer to handling young people today? None of her friends had the answer either and she had heard that things were worse back in the United States than in France, where at least the family structure was stronger.

"I'm going to the office," she told Simone. "But telephone me immediately if you hear from Nicole."

By evening there was still no word from Nicole and she was frantic. She called Claudette and found out that she had not seen Nicole since they parted at the Place Denfort-Rochereau. She picked up *Le Figaro* and studied the picture of Nicole and the others in front of the Lion de Belfort statue listening to Daniel Cohn-Bendit. She looked at Marc.

"Could she be with him?"

Marc's expression was grim. "It's a possibility."

"Then what should we do?"

"There isn't much we can do at the moment but wait."

My little Nicole, I'll never get angry with you again if only you're safe, she thought, with visions of a young girl's body being fished out of the Seine. Just then the telephone rang. She jumped.

Marc got to it first. "Yes? Yes, this is Marc Saint-Céran speaking . . . I see . . . Yes, I understand."

"What is it?" Ardith whispered in alarm.

Marc cupped his hand over the receiver. "It's the police station."

Ardith gasped.

"It's all right. Well, it's not exactly all right, but they have Nicole there. She's been arrested."

"For what?"

"I'll tell you in a minute." He continued to talk to the police officer, then he put down the receiver.

"What's happened?"

"Nicole is in a jail cell with some other students. They were marching up the Boulevard Saint-Michel singing the *Internationale* and throwing stones at buildings and at the police."

Ardith sank down on the couch and put her hands over her face.

"I'll go get her," Marc said.

"I'll come with you."

"No, you stay here. I'll deal with it."

Nicole looked dirty and unkempt, her expression sullen. Ardith started to embrace her but she turned her cheek.

"I'm going to take a bath," she said.

Ardith looked at Marc and then back at Nicole.

"We'll finish our talk later," Marc said. "Go get cleaned up."

Nicole left the room and Marc threw up his hands. "You should have seen her friends. You'd think they were fighting for some great cause instead of acting like a bunch of spoiled brats!"

"Will she have to appear in court?"

"Fortunately, no. Since Nicole is under age, she was released in my care and she won't have a police record. With the others it's a different story. They were all university students and they'll be fined for their unruly behavior."

Ardith sighed.

"However, by the time I'm through with Nicole, she may wish she were back in that cell—"

"Marc, please—" Ardith hesitated. "Don't you think you're being a little too harsh with her?"

"And how should I act? Pleased that my daughter was picked up by the police?"

"No, I didn't mean that—"

"The trouble with young people today is that they have no respect for the law. Rules mean nothing to them."

"I know. It's hard to make them listen to anything."

They heard a sound and turned around. Nicole was standing in the doorway.

"I'm sorry, Papa and Maman, I didn't mean to upset you so and cause so much trouble."

"You realize the seriousness of what you did?"

"Yes, Papa. And I'm truly sorry. It won't happen again.

"I should hope not," Marc said, and Ardith noticed that he was struggling to appear firm. "Now, go get out of those filthy clothes."

CHAPTER SIXTY-TWO

Paris 1974, a Sunday morning in early March. The bare branches of the trees shivered in the wind and melting snow covered the ground. Ardith and Joe Kreskie got in the small white Renault and Joe waved goodbye to Marc standing on the curb in front of the apartment.

"Bon voyage," Marc called.

"This visit was much too brief," Ardith said, as she pulled away from the curb and started down the Avenue Foch. "Next time I hope you can stay longer. And bring Helen with you."

"I'd like that and I know Helen would. But this was a business trip. And I have to be back for my grandson's christening, don't forget. As soon as I give my report to Congress on the Middle East."

"Do you think we'll ever have peace there?"

"I'm afraid not, at least not on any permanent basis. I think that's where the next big one's going to start. And it will be over oil." Joe had white hair now and wore glasses. He had been in Congress for over thirty years and was one of their most distinguished senators. "We've become dependent on Arab oil and if the Soviet Union ever controls the oil fields of the Middle East—"

"Do you think it could happen?"

"We can't allow it. The survival of the United States and the free world depends on oil."

"That sounds like something Grandfather would have said." They were passing the Arc de Triomphe. "It's strange, but I've been thinking a lot lately about the Wyman family. And Grandfather. I even had a dream about him the other night."

Joe was silent.

"Do you still resent him?"

"After all these years? No, I got over that a long time ago. He was the product of his times, and it shaped his thinking and attitudes. I don't blame him anymore for what he did."

She turned onto the highway leading to Orly Airport. "The times do shape us, don't they? It's a different world now. So very much has changed. And especially for women."

"Yes, they don't want to be wives and mothers these days. I was beginning to wonder if I was ever going to have a grandchild. Margaret wanted to get through medical school and establish a practice before getting married and starting a family, and Kathleen is in law school and has no plans for marriage."

"It's the same with Nicole. She graduates from the Sorbonne in three months and then she wants to become an architect."

"And you — you like working, don't you?"

"I love it. It's exciting going to the office each day and meeting a challenge. And luckily I have a very supportive husband. Did I tell you I'm going to open my own literary agency?"

"No, you didn't. That's great. When?"

"In a few months. I'm getting it organized now. I've found an office on a quiet courtyard near the Luxembourg Gardens."

"I wish you a lot of success with it."

"Thank you, Joe. It's so good to be able to talk to you. You're the only cousin I'm close to. It's as if the others don't exist. I haven't seen or heard from them in years and I don't really want to."

"Do you think you'll ever move back to the United States?"

"I've thought about that. And I miss it—sometimes. But Marc's roots are here and it's been my home for twenty-five years. That's a long time."

He smiled. "My expatriate cousin."

"It's too bad you had to be here in March when we have such dreary weather." She turned at the arrow reading: ORLY. "At least there isn't much traffic this morning. We're almost there. Your plane to London leaves at 11:30, doesn't it?"

"If it's on time. It's coming from Istanbul."

"Why Istanbul?"

"They're putting us on a Turkish plane because of the British Airways strike. It's picking up passengers in Paris and going on to London. They told me when I checked on the telephone this morning."

"I've never flown on a Turkish airline."

"Neither have I, but it's only an hour's flight, so it can't be too bad."

She pulled up in front of the airport. Joe got his suitcase and briefcase and kissed her goodbye.

"Have a good flight to London," she said. "And another one home."

"I will."

"And give my love to Helen and the girls. Oh, and kiss the grandson for me."

"I'll do that. Goodbye, Ardith. And thanks again for everything."

A Japanese tour group was getting out of a bus ahead of her. The last she saw of Joe, he was towering above them as he walked into the airport.

Joe fastened his seatbelt and opened his briefcase. He was glad he had been given a window seat. He could go over his report and get some work done before he got to London.

Passengers were coming in and it looked as if the DC-10 would be full. He was hoping that the seat next to him would be empty, but a British rugby team was just coming on, still in uniform, and one of the men had the seat beside him.

There were a few Turkish passengers remaining from Istanbul, but most of the passengers seemed to be getting on in Paris. He noticed several stunning tall model types and the Japanese student group he had seen earlier in the airport.

"We were lucky to make it," said the English rugby player, as he stored his gear in the overhead bin and slammed it. "At first they told us the plane was full, what with British Airways still on strike."

I hope that fellow's not going to keep up a conversation for the entire flight to London, Joe thought, as he settled himself with his papers. Maybe if he sees that I'm busy. . .

"Let's have a cheer for the Suffolk team!" the rugby player shouted to the rest of his group. "We'll have a big celebration in the old home town tonight."

A Turkish stewardess came up.

"Will you please sit down, sir? We want to get everyone on so that we can take off on time, and you are blocking the aisle."

"Sorry, Miss. Say, you're pretty. I've never flown on a Turkish airline before. Do they all look like you?"

"I don't know, sir. This is my first flight."

"Well, now! Just so it isn't the pilot's first flight." He laughed.

"Oh no, sir, the captain is a very experienced pilot and the DC-10 is a very good plane."

"I'm glad to hear that." The rugby player sat down. "We won our match, as you've probably guessed," he told Joe.

"Congratulations," Joe replied without looking up.

"Say, don't I know you? No, I know what it is—I've seen you on the telly. Aren't you an American politician or something?"

There'd be no work on this flight. Joe put the papers back in his briefcase and snapped it shut. "I'm Senator Kreskie," he said. "I'm sure some of my opponents refer to me as 'or something.' " He smiled. "I used to play football once. In my college days."

A buzzer rang and a stewardess rushed forward to the cockpit. The engines started. Across the aisle the students were chattering in Japanese and laughing.

"Alfie Meacham." The rugby player held out his hand. "Looks like we're taking off."

It had been a long time since he had been so enthusiastic about sports, Joe thought. Maybe it was having daughters instead of sons to play ball with and roughhouse. But now he had a grandson. Daniel. Oh, Danny boy, he hummed to himself. He could hardly wait to see him. What fun they would have together! In a few years he could take him to football games.

The DC-10 was racing down the runway.

One of the models in the seat ahead of him was checking her make-up.

The plane lifted off and he could see the Seine below and beyond the French countryside with patches of ice on the ground.

He opened the copy of *Time* that he had picked up at Orly. It was full of the Watergate hearings. They were talking of impeaching Nixon. Impeaching the President of the United States, possibly sending him to jail—what a national disgrace! But it could happen, for Nixon would never resign. Being President meant too much to him.

Over the years there had been suggestions that he run for President, but he had squelched them for various reasons. One was his illegitimate birth. He had seen how nasty presidential campaigns could get and he didn't want his mother's name dragged through the mud. Also, a campaign was expensive and he wasn't a wealthy man. But he had done what he wanted in life and he still had his self-respect. That was a lot — hell, it was everything! He'd been an effective senator, served on some important committees, been an active conservationist and at sixty-seven, God willing, he still had useful work ahead of him.

They were climbing higher.

Then, suddenly, there was the sound of an explosion and a rush of cold air into the cabin.

Alfie Meacham looked over his shoulder. "What was that? It sounded like a bomb. My God!"

The model screamed. "We're going to crash!" She put her hands over her face.

The plane was now out of control, hurtling downward. Joe saw a forest below, the stark leafless trees rising to meet them. Some passengers were crying, others praying.

The pretty Turkish stewardess had a look of terror on her face.

It was ironic, he thought, that his life should end violently, like his father's, in a forest in France. He would never see his family again or play with his grandson, the grandson who had been born while he was in the Middle East.

So be it. It was out of his hands now. He just hoped it would be quick.

Then, just before everything went dark, he suddenly saw a golden light and heard a woman's voice saying softly, "Come, Joey, we're going home now."

WORST AIR CRASH IN HISTORY KILLS 346, read the headlines around the world.

In Ankara the Turkish communications minister, Ferda Guley said, "Considering the world situation, we are not ruling out sabotage."

A Frenchman who was out for a Sunday walk with his family said he saw the huge plane in difficulty, but heard no explosion before the accident.

Parts of the red-and-white plane were jammed between trees. Cushions and other material from the interior hung over the stark winter branches, along with bodies and pieces of bodies. More bodies were scattered in the forest of Ermenonville, a favorite picnic ground for Parisians.

A boy walking his dog in the woods found, next to a torn-open leather briefcase, a sheaf of papers almost intact.

Report on the Middle East Situation
by
Senator Joseph Kreskie

CHAPTER SIXTY-THREE

During the night, when the train jolted to a stop at a station, she heard them speaking French instead of German, so she knew they had crossed the border.

Now she lay back against the pillow on her berth watching the French countryside speed by, flat green farmlands with red and gold trees seen through a mist in the distance, the sun trying to break through patches of gray-blue clouds. She listened to the click of the train wheels carrying her toward Paris and thought how trains always made her nostalgic.

She remembered the whistle of the train across the Allegheny River in her childhood, the train leaving her father in New Orleans, and it was on a train that she first met Joe and learned he was her cousin.

His death had hit her hard and made her wonder again why tragedy seemed to stalk the Wyman family. It had been seven years since that terrible Sunday when his plane crashed on take-off from Orly. She still missed him. He had been like the brother she never had.

She drank the orange juice the porter brought, spread apricot jam on a piece of dry white toast, and stirred the coffee in a red plastic cup. She could have flown from Paris to Frankfurt in an hour, but she preferred the train. It gave her time to think.

She was on her way back from the Frankfurt Book Fair. It was held every October and publishers and booksellers and agents gathered from all over the world to sell books. Her literary agency was well established now and she had made some good deals for her clients. She could hardly wait to see Marc and tell him all about it.

I'm a lucky woman, she thought. In spite of everything that happened earlier in my life, it's all come out all right. She and Marc had been married thirty years and she was still as much in love with him as the day they met.

He was no longer with the government, but on the board of a French aerospace company. Nicole was twenty-eight now and an architect. Tom had graduated magna cum laude from Princeton and was working for Exxon in Saudi Arabia. Sometimes she had dreams that her children were small again. She had loved those years, but time moved on, and now they were grown and on their own. And she had her work to keep her busy.

She thought of the grandmother for whom she was named, who had no life of her own but lived only for her husband and children. And her own mother, who built her life around a man who disappointed her. She recalled her own youth and the debutante balls. Every mother's dream in those days was that her daughter would make a brilliant match.

Now all that had changed, and thank God, she thought. Women had a choice, they did not have to get married, no one was forced to have children. Nicole had a good job in a field that used to be considered only for men, she had a boyfriend with whom she was living, but no plans for marriage. And Joe's daughter Kathleen was a lawyer and planning to run for Congress.

Today, women could do almost anything, aspire to be an astronaut, a Supreme Court justice, anything they dreamed. What had been an impossibility when she was growing up, now loomed on the horizon.

President Kathleen Kreskie. Why not? Other countries had women heads of state. Who knows what could happen in another twenty years?

The mist outside had turned into a heavy rain. Ardith put on her raincoat and looked eagerly out the window at the red-roofed houses as the train approached Paris.

In a few minutes she would be with Marc again.

He was not at the station. She looked up and down the platform, but there was no sign of him. Strange. Possibly something had come up at the last minute and he had been unable to meet her, she thought, as she looked around for a porter. Yes, that must be the reason.

She saw a porter in the distance and tried to catch his attention. He acted as if he didn't see her. Gone were the days when porters fought for the chance to carry your bags. Never mind, she could manage. She snapped the long leash on her suitcase, thankful that she had recently put wheels on it, and pulled it along the platform to the gate. Possibly Marc was waiting for her there.

But he was not. A porter approached her and offered his services.

Where were you when I needed you? she thought.

"*Un taxi, s'il vous plaît,*" she said.

A strange foreboding swept over her as soon as she entered the apartment.

"Madame, we tried to reach you," the maid said, "but on the train it was impossible—"

"What is wrong?" Suddenly her hands felt wet and clammy. "What has happened?"

"It is Monsieur." She burst into tears.

And then she saw Nicole. What was she doing here?

"Maman." Nicole threw her arms around her and her cheeks were wet. "Papa is gone."

"Gone?"

"Monsieur had a massive heart attack last night," the maid said. "We got him to the hospital, but it was too late. There was nothing to be done."

Ardith stared at the two of them. No one spoke.

"It's not true! Tell me it isn't." She looked around wildly, then screaming like an animal in pain, she ran through the apartment.

"Marc! Marc!"

His clothes were there, his pipe, everything looked the same, as if he had just gone out and would be back. But he was not coming back, he was never coming back.

Never.

The word reverberated in her brain and the pain was more than she could bear. She clutched her head, the room started to whirl, faster, faster, she was on a carousel, but there was no brass ring for her to catch, nothing but emptiness. . .

Nicole grabbed her. "Maman, please lie down." She looked at Simone. "Telephone the doctor."

"I don't want a doctor. I want Marc! It isn't true, I simply won't believe it!"

"Come, Maman."

"But he was in perfect health. He'd never had any signs of heart trouble." Her voice echoed in a cavern, a stranger's voice, lost.

Nicole helped her to bed, the doctor came and gave her a shot, the pattern of her life was repeating, she thought, as the needle went in, and then all was oblivion.

* * *

The cemetery of Père-Lachaise. Cobblestone walks shaded by ancient trees winding past ornate tombs and statues. When she first came to Paris she had wandered through it with a map the attendant at the gate gave her, looking for the graves of Chopin, Balzac, Isadora Duncan, Oscar Wilde, for here were buried the famous and infamous, and she had thought: What a beautiful final resting place.

Now she stands, veiled in black, leaning on her son and daughter for support, as Marc's casket is lowered into the grave. The sky is the color of pale blue hydrangeas, there were urns of blue hydrangeas on the marble staircase of the Villa d'Este where she and Marc spent their honeymoon, she recalls. They had drunk champagne in their room overlooking Lake Como, they had made love . . .

And now, the shovelful of earth, the last farewell, their life together finished.

A black cat crawls out from behind a tombstone and looks at them, then scampers off chasing a bronze leaf. An old woman passes carrying a bunch of lavender chrysanthemums, her flesh like wrinkled tissue paper, barely covering the bones. For an instant their eyes meet and Ardith shivers.

Only a few days ago I was happy and now Marc has been taken from me.

She feels drained of all emotion, weightless, like a flower petal floating on a pond, drifting without direction, life goes on around her but she is no longer part of it.

"Maman, are you all right?"

Tommy grips her arm. How sweet he is, how concerned. He is taller than Marc. Than Marc was, she reminds herself. She nods. There is no ground beneath her, she is not conscious of walking to the black limousine, she feels cold, icy cold, she cannot stop shivering, they tuck a robe around her, and the sad procession leaves Père-Lachaise.

CHAPTER SIXTY-FOUR

Snowflakes drifted across the Place de la Concorde and Paris was cold that winter and dreary, but somehow she managed to get through it, and finally spring arrived and daffodils burst forth in the Bois de Boulogne and Nicole had an announcement.

"Alain and I have decided to get married," she said. Alain was the lawyer with whom Nicole had been living for two years. Ardith had tried to be modern about it, and she knew that Tommy had live-in girlfriends, but somehow it was different with your daughter. And it had upset Marc dreadfully. Memories returned, Marc holding Nicole as a baby, smiling proudly. Her first communion in a white dress and veil. . .

"You like Alain, don't you, Maman?"

Startled, she returned to the present. "Why yes, of course."

"I'm glad." Nicole kissed her. "We want your blessing."

"When is it going to be?"

"We thought the first week in May. Just immediate family and a few close friends. I want Tommy to give me away, if he can get back from Saudi Arabia."

"And now that you've decided about your life, I've been doing a lot of thinking over the past months about what I'm going to do with the rest of mine. Paris isn't the same for me without your father, and I've been considering moving back to the United States."

Nicole looked surprised. "Where would you live?"

"At Llantarnam."

"Llantarnam?"

"Your great-grandfather's cottage in Pennsylvania."

"But what would you do there? You have your agency here, your friends—"

"I'd turn my clients over to another literary agency. I've been considering it for a while. My heart just isn't in it anymore. And I want to write a book. That will take time—and solitude."

"What kind of book?"

"A novel. About the early oil business."

"But you haven't been back to Pennsylvania in years."

"No, but I still own the cottage, along with my cousins. I've been paying the taxes on it and I'll buy them out."

"And what about the apartment here?"

"I'll let you and Alain have it as a wedding present."

Nicole looked stunned. "I don't know what to say."

"Unless you don't want it."

"Yes, that would be wonderful. We were going to look for another place because Alain's is just too small. But are you sure?"

"Quite sure. I'm rattling around here all by myself. Just save me a guest room for an occasional visit. Now, call up Alain and tell him that I'm inviting you both out to dinner tonight to celebrate."

Yes, she thought, that is what I want to do with my life now, throw all of my energy into writing. And if I get tired of the cottage year-round, I can rent an apartment in New York and use it just as a summer place.

She could hardly wait to see it again after so many years, to roam through her beloved Allegheny woods and pick wildflowers, to canoe on the river. And it would be the perfect place to write her book, for no one would disturb her there.

Paris was a city for lovers, not a city that she wanted to grow old in. Alone.

But several days later an ominous letter came from the Oil City Bank with a paper for her to sign. Cordelia wanted to sell Llantarnam and her consent was needed. A legal-looking document was enclosed for her to sign.

She threw it down in a fury and wrote a letter to Cordelia, who now lived in New York. Then she tore up the letter. A personal visit would be better, and she could also take care of some business for her clients and talk to a publisher she knew about her projected novel.

She called Air France and made a plane reservation.

*   *   *

Cordelia had gotten very stout since she last saw her and resembled her Uncle Hubert in more ways than one, Ardith thought, as she sat in Cordelia's antique-filled Sutton Place apartment looking out over the East River.

"I still can't understand why you'd be interested in the place," Cordelia said. "After all, you've been living in France for thirty years—"

"That was because of Marc."

"The cottage isn't worth much on the market, but the wicker furniture in it would bring a fortune today."

And you'd like to sell it, wouldn't you? Ardith thought, remembering the time Cordelia scared her with a toad and made her drop and break her favorite doll. "I want the cottage with all the furniture, just the way it was when grandfather had it," she said.

"It needs a lot of repairs. The roof is in terrible condition—"

"I'll have that fixed, and anything else that needs doing." Her oil stocks were paying good dividends, thank heavens, and with the recent sale of a client's book for a film, she was in good shape financially. But with a Socialist Government now in France confiscating everything, she wasn't making her move any too soon.

"I'll have to check with Abigail and Jessie," Cordelia said. "After all, we all own the cottage jointly."

"Do they go there often?"

"Hardly ever. The place has changed. New families have moved in, not the same class of people as in grandfather's time. I don't think you'd be very happy there."

"That's for me to decide, isn't it, Cordelia? Now, I'm going to have an appraiser go over everything, and then we'll have the papers drawn up. Who has the key?"

"I have one here, of course, and the Oil City Bank has one—"

"Then I'd like to have a duplicate of yours made to take with me. I'm going to drive there the day after tomorrow and look things over and I want to take possession not later than June first."

"That may be a little difficult," Cordelia said.

Ardith ignored her. "I'm returning to Paris for Nicole's wedding next month, and then I intend to move into the cottage."

"You'll stay there in the winter as well?"

"And why not?"

"You'll freeze. And you'll be snowed in for weeks at a time. The roads are impassable."

Fine, that's just what I need, she thought. I'll be able to concentrate and get a lot of writing done, maybe even finish the novel. "I'll see that I have plenty of wood and I'll get electric heaters for the rooms," she said. "And I plan to buy a four-wheel-drive station wagon. I'll get it when I'm in Oil City, or at least order it."

Cordelia lit a cigarette and then started to cough. "I see you've thought all this out, Ardith."

"Yes, I have," she said, getting up. "I'll have my attorney draw up all the papers and you can inform Abigail and Jessie of my intentions. And now, may I have the key to the cottage?"

"You always were an odd one, Ardith. Not like the rest of the Wymans. But if that's what you want to do—" She shrugged. "I'll get you a key. I have a duplicate."

EPILOGUE

She stood on the dock and looked across the river, recalling the small lonely girl of long ago who waited for the train and waved to the man in the caboose. There were no trains anymore, only tracks grown over with grass. But she was back and she had survived. Her life had come full circle. And she thought how we all walk that narrow precipice along the edge of the cliff between sanity and madness. Some fall into the volcano, others survive. In life there is nothing permanent to cling to, no handrail that can keep us from falling into the abyss save ourselves. Loved ones fail us, fortunes are swept away in the tide, what we cherish most is taken from us.

What is the answer? she wondered, looking around at the woods, hearing the river sounds. Is it a spiritual faith that keeps some going while others drift in emptiness, clutching for what eludes their grasp?

Here at Llantarnam she felt most herself, in touch with nature and God. She derived a strength from the place and here she would remain. She was alone, but she was not lonely. In the spring, her novel would be published. It had taken her longer than she had expected to write it, but out of her childhood memories and imagination she had created her grandfather's world, a world that no longer existed, but one that had touched her and shaped her life.

She leaned down and picked a wildflower growing by the edge of the dock, and then she turned and walked up the stone steps back to the cottage.

www.ingramcontent.com/pod-product-compliance
Lightning Source LLC
Chambersburg PA
CBHW020426030726
47495CB00006B/1673